23 Nov 1994

To one of the unsung heroes —
GEORGE J. MACZALI, U.S.M.M.
Lest we forget!

Ray Thompson

THE
WATERY
HELL

Also by Ray Thompson

After 1883

The Feisty Veterinarians of New Jersey

The Good Doctors

THE WATERY HELL

by
RAY THOMPSON

CB
Creative Books
Joppa, Maryland

All characters in this novel are fictional except for leaders of governments and some high-ranking military officers of World War II. Those readers who served in the United States Merchant Marine and the Navy Armed Guard in that war will recognize incidents that may parallel their own experiences. They also will recognize a chronological compression or elongation of some events, particularly the transit time of some voyages. While this is a work of fiction, much of it is based on actual events, although the names of persons, living or dead, locales and dates may have been changed.

All rights reserved including the right to reproduce this book or portions thereof in any form whatsover. Published by Creative Books, Inc., 419 Timber Lane, Joppa, MD 21085.

Copyright © 1993 by Ray Thompson
Cover Design © 1993 by Brian Hope

Thompson, Ray
  The Watery Hell, a novel / Ray Thompson.

ISBN 0-9637031-0-2

Library of Congress Catalog Card Number: 93-90396

10 9 8 7 6 5 4 3 2

Printed in the U. S. A.

TO

Earve P. Higgins, a merchant seaman,
and Vernon Camp, a Navy Armed Guard,
among those killed when two Japanese Kamikazes
heavily damaged the S. S. *Leonidas Merritt*,
a Liberty ship, at Leyte, Philippines,
on 12 November 1944.
They were shipmates and good friends
and have not been forgotten.

ACKNOWLEDGEMENTS

With gratitude to Dr. John E. Hayes, a veterinarian in Virginia, who generously loaned his extensive World War II library for research; Captain Brian Hope, of Project Liberty Ship, Baltimore, for editing to asssure proper sea language and for the cover design; Joseph B. Vernick, chairman and national director, Merchant Marine Veterans of World War II, San Pedro, CA and a Japanese POW for three and one-half years, who likewise made many fine editing suggestions; William Karditzas, of the Naval Station, Annapolis, for providing technical information on a Liberty ship's guns; Charles A. Lloyd, chairman and secretary of the USN Armed Guard WW II Veterans, of Raleigh, North Carolina, whose publication, *The Pointer*, was a rich source of real life stories about merchant ships and the Navy Armed Guard who sailed on them; my daughter, Mona-Rae, who assisted in the research; my brother, John, whose eagle eye caught many typos in the final draft; and my wife, Nancy, who steadfastly refused to read a line until this book was published. Okay, Nancy, it's reading time.

Ray Thompson
Fallston, Maryland

PROLOGUE
The Birth of a Ship

THE LIBERTY SHIP

She was conceived in haste without the usual tender caresses and gentle words associated with love. That love would come later as men boarded her but, for now, her fetus grew in a hurry with no predetermined gestation period. Her birth date was 112 hours to 100 days from conception, depending on the resources of the semi-skilled laborers who attended her and whether all the parts of her anatomy were in the right place at the right time. The average gestation period was 58 days. When she was born, she weighed 3,337 tons and measured 441 feet, 6 inches long, with a beam of 56 feet, 10 3/4 inches.

She was a Liberty ship.

In all, 2,751 Libertys were born in four years at eighteen shipyards across the United States in what has been described by some marine historians as the largest and fastest shipbuilding program in history. The first of this huge family of cargo-carrying vessels was the S. S. *Patrick Henry*, launched at the Bethlehem-Fairfield Shipyard in Baltimore, Maryland, on 27 September 1941. The United States was not yet at war, but most of Europe had already fallen under the blitzkreig of German troops. Hitler's Panzer tank divisions had invaded Russia and a defiant England was being pounded by the German Luftwaffe. Allied forces in North Africa were struggling to regain ground lost to the Germans. It was only a matter of time before the United States would be drawn into World War II and President Franklin Delano Roosevelt called for a "bridge of ships" to carry bombs, ammunition, tanks, jeeps, trucks, landing craft, airplane parts, food, clothing and troops to faraway places around the world. He wanted a ship that could do that job efficiently and be constructed quickly.

American engineers went to their drawing boards and hastily came up with the blueprints for a ship based on an old British tramp steamer, modified to utilize American standards and mass production methods. The reciprocating steam engine was chosen because of its simplicity of operation and ease of procurement. It had five deep cargo holds and its lines were not particularly graceful. Roosevelt later described the Libertys as "ugly ducklings."

After the Japanese attack on Pearl Harbor on 7 December 1941, the Liberty shipbuilding program was accelerated at existing shipyards and at emergency ones quickly thrown up in ports on the East, West and Gulf coasts, with three workshifts hammering, welding and riveting around the clock, seven days a week.

No sooner was a Liberty launched than its crew of 41 merchant seamen boarded to ready the ship for sea. Finding men for this huge fleet of Libertys and other cargo-carrying vessels was difficult. In 1941, the United States Merchant Marine included about 65,000 men and a few women. Many of the unlicensed crew were professional seamen with no family or shoreside ties, adventurous and restless, the kind of men who loved their freedom and hated restraint. Their ages ranged from 15 to more than 60; some were in their seventies. Most worked hard at sea and drank even harder ashore. A few were alcoholics or emotionally unstable. When the United States entered the war, even these misfits were needed to fill the number of bodies required by law before a ship could depart port. So desperate was the need that men with sea experience were paroled from federal and state prisons. Some professional seamen, drafted into the Army, were discharged to go back to their ships or new ones.

In 1942, the United States Maritime Service was established to help fill the need. Three training schools for unlicensed deck and engine room hands, cooks and messboys were hastily constructed at Sheepshead Bay, Brooklyn, New York; St. Petersburg, Florida; and Avalon, Catalina Island, off the coast of California. Officer and officer cadet schools also were hurriedly organized and in 1943 the United States Merchant Marine Academy was established at Kings Point, New York.

When America entered the war, most of the cargo ships in service were old, rusty and had no weapons to defend themselves. If any guns were on board, they were probably .45 Colt automatics or smaller pistols kept in the captain's safe or smuggled aboard by seasoned crew members who knew the personal safety value of carrying weapons in foreign ports of call. A few vessels were quickly armed with one or two 50-calibre machine guns, woefully inadequate to protect against attacking aircraft and utterly useless against submarines.

The Liberty ships were more heavily armed, with at least eight 20-millimeter, one forward three-inch-fifty and one aft five inch thirty-eight anti-aircraft guns. These weapons were manned by small, hastily trained Navy Armed Guard crews, supplemented by young merchant seamen given a short gunnery course at the maritime training schools. Whatever their armament, the merchant ships faced a fierce onslaught of torpedoes, mines and bombs and the seamen had their own now famous battle cry: **"Damn the torpedoes; full speed ahead!"**

By the end of the war, the Merchant Marine delivered an average of 8,500 tons of war materials every hour, 24 hours a day. More than 4,000 Allied merchant ships were lost, 820 of them American. Hundreds more United States vessels were crippled, but managed somehow to return to safe harbor. About 215,000 served on American merchant ships during World War II. The Merchant Marine Combat Bar, issued to the crew of a ship attacked, damaged or sunk by the enemy, was awarded to 103,052 seamen, almost one out of every two. Three of those bars went to women serving as stewardesses when their vessels were torpedoed. One was killed in a torpedoing on 30 June 1942, and a Liberty ship, the *S. S. Mary Cullom Kimbro*, was named in her memory. With her death, the federal government forbid women to serve on merchants ships for the duration.

At least 6,795 American merchant mariners were killed in action or reported missing and presumed dead, one out of every 32 who served. Thousands more were wounded. A reported 649 were prisoners of war. Some died on unmarked Japanese prison ships torpedoed by unsuspecting American or British submarines. Two were beheaded on Wake Island. The Navy Armed Guard, in which 144,970 men served, counted 1,810 dead, one in every 84.

The casualty rate among merchant seamen was higher than all of those killed in the Army, Navy, Marines and Coast Guard combined (one in 57).

Yet, they were not servicemen. They were civilians assisting in the war effort, but were subject to military court martial.

There was a myth during the war, and it unfortunately continues today in some circles, that merchant seamen were paid far more than members of the armed forces. There *was* a differential in pay, but it was negligible. A Navy seaman first class, single and without dependents, serving as an Armed Guard gunner on a merchant ship, was paid $79.20 monthly, including sea pay. If married, with one child, he received an allowance of $80 monthly. Married or unmarried, an ordinary seaman in the Merchant Marine was paid $82.50, plus bonuses ranging from 40 to 100 per cent while in or traveling through specified combat areas. There were no allowances for a wife and children.

The seamen, however, did not have the same benefits as the Navy men or those in the Army and Marine Corps.

Those in the military received free clothing and a monthly clothing allowance. The seamen paid for their own clothes, shoes, overcoats, gloves and foul weather gear. They paid for their own medical and dental needs, for eyeglasses. There was no free postage. They could not enter a U. S. O., were denied access to most American Red Cross facilities and there was no reduction in train and bus fares. No G. I. Bill of Rights for education or house purchases after the war.

Worse, their pay stopped the moment their ship was sunk! No pay no matter how long they spent in a lifeboat, on a liferaft or as a prisoner of war!

They were not paid when they signed off a ship for shore leave. (Those in the military were paid for 365 days a year.) The merchant seamen could take up to thirty days vacation *without pay* each year. Any days longer than that subjected those of draft age who were physically fit to a call for possible military duty from Selective Service. Others above draft age could take all the time they wanted. Many, however, found that, in a week or two, or even just a few days, their money was spent. So they went back to sea again.

Merchant seamen were finally recognized as veterans by an act of the U. S. Congress in 1988, forty-seven years after America's entry into World War II and after many thousands of those who served had passed away.

The foregoing is fact. The following is fiction. It is the story of a seafaring family, a father and two sons, who took Liberty ships and crews to war in the Pacific Ocean against the Empire of Japan and in the Atlantic Ocean against the Third Reich.

A war seamen called "The Watery Hell."

LOG BOOK ONE
5 February - 22 March 1942

Hades is relentless and unyielding.

-- Homer

5 February 1942

2100 HOURS
Four Nautical Miles off the Coast of North Carolina
"Dummkopf bastard!" Lieutenant Commander Reinhard Barnschmidt swore as he tossed the shortened, burned out cigar to the water churning around U-84-B. His executive officer was startled.

"Who, Mein Capitan?" the exec asked, his voice anxious with respect.

"Admiral Donitz! The bastard!"

The young lieutenant was startled again. Admiral Karl Donitz is the head of the submarine arm of the German Navy and officers are not expected to talk in such disrespectful terms, even if they don't like the man.

"Sir, I thought you and the admiral are friends. He sent you a bottle of twelve-year-old Scotch before we sailed."

"I thought so, too," Commander Barnschmidt said angrily, putting a gloved hand on the steel railing of the submarine's cigarette bridge and feeling the bitterness of the 22-degree Farenheit cold. "I had not opened our orders when the bottle arrived. The bastard knew I couldn't open them until we moved into open sea outside Wilhelmshaven. That's why he sent the Scotch. He wanted to soften me up for this rotten assignment. He didn't give a damn about me or this boat!"

He pounded his fist on the railing.

"I wanted . . I asked him personally for another wolfpack command. That's where the action is, Lieutenant. With a wolfpack in the North Atlantic. Or the Barents Sea. That's where I was on my last assignment. Great hunting grounds! But that harebrained admiral sent me here. No command. Just a single U-boat with no ships to sink."

"Sir, you're one of the admiral's best submarine commanders," the lieutenant said tentatively, cautiously. "You already have twelve ships and forty-nine thousand tons to your credit. I'm sure he thinks the East Coast of the United States is an important assignment. That's why he picked you."

"Important? It's been five nights since we arrived here. Where are all the solo ships he claimed are running up and down the coast? We haven't seen any. Not one! Not even garbage tossed overboard. Not even a convoy! The Americans know our U-Boats own the North Atlantic and it's not safe to keep letting ships try to cross it without an escort. Maybe no ships are leaving port alone. Is that what's happening?"

The bow lookout answered his question.

"Capitan! Ship on our port beam. Two, two and one half miles. I think it's a tanker!"

Barnschmidt put binoculars to his eyes, thanking whoever sets up such luck for submarine captains for the glowing shoreline that silhouetted the ship. *Yes*, he mused after a few seconds, *it is a tanker. The coastal type. Twenty, thirty years old. About three thousand tons, filled with thousands of barrels of crude oil.*

"Lookouts below!" he called fore and aft.

The men raced for the warm comfort of the submarine's bowels. Barnschmidt pushed his exec to the ladder.

"We must hurry, son. This could be our first victim on this patrol."

When the lookouts had scrambled below, he took another look at the tanker. It would be a prize.

"Submerge! Submerge!" he ordered as he grabbed the hatch lanyard and began closing the hatch cover above him.

He could feel the adrenalin flowing and he started to smile.

Maybe, just maybe, this assignment won't be so bad after all.

2110 HOURS
In the Same Waters
There was no warning. Two torpedoes hit the S. S. *Terrapin* within four seconds of each other, the explosions tearing through the tanker, flinging men overboard or to the decks. Flames leaped four hundred feet into the dark night air. Burning oil cascaded back down with the water to ignite the ship from bow to stern and engulfed several men struggling in vain to swim clear of the fiery furnace.

Boatswain Jim Davis was on the fantail, taking his

customary inspection stroll around the deck before turning in, when the torpedoes struck near the bow and midships. Tying the ribbons on his lifejacket, he ran across the steel catwalk toward the bridge, flames licking at his every step.

Can anyone be alive? he asked himself, knowing instinctively there would not be many survivors. The ship was an inferno. He saw that both lifeboats, port and starboard, were ablaze. As he neared the deckhouse, his eyes fastened on a liferaft not yet touched by fire and quickly cut it loose, letting it plunge into the ocean twenty feet below. *That may be our only hope,* he told himself as he ran toward the steel ladder leading to the bridge.

Blackened bodies, bursting like cooked sausage, sprawled across the deck. He did not recognize any of them. Jim visualized the terrible fate that befell the black gang, the men below decks in the engine room where the second lethal torpedo hit. Crushed by collapsing steel. Scalded to death by the steam from ruptured boilers. Or drowned by the in-rushing sea. He hoped their deaths had been quick and merciful.

A figure stumbled out of a smoke-filled passageway, face blackened, shirt on fire, voice screaming:

"Help me! Oh, God, help me!"

Jim took off his lifejacket, wrapped it around the man's chest and threw him to the deck, rolling his body over and over to douse the flames. The steel deck was hot enough to fry bacon and Jim burned his hands.

"Sandy," he called. "It's okay. The fire's out on your clothes. Come on! Stand up, man! You'll burn to death on this deck!"

He helped Ordinary Seaman Walker to his feet.

"Bo's'n!" the seaman shouted, his voice filled with fear. "They're all dead on the bridge! The captain! The third mate! Tom Marshall! Everybody! It's a furnace 'tween decks! Nobody can make it!"

Jim could smell the stench of charred flesh and knew there was no hope for anyone on the bridge.

"The bow?" he asked anxiously.

"The fire's worse than here!" Walker said. "Anyone there either jumped overboard or . . or is dead. What about aft?"

There was another thunderous explosion. A huge ball of flame engulfed the stern, then rose skyward five hundred feet or more.

"If anyone was there, he's gone now," Jim said sorrowfully. He instinctively knew there were only a few minutes, if they were lucky, before the ship would explode in one more lethal blast before sinking.

"Over the side!" he ordered. "Over the side and make for the raft!"

Walker jumped feet first. Jim followed, clinging to the lifejacket with one hand. By the time his head came above the surface, he had swallowed a mouthful of oil.

"Just what I needed!" he spat, but the nauseating taste stayed with him and he wanted to vomit.

The two men, splashing with bare hands the burning oil on top of the water to clear a fire-free path in front of them, reached the wooden raft at the same time and Jim helped the young seaman to its eight by ten foot strutted deck.

"Here, take this and put it on," he said, handing the lifejacket to the youth. He scrambled aboard the raft himself, his agility belying his fifty years. Pulling one paddle from a wooden pocket and pointing to the other, he ordered: "Start rowing! We've got to get away before she blows!"

They paddled furiously, skin tearing from Jim's scorched hands with every stroke.

"Wait for me! Wait for me!" a voice cried to their port.

They stopped and a man Jim recognized as an engine room watertender grabbed the raft's side and struggled to climb aboard, his oil-covered hands slipping twice before Sandy hauled him up by the armpits. Two other men followed quickly. They were messboys from the steward's department and, like the watertender, had no lifejackets.

"Thank God!" one of them prayed, trembling. "I couldn't have swum another foot."

He rested a moment, elbows on the raft's deck, before pulling himself on board. He was naked to the waist and shoeless, much of the skin burned from his chest and the soles of his feet.

"I was sleeping when . . when . . I didn't think anyone would make it."

"Any others out there?" Jim asked.

"Dun . . Dunno," the watertender sputtered. "I didn't even see these guys."

"We have to move further away," Jim coached, handing his paddle to the messman who had not been burned.

"The ship'll blow any second and we'll be sucked down with it!"

The two seamen stroked in unison, the intense heat broiling their backs as they moved away from the burning ship. Jim hoped others would be found in the water and that the raft would get far enough away before the ship exploded for the last time. *Another hundred yards should do it. Maybe.* Each stroke seemed an eternity.

In his thirty-two years at sea, he had never seen such destruction. This was his first sinking, although he had made eight trans-Atlantic crossings during World War I when the Germans first discovered the awesome power that could be unleashed from underwater craft. In 1933, one of his ships had grounded on a reef in the Aleutians and there was some minor damage. Hurricanes and typhoons had snapped booms off other ships, but nothing could compare to this watery inferno.

Another deafening explosion ripped the night air and the two oarsmen pulled harder, chopping their blades into the relatively calm waters of the Atlantic Ocean. A shock wave lifted the small raft out of the water and the seamen held on to each other and to the strutted deck. Balls of flaming oil hit the water around them.

"Look, she's going down!" the watertender shouted.

Jim stared ahead, not turning to look. He did not want to see the death throes of the ship on which he had served these past three years, carrying crude oil from Caracas to Baltimore and going back down again, empty. This time they were fully loaded and would have made Baltimore day after tomorrow. There, in the Bethlehem-Key Highway Shipyard, the Navy would have overseen outfitting the tanker with four 20-millimeter and two three-inch-fifty guns.

A lot of good antiaircaft guns will do a coastal tanker, Jim had mused when he first heard of the plans. *There are no Nazi aircraft near United States shores. Not yet!*

Still, he had been looking forward to the ten-day layover, the longest he would have stayed ashore in four, five years. It would have given him time to get to know his only grandson better.

Baltimore. Jim's home. He had been born there, the son of a deckhand who served mostly on sailing ships, the last being the four-masted *SV Arthur P. Johnson.* At age 68, after fifty years at sea, the elder Davis "swallowed the anchor," signing off that schooner to retire two weeks before the Japanese attack on Pearl Harbor. Three days later, the old man died in his sleep. Heart attack. Jim thought then his father's death was preordained. The 735-ton *Johnson* was sunk on 12 January 1942, en route to her home port in Baltimore from Turk's Island, deep laden with salt. There were no survivors from her eight-man crew. At least, Jim consoled himself, his father was not fish bait in the ocean, but was buried in Baltimore's Druid Ridge Cemetery, alongside his wife who had died of leukemia two years earlier.

Squatting on the raft, he likened the sinking of the *Terrapin* to the time in 1925 when his wife, Marie, left him. Only twenty-nine and married to Jim for eleven of those years, she had tired of a life with a husband who was a stranger, gone to sea for long months at a time. When he refused her repeated demands to get a shoreside job, she obtained a divorce and left Baltimore, and her two sons, looking for a more normal relationship while she still had what she called "the best years of my life ahead of me." Marie Davis moved to Butte, Montana, and within a few months had married a wealthy rancher. Jim's ego had been crushed. It never dawned on him that he may have been selfish by living as he wanted to and not giving thought to the lonesomeness she must have felt while he was at sea or in some foreign port. He had not remarried. He sold his home in the port city and sent his sons to live with a younger sister a few blocks away. He had come to realize that marriage and the sea are like oil and water. They don't mix. Many of his shipmates were loners who never married or, like him, were divorced. They sought the quick thrills and comforts of women in port, particularly on The Block, Baltimore's red light district with its striptease joints and two-dollar prostitutes, not far from the docks.

Unlike the rest of the crew, Jim avoided relationships with women, devoting his life to the sea and, by long distance correspondence and occasional time ashore, raising his sons with his sister's help. Billy and Frank had joined him in the Merchant Marine and were now on other ships. He had not seen them since last October, two months before Pearl Harbor. Both were at sea when their grandfather died.

If anything like this happens to them, Jim agonized, *I won't be able to live with myself.* He looked to the heavens. *Dear God, let them be safe.*

"Hey, she's going down bow first!" the watertender called, his voice screeching. "Her stern's pointing straight up!"

"Keep rowing!" Jim ordered, reaching for a tin of water.

He swished a mouthful to rid it of the foul oil taste still there. It helped a bit and he passed the tin to the others. He kept his eyes forward, squinting, searching the sea, looking for other survivors. He could see none and there were no cries for help. There was only a loud gurgling sound, like a gutteral voice from the ocean bottom, as the 3,000-ton tanker seemed in a hurry to go below and find Davy Jones' locker. Oil still burned in a wide circle on the surface.

His eyes fastened on an object moving slowly and rising higher out of the water as it came closer to the raft. He stood up. A submarine's conning tower broke the ocean's surface not one hundred feet away. The hatch opened. Two men scrambled to the deck, ran a few yards on its slippery surface, stopped, untied ropes holding canvas covers on two .50-calibre machine guns and pointed the weapons at the men in the raft.

My God, Jim swore silently, *they're going to kill us!*

The four other men turned their eyes away from the tanker, its stern now sticking three, four feet out of the water, like the hardback shell of a turtle, probably resting its bow on a shoal.

"What is it? I can't see." Ordinary Seaman Walker was frightened. After staring at the fire, his eyes were not as accustomed to the darkness as the boatswain's.

"Quiet!" Jim ordered. "The submarine's surfaced."

"What's he going to do, Boats?"

"Be calm. Maybe he just wants to talk," Jim hushed

He was afraid, the normal fear of a man who knows he may have only a few seconds to live, the kind of fear all men feel in war. He knew, though, that as the ranking seaman, the main thing was to appear calm and not show that fear to the others. That took a lot of will power as he watched two machine guns being trained on the raft.

Another figure climbed out of the hatch and walked the few steps to the cigarette bridge. He waved a hand and a bright searchlight beam encircled the liferaft. Another motion and the submarine moved closer until it was only thirty feet away.

"Halte!"

The boat's engines went silent.

"Good evening," the man called in English. There was hardly a trace of a German accent. "Are you the captain?"

Jim could not see the man or the submarine, so blinding was the beam that he had to shield his eyes with his hands. As if in response to his movements, the searchlight was turned off. The man switched on a flashlight, focusing it on Jim.

"I repeat. Are you the captain?"

"No. The captain's dead."

"I regret that. Your rate?"

"Bo's'n," Jim said, eyeing the man warily.

"Any other casualties?"

"We are the only survivors."

"Again, I'm sorry. Any of you hurt?"

"No. A few burns. That's all."

"Can I offer assistance. Water perhaps?"

Jim looked at the water tins. They were intact. "We have enough."

"Medical supplies for the burns?"

Jim examined the first aid kit. "We've a good supply of salve and bandages."

"Lifejackets?"

"Only one."

The captain called below for four lifejackets.

"Blankets? It's already below freezing. Twenty-two degrees Farenheit."

"None."

Another order went below.

"Your ship's name?"

Jim did not respond.

"Come now, Bo's'n, it's for the log," the captain demanded authoritatively. "No harm in her name now. She's already at the bottom."

Out of the corner of an eye, Jim saw one of the guns move up and down. He was aware the War Department refused to publicly release the names of merchant ships sunk by the enemy. He knew, too, that telegrams sent by the Navy to the families of men lost in a sinking cautioned against revealing the ship's name "lest comfort be given the enemy." He kept his silence. The gun moved up and down a second time. Jim looked at his raftmates. *Maybe the submarine captain is right*, he allowed. No sense encouraging his wrath and adding five more names to the casualty list.

"*S. S. Terrapin,*" he said reluctantly, feeling a bit like a traitor to his country. Then, to ease his guilt: "We had no guns."

"But it is war, no?"

There was no sarcasm in the captain's voice, just pride.

Another man came on deck, tied four lifejackets together and tossed them toward the raft. They hit the water just inches away and one of the messboys quickly recovered them. The submariner had better aim with the blankets. They landed in the middle of the raft.

"If we were further out, I'd offer to take you aboard. As it is, we're only four miles due east of Wilmington, North Carolina. I'm sure you know that, Bo's'n. Someone's bound to have seen the explosions and help will be on its way shortly," the captain said reassuredly.

It was true. Jim could see the halo of light over the shoreline.

"Honestly, I think your fellow Americans don't know there's a war on," the captain continued. It was almost a complaint. "They leave their lights on at night and you were clearly silhouetted against the horizon. An easy mark. Easy. Like knocking over ducks in the shooting gallery at Coney Island."

He lifted his two hands as though sighting a rifle.

"Bang!"

He childishly mimicked the sound of a gun, drawing his right index finger toward his thumb.

"That's my favorite place in New York. The shooting gallery gave me good practice for the job I do now. Went to Fordham University and graduated in thirty-six," he boasted.

"I wish I had a gun," the watertender muttered.

"Quiet!" Jim ordered.

He was fuming himself, but held his tongue. Not twenty feet away stood a man who had just sunk his ship, killing twenty-seven unarmed men, and who was talking as though he and the boatswain were old college buddies knocking back casual beers in a Times Square bar. It was crazy.

"Sorry we had to do it," the captain apologized. "But, as you Yanks say, 'all's fair in love and war.' Tell your Mr. Roosevelt that U-Eighty-four-B is out here. Reinhard Barnschmidt, Lieutenant Commander. U- Eighty-four-B. Remember that."

"I'll remember," Jim called back. "I'll remember."

I will too. There has to be a way to get even. U-Eighty-four-B. Reinhard Barnschmidt. You bet I'll remember.

"You're our first ship on this patrol. We fired two torpedoes and hit with both. Good shooting, don't you agree?"

The captain laughed again.

"Captain," Jim called evenly, surprising himself that he wanted to say anything more to the man.

"Yes?"

"Sir, you have seen my face. You have seen all our faces. Would it be possible, Captain, to see your face?"

"Why?" the captain asked, curious.

"Because, sir, I would like to see the face of my enemy," Jim said humbly.

"But we are not enemies, Bo's'n," the captain said warmly. "We are just bit actors in a small scene in a big play."

"True," Jim said agreeably. "But you are the victor and we are the vanquished. This is your big scene. The spotlight should be on you."

"Well said," the captain agreed boastfully.

He raised the flashlight and played the beam on his face, bowing and smiling as if taking applause from an admiring audience.

"A bit further away, Captain," Jim suggested. "The light casts too many shadows."

The flashlight moved and Jim got a better look at the cleanshaven face of Lieutenant Commander Reinhard Barnschmidt. It was thin. The man appeared to be about thirty, with short blonde hair and bright blue eyes. His uniform was impeccable. A small mole marred his left cheek. Not the perfect Aryan.

"How's that?"

"Bravo!" Jim said, applauding, playing the role of an enthusiastic theatregoer.

"Thank you, thank you," Barnschmidt said, bowing and turning off the light. "You appreciate a good act, I can see. Now, my friend, we've . . ."

The captain hesitated.

"We've got to go now. Don't want to be here when your rescuers show up. Wouldn't be healthy. For us."

He laughed goodnaturedly and waved.

"Wiedersehn . . and good luck!"

With that, the U-boat commander dropped out of

sight. The gunners covered their weapons, ran to the hatch, climbed in and, as the 740-ton boat slipped slowly beneath the waves, the last one grabbed the hatch lanyard and closed the hatch.

"Crazy sonofabitch!" the watertender swore.

Jim sat down and drew a long breath.

"That captain's right, though," he said tiredly. "We were sitting ducks. Those lights make easy targets of all ships running up and down this coast."

"Torpedo Alley, for sure," Seaman Walker said. "People are probably standing on the beach now, still applauding the fireworks."

So many American ships are being sunk close to the shoreline from Florida to Boston that seamen have dubbed that stretch of water "Torpedo Alley," declaring it is easier for a German U-boat to sink a ship there than to get a strike rolling a ball down a lane in a ten-pin bowling alley.

Jim looked around. There was no more fire, no floating debris. Only silvery streaks cast by the half moon above mingled with a large oil slick rolling toward shore. He cursed the politicians who would not accept a Navy recommendation for a complete blackout of coastal cities, from the Gulf to Boston. Such a blackout, he knew, would help protect the ships, but would be politically unwise. It would hurt the morale of American voters, particularly the businessmen who claimed turning off their lights would hurt them in their pockets. Some of those businessmen, hotel owners in seaside resort cities, complained that the fuel oil from torpedoed ships was fouling their beaches. It didn't seem to matter that dead seamen were associated with the oil, that with each sinking America might be losing the war. Some tourists also complained when a seaman's body washed up on a beach. These were the people who put politicians in office and who were sure the enemy would never land on their country's shores. There were no bulwarks to protect against that possibility and Jim was not so sure it wouldn't happen. Nazi submarines were frightenly close and could easily land a terrorist party as a first step.

He squatted on the raft.

"Reinhard Barnschmidt," he muttered almost to himself.

"Who?" the watertender asked.

"Lieutenant Commander Reinhard Barnschmidt. U-

Eighty-four-B. I've got a score to settle with him."

His raftmates guffawed.

"How you gonna do that?" Seaman Walker asked incredulously. "You'll never see him again less'n you're on the receiving end of another of his torpedoes."

"Maybe that way. Maybe not. But I feel in my bones Barnschmidt and I will meet up again one day. You can bet on it!"

"What odds you givin'?" the watertender said assuredly.

"No odds. No money," Jim said slowly. "It's a personal promise to our dead shipmates."

He began carving the name on one of the raft's wooden struts. The others fell silent. What Jim had to say had sobered them. Then they saw a tiny light probing back and forth a couple of miles away.

A Coast Guard rescue boat was heading their way.

2145 HOURS
Aboard the U-84-B

"Forgive me, Mein Capitan," U-84-B's executive officer said almost apologetically. "It is not my place to criticize, but I do it constructively for your benefit. For your career. I do not think, sir, that you should have given your name and shown your face so boldly to those men."

"Why not?" Barnschmidt demanded. "I want their president to know I'm out here, off his shores, sinking his merchant ships. It will give that pompous, cigarette-smoking cripple another name to worry about besides the Fuhrer. Barnschmidt. Reinhard Barnschmidt. That's a name he'll hear a lot more about."

He poked a finger at his young exec.

"Besides, It's great being back in action. How glorious it is to sink a ship! I had almost forgotten the thrill."

The exec smiled knowingly.

"I'm glad, sir. If you do it right, and I know you will, you'll break all kinds of records in tonnage sunk right here, right in Mr. Roosevelt's front yard."

He paused, unsure that he should press the matter of his captain's egotism.

"Still, there was something in that bo's'n's tone of voice, his playing up to you, that troubles me. I fear your boasting will come back to haunt you."

"Nonsense!" Barnschmidt shouted.

"I have a feeling that bo's'n wanted to see your face so

he could recognize you later."

"Utter stupidity!" the captain laughed. "Americans have short memories, my friend. Remember how easily they forgot the last war and isolated themselves against the rest of the world? Come, now, Lieutenant. After a few drinks ashore, that bo's'n probably will have trouble remembering his own name!"

What the captain said made sense, but the exec still wondered if the man's boastfulness would reap trouble in the weeks and months to come.

A feeling in his gut said it could.

2158 HOURS
Reykjavik, Iceland
The convoy, with thirty-four cargo ships flying the flags of seven nations, and eleven warships, most of them British Royal Navy, began moving out of the teeming harbor. It was not exactly a precision-executed maneuver despite the endless planning in the endless convoy conferences. Some of the merchant ships moved out too quickly and were reprimanded by flashing Aldis lamps from the COMCONVOY's cruiser to "stay put" until their turn came to form up with the others. A few ships moved into positions assigned to others and were just as quickly warned by the same signal lights to "get to your proper place." Other captains held back, not particularly in a hurry to enter waters that, for now, belonged pretty much to the enemy. Within two hours, when all had passed through the harbor's mouth, with its mines and nets placed strategically to keep enemy submarines out, the warships, like mother hens, will shepherd the merchantmen into a loosely knit but orderly formation.

Then, like a school of dolphin chasing each other, Convoy 37B will begin a ten-knot dash across 1,500 forbidding miles to Murmansk, Russia.

None of the men on the ships, not even forever optimistic Chief Engineer William "Billy" Davis on the Liberty ship, *S. S. Elihu Nicholson*, thought this voyage would be a routine crossing of the North Atlantic and Arctic Oceans. Billy had been to Murmansk before. And to Archangel, Russia's other northern deepwater port. In peacetime. He knew about the violent storms with waves as high as sixty feet, the blinding snow and the floating ice that buffeted ships and sometimes sank them. He had not yet, however, met the Nazis. The United States had been at war just two months, but he had heard all sorts of horror stories about German submarines, some of the U-boats perhaps lurking only a few nautical miles outside Reykjavik, and their screeching dive bombers, sure to come after the convoy when it reaches the Barents Sea.

Is this trip really necessary? he asked himself flippantly, shuddering, knowing it was, but fearful it would be cold and bloody. He could take the cold. The blood worried him.

For the past two hours, he had watched silently as the third assistant engineer and the black gang on the 8-to-12 watch fired the *Nicholson's* two oil-burning boilers which fed the huge three-cylinder reciprocating steam engine. The third assistant knew his job and Billy let him do it. He had originally planned to take command of the engine room when the Liberty ship left Reykjavik. It was rightfully his domain, one he had earned. For nine and one half years he had worked up from unlicensed crew to licensed officer. Then, a month ago, he took the chief engineer's examination and won the top job in the sweaty below decks where engines give ships power to move from one port to another. But sitting with the captain in the convoy conferences the last two weeks had changed his mind about taking over from the third assistant engineer.

That's why I have assistants, he reassured himself. *They leave me free to do the things I couldn't otherwise do on this ship.*

This was his first convoy and he wanted to be on deck when it moved out where he could get a firsthand view of how it fit together. He envisioned the ships as pieces of a jigsaw puzzle being moved into place by an invisible hand.

He liked jigsaw puzzles.

The third assistant signalled a thumbs up. Billy whistled into the tube to the bridge.

"What's up, Billy?" the captain called back.

"Steam's up. Full. She's yours whenever you're ready."

"Good. We're ready to pull out soon's COMCONVOY gives the order."

"I'm on my way topside to see how you deck apes pull this convoy off."

Billy heard the captain laugh as he turned, waved to the third assistant and moved up the steel ladders leading to the bridge deck. Before he got out of the engine room he heard the familiar ringing of the telegraph. *Half Ahead.* He felt the vessel jump and glanced at his watch. 2200 hours. They were underway right on time.

Two minutes later he stepped into the wheelhouse.

"Evening, Slim," he called to the portly officer holding a steaming mug of coffee and peering out a small porthole on the starboard side, eyes intent on the unfolding drama of more than a dozen ships steaming out of the harbor.

Why Third Mate Glen Stevens was nicknamed "Slim" no one on the Liberty ship knew. At twenty-two, his five-foot eight frame packed 220 pounds, maybe more. He had what some people would call a "barrel chest."

"Evening, Chief," Slim answered, motioning to the chief engineer to draw himself some coffee. "We just . . we just pulled . . hoisted the anchor."

He was nervous and it showed in a halting, unsure voice, raspy from smoking too many cigarettes.

"Your first trip to Murmansk?" Billy asked in a fatherly tone.

"My first trip anywhere. They graduated my class early."

"What school?"

"Pennsylvania Maritime Academy. Wasn't do out "til May, sir."

That explained the young mate's nervousness, a condition Billy was sure would increase in the days ahead on the watery road to the Soviet Union's most important deepwater port. It would not be an easy voyage and it would test the green mate's book-learned knowledge of how to handle a 3,337-ton cargo ship, laden with supplies of war, in a raging sea in sub-zero temperatures. It would also test his courage. The Russians, fighting desperately to hold back the blitzkrieging German army on land, needed products from the small but building American war arsenal. They could only get those products from merchant ships running through the normal hazards of storms and Arctic ice, and the more dangerous gauntlet of U-boats and torpedo planes, to reach Murmansk and Archangel.

Billy conceded that the ships, their cargoes and crews might have an easier time reaching Persian Gulf ports. Even with the German and Italian submarines in the Mediterranean, the weather would be less hostile. But the rail lines and roads that stretch from the gulf to interior Russia are totally inadequate to carry the huge stores of weapons, munitions, vehicles, food and clothing its army needs. There are better roadways from the northern ports.

"It's just as well you got out early," Billy said. "You'll pick up a lot this trip you wouldn't have learned at the academy. There's nothing better than a run to Murmansk for on-the-job training."

The COMCONVOY (commander, convoy) cruiser's klaxon horn burped noisily, staccato like, and colorful flags flapped wildly, ordering the ships to *"take up formation."* They began lining up in seven columns of five each, with the COMCONVOY in the center of the front line.

"Bring her to starboard and line up behind that Danish freighter," the captain called from the flying bridge. "She's flying number thirteen."

"I've already learned one thing," the mate said, searching with binoculars to identify the Danish ship and, finding it by the signal flags strung from its foremast, he gave a new heading to the helmsman. "To be grateful we didn't draw that freighter's unlucky number or cargo. She's loaded with ammunition."

"Superstitious?" Billy asked.

The mate's face reddened.

"I hate to admit it, sir, but . . yes, sir. Particularly the number thirteen. There were thirteen kids in my family and guess what? I'm the youngest. Number thirteen. Ever since I was born the family's had nothing but troubles. Two of my brothers died. My dad was out of work most of the Depression. Mom's suffering bad with arthritis she says she got when I was born. For sure, thirteen is not my lucky number."

"Let's keep that our secret," Billy offered.

"Thanks," Slim said with a sigh of relief, turning his attention to the ships surrounding the *Nicholson*.

Each had been assigned a number in the formation and flew one or more signal flags for others to see that number. While still in the harbor where it was safe to use them, searchlights played back and forth, quickly touching the flags like huge dancing fireflies as each captain or mate, straining with binoculars, identified the ships forward, astern and to starboard and port. A lot of planning had gone into the ship assignments.

When they reached open water, the five ships in each line would space themselves five hundred yards apart, forward to aft. The next row of ships, also five hundred yards apart, would line up one thousand yards away; the next row another thousand yards, and so on. Ammunition ships, oil tankers and vessels loaded with tanks, guns and other critical materials would hide in the middle of the formation where they were less likely to be the targets of German U-boats. Ships carrying expendable raw materials such as ore and foodstuffs would reluctantly move to the convoy's outside edges. The *Nicholson*, its holds and decks crammed with Lend-Lease tanks, trucks, tractors, crates filled with field telephones, several thousand miles of telephone cables and one thousand batteries, drew a spot in the third column from starboard, fourth in line. Not a bad position considering the size of the convoy. No one envied the two ships posted for the last spots in the outside starboard and port columns.

The "coffin corners."

"I've learned another thing," the mate said.

"What's that?"

"The Old Man is a stickler for the book."

"You called that right," Billy said. "The captain's from the old school and doesn't take kindly to anyone who doesn't know that book."

"Even if he's wrong?"

"Even if he's wrong!"

The moment the ships were in position, another flag ordered: *"Full ahead. Maintain your distance."* They moved out quickly, stretching over an area three miles wide. The escort commander, on one of the two Royal Navy cruisers, rode up front, on the port side. Five British destroyers began patrolling in elliptical patterns five thousand yards away, positioned to try to prevent attacks from the front. Four Canadian corvettes patrolled in similar patterns ten thousand yards further out, their eyes on the flanks and rear. A small coal-fired fishing trawler darted past the *Nicholson*, starboard side, heading toward the rear of the column.

"What's that?" the third mate asked eagerly. "A supply boat bringing a lunch bucket someone forgot?"

Billy chuckled.

"Her captain wouldn't appreciate that description. She's a rescue ship. Free Dutch. Seven are going with us."

"Seven?"

"Two are Dutchmen. The other five are Free French and Free Polish. They get at the end of each of the convoy's columns and they're responsible for the ships directly in front of them. In her case, five. We're one of them. We get hit, she moves fast to pick up survivors. If there are any."

Slim winced.

"I know," he said. "They taught us at the academy that we're not supposed to help any ship that gets hit in a convoy. No matter what. Seems damn callous to me."

"Maybe so, Slim. But you've got to think of your own crew. It's too risky for them. You won't have time for grandstanding. You leave that job to the rescue ships. Besides, a man can't survive for more than a couple of minutes in Arctic waters."

He was right. Convoy rules dictated that those ships unfortunate enough to be hit by a torpedo or aerial bombs, and the men on them, are to be left to their own destiny, the rescue ships and God.

Slim nodded his understanding, drew a Chesterfield cigarette from a shirt pocket and fumbled in his trousers side pockets until he found his Zippo lighter. Crouching almost to the deck, he cupped his hands and lit, drawing hard to make sure. An eerie red glow covered his face.

"They teach you that at the academy?" Billy asked sharply.

"No," the mate said, straightening and taking a long draw on the cigarette, his right hand cupped over his mouth. "Figured it out myself. We can't smoke on deck at night because they told us a flame from a match or lighter can be seen for five miles at sea. I personally find that hard to believe, but being a three-packs-a-day smoker, I need my cigarettes when I'm up here. I figure that by bending over like that, behind the bulkhead and cupping my hand tightly, it's impossible for anyone to see a light."

"You're wrong!" Billy countered. "Dead wrong and you're about to find out just how much!"

The door to the wheelhouse opened quickly and the captain stormed in, fuming.

6 February 1942

0600 HOURS
Bel Air, Maryland
"I just don't understand the urgency," Lynne Margaret

Davis called from the bedroom. "Your father's tanker is due in Baltimore sometime tomorrow, if he's on his regular schedule. Why can't you wait to see him?"

"Can't," Frank answered from the bathroom, pausing in the buttoning of the short sleeve shirt to the white uniform Lynne had a tailor make without a fitting. She had done it surreptitiously while, for the past 27 days, he had studied for, taken and passed the master's licensing examination. The uniform fit perfectly, complementing his six foot, one inch broad-shouldered frame, but he wasn't anxious to wear it. Most Merchant Marine officers, except those on passenger ships in peacetime, don't wear whites, he had told her. Or any uniforms. Too ostentatious. Too Navy. Too military. A newly-licensed ship's master is often seen by the crew as too eager to show off his new authority. The new uniform, with its black shoulder epaulets with four gold stripes and its white hat, with company insignia, black brim and gold braid, said just that.

"Why can't you, Frank?" his wife demanded. "You haven't seen Dad for over a year. Another day before you reach your ship won't matter."

Captain Frank Davis knew then that Lynne didn't understand the nature of war. There is an urgency to everything. To building a war arsenal. To drafting civilians and training them to be warriors. To moving supplies and troops thousands of miles. To probing, testing the strength of the enemy. To hitting the enemy hard. To killing. Or being killed.

"I'd like to, hon," he said. "You know that, but I'm to report to the *Bennett* in San Francisco day after tomorrow. My flight leaves Harbor Field at nine. With layovers in Chicago, Denver and Salt Lake, I'll make Frisco just in time 'tho I won't board the *Bennett* 'til after noon. There's not another plane out for two days. I can't be that late."

It's as simple as that, he told himself. It wasn't as simple for Lynne Margaret.

"You're a captain now! Surely your new rank has some privileges. Dad should see you in your new uniform. He doesn't know you have your captain's license. He'll be so proud."

She got up from the bed and walked to the closed bathroom door.

"Besides, I think it's stupid for you to fly in one of

those awful things across the country. You should take the train."

She was afraid of airplanes.

"Why do they have to send you way out there? Don't they have any ships here? Lord, they're launching a new one almost every day in Baltimore. Surely they could assign you to one of them."

"Maybe Dad won't get in tomorrow," Frank ventured. "The *Terrapin* could get diverted to another port. That's happening a lot these days."

"He'll be home all right. He's made it here every six weeks for three years. What makes you think this trip is any different?"

Frank didn't answer. He knew Lynne was getting worked up and he had learned, in four years of marriage, to keep his silence until her anxiety passed. Lynne went back to sorting his clothes and was quiet for several minutes.

"I guess you're right," she admitted grudgingly. "There's a war on. Lots of families are separated. For the duration probably." She put three khaki shirts on the top of the dresser. "Is the *Bennett* a new ship? Is that her full name?"

"No to both," Frank answered, buckling the black belt. "She's the *Andrew Bennett* and she was delivered to the company in early January from the shipyard in Los Angeles."

"Doesn't she have a captain then?"

"She did, but a terrible thing happened to him. She was on the return leg of her maiden voyage to American Samoa when he died of a stroke. Fell from the captain's chair in the wheelhouse and was dead three hours later. He had no wife, no family and they buried him at sea. Sad. The chief mate took over the bridge and, now, I'll relieve him. I don't look forward to that."

"Why?"

"Because I'll be relieving The Spoon."

"The Spoon?"

"Yeah. John Speer, my roommate at the Academy. You remember me talking about John."

"Yes, but I don't remember you ever calling him that. How'd he get that nickname? "

"He was -- is -- a bright guy. Has a high I.Q. with lots of money to boot. Tall, dark, handsome and a real Errol Flynn with the girls. You name it, honey, he's got it.

Anyway, he seldom cracked a book, but he always had the right answers in class and for exams. Everyone said he spooned the answers up from his rectal orifice. The Spoon. Get it?"

"Heavens, Frank, that's a horrible name to give someone! At the academy, you probably called it just what it is. A . . s . . s."

She curled her lower lip as she spelled the word and the letters came out in a distorted wheezing sound.

"We did. But this isn't funny, Lynne. He was the chief mate and became acting captain when the old man died. Now I relieve him and he goes back to being a mate. When I heard I was to take command of his ship, I almost turned down the job. He'll probably sign off when he learns I'm coming, if he hasn't already. I wouldn't blame him. Everyone in our class predicted he'd be the first to make captain. My being his boss won't go down very well. I'm not happy about it."

"Why not? He'd do it in a second if the situation was reversed. He obviously hasn't passed his captain's exam. Couldn't spoon up enough right answers, I guess," she smirked. "You did, so don't go feeling sorry for him."

Frank opened the bathroom door, stepped into the bedroom, stopped abruptly and stood tall.

"I won't," he promised, his voice filling the room.

Lynne turned, saw him and jumped up.

"Oh, my God!" she exclaimed. "You look great!"

Frank grinned.

"Just great!" She touched the uniform fabric. "The tailor did a fantastic job!"

"How'd you get him to do it, Lynne, without a fitting?"

"Easy. I took a pair of your old khakis and told him to make a uniform a size smaller. I wanted a snug fit, not the loose way you wear things. He made it just right. I'm so pleased."

"You're a marvel."

"And you're a handsome captain," she said warmly. "Because you are, here's your other gift."

She bent down and reached under the bed.

"Another gift?"

"Yes. This."

She pulled out a large suitcase and he knew immediately it was expensive, handtooled from fine, light brown leather with four encircling blue bands somewhat like the four stripes on his shoulder epaulets.

"I can't use that, Lynne," he groaned. "It's too big. I prefer my seabag. Besides, it's too expensive."

"It's not. I bought it, and the uniform, with pocket money I saved and because I'm proud of you. You can't refuse this, Frank. I won't have you carrying your things in that beatup bag like you've been doing. That's not becoming of a captain. Besides, there's something special inside, just for you."

She winked, smiled mischievously, picked up the luggage bag, placed it on the bed and lifted the top.

"Look, darling. Here's something special to remember me on lonely nights."

Frank looked into the cavernous bag, gulped, stared long at the photograph in the gold frame and turned, red-faced, to his wife.

"My God, Lynne, you're almost nude!"

It was an accusation. She giggled.

He picked up the frame and stared long at the black and white study of his wife. It was unlike anything she had ever done before, entirely out of character. It was her habit to undress alone in the bathroom, returning to their bed after showering and putting on a long nightgown. He could remove that nightwear only after the lights were turned out. They never made love during the day. The photograph revealed more of her than he had ever seen in daylight, more than he saw when she wore a swimsuit at the beach.

"I don't like to be looked at when I'm nude," she had explained on their wedding night.

They were married by a justice of the peace in Elkton, Maryland, a mecca for those on the East Coast who didn't want to wait the normal three days after obtaining a license. Frank wanted a church wedding but, in that logical way that always got Lynne exactly what she wanted, she insisted on the civil ceremony.

"You have no family, at least at home," she had pointed out. "It doesn't matter to my family where we're married. A peace justice is just as legal and, besides, I don't want to wait another minute."

They didn't. The five-minute ceremony was performed that day and they spent a three-night honeymoon at her uncle's seashore house near Rehobeth Beach, Delaware. Frank went back to sea the fourth day. Although neither was particularly religious, and seldom went to church, they did have a religious ceremony on their first anniversary. In Frank's Lutheran church. They had a second honeymoon in the bridal suite of the fancy Southern Hotel in downtown Baltimore. For five nights. That was when Frank, Jr., was conceived.

"My God," he exclaimed again.

The photograph reminded Frank of the suggestive pinup posters of actresses that are becoming so popular with American servicemen. Lynne was dressed in flimsy see-through panties and an open-lace bra that barely concealed her breasts. He contemplated the face staring back at him. It was a pretty face, with long, straight hair, lean, nicely proportioned figures that showed her cheekbones, a small pugnose, a soft curve of the chin, innocent eyes and pale skin. He took in the wide mouth with soft outlines, brightening with the beginning of a smile.

A sensuous smile, he thought, and felt a rising in his groin.

"When? Where? Why?" he gasped.

"The day after you got your captain's license. Last Wednesday."

She leaned over, touched his chest lightly, then began unbuttoning his shirt.

"At the studio on Charles Street where Alice works. She was with the photographer though. Spoilsport!"

She feigned annoyance at her sister.

"Gosh, Frank, to think you're a captain at age twenty-six gives me the goosebumps. You can see them in the photograph."

She unfastened another button.

"I'm not so special, honey," he said, trying to ignore her moving hands. "It's happening to a lot of us in this war. So many ships are coming off the ways they can't find enough experienced engineers, mates and masters. They move us up fast. They're going to need a lot more before this fight is over."

"And Billy made chief engineer just a month ago!" she said, unfastening another button. "Won't your father be proud? He doesn't know about Billy either. I can't wait to tell him."

Frank's brother, Billy, two years older, quit high school in 1931 and sailed out of Baltimore as an engine room wiper on a rusty tramp, loaded to her marks with coal, bound for Copenhagen. Their father, a seafarer since before World War I and a boatswain in charge of the deck crew for as long as they could remember, was on a voyage to Hong Kong when Billy took off. He had encouraged the boys to seek a life at sea when they grew up, but was like a raging hurricane when he learned of his eldest son's sudden departure. He hadn't expected Billy to quit school.

"You'll stay in school, you'll graduate and, then, if you still want to go to sea, you'll go to the New York Maritime Academy!" he had stormed at Frank as though his youngest son had been the guilty one. "By God and all that's right, you'll get an education! You'll learn a lot more and you'll start as an officer, deck or engine room, your choice. I won't have you sailing as a deck ape, like me, or the black gang like Billy."

His words were final.

Frank did go to the academy, at Fort Schuyler, New York, graduating with a third mate's license and even more enthusiasm for a life at sea. Shipboard jobs were scarce in 1936 and he had to settle for a job as ablebodied seaman, in the unlicensed deck crew, on his first trip. The four-month experience hauling three-inch hawsers, chipping rust off hulls, standing at the helm and living in crowded, sweat-scented foc'sles gave him a deep understanding of how the unlicensed crew worked and lived. That helped gain a greater respect for the crew and, in return, for himself when he finally sailed as a third mate and earned successively higher licenses. America's entry into the war had speeded the process.

His shirt was completely unbuttoned and he tried halfheartedly to remove the slender hand Lynne thrust inside, slowly stroking the black hairs on his chest.

"And because I don't want you to forget me on this voyage," she whispered, tugging to loosen his belt.

"I could never forget you," he protested. "But please, pugnose, I just got dressed and have to pack now. The plane takes off from Harbor Field in . ." he looked at his watch . ." in two and one-half hours. There's no time for what you want."

She smiled the almost smile in the photograph.

"A repeat of last night will only take half an hour, silly. Junior will sleep past that. All of your clothes are on top of the dresser. When we're through, I'll finish packing while you dress. We'll make it in plenty of time. The airport is only thirty-five minutes away."

"Forty-five!"

She took one of his hands gently and led him to the bed.

Her sexual appetite has increased enormously, Frank thought as he stepped out of his shoes and pulled down the trousers he had put on just a few moments ago. *Why?* Before, in the week or so between other voyages, she was reticent, shy, and he felt lucky if they had sex once or twice. This time they had made love no less than twenty times in the nearly four weeks he had been home. *Oh, well,* he told himself, *women supposedly get more sexually aroused as they get older.* He remembered reading that somewhere and wondered if it was true.

He got into the bed.

0845 HOURS
Wilmington, North Carolina
A 1940 Chevrolet sedan with U. S. Coast Guard insignias painted on the two front doors stopped in front of the emergency room at Wilmington General Hospital.

"Here we are," the uniformed driver told Boatswain Jim Davis, sitting in the front passenger seat. "It's a good hospital considering the size of this city. They'll take good care of you."

He didn't get out to open the passenger door. Jim struggled with the handle for a moment. Both hands were swathed in one-inch gauze and none of his fingers were free. Ointment had been applied to his burned hands at the Coast Guard station to which he and the other four survivors of the S. S. *Terrapin* had been taken. The officer of the day had wrapped the boatswain's hands with the small gauze, the only size available in the station's first aid kit. It was not a very professional job.

"Need some help?" the driver finally asked.

"No, I think I've got it now," Jim said, pushing the handle all the way down until he heard a click and using his right shoulder to push the door open. "Thanks," he said, not looking back at the Coast Guardsman and using his shoulder to close the door again.

He walked straight to the emergency room entrance. Inside, he approached the registration desk.

"I'd like to see a doctor," he said simply.

"Your name?" the bespectacled woman behind the desk asked.

"Davis. James Charles."

She wrote his name on a sheet that looked like a ship's manifest.

"Have a seat," she directed. "We'll call you."

Jim sat in a chair in the far corner of the green-painted room. *What a terrible color,* he thought. It reminded him of a drunken seaman's bile. He surveyed the others waiting in the room. Two mothers with crying babies. A very pregnant teen-age girl, seated between a stonyfaced man and a distraught woman. *Angry parents,* he guessed. A Negro with a deep cut on his right forearm, blood oozing from what looked like a knife wound. The man pressed a dirty handkerchief against the wound and Jim shook his head, concerned. *You damn fool! You're only making it worse!*

It was nearly an hour before Jim's name was called.

"Report to the nurse inside that first door," the woman instructed, pointing. "She'll get all the information the doctor needs."

The nurse took his vital signs. Blood pressure. Temperature. Pulse.

"What's wrong with your hands?" she asked.

"Burned."

"With what?"

"Oil," Jim answered.

"How'd that happen?"

Jim hesitated.

"Look," the nurse said impatiently. "I need to know for the doctor."

"My ship was sunk last night."

"Were you on that ship?"

"What ship?"

"The one blown up off the coast about eleven o'clock?"

"Yes."

"I saw that!" the nurse said excitedly. "My boyfriend and I were . . well, we were at his place on the beach. All of a sudden we saw this ball of fire way out on the water. And more balls of fire, one after the other. It was spectacular! Beautiful!"

Jim stared into her dancing eyes.

"Twenty-seven men died in that *beautiful* fire," he said quietly.

"Oh, my gosh, I'm sorry. How stupid of me. It must have been terrible."

Jim didn't answer.

"Dr. Shaw," she called to a man across the room. "Look at this patient, will you? He was on that ship I told you about. The one blown up last night."

"By two torpedoes," Jim said mildly.

"By two torpedoes!" the nurse shouted and three other women came running across the room. Norman Shaw, M.D., followed.

"Was it exciting?" a nurse's aide asked.

Jim looked at her. Young, probably no more than nineteen. Pretty. Definitely pretty, with blonde hair, blue eyes, an innocent expression and large breasts. He didn't answer, but his eyes told her it wasn't exciting. It was hell.

"Sorry," she fumbled.

Dr. Shaw slowly and gently unwrapped the loose gauze from Jim's hands and forearms.

"Nasty looking," he said with emphasis. "Third degree burns are always nasty."

He saw Jim flinch as he got closer to the skin.

"Hurt?"

"It's okay," Jim said.

"Don't try to be a hero here," the doctor cautioned. "The place for heroism is out there."

He pointed a finger out the window.

"Looks like you may have been one."

Jim kept quiet.

"They give you anything for the pain at the Coast Guard station?"

"Aspirin."

"Aspirin? You need something stronger than that. Nurse," he called to the young and pretty one. "Get me one-quarter grain of morphine."

Turning, he said to Jim: "We'll give you a little now and some more later, in about forty-five minutes or an hour. Should help ease the pain."

"I can live with it," Jim said bluntly.

"Maybe so, but here you get the works. Burns like these are open wounds without danger of hemorrhage, but there's always a good possibility of shock and infection. You're probably past the danger point for shock, but we've got to protect against infection." The doctor finished unrolling the small gauze. "These kinds of burns are among the most incapacitating types of injury until they're healed. That'll take several weeks, maybe more. And, I want you to know, straight out, there's a good chance you won't ever have full use of these hands. They're also apt to be disfigured."

"Glad it wasn't my face then, " Jim said gratefully.

The nurse came with the morphine.

"Here," Dr. Shaw said as he stuck the needle intramuscularly in Jim's left upper arm. "Two, three minutes, much of the pain will be reduced. You may get a bit drowsy."

He picked up Jim's right arm gently, examining the hand.

"This one's worse. It's pretty well cooked, charred. The left hand's blistered but the burn hasn't gone as deep."

Jim nodded.

"Gauze compresses?" the doctor asked a nurse and, one by one, he covered the burned area on the right hand, then washed the skin surface around the burn with soap and water for several inches. "The gauze compresses prevent the water and soap from touching the burned area. They'll come off in a minute."

"Oh," Jim said. It made sense.

The doctor removed the compresses and did not attempt to remove dirt and other debris from the burned area, although he carefully washed away some of the oil around the wound with the help of rubbing alcohol. The charred and blistered area would protect the underlying tissues against entry of germs until a dressing could be applied. He sprinkled sulfanilamide, about ten grams, on the burns.

"Marvelous product, this sulfanilamide," he said, being sure he didn't sprinkle too much on one place. "Can be used for almost any wound and even treats syphilis. That's some combination!"

Jim felt he was in a medical classroom, being lectured by a professor. He wondered if the doctor gave the same sort of running account of treatment to all his patients.

Dr. Shaw applied new sterile gauze compresses coated with petroleum jelly, covering the burned surface and an area two or three inches beyond. He placed gauze carefully between the fingers, so the two raw surfaces would not touch each other and grow together. By the time he was through, he had applied six thicknesses of the compresses to the right hand, added a large resilient gauze pad made from cotton wrapped in gauze and secured all these compresses firmly, but not tightly, with an elastic roller bandage. He did the same thing to Jim's left hand and, when finished, the boatswain looked as if he was carrying two large hornet's nests.

"We've got to leave those dressings on for about ten days, unless we see signs of infection developing. We'll put on a lighter dressing if everything's okay. We'll keep you here at least until --- "

"I'd rather go home," Jim interrupted. "To Baltimore."

"Out of the question!" the doctor snapped. "You won't be able to do much in the way of eating, drinking, dressing, opening doors and the like. I've got to keep you on antibiotics to ward off infection. We'll make you comfortable. We'll get you a private room if you want."

"A private room? I can't pay for one."

"You don't have to pay. We don't have a military hospital around here so we provide medical aid to servicemen until they can get to an Army or Navy base."

"But I'm not in the military. I'm a merchant seaman," Jim protested.

"So?"

"So we have to pay our own hospital and doctor bills."

"I don't believe it. You were torpedoed by a German submarine."

"That doesn't put me in the military. I'm a civilian, like you."

Dr. Shaw shook his head.

"That doesn't make sense. Good Lord, after what you've been through, one'd think you're entitled to free medical care!"

"It doesn't work that way, doctor. We get paid union wages and we pay our bills, like any working stiff. So, now, you know why I can't stay here."

"Not so fast, Mr. Davis. Like I said, you're in no condition to dress, eat, drink or do a lot of things yourself and you've got to be put on antibiotics. I'll work something out with the hospital administrator. Meanwhile, we're putting you in a private room."

"No," Jim said flatly. "I won't take charity."

"You're not getting charity. I told you I'd talk to the administrator. Trust me," the doctor said.

"Okay, Doc, you win," Jim finally said, inwardly a bit relieved. "But only for a few days and I warn you. I'll try to sign you up on my next ship. We need doctors. Problem is, they won't put doctors on merchant ships. Not enough men to warrant one. So we'll get you a purser's certificate. Pursers aren't real doctors, but most are in charge of the medicine chest. They know a bit of first aid and they hand out aspirins. Minor illnesses only, though. Nothing major. No surgeries. When you're out to sea, Doc, you can offer some real medicine to the crew. They'll love it."

He looked out the window.

"You'll find a serenity at sea you won't find in this hospital."

"Serenity? With ships being blown up like yours? No thanks. I'll stay right here."

0930 HOURS
Room 419, Wilmington, NC General Hospital
Alone in the private room, Jim stared at the ceiling and began reliving the frightening ordeal that began eleven hours ago. He vividly recalled the shock of the two torpedoes exploding into the hull of the *Terrapin* . . the sickening sights and smells of dead shipmates burned to a crisp . . the deaths of twenty-seven of those shipmates . . the fear that he and the other four survivors would not get far enough away to avoid being sucked into a whirlpool as the ship sank to her watery grave . . and his anger at the boastfullness of the captain of U-84-B.

Lieutenant Commander Reinhard Barnschmidt.

Jim's eyes narrowed. *The man had no remorse, no guilt about murdering so many unarmed civilians*, Jim thought, remembering his promise to get even some day. He hoped it wasn't just another hollow promise, but he wondered how he could keep it. He began thinking about ways and began to yawn spaciously. Drowsiness, a side effect of morphine, took precedence and he fell asleep.

Getting even with Lieutenant Commander Reinhard Barnschmidt would have to wait.

8 February 1942

0830 HOURS
Treasure Island, California
"But, Commander, sea duty's not for me," implored Lieutenant (j.g.) Harold Ross Hamilton, U. S. Navy Reserve, protesting his continued assignment as gunnery officer on the *S. S. Andrew Bennett*. "It makes me sick all the time."

Commander Horace Theodore Roosevelt, no relation to United States presidents, past or present, closed his eyes and turned his head away from the officer standing at attention in front of him. Roosevelt's responsibility with BuPers (Bureau of Personnel) at Treasure Island was to provide Armed Guard crews for merchant ships sailing from the West Coast. He was convinced the officer was a poor example to wear the Navy uniform, but good or poor, he needed a gunnery officer on every ship.

"Stop whining, Lieutenant!" he rebuked. "It's not becoming."

"Commander," Hamilton said slowly, trying to regain his composure, "when I joined the Navy Reserve two years ago they didn't tell me I had to go to sea. I was assigned to the public information office and that's what I did up to two months ago. Writing brochures and speeches for the brass. Then the war came and they assigned me to the *Bennett*. I've never fired a gun with real ammunition, not even in the short training course they gave me. I don't know what I'll do if I ever have to fire a real gun."

"You won't be personally firing the ship's guns, Hamilton. That's what you have gunners for," the commander said, dropping his tone one octave to show his growing impatience.

"Please understand, Commander," the lieutenant pleaded. "I was seasick every day on my first trip out and I couldn't -- didn't -- come out of my cabin very much. I got to the officer's wardroom only twice. I tried to get some solid food in me. It didn't work. I can't hold anything down. Not even crackers and dry bread. A drink of water makes me throw up. Sir, I clean up my own vomit. I don't want the men to know I get so sick."

"You don't look sick. Eat anything today?"

"I had some dry toast and a couple spoons of tea for breakfast. I still feel I'm on a rolling ship in a heavy sea. My stomach's terribly upset."

The commander shook his head, unbelieving, and scribbled notes on the record in front of him.

"Noted all that, Lieutenant, for your fitness report," he said, his head down.

"Sir," Hamilton said abruptly. "I want to resign my commission."

Commander Roosevelt didn't bother to look up. He had heard such requests before, from men who claimed to be conscientious objectors or who couldn't face the thought of going into battle. He pegged Hamilton as the latter kind of coward.

"Well, Lieutenant," he said slowly. "You can file your request through channels. I won't comment on how it will be received upstairs."

He finally raised his eyes, picked up his pen and pointed it at the lieutenant.

"Such a request takes time for processing. Standard procedure, you know. In the meantime, Hamilton, understand this: There's a shooting war going on. A real war. You're in it. For now anyway. Better get back to your ship. I understand her new captain will come aboard sometime today. I will not be embarrassed by having him think the Navy let him down by not supplying a gunnery officer. You're still it, Lieutenant."

There was no pleasantness in his voice.

0930 HOURS
A San Francisco Dock
Gunner's Mate First Class Charlie Hunt dropped his seabag at the top of the gangway and smartly saluted aft.

"Permission to board, sir."

"Permission granted," the watch seaman answered.

Hunt picked up his seabag and, with a gait that said he knew exactly where he was going, strode quickly to one of the Navy Armed Guard foc'sles on the aft main deck. He walked with a limp, hardly noticeable, favoring his left leg. He had been briefed at Treasure Island that he would be replacing a gunner who had manned the number eight 20-millimeter gun on the *S. S. Andrew Bennett*. Like the others in the Armed Guard complement -- nineteen gunners, a signalman and a gunnery officer -- he had volunteered for this duty. Volunteered, even though the Navy had been honest enough to warn that duty on a merchant ship was one of the most dangerous assignments in that service.

Inside the small cabin, he saw another gunner sitting on a lower bunk, writing on a tablet.

"Carter's bunk?" he asked.

"Top mine," came the answer.

Hunt took the three steps to the bunk and tossed his seabag on top the thin mattress.

"I'm his replacement. Heard he committed suicide. What happened?"

The other sailor didn't look up.

"Blew his brains out with a forty-five."
"Why?"
This time the man did raise his eyes, then stared at Hunt blankly.
"Who knows? He didn't leave a note. I think it was girl trouble. He had one here in Frisco. Talked about her all the time last trip. Said he was gonna marry her. Went ashore soon's we got here two days ago, came back yesterday morning, went to his tub and shot himself. Wasn't much left of his head."
He went back to his scribbling.
Hunt thought about that a moment.
"No girl's worth doing that," he said.

1200 HOURS
Oakland, California
The noonday sun mixed with the breeze and painted a tapestry of dancing tree limbs on the redwood picnic table. Marilyn Littman tried to catch one of the shadows with her right index finger as she listened with one ear to the car radio playing *I Don't Want to Walk Without You* and with the other to the pleadings of Ordinary Seaman Mark Anthony Durante.
"But, Marilyn, we're sailing tomorrow, I think, and I can't get off the ship again. This is our last chance."
"I suppose that means you want to throw me into those bushes right now and take it from me," she said matter-of-factly.
"No, no, not like that! I have a feeling about this trip, a premonition that something bad is going to happen. I can feel it in my bones. It's like . . well, Marilyn, please, I want you before . . before . ."
He stopped and, with his eyes, told her he didn't think he'd be coming back again. Tony was an ordinary seaman on the *Bennett*'s maiden voyage and that was his first trip. He was seventeen and acutely aware he might not reach eighteen.
"Every guy says that these days," she pouted. "Just to make out."
"But it's true and . . Hey! What do you mean 'every guy?' You been seeing other guys while I was gone?"
"No, silly, and calm down. I've been your girl since the sixth grade. You know I love you, that there's no one else. There never will be. I've promised to marry you. What

more do you want?"

"I want you now."

"You've promised you'll take thirty days shore time after this trip. We'll be married then."

"We could be gone a year. Maybe more. Why can't we do it today?" he asked impatiently.

"Oh, Tony, Tony! When will you understand? I want to be married in white."

"Well, you can be. No one but us will ever know."

He timidly reached over and put a hand on her left breast, softly fondling it. She had let him feel her like this a couple of times before, but as soon as her breathing became heavier and faster and he tried to touch between her thighs, she would ask him to stop. He always did.

"You'll look beautiful in white," he said, his hand moving to her right breast.

She removed the hand gently, but firmly, and held it, his use of the word "beautiful" making her laugh. Plain would be more like it. Plain Marilyn. No one but Tony would ever call her beautiful. Short blonde hair, round face, hazel eyes, curved nose, chubby body with big dimples on her elbows and knees. Thick eyeglasses in metal frames that made her face seem larger than it was. She wanted to lose thirty pounds before the wedding and already had begun to diet. She refused milk shakes, even a Coca-Cola, on this picnic, settling for carrots and unsweetened lemonade. He drank a couple of beers, ate three ham and cheese sandwiches and finished off with several slices of cheesecake she had baked. Marilyn was a good cook. She would make a good wife.

"Don't bullshit me, Tony," she said. "Beautiful I'm not. But I am a virgin. I'll be one on our wedding night."

There was distant rumbling of thunder.

"Besides, we'd get wet doing it out here," she said pointedly.

She's weakening, Tony thought and his hopes were raised. He looked at the sky.

"The rain won't come for half hour at least," he said confidently. "We can do it before then."

Her body stiffened. His words implied he would hurry the loving. She stood up, hands on hips, and shouted defiantly into his face:

"If you think, Mark Anthony Durante, it's only going to take a half hour to take away my virginity, you're wrong! Dead wrong! I want more than that!"

He knew he had lost. He couldn't budge her from the Catholic tenet that a woman had to be pure and unbroken "down there" when she married. The nuns drilled that into the girls' heads at the high school both had attended in Oakland. The priests talked celibacy to the boys, but mainly explained it in dirty jokes. He raised his arm, caressed her head and sighed.

"Marilyn, I'm one too. So help me, I'll still be one when I come back." He sucked in his breath. "If I come back."

"You will," she whispered, touching his cheek. "You will. God meant for us to be married and God takes care of the people He loves and who love Him. Nothing's going to happen to you. I have faith."

She kissed him tenderly.

"You'll see, darling. You'll see."

1230 HOURS
Aboard the S. S. Andrew Bennett

Ordinary Seaman Gary Benson was dumbfounded at the Navy gunner's statement.

"You've got to be kidding, Cookie!" he admonished.

"No, it's true, Gary. I never heard of the Merchant Marine 'til I volunteered for the Armed Guard," Seaman First Class George Cookman said seriously. "When did they set up this service?"

"Jesus, Cookie, there's been a merchant marine for a thousand years. More even."

"You're kidding!"

"Ever hear of Christopher Columbus?"

"Sure."

"The Vikings?"

"Yeah."

"Noah's Ark?"

"Good God, yes!" The last question exasperated the Navy man. "What's the Ark got to do with it?"

"In a way, it was God's merchant marine," Gary said, satisfied and condescending.

There was a flicker of surprise in Cookie's nicotine-brown eyes. The two men, one in Navy blue workclothes and the other in civilian dungarees and white undershirt, were on a coffee break, standing on the stern of the *Bennett* and watching longshoremen load the ship. Both had been assigned to the ship three months ago, on its maiden voyage. Benson in the merchant crew. Cookman in the Navy Armed Guard.

"Well, the Ark was a ship," Cookie admitted. "But I still don't see -- "

"Every country surrounded by water has had a merchant marine ever since man learned to build boats and carry himself and his possessions from one place to another over water," Gary interrupted.

He was relishing this conversation. He had already established himself as the ship's philosopher despite his tender nineteen years. Tall, witty, a high school graduate, and articulate, he had deep penetrating eyes that looked squarely into the eyes of those to whom he talked, and listened, and one knew he absorbed every nuance of every word. Spoken or unspoken.

"Trade between countries is the bulwark of the world's economy," he continued. "Most of that trade is carried on ships."

"Okay, okay, but we're in a war. How come these merchant ships aren't part of the military? They're in combat, they need Navy gunners on them and Navy ships protect them in convoys. So why aren't they in the Navy?"

"That would take hours to explain, Cookie," Gary said softly. "Hours."

"Well, put it in a nutshell."

Gary thought a long while, probing for a simple answer.

"Look," he finally said. "The Merchant Marine has been run by private shipping companies ever since this country was born. Our government wants to keep it that way. No sense putting these ships in the Navy and then giving them back to civilian hands after the war. Some people want that to happen, but that would be stupid the way our government wastes money and men. If the Navy took over this ship, it would put a crew of one hundred fifty aboard instead of the forty-one we now have. Takes three Navy guys to do the job of one merchant seaman."

He put up a hand to stop his friend from answering that insult.

"Don't ask me why. Government, whether federal, state or local, always needs more people to do a job than private business. It's a fact of political life. The Navy would have to refit the ship for the larger crew. More money. Things are screwed up enough without that."

He paused, brushing a finger over his right eye.

"We built a strong Merchant Marine in World War I with Navy gunners like you on the ships, but when the war was over we let it fall apart. Scrapped most of the ships. Sold others to foreign countries. It was damn foolish of our government. Now we've got a bunch of old ships, many made of wood and damn few with guns like this one."

"It's hard to believe the country's done that and especially that most cargo ships don't have guns."

"We've got to build the Merchant Marine all over again. That's why we're building Liberty ships like the *Bennett*."

"She sure is a beautiful ship," Cookie said.

"Yeah. The country's planning to launch at least two of them every day. More even."

"That's a lot of ships."

"Sure is, but they've figured a way to mass produce them. A guy named Kaiser has a couple of shipyards where he builds a ship in sections, then hoists the sections with cranes to be joined together in the drydock. Trouble is the country doesn't have enough men to sail the ships they're building."

"Geez, Gary, why'd you join the Merchant Marine? You're smart, not like most of the crew. Some of them don't even know how to read. You're young. Most of the others are old and uneducated. You don't fit in. Was it for the money?"

"Hell, no, Cookie! The money's not important."

Benson was disappointed. Differing pay scales sometimes caused friction between merchant seamen and the Armed Guard. Seamen's salaries were more than four times the pay for Navy gunners. Gary had thought Cookie too good a friend to bring up the specter of that problem.

"Then why?"

"The Army turned me down," Benson said sharply. "Flat feet, would you believe? So I got my seaman's papers. I couldn't sit this war out in the States. If I wanted money, I could make a lot more working in a shipyard, building Libertys, or in a factory building tanks. That's not for me and it's not for a lot of guys like me. You're going to see a lot more of us in the Merchant Marine."

He paused again, giving more thought to what he wanted to say.

"There's a lot of action on merchant ships and I want to be in on some of it."

"So do I, Buddy!" Cookie said loudly. "So do I!"

1300 HOURS
At the Ship's Gangway
As he neared the top of the *Bennett*'s gangway, Captain Frank Davis was tired after the long, turbulent cross-country flight on four DC-3s and more than just a little apprehensive about his new command, his new responsibility. Frank mentally wished he was carrying the more familiar seabag instead of the suitcase. He wished even more that he had not worn the white uniform Lynne had tailored for him. It already was dirty and he felt self-conscious, embarrassed. He was sure he would never put the whites on again. He straightened his shoulders, pulled in his stomach and filled his chest with air as his feet hit the ship's steel deck. He saluted the aft colors.

"I request permission to come aboard."

"Permission granted, sir," the watch seaman said stiffly.

He was not accustomed to such formality. Nor to a white uniform.

Frank looked aft and saw a Sherman tank being lowered from the steel jumbo boom into the number four hold. Another was just being lifted over the rail by a dock crane, headed for hold number five, and longshoremen were securing a number of other tanks on the port aft main deck. There was an enormous straining and rumbling from the steam-driven cargo winches.

"I'm Captain Davis," he said, his eyes riveted to the scene on the deck.

"We've been expecting you, sir. I'll send for the chief mate."

"No. I want to go to my quarters and freshen up," the captain said. "I'll look up the mate shortly."

He turned around and fastened his eyes on the seaman. The man appeared to be in his forties. Both forearms were heavily tattooed with interweaving blue snakes, each with red forked tongues. Tiny black spiders were on all ten fingers, just above the knuckles, and Frank was sure there were more tattoos on other parts of the man's body. A bandage ran down the side of his face, almost from his right eye to under his chin. Small splashes of dried blood showed through the gauze. His eyes were dark, piercing, and seemed to say, *don't screw with me.* The bandage said someone had tried.

"Your face, seaman?" Frank questioned.

"It's nothin', sir. Just a scratch," the seaman smiled

sheepishly. "Some nutty Navy bums . . excuse me, sir . . some Navy sailors got a bit stupid in a bar las' night an' one of 'em was crazy enough to question our patriotism. Called us 'draft dodgers.' Ha! That's nuts! We got an ex-Navy man with a pegleg, a watertender with one arm an' a chief engineer who's seventy-one. He swallowed the anchor more'n ten years ago, but came back after Pearl. Call those guys draft dodgers?"

He snorted.

"An' me, sir? Been torpedoed twice already. Once before we got in this stupid war . . excuse me again, sir . . an' my last ship. Imagine those bastards sinkin' one of ours an' we was neutral! Two ships in five months. Swabbie called me a draft dodger. Hell, at forty-seven, the Army wouldn't 'ave me. Too old. Don't blame 'em. I wouldn't be much good as a soldier. Been goin' to sea since I was fourteen."

He balled up his fist and punched at an imaginary jaw.

"I didn't like his mouth so I hit'im. A couple of times. Scratched me with a broken bottle, he did, but I bet he's in a Navy hospital this mornin'." He laughed with satisfaction. "We got out before the Shore Patrol got there."

It was a long speech to justify his barfight. It also gave Frank his first insight into some of the crew.

A pegleg deck seaman. An engine room watertender with one arm. A chief engineer who should be home sitting in a rocking chair. In front of him, a seasoned deckhand who apparently likes to use his tattooed fists as weapons. Captain Davis studied the man. At six foot two, about two hundred twenty pounds, he was built like a heavyweight boxer. Older, but well muscled, with a ruddy, rounded face. His complexion was dark and wizened from too much sun and salt spray, almost shrouding the tattoos, but he looked to be in good physical shape. His hands were oversized, like sledge hammers. Not a man to trifle with in a bar or back alley. Or any place.

"I don't like my crew fighting in bars," Frank said softly, but with authority. "Particularly with the Navy. Not good for our reputation. Besides, we've got Armed Guard aboard."

"Oh, they wasn't Armed Guard. Gun crews on these ships know better. Some may be jealous 'bout our pay . . can't blame 'em 'cause they're underpaid . . but they know we ain't here to dodge the draft. Those jerks were from that cruiser over there."

He pointed to a Navy ship at anchor.

"Your name, seaman."

"Jones. Joseph Aloysius Jones." He winked.

The name seemed fictional enough to be an escape from a wife or perhaps the law. In any case, Frank understood. He had met men like this before. They are running away from something or someone, but certainly not the war.

The captain nodded, then said with only a trace of harshness:

"Under the circumstances, Jones, you may have been justified. Your chances of being killed on a merchant ship are higher than in the Army or even on that Navy ship. But, still, I want no more barfights under my command."

He bent to pick up his suitcase.

"We'll get that, sir." Jones moved quickly, hoisting the heavy luggage as though it was a bakery bag of creampuffs and pointed it toward a barechested seaman lounging on the nearby starboard rail.

"Wilson, carry this to the captain's quarters, will ya?"

Harvey Wilson walked over quickly, saluted awkwardly, grabbed the suitcase and lifted it with two strong hands to hide his naked chest.

"New suitcase, sir?" he asked casually, probing to learn something about the new skipper.

Frank didn't know how to answer. He looked hard at the seaman who appeared to be twenty or younger. Wilson was of medium height and strongly built, with yellow hair, bright blue eyes and soft features. His complexion was fair with a vaguely reddish hue that went with good health and, despite his modest bulk, he displayed a body that kept itself in good shape. A baseball cap tilted rakishly on the back of his head. The only detractions Frank saw before Wilson hid his almost hairless chest with the suitcase were a long scar running down the right side and two tiny bluebirds tattooed above the nipples. The scar was ugly and the birds seemed incongruous to the rest of his body.

"Let's find my quarters," was all Captain Davis said.

He strode quickly into the midships passageway, knowing exactly where to find his new quarters. Up the ladder to the bridge deck, starboard side, aft the chartroom. His last ship, too, had been a Liberty, one of the first built, and most of these "ugly ducklings" were exactly the same.

Frank's thoughts raced. He had not answered Wilson's question on deck, abruptly cutting off the conversation. Frank was sure Wilson and Jones knew he had just obtained his master's license. The white uniform gave that away. The new suitcase said without words that he was either trying to show off his new rank or that his previous clothes and seabag had been lost in a sinking. The latter was a familiar story these days.

Out on deck, Frank wasn't prepared to answer. He had been taught at the maritime academy, and knew from experience, that a captain's personality and character are important for the morale of the crew. In the week since he received his license as master of steam and motor vessels, any gross tons, upon oceans, he understood for the first time the axiom that a captain must stand apart from the crew, that he not develop too close a relationship with any of them. He also had been taught that sea law dictates a ship's captain is the jury, the judge and, if necessary, the executioner of his subordinates. He knew, however, that the Merchant Marine was more tolerant in matters of shipboard conduct than the Navy, more tolerant than itself had been a half century ago. In large part, this relaxing of custom was due to the unions which, since the strikes of the early thirties, had become more vociferous and demanding. Too serious a discipline of a man by a captain at sea could lead to a confrontation with the union when the ship returned to port.

Still, because of custom, command at sea is among the loneliest of all professions and Frank's gregarious nature went against the grain, a trait that was sure to make his job more difficult. He realized that one of the things he had lost when he earned his captain's papers was a sense of belonging, of being a member of the team. He could no longer sit in the galley, as he had when he was a mate, swapping jokes, tall stories or just having that sense of being a part of the crew.

In a way, he resented his new role.

He wanted to be on friendly terms with his crew, particularly on this first command, wanted to earn their respect, wanted them to like him. Above all, because he was so young, he did not want a lot of speculation about his character or experience. Merchant seamen, whether boy or old salt, had an uncanny way of combining fact with fiction when it came to officers. Especially captains. His youth would be a problem, particularly among the older, more seasoned seafarers. He wasn't the youngest captain in the Merchant Marine. He knew two who were twenty-four and heard that one was only twenty-two. Surely, those masters younger than he also had the same problem of being accepted by their crews. Frank needed some way to let them know that, although only twenty-six years old, he had enough knowledge, experience and self-assurance to take them into harm's way and do his best to bring them back safely.

The solution came sooner than he expected. As he started up the second ladder leading to his quarters, he saw two legs starting down, then pulling back. When he reached the top, he heard a raspy voice.

"Holy Jesus! It's Baby Ruth!" The seaman seemed incredulous at first, then embarrassed. "Oh, sorry, sir. I didn't mean . . "

Frank looked at the face of the voice and immediately recognized the deck engineer from his last ship. The "donkeyman" was part of the engine crew, but responsible for the maintenance of the steam-driven cargo winches, windlass, warping winch, steering gear, all machinery on deck.

"It's Phipps, isn't it? Nelson Phipps? Donkeyman?"

"Yes, sir."

"How come you're here in Frisco? I thought you shipped out on the East Coast."

"Did, sir, but that North Atlantic was getting too cold for me. Especially that last trip. Wow! You know what I mean, sir. My home's in Provo, Utah, so I went there when we got back to New York after the *Hennessey* . . well, you know. Saw my parents and an old girlfriend -- she's married now -- found a new one and signed on this Liberty yesterday. Deck engineer again. Thought I'd enjoy the warmth of the Pacific for awhile."

He held his arms upward, then wiped his forehead, pantomiming his need for the heat of the sun.

"Baby Ruth? Is that what the *Hennessey* crew called me?" Frank asked.

"Well, you see, sir. You're from Baltimore and Babe Ruth's from Baltimore. The baseball player, you know, and, well, you were so young to be the chief mate and, well . . "

He struggled for the right explanation and found none.

"Gosh, those four gold stripes look mighty good on you, Captain."

Phipps turned to Wilson.

"He was chief mate on my last trip."

He turned back to the captain.

"Congratulations, sir. We're lucky to have you as our skipper."

He ducked down the ladder, whistling.

Frank happily bounced the remaining few feet to his stateroom. Having Deck Engineer Phipps aboard was a stroke of good luck. After what happened on the last trip, the donkeyman, he was certain, would help solve the problem about the crew accepting Frank's age. As he turned the doorknob, he looked back at Wilson.

"You an ordinary seaman?"

"Able-bodied," Wilson said proudly. "Got my ticket last week. Came aboard two days ago."

"Where you from?"

"Oklahoma, sir. A farm near Cushing. Ever hear of it?"

"About fifty miles northeast of Oklahoma City," Frank said without hesitation. "Cushing's a long way from the ocean. Why'd you join the Merchant Marine?"

"I tried to enlist in the Army on December eighth. I wanted to get into the war after what those Japs did, but they wouldn't take me. Said I was too young. I'm sixteen, sir. Figured the Navy would say the same thing so went down to Houston where I heard they needed merchant seamen. They weren't as particular and gave me ordinary seaman's papers right away. I like it better than the farm."

The captain took an immediate liking to the boy who was younger than he had thought. He appreciated his youthful innocence and straightforward honesty. He wanted to chat more, to get to know him better, but knew he had to keep a captain's distance. Besides, he had a new ship to ready for departure. He opened the door and stepped inside the quarters that would be his home for only God knows how long. Wilson set the suitcase down and crossed his arms over his chest. The beak of one tattooed bluebird peeked out.

"Anything else, sir?"

"Nothing now. But, Wilson, I want you to wear a shirt on deck when we're in port. At sea, too, with the sleeves down, hot weather or not, in case we see any combat. Protects against gunpowder flash burns. And ask the purser to get the officers together in the saloon in an hour."

"Sir, all the officers but the chief engineer and chief mate are ashore. Expect the others won't be back 'til very late or 'til tomorrow morning. The chief mate said we'll be shoving off soon and told the officers to be back aboard by oh eight hundred. They've all got wives or girlfriends ashore."

His eyelids flipped up and down nervously.

"We don't have a purser assigned yet," he added apologetically.

"No purser? What happened to the last one?"

Wilson hesitated.

"The way I hear it, sir, he blamed himself for the captain's death. I'm sure you know the Old Man died of a stroke before the ship got back."

Frank nodded.

"As the ship's doctor -- and you know yourself, sir, pursers aren't real doctors -- he thought he should have done more to save the captain. He never saw anyone suffer a stroke before and didn't recognize the symptoms. The skipper was unconscious. They say that after he got the captain to the sick bay he kept reading the book in the medicine chest and, while he was doing it, the Old Man died. He signed off soon as the ship docked. Some of the old crew thinks he won't sail again."

Frank nodded again, understanding. The purser is a staff officer, the ship's administrative officer, who also doubles on most ships as a "doctor." Any officer with an ounce of first aid training was given the job, sometimes the Navy gunnery officer, but it mostly went to pursers. Some were given short courses in emergency medicine at sea. Others qualified for a purser's certificate because, in addition to their administrative talents, they had taken a Red Cross or had earned a Boy Scout merit badge in first aid. To help them, all ships carry a book, *The Ship's Medicine Chest and First Aid at Sea*. It describes in simple and nontechnical language the diseases and medical emergencies most commonly encountered at sea, the signs and symptoms by which they are recognized and directions for first aid and follow up or prolonged emergency treatment until a port is reached. With wartime radio silence on ships, a purser has nowhere to turn for advice except the book. On most Libertys, there is a hospital -- actually an aft cabin on the main deck filled with medical stores and four pipe berths. It is tough on pursers with an extremely ill patient, particularly one needing an operation. Appendicitis. Ruptured colon. Some patients die before a ship reaches port where a real doctor can be found. It is natural for the purser to feel guilt.

What's wrong with the steamship company that it hadn't immediately assigned a new purser? Frank asked himself. He would have to call the company this afternoon.

"Post a notice at the head of the gangway for an officers meeting tomorrow at ten thirty hours in the saloon," he told Wilson. "Breakfast will be over by then. Also post to the crew that everyone's to be aboard by sixteen hundred tomorrow."

"We sailing tomorrow night?" Wilson asked.

"You know better than to ask that," the captain said sternly, turning to hoist his suitcase to the bunk.

"Yes, sir." Wilson crossed one arm over the tattoos, turned smartly and walked out of the cabin.

Alone, Frank smiled to himself. He hadn't had to answer Wilson's questions after all. He was sure Deck Engineer Phipps was already spreading the word about what happened on his last trip, about the torpedoing. Frank had been going to sea long enough to know that the story, magnified with each telling, would work its way around the ship like wildfire in a wheatfield.

"At least they'll know I wasn't in command when she took those fish," he said aloud.

Older seamen get spooky around a captain who loses a ship and survives to talk about it. Somehow they cling to the absurd notion that he should go down with the ship if any of the crew dies in the attack. No such stigma is attached to other deck officers who survive torpedoes and sinkings. Frank knew, too, that A. B. Wilson would tell the others that the new captain cared about his crew. Witness the banter about Wilson's hometown. He was sure the seaman would also say the captain was stern and knew what he was talking about. Witness the bit about Wilson's shirt. Frank felt smug.

He studied his new quarters. The sleeping cabin was an exact replica of those on all Libertys. A large bunk against the outboard steel bulkhead, with four storage drawers below. A porthole over the bunk, with a blackout cover for use at night. A small wardrobe for hangup uniforms and coats, a settee covered with green imitation leather and a door that led to a shower, wash basin and toilet. One of the perks of being captain was having the only private head on the ship. Forward the sleeping cabin was a private office with desk, cushioned swivel armchair, straightback wooden chair, filing cabinet, safe and some bookshelves. The chartroom was adjacent and forward. The rooms were separated with one and one-eighth inch plywood joiner bulkheads.

Only a few feet from his stateroom was the wheelhouse. Frank walked there, touched the telegraph to the engine room, the compass housing and the familiar spokes of the huge wooden steering wheel. Grasping the wheel with both hands, he began to feel for the first time the awesome responsibilities of being a captain. His eyes roamed the wheelhouse, resting for a moment on the chair in the aft port corner. The captain's chair. Probably the same one from which Frank's predecessor fell when he was stricken. Frank shuddered. *Was his death an omen of what's to come?* He turned quickly, shunting aside the thought, and walked to one of the small forward portholes. He knew their size restricted vision and much of the time, except in extremely bad weather, the ship would be conned from the monkey bridge topside. He took a deep breath. His nostrils filled with the salty and pungent harbor breeze. The deck underfoot felt good. He touched the bulkhead with a gesture of intimacy, feeling the bond between himself and the ship.

Regardless of what happened to the previous captain, this is where I belong, he thought.

He remembered the day after he got his master's license, when he was asked to come to the Schelling Steamship Lines' office in Baltimore and was handed an envelope addressed to Captain Francis James Davis. The letter inside was headed, "ORDERS TO ASSUME COMMAND," and Frank remembered choking up, his eyes getting blurred and his heart pounding. He was doing the same thing right now.

He returned to his sleeping quarters and plunged into unpacking with vigor, changing in the process from the whites to older, rumpled khakis. When he got to the bottom of the suitcase, he found two photographs. The one with Lynne in her daring pose, now bearing the inscription, *Darling, I'm waiting impatiently,* penned across her legs. The other a three-quarter portrait of Lynne's face, her eyes staring so that no matter which way he moved his head her eyes followed him. There was no inscription, but a note was taped to the back. *I know you can't put that other photo on view for the officers and crew though it's a spicy thought. This will be better to hang in your cabin. Stow the other, but promise you'll peek at it every now and then.*

Frank laughed aloud. His wife sensed -- no, knew -- the limitations of command, the perceptions others would have of him if they saw the near naked photograph of her. He took a roll of Scotch tape from the desk and mounted Lynne's smiling face on the bulkhead at the foot of the bunk, where he could look at her the last thing before sleep and the first thing when he woke. The portrait filled the room with her presence.

A small package was at the bottom of the suitcase, wrapped in tissue. *What the hell?* he thought, picking it up gingerly, laying it carefully on the bunk and carefully removing a yellow ribbon. Opened finally, he lifted a pair of net panties, pale blue, and an open-lace bra of the same color.

"I'll be damned!" he chuckled.

He sniffed the panties, immediately was embarrassed and quickly rewrapped them in the tissue, then placed the package atop the naughty but nice photograph and rewrapped everything with newspaper. He lifted the shirts in the bottom right hand drawer under the bunk, placed the valuables underneath, restored the shirts and patted them as if to assure they would protect his secret.

"I'll be seeing you, honey," he promised the photo on the bulkhead and left for the saloon.

Chief Mate John Speer was alone there. A plate of tuna fish salad and hard-boiled eggs was on the table in front of him, untouched. He held a half empty glass with a light brown liquid in his right hand and he was smoking the tail end of a cigar, staring at the ceiling. A strong smell of whiskey permeated the officers dining room.

"Afternoon, Spoon," Frank said, offering a hand and smiling fraternally.

The mate didn't take the hand. He took another drink from the glass and eyed Frank warily.

"When I heard you were coming aboard I thought about signing off," he said tersely, "but then I figured anyone who needed my help as much as you did at the academy will need me on this ship. So I made a deal with myself. Promised I'd stay if you'd agree never to call me by that name. 'Mister Mate' is what you call me. I call you

'Captain.' Is that a deal?"

Frank was surprised at his old roommate's abruptness. He sat down, scrutinized the man's face, absorbed. The old friendship seemed to have vanished.

"Deal," he said.

The mate finally clenched Frank's hand, firmly.

"Welcome aboard, then."

His face was passive and there was no smile. Frank was partially relieved.

"How's your love life these days?" he asked casually, hoping to brighten the conversation.

"Ain't got one," Speer said bluntly.

"You're kidding!"

"No. I'm through with women."

"Through with women?" Frank scoffed. "You? The class swordsman?"

He didn't understand. He could hear anger in the mate's words. *Why?* The man not only had been the academy's brightest cadet, but he scored, or said he did, every time he went out with a woman. He had a habit of pasting a gold star on the inside lid of his footlocker after each conquest. The lid was covered with gold before he finished his third year. *What had happened to sour him?*

"I don't believe it!"

"I don't want to talk about it," Speer said, taking another cigar from his shirt pocket and chomping on it nervously. "Heard you made quite a splash when you came aboard," he said slyly, changing the subject.

"Oh, you heard about the whites? Lynne made me wear them."

The mate rolled his eyes.

"That's one reason I haven't married," he crowed. "I don't want any damn woman telling me what to wear. That was a stupid thing you did, Captain. Pardon me for saying so. The crew's gonna laugh you down. Some don't have respect for fancy uniforms. Or any uniforms. They're union men and you know how much the unions don't want us wearing uniforms. We've always been civilians and we should stay that way."

Frank managed not to flinch at the rebuke.

The chief mate is right. The Merchant Marine should remain in private hands, he conceded, *not be run by admirals or generals in the War Department. There's enough fouled up bureaucracy now with the Coast Guard giving examinations for seamen's licenses, the War*

Shipping Administration deciding which steamship companies could receive contracts to sail these government-built ships, the Army and Navy chartering them and the Army sometimes countermanding Navy orders, commandeering ships to carry the cargoes of a few generals who think the Libertys are their own personal possessions.

"No more whites," Frank promised, getting back to the conversation. "Just khakis. No rank insignia either except when I go to convoy conferences. It's expected then."

"Understood."

The mate puffed at his cigar, then took another drink. He was a well built man, six feet tall and weighed one hundred eighty-five pounds. He had a handsome face, but with a nose a bit too large, and deep brown hair. He was trim and well muscled, the result of an exercise regimen that kept him in the same shape he had been at the maritime academy where he played football and baseball, swam, ran track and dabbled in boxing. He looked the same as he did then, although Frank sensed a tension perhaps attributable to more than having to serve under a former roommate. There was more arrogance. Anger.

"And don't ask me why I don't have my captain's license," the mate said more loudly. "I'll tell you straight. I've seen captains break down with the stupid way the government's running this war. I think I do better at taking over when they can't handle things -- gives me a sense of superiority -- but I don't risk the ripping they take from those damn admirals and generals who look down on merchant seamen. I once thought I'd like to make captain, but not now. I'll stay a mate and when this fucking war is over I'm carrying an anchor on my shoulders, walking inland and, when someone asks me what it is, I'll drop the goddamn thing and settle right there."

He laughed.

"I never thought, though, I'd ever have to serve under you. Maybe I should pick up that anchor now."

"I'm glad you're on my team," Frank said seriously. "I'll need your help."

"Damn right you will. This ship's got problems."

"What kind?"

"How much time you got?"

He paused and they looked at each other, he almost apologetically, Frank with concern.

"She has a few quirks, like most ships. Every now and then she gets sluggish when making turns. Doesn't respond quick enough. It's as if she has a mind of her own. Stubborn, like a woman. Or maybe she's tired and doesn't want to wear herself down. It's uncanny. Still, for a ship built in thirty-seven days, she does her best."

"I'm sure," Frank said, but his voice was troubled.

"She doesn't take too well to rough seas. Not as stable as most Libertys. That was tough on the crew last trip. Most of them were seasick on our way to Pango Pango, more so during the storm we went through halfway across. Christ, we smelled like a garbage scow!"

He pinched his nose as if to block out an offensive odor.

"We had a crack in the hull, just forward the bridge, starboard side, during the same storm. I wonder if she'll stay together in another one."

Frank felt his first pang of alarm.

"We had trouble with one of our boilers on the way over and we had to shut it down three times until we found out why," the mate complained. "Grease! Goddamn grease was fouling up the boiler water! Protective grease the shipyard workers forgot to remove when the boiler came from the factory. We cleaned out nine buckets in Pango Pango and didn't have any trouble on the way back."

He relit the cigar with his Zippo, studying the first puff of smoke, thoughtfully, and turned to look at Frank, more thoughtfully.

"Our crew's not exactly a captain's dream," he said, narrowing his eyes. "Mostly oldtimers, a few rookies, some able men, a couple of misfits. Nearly half signed off when we got back, saying a captain dying on the bridge is a bad omen. Maybe they're right. You heard about it?"

Frank nodded.

"Hell, he was sixty-six, overweight, drank too much and had high blood pressure," Speer went on. "What can you expect? Well, anyway, we put out a call for new crew members and what the unions sent us as replacements didn't improve our lot except for two good A.B.'s. Both are survivors of sinkings. Wilson and Jones. Wilson was wounded. Spent eleven days in a lifeboat with nine others before being picked up by a Navy PBY. Solid man. Jones looks like a top seaman but I've already noticed he likes his Scotch too much. I shouldn't complain. I'm getting to like it too."

He took another swallow.

"Problem is, Jones has a real romance for alcohol, barfights and altercations with police. Had another fight just last night with some Navy guys."

"I know," Frank said, remembering Jones' account of the fight, but he mused silently about Wilson. Eleven days in a lifeboat, wounded and the man had said nothing about it when they talked earlier. That said something about his courage. It also accounted for the scar.

"On deck, the second and third mates are capable enough," the mate continued. "The second's been going to sea more'n thirty years. Quiet fellow named Roscoe Turner. No relation to the barnstorming aviator. He's visiting his mother now in Pamona and will be back tomorrow morning. The third's a bit timid despite his name. Benjamin Franklin Franklin. Some moniker, huh? Graduated from the California Maritime Academy and signed on last trip. Even with a couple of months under his belt, he's still unsure of himself. I try to spend a lot of time with him on the bridge. A few more trips, I think he'll get the hang of it. Bo's'n Hank Burleson is topnotch. We've also got two good ordinaries who stayed on from the last trip. Tony Durante and Gary Benson. Young, but they're both hard workers. Benson's bright. He's already got a reputation as the ship's lawyer, but he's not a wise guy. I think he's material to make officer."

"Sounds good," Frank said. "What about the engine room?"

"Most of the black gang has experience. Not a young one in the lot except for a wiper. The others are old seadogs, including a watertender with one arm."

"The chief engineer?" Frank asked.

"Klaus Huben? Good man, but old. He came out of retirement but should'a stayed home. His arthritis slows him down and sometimes I think he won't make it into the engine room. He does know ship's engines and works harder than any other man. I like to go to sea with a man like that. He's a stubborn Dutchman, though. You'll have to deal with that."

"What about the purser's slot? I'm told the last one quit."

"Yeah, he had a rough time over Captain Wolff's death. Couldn't take the old man's dying. I've called the company. They're sending one over this afternoon. Young fellow named Tanner. I hear he was a pre-med student at the University of California when he decided to sign on a ship."

"Great! You've saved me a call to the company. I'm glad to hear he has some medical training. We'll need him for doctoring duties. I hear we have a pegleg aboard. Deck or engine?"

"Deck. Everingham is an ordinary seaman, one of the replacements the union sent over. Was in the Navy eight, ten years. Lost his right leg below the knee, a year before Pearl, in some kinda shipboard accident. The Navy gave him a medical discharge when he got out of the hospital. Told me he likes the sea so much he got his ordinary's papers soon's he could walk with the prosthesis. Doesn't have a pegleg though. He has an artificial one. I told him he'll go on the four to eight watch so's he wouldn't have to work too much, but he said he doesn't want that. Said he'll ask for overtime work every day but Sunday. Then you know what he did? He climbed up to the crow's nest. It's hard to tell he doesn't have two real legs. Looks like a helluva man!"

"Any troublemakers?"

The mate hesitated before answering.

"Wish you hadn't asked. We've got a new deckhand. An A. B. the union sent over as a replacement. Name's Robinson. He was serving ten to twenty years for killing a man in a federal post office, but was paroled to this ship because he has seaman's papers and more'n ten years sea experience. I guess that counts for something."

"How can they send us a man like that?" Frank demanded, worried.

"Where you been, Captain? The goddamn politicians let the Merchant Marine go to pot after the last war and, with all the new ships being built, there just aren't enough experienced men to sail them. We're begging, borrowing and stealing to fill crews. Hell, hundreds of guys are being paroled from prisons because, at one time, they sailed. Look, no matter what kind of men we have, you've got to give them credit. They may be rough, they may be hard drinkers, they may be whoremongers, but, damn it, they ain't afraid to sail! Weren't for them this country would be in deeper crap than a horse in a dirty stable. You can't move ships without men."

"You're right," Frank agreed.

He knew the manpower situation was critical. Even men with sea experience who had been drafted into the

Army were being discharged to go back to their jobs on ships.

"Most of the old seamen I've seen have a lot of guts," Frank said. "They don't seem afraid of death. They accept the torpedoes as much as the reefs and storms. Same thing's true of the young ones."

He paused, closing his eyes and pinching the bridge of his nose.

"We'll be getting some fresh blood soon, though. I hear the new United States Maritime Service is setting up some training schools for deck and engine hands. They'll be like Navy boot camps and we'll be getting some young men."

"Yeah, probably castoffs the Army and Navy won't take," Speer countered.

"No, not really. There will be a few of those, of course, and we'll get a lot of seventeen-year-olds too young for the draft. There's talk of letting sixteen-year-olds and even kids of fifteen sign on. These young kids aren't afraid of anything. That's the bright side. Speaking of the bright side, we've got a good donkeyman. He was on my last ship. Phipps knows his deck machinery so well he can take it apart and put it back together blindfolded."

"That's good!" the mate said. "We've got trouble with the aft winches."

He stood up, went to a cabinet and poured more Scotch into his glass.

"Want some?"

"This a wet ship?" Frank asked, declining with a shake of his head.

"The hard stuff's in port, stateside. But the medicine chest has a few bottles, strictly for medicinal purposes. That's what I use it for. To cure my ailments." He laughed as if he had played a joke on himself. "The crew gets a ration of a case of beer once a month if they want to buy from the Slop Chest. Want to change that?"

Frank looked around the room to ponder his reply. He rubbed his chin for a moment before turning back to his chief mate.

"No."

"Good thing," Speer said. "Cribbage, poker, Monopoly and beer are the only relaxation for the crew. Not much other recreation. Beer is profitable for some of the men. They pay a buck and sell the case for four, even five. Like cigarettes. They pay fifty cents a carton. That can buy a longshoreman's daughter in most any port."

He grinned. Frank thought such a barter was sad.

"One more thing you should know," the mate added somberly. "One of the Navy gunners shot and killed himself the day after we docked."

"God!" Frank moaned, slumping back in his chair. "Why?"

"Don't know," Speer shrugged. "Shot himself in the head. The Navy took his body off, said it was a suicide and we wouldn't be held up by an inquiry. His replacement came aboard this morning. The gunnery officer, Lieutenant Hamilton, is a weak sister type reservist. He didn't hold one gunnery drill all last trip. We don't even know if the guns will fire. He spent most of his time in his cabin. Something's wrong with the man, I'm not sure what. We can't count on him much if we see any action. I think he's scared shitless."

All the elation Frank felt when he entered the saloon was gone.

"Sounds like this ship has more than it's fair share of problems," he said.

"Hell, Captain, that's what I've been telling you!" John said. "They shoulda christened her the *S. S. Bad Luck.*"

He pointed to the brass plate and some framed words posted on the saloon's aft bulkhead.

"You should read why they named her the *Andrew Bennett*." he said. "Might give you one explanation why we had so many problems."

Frank looked askance at his chief mate, then got up and walked to the bulkhead. The brass plate was engraved simply:

S. S. Andrew Bennett
Built for
U. S. Maritime Commission
Hull No. 8
by
CALShip, Los Angeles, California
January 1942

Frank's eyes moved to the short biography printed in bold black letters inside the glassed frame. Like most Libertys, the ship was named after a distinguished American, a deceased American, whose biography was posted in each Liberty's saloon.

ANDREW BENNETT
1842-1864

At age twenty-two, Major Andrew Bennett commanded an advance unit of Union soldiers encamped on a hillside three miles from Gettysburg, Pennsylvania. They had been at that position nearly a week, sent ahead by a Union General whose intelligence led him to believe Confederate forces were being moved into the peaceful South Central Pennsylvania countryside. The General was right and Union troops were called in from all directions. A big battle, one of the worst of the Civil War, would soon take place. On their fourth day on the hill, Major Bennett's troops had the misfortune of being discovered by a company of the Confederate Army. He had sent a courier to the General's headquarters with a message detailing the strength and position of the Rebel forces. The courier was intercepted and, after being shot in the back of the head, was tied to the saddle of his horse which was then pointed toward the Union position. The horse walked back to Major Bennett's unit, giving away its position and leading the way for a Rebel assault the next morning. Major Bennett's men held their ground. In all, eight assaults were mounted during the next two days. Major Bennett, his men running low on ammunition, sent another courier through the Confederate lines, detailing the size of the enemy force and appealing for ammunition and support. The second courier made it and the General was able to shift his forces to prepare for the Rebel threat from that direction. Yet, he was unable to get ammunition or reinforcements to Major Bennett's beleaguered men. In the final assault on the hillside, all the Union soldiers, including Major Bennett, were mortally wounded. The Battle of Gettysburg began the next day. Through their steadfast courage and bravery, Major Bennett and his entire unit paid the ultimate sacrifice, but, before doing so, gave their comrades-in-arms sufficient intelligence to provide a major advantage in that famous battle, undoubtedly saving hundreds of lives of Union soldiers.

"Heroic guy," Frank said. "Sounds like he didn't have much luck."

"That's why I thought you should read it," Speer said. "Maybe Major Bennett's ghost is on this ship passing his bad luck down to us."

"That's ridiculous!" Frank said.

"Maybe. The major's number was up that day. So were the numbers of all his men. They say God keeps a book up in Heaven that lists, when a person is born, exactly how that person will die, and when."

"I don't think that's true," Frank said, sitting down again. "God can't possibly have the time to list all those circumstances on every baby that's born. There are millions of people on this earth. Hundreds of thousands are born every day. If He took the time to do that, He'd have no time to listen to our prayers and answer our requests for help. No, there's no way He can put a man's name on a bullet like some say He does."

"His angels do that," John joked.

"This is no joke," Frank shot back. "You've spelled it out. Something is wrong on this ship and I don't think it's Major Andrew Bennett's doing. He's long dead and I don't believe in ghosts."

"Some people do. At least a ghost is one explanation for all the problems we have," the chief mate said. "The major's ghost is probably aboard."

There was a loud crash as a tall, heavy Negro dropped a pot of coffee on the deck.

"My Gawd! Ah knows now why this ship's so jinxed! There's a ghost aboard!"

"Where'd you come from?" Captain Davis asked, surprised at the intrusion.

"The galley, suh. Ah's a cook." He began cleaning up the spilled coffee with the white apron of his trade. "Ah's sorry about this, suh, but when ah heard the mate say there's a ghost aboard ah got shook."

"Don't pay any attention to the mate," the captain said. "There's no such thing as ghosts."

"Ah don' know, Captain," the Negro said. "Ah's heard some people comes back 'cause they ain' satisfied wit what happened to them when they was alive. Maybe the major wasn't satisfied."

He hurriedly left the saloon.

"Who was that?" Frank asked.

"Overall, the second cook and baker."

"All we need now is to have him spread a rumor there's a ghost on this ship!" Frank complained

"His kind gets spooked over most anything," the mate said. "The crew won't pay any attention to him."

"I hope," Frank said, standing up and staring intently

at the roommate he had once called The Spoon. That nickname, ironically, seemed appropriate now. Chief Mate John Speer had spooned up a lot of what Frank needed to know about his new command and what he learned did not help build his confidence.

"Even without a ghost, you've painted a very glum picture, Mister Mate," he said frowning. "Thanks for staying on. I'm going to need you."

"Told you that to start with," the mate crowed.

1330 HOURS
In the Captain's Quarters
Captain Davis, pondering all the ship's problems outlined by his chief mate, sat on his bunk staring at the photograph of his wife taped to the bulkhead.

"God, Lynne!" he said uneasily. "Looks like I've walked into a hornet's nest. I really need you now. Wish I could talk to you about it."

He knew he would call her in a couple of hours but knew, too, he wouldn't paint a pessimistic picture. That would make his being at sea more difficult for her. He would try to be cheerful and keep the conversation short to avoid too many questions.

Two sharp knocks on the door interrupted his reverie.
"Come in," Frank said.
The door opened and the second cook and baker entered, carrying a small tray with a large mug of coffee, a pitcher of cream, a bowl of sugar, a spoon and a ham and cheese sandwich, on rye.

"Ah heard, suh, yo' missed breakfast an' didn' take any lunch, but figgered yo'd like a snack 'fore supper. Didn' know how yo' takes it, suh, so brought all the fixin's."

"I take it black," Frank said, picking up the steaming mug.

"That fits. Strong men likes their coffee black."

The man grinned, an almost toothless grin, and there was the stale smell of whiskey on his breath. His skin was not black, but the color of an old penny. He was about forty and his kinky hair was black with some tinges of grey.

"Heard, suh, youse a strong man. That yo' last ship took three torpedoes an' yo' captain had two broken arms an' a broken leg. An' yo' tied 'im on yo' back an' carried 'im down a rope to the liferaft. That true, suh?"

He didn't wait for an answer.

"Must've been tough, with the ship sinkin' an' all those fires. Bet, too, yo' likes yo' beef rare."

"That I do. You're the second cook and baker?"

"Yes, suh. Ah makes real fine pies, if ah say so maself. Been cookin' for more'n twenty years an' heard they needed cooks on these ships. So ah signed up right after Pearl. It's the same as cookin' asho', 'tho with the stores they give us, we's can't promise gourmet meals. We'll have fresh eggs the first several weeks or so an' we's got a good supply of fresh potatoes, brussel sprouts, carrots. An' some T-bone steaks in the freeza'. After that, powdered eggs, powdered milk, powdered potatoes an' everything else from cans. We'll try to spice it up with diff'rent herbs but, all the same, it'll taste like powder," he grunted.

"I'm sure your meals will be fine," Frank said, wondering if it was true that powdered eggs ruined a man's virility.

"What's your name?" he asked.

"Zachary Overall, suh, but most everyone calls me 'Bib.'"

He pulled on a strap of the overalls he was wearing under the apron.

"Like these overalls, yo' know. Bib Overalls." He laughed. "Ah don't mind. Been called 'Bib' since ah was a little kid. Lived on a farm in 'Bama where ma mama was the cook. Began wearin' those overalls when ah was two. Ma mama thought they was cute an' fit ma father's name, 'tho they wasn' married. Ah'm also the washerwoman, suh, fo' some of the crew. Ah'll do yo' wash if'n yo' don' mind ma trailin' yo' clothes wit a line off the stern. Gets clothes really clean that way. An' as far as ah know, ah'm the only guy wit an iron aboard. Ironed clothes fit better."

Or, Frank mused, *the clothes will be in rags after a few draggings off the fantail.*

"I'll take you up on that, Bib." He looked at his watch. "What time is supper?"

"Five o'clock, suh. We serves on time."

The second cook and self-described washerwoman turned and started to leave. He hesitated, turned around again and flashed a nervous smile.

"One mo' thing, suh. Yo' thinks there's a ghost on this ship?"

Frank held back a laugh.

"Forget the mate's ramblings," he said. "He was just joking about why the ship had so many problems last trip."

"If yo' says so, suh," the cook said and left the cabin.

Frank grinned broadly. Despite the second cook's concern about a ghost, his compliments were just what the captain needed to boost his morale after the disturbing conversation with the chief mate. Obviously, Phipps had run true to form. The deck engineer had already established the captain as something of a legend and, despite his youth, Frank felt he was well on his way to being accepted by the crew.

A comfortable way to start a voyage, he thought.

9 February 1942

2300 HOURS
In the Bennett's Chartroom
Captain Davis and Chief Mate Speer were in the chartroom, an hour before the *Bennett's* scheduled departure. A team of carpenters had just left after building catwalks the length of the fore and aft main decks, with small arteries reaching out to the guntubs. They would help the crew and Armed Guard move around the ship quickly, without facing the obstacles of the tanks on the deck. The last of the cargo was tied down. Steam was building in the boilers.

"Let's get some coffee," Frank said, heading toward the saloon. "The harbor pilot will be aboard in half an hour."

"I'm with you," the mate said. "I could use some."

In the saloon, Chief Engineer Huben sat in his regular chair, laboriously writing a letter. Second Mate Turner ate a late night sandwich. The new purser, William Tanner, sipped a cup of tea and studied the ship's medical book. Third Mate Franklin set a pot to perk and the fragrance of brewing coffee filled the room.

"Smells good," Captain Davis said.

"My own special blend," Franklin smirked. "A secret recipe. I'll let you in on one thing. There's more than coffee grounds in it."

When it finished perking, he poured cups for the captain and chief mate.

"Want some, Chief?" he asked the chief engineer.

"No," Huben answered. "It will keep me awake. Thanks

anyway. I write my sister a letter. Can we get it mailed?"

"Sure," Captain Davis said. "We'll ask the pilot to take it back with him after he gets us out of the harbor. Coffee, Mr. Turner?"

"Thanks. I got my cup from the galley. Didn't taste as good as that coffee smells." The second mate emptied in a saucer the little left in his cup and held it up for the third to fill.

"What about you, Mr. Tanner?"

"Thanks, Captain, but coffee doesn't sit well with me," the purser said. "I take tea with cream, the English way."

The captain raised his coffee mug.

"Here's to good sailing."

"Salute!" Speer said.

"Slainte!" Turner said.

"Down the hatch!" Franklin said.

Tanner lifted his teacup.

"To luck, the American way."

"We're going to need it on this trip," Frank said after each had taken a sip.

"Why this trip?" Turner asked.

"Because the Japs are as good as the Germans in submarine warfare."

"Impossible!" Turner said skeptically. "Their subs aren't as sophisticated."

"They must be," Frank said. "We've lost twenty-two ships in the two months since Pearl and ten of them were sunk by the Japs."

The third mate winced.

"I didn't know it was that bad," he said trembling.

"That was only American ships," Speer said. "Just as many, if not more, Allied ships were sent to the bottom."

"How can we win this war if that many ships get sunk?" the third asked. "That's a lot of cargo lost, not counting the men."

"It will be difficult," Frank answered. "We've just got to build more ships and give them better convoy protection. The U. S. Navy's working on that."

"We going out in a convoy?" the third asked hopefully.

"No," the captain said, "this trip's solo."

The chief engineer stopped writing and turned his eyes to the young mate.

"Not to worry, son," he soothed. "You get used to the fright after the first attack."

The old man had been torpedoed twice in World War I.

2400 HOURS
San Francisco Harbor
Chief Mate Speer gave his familiar order: "Fore and aft, bo's'n, all hands!"

The hawsers were cast off. On the flying bridge, the mate reached for the engine room telegraph and rang "Slow Ahead." The S. S. *Andrew Bennett* glided away from the dock, the helmsman taking orders from the harbor pilot.

Captain Davis stood alone, twenty feet away, not thinking about the departure, as he should, but brooding about all the things stored in his mind the last two days. He had command of a nearly new ship whose captain had died on its maiden voyage. A ship with physical problems. One crack in its hull, now patched up. Grease fouling up the boilers. Aft winches not working properly. A gunnery officer with weak knees. A Navy gunner committing suicide. An aged and arthritis-crippled chief engineer. A deck seaman who likes to use his fists. Another deck seaman with an artificial leg, an engine room watertender with one arm and a paroled killer.

What the hell is going to happen this *trip?*

10 February 1942

0500 HOURS
In the South Pacific
The second cook and baker ran to the wheelhouse, frightened.

"Youse got to get 'im out of ma galley!" he pleaded with Second Mate Turner.

"Who?"

"The ghost!" Bib panted.

"Ghost? What ghost?"

"Major Bennett! He was standin' there, not smilin', lookin' at me an' he put up his hands like tellin' us to go back! Ah ran up here. Youse got to get 'im out, suh!"

Turner had heard the rumor started by the chief mate about the ghost of Major Andrew Bennett, a story that had been repeated by many in the crew. He had thought it nonsense, but now here was one of the men claiming to have actually seen the thing.

"What's he dressed like?" he asked, holding back a laugh.

"It was hard to tell, suh. He don' seem all there. Sort of shadowy. But ah thinks he has on a blue uniform wit' gold buttons an' a choker neck on his blouse."

A Union soldier's uniform, the mate thought. *Major Andrew Bennett was a Union soldier. It can't be! There's no such thing as a ghost.*

"Does he have on a hat?"

"No, suh. No hat. His face is kinda bleary an' it looks like he has yellow hair. But he's blurry."

Blurry?

"Did he say anything?"

Bib hesitated.

"Not's that ah could hear, suh. He keeps pointin' . . pointin' back. Ah asks 'im if he means San Francisco. He shakes his head 'no' and points even further back."

The cook stretched his arm overhead and over his back, apparently trying to imitate the vision.

"Ah doesn't know what he means."

This is getting more ridiculous! Turner thought.

"Hurry, suh, youse got to do somethin'!"

"I'll go down with you, Bib, and ask him to leave," the second mate said soothingly.

A ghost? Inpossible! But, Holy Christ, what will the rest of the crew do when they hear about Bib's unwelcome galley guest? Some seamen are superstitious as hell!

11 February 1942

1900 HOURS
In the North Atlantic

Third Mate Stevens sat on his bunk smoking a Chesterfield, his third in the last fifteen minutes. He wasn't enjoying it. After the incident in the *Nicholson*'s wheelhouse, when he had been caught lighting a cigarette the night Convoy 37B left Reykjavik, Iceland, the captain had forbidden his smoking "any place on this ship but in your cabin."

"I'm a nervous wreck," Slim had told Billy at dinner, showing Chief Engineer Billy Davis his trembling hands. "The old man is unfair. He hasn't stopped anyone else from smoking wherever they want."

He pointed to the radio operator.

"Sparks lights up any time."

"Not any place," Billy said. "Sparks doesn't smoke on deck at night. He's been sailing long enough to know the glow from a cigarette can be seen miles away by a sharp lookout. He also doesn't throw a cigarette overboard any time, day or night. It could hold together long enough for a U-boat captain to see it and know a ship isn't far away."

Slim thought about that.

"I don't see where that can happen in the storms we've been going through. The ocean's so rough a sub couldn't ride on the surface."

"You're right," Billy agreed, "but the captain's trying to teach you a lesson. One doesn't light a cigarette if that puts the lives of the rest of the crew in danger. In fact, Slim, you should know the COMCONVOY has standing orders that gunners on the destroyers are to shoot at any light showing on a ship at night. That means from an open porthole or a cigarette."

Slim winced. He hadn't heard about that order. He thought he was prepared to face torpedoes from an enemy under water. But he wasn't ready to have protectors on friendly ships shooting at him.

14 February 1942

0630 HOURS
Trondheim, Norway

Major Herman Rall paced back and forth in the small shed that served as the weather station at Trondheim, a Luftwaffe airfield in one of the many fjords on the Norwegian coast. Through the shed's window he could see the monstrous 42,500-ton German battleship, *Tirpitz*, hiding from the Royal Navy. The Alta Fjord provided easy exit for German ships, but was heavily guarded against attack from Royal Navy guns. Adolf Hitler saw battleships as symbols of power, but was still shaken by the loss of his most majestic and powerful one, the *Bismarck*, on 24 May 1941. The German fuhrer recognized then his battleships were so outnumbered by the British he dared not risk them in a naval battle. Instead, he decreed they must never be sent out on missions against a potentially superior Allied force. None could sail without first getting his personal approval. The British and Americans, unaware of Hitler's decree, knew of the *Tirpitz*'s safe haven in the fjord and were concerned it might come out to do battle against a convoy, standing far off and out of range of the escort ship's guns.

It was Major Rall's wing of torpedo and dive bombers, however, that sallied forth from Trondheim to chew up convoys on the long last leg of the route from Bear Island to Murmansk.

The *Tirpitz* stayed in its safe harbor.

"Well?" Major Rall demanded.

"There is a break in the weather this morning," said the sergeant in charge of the weather station. "A warm air mass is moving fast, coming from the west, pushing the snow and rain inland. The snow has stopped and we haven't had sleet for more than four hours. The skies are clearing fast and I'm sure it will hold."

"It's about time!" Rall stormed. "We haven't put a plane in the air for seven days. Seven days! Did you hear that?"

"Yes, Herr Major," the weatherman answered, "but today'll be good flying weather."

"Good," the major said, raising his right arm in a stiff salute. "Heil Hitler!"

He strode quickly to one of the airstrip's hangars. There, he ordered the pilot of a FW-200 Condor long range reconnaissance plane to take off to search the waters within the range of his torpedo and dive bombers.

0811 HOURS
Barents Sea
Keen-sighted lookouts on the corvettes spotted the Condor circling to starboard, out of range of their antiaircraft guns.

Convoy 37B had been spotted.

For six days, the lines of ships had moved steadily across the North Atlantic and Arctic Oceans in the face of violent storms that battered the ships and sometimes scattered the convoy for what seemed endless hours until they were shepherded into formation again by the escort vessels. Some of the seamen called the weather "hell below zero" and the lookouts grew face masks of icicles. All of the crews, above and below decks, wore lifejackets at all times -- in the sack, in the mess, in the head and on watch. The kapok jackets were cumbersome, but the men were grateful there had been no sign of the enemy.

When the watches changed at 0800, the convoy was less than sixty miles from Murmansk. The snow and sleet had stopped abruptly six hours before and there was only the grey stillness common to the Arctic winter. All color was drained out of the sky and there were only different shades of grey. There was no wind. Even the heavy seas abated and, with the calm, the crews on all ships were tense.

This kind of weather favored the enemy.

The sirens of the escort ships wailed the alert and general quarters was sounded. Men not on duty but already dressed stumbled out of their bunks or up from their chairs, grabbing helmets, lifejackets and extra clothing for protection against the cold blasts of winter on the open decks. On the *Nicholson*, the purser ordered the cook and galley crew to break out bandages, splints and anesthetics and had them cover the saloon's and crew's mess tables with blankets in case the ship was hit and there were casualties. It was a therapeutic activity he had devised to keep the men busy, their minds off the attack and to reduce their fear. He hoped it would work.

The deck crew went to battle stations at fire hoses, lifeboats and guntubs to assist the Navy gunners. Below, in the engine room, the black gang could only listen and wait, hoping no torpedo, from a submarine or torpedo plane, would find the *Nicholson* a mark.

Lookouts and the Navy gunners scanned the sea and horizon, some with binoculars, looking for the telltale ribbon of white foam that signalled a moving submarine or flecks in the sky that signalled attacking planes.

It was not enough.

The shrill, shrieking engine of a Junkers-88 dive bomber broke the eerie silence, plunging out of the low-hanging clouds toward the Danish freighter forward the *Nicholson*. There was a violent explosion and the freighter, fully loaded with munitions, disappeared in a tall pillar of smoke. Debris rained on the decks of the Liberty ship. The dive bomber seemed to hang motionless, then somersaulted above the smoke, its pilot having only a few seconds to savor the thrill of the kill before crashing into the water. There had been no antiaircraft fire from any of the ships. In thirty seconds it was over. There was nothing left. No wreckage, no flotsam, no survivors, no smoke. Only a ripple of oil on the surface of the sea where the ship and its killer had been.

Fourteen more dive bombers and torpedo planes came at the convoy from the east, in formation, only thirty to fifty feet off the water, their wing guns spraying decks, and dropping chain bombs, stick bombs and aerial torpedoes. Their marksmanship was not as accurate as that of the first Junkers, perhaps intimidated by the fierce fusilade of ack-ack from the convoy's guns, all firing at once. The escort ships, except for the rescue vessels, were heavily armed, as were the five Libertys, but most of the other merchant ships had no guns. A few had creosote poles fore and aft, rigged up to look like guns.

Whoever dreamed up that outrageous scheme, Billy often thought, *was either a fartbrain or liked his whiskey heavy, straight and in abundance. Submarine captains and dive bomber pilots are not scared off by signs of guns, real or otherwise, on a cargo ship's deck.*

There was a cacophony of roaring engines, chattering antiaircraft guns and thundering explosions as the air attack mounted. Bomb after bomb hit the water close to the ships, creating huge geysers and rolling the vessels like matchsticks. Fifty-pound bombs, tied with chains a few feet apart, hit an American Hog Islander, the last ship in the starboard column. In the "coffin corner." Each impact caused another shuddering explosion on the Hoagie's forward deck. Her number two mast crashed over the port bulwark. Fires raged and smoke curled high as the ship began listing to port. A rescue vessel headed for it, ready to take on the crew if they took to the lifeboats.

A Liberty two ships in front of the *Nicholson*, its forward three-inch and starboard 20-millimeter guns firing almost blindly at a Heinkel torpedo dive bomber, seemed to rise slowly out of the water as she was struck midships and broke in two. Liferafts were dropped and men jumped into the freezing waters, like terrified mice, their hands tightly clasping the tops of kapok lifejackets to prevent broken necks when they hit the water.

Another rescue ship raced to the Liberty's aid.

Two Junkers headed for the *Nicholson* and both unleashed loads of stick bombs.

"Goddamnit, they're after us!" someone screamed.

The first bombs hit the water, exploding forty feet abaft the starboard beam, but the second pilot had better aim. A cluster of bombs hit between the number two and number three holds and the starboard side of the flying bridge, blowing the Navy gunners and their merchant seamen ammunition loaders out of the guntubs and throwing them into the sea. Another cluster of bombs hit the flying bridge again, sheering off a quarter of its deck and most of the starboard wheelhouse bulkhead, totally destroying the chartroom. Four more loud concussions trembled the ship, starting fires on the bridge and lower decks, Billy's stateroom on the port side and in the saloon. All of the starboard passageways were ablaze. Screams of wounded men rose above the engine noises of the bombers, the crackling fires and the pouring water from hoses already played out by the boatswain and several of the deck crew.

The attacking planes withdrew as suddenly as they had arrived.

"The captain's dead," a voice screamed from the *Nicholson*'s smoking chartroom. "So's the chief mate. Christ Almighty, his head's been blown off!"

Third Mate Stevens, who took the bridge from the second mate only minutes before the attack, cringed. For a moment, he was lost in himself. They had not taught him at the Pennsylvania Maritime Academy what to do on the bridge when a ship was damaged. Particularly a bridge without a captain. He remembered how angry the skipper had been that night coming out of Reykjavik harbor when he stupidly lit up a cigarette in the wheelhouse. The captain had forbidden him to smoke any place on the ship except in his cabin. That order had been hard on him but, despite it, he always had a partial pack in a shirt pocket, taking one occasionally and holding it unlit in his mouth. He looked at his hands. They were trembling and he reached for a cigarette. Lighting it, he took a long draw and blew out a cloud of smoke. Feeling steadier, he called for the boatswain.

"Give me a damage assessment," he said, trying to make the words come out calm. Then, whistling into the speaking tube to the engine room, he asked: "Any damage below?"

"None, Slim," came back the muffled voice of the second assistant engineer. "Some debris came down one of the vents, but no one's hurt. What's it like up there?"

"The captain and chief mate are dead." He heard a gasp through the tube. "We've a lot of fires, but they're coming under control. Bring us to half ahead."

He wanted to slow down, to assess damage and to await orders from COMCONVOY.

Where is the second mate? he asked himself,

surveying the scene, wondering what his next steps should be. One of the rescue vessels raced toward the *Nicholson*'s side.

The boatswain ran up and hurriedly gave his report.

"You know the captain and chief mate are dead. So's the gunnery officer. The two Navy guys and two seamen in guntubs three and five were washed overboard. No sign of them in the water. Two ordinaries, the chief cook and an oiler are dead, cut to ribbons at their G. Q. stations. A messboy is dead just outside the charthouse. Must have been taking coffee to the captain, though why at the time I don't know. Anyway, the coffee pot's still clutched in his right hand. Why in hell was the captain in the chartroom at a time like this?"

He didn't wait for an answer.

"The third assistant engineer is hurt bad. He was on deck and took some bullets in his stomach. A huge piece of shrapnel is stuck in his left thigh and he's unconscious. Three other seamen and a Navy gunner also are hurt and the purser has all of them in the crew's mess. Far as I know, everyone else is accounted for."

He stopped, catching his breath, a subdued fear showing in his eyes. He rubbed his left forearm and the mate could see a small trickle of blood.

"Two lifeboats were blown overboard, including the one with an engine. You can see for yourself, sir, the entire starboard side of the wheelhouse has been blown away. We've lost booms on the forward and main masts. Most of the tanks on the starboard foredeck are damaged. The wheel and compass housing on the monkey bridge have been blown away. It's hard to tell, but there may be some structural damage to the hull, starboard side. It looks like only above the water line. I'm not sure. I don't think we should risk full speed until we check that out in port where we can lower a seaman over the side and inspect her more closely. All the bombs hit above decks."

He paused again, rubbing his left forearm.

"At that, sir, we're lucky. We can make port if they don't come back."

Slim nodded and lit another Chesterfield.

"Where's the second mate?" he asked anxiously.

"Oh, Christ, I forgot! He's down near the food lockers, scared stiff, babbling like a baby. Won't come up on deck. The purser's given him a sedative and asked one of the messmen to stay with him. I don't think he's a coward, sir," the boatswain added, trying to excuse the second's behavior. "Shell shock, I think they call it. I understand he saw the chief's severed head and ran below decks. A helluva thing to see. This is his first taste of war."

Slim felt like throwing up. This, too, was his first glimpse of hell.

"Looks like you've been hit," he said, pointing to the boatswain's bleeding forearm. "Better see the purser."

"It's nothing, sir. Just a scratch and not from that damn Nazi plane. Cut myself pulling a fire hose from its stanchion. Stupid! Real stupid! I won't get a medal for this."

He laughed at himself and the third mate responded with a weak smile.

A corvette came alongside, to starboard, blinking a message. Flags, the Navy signalman, read the letters, wrote down the brief message, acknowledged, walked over to the mate and handed him the scrap of paper.

Need help? the message read.

"Do we need any help, sir?" The Navy signalman's tone suggested ridicule of the sender.

Slim looked at the boatswain a few seconds, then fixed his eyes on Flags.

"What the hell does it look like?" he shouted, throwing up his hands.

The scivvy waver shuddered at the mate's intensity.

Slim shifted his gaze to the corvette, trying to calm his rising temper. *Christ, they can see we need help,* he told himself. Then, *Easy, boy, you're acting like a kid. They mean well and you should not have spoken so sharply to Flags. The man was only delivering a message.*
Despite the cold, he was perspiring. He mopped his brow with a handkerchief.

"Send this: 'Eight dead including captain and chief mate. Four wounded, one critically. One other in deep shock. Five missing, presumed lost. Fires under control. Most cargo intact. Major damage wheelhouse and forward deck. Monkey bridge wheel and compass destroyed. Suspect structural damage to hull. Will slow us. Can't keep up with convoy. Appreciate escort Murmansk, if possible.' Sign it 'Third Mate Glen W. Stevens.' "

"But you're in command now," the boatswain protested. "You should sign it 'captain.'"

Slim was startled. He hadn't realized that, with the captain and chief mate dead, and the second officer incapacitated, he was in command of the ship. It was an awesome responsibility and it frightened him. He fell silent, looking exhausted, dark rings already developing under his eyes. He felt ten years older and he rubbed the beard he had grown to protect his face against the bitter cold of the Arctic winter.

"I may have the bridge now," he said finally, slowly, measuring his words, "but I'm certainly not the captain. I'll just get us to Murmansk. It's only a few hours. They'll assign a real captain. There's probably a few there who've lost their ships and need a way back home."

He turned to the signalman.

"Send the message as I gave it to you." He sat in the skipper's chair and took a deep breath. "We'll make Murmansk by mid-afternoon if they don't hit us again," he told the boatswain.

He had a feeling the ship was not traveling to Murmansk but to its own Armageddon. He lit another cigarette, inhaled deeply, blew out a cloud of smoke and studied the debris in the wheelhouse, mentally wondering if the carpenter could rig up wooden bulkheads and fill in the missing flying bridge deck. His eyes narrowed at the mangled forward booms.

"What I wouldn't give for another snowstorm right now," he muttered, exhaling the cigarette smoke slowly through his nose.

The signalman came back.

"The corvette will stay with us into port, sir. No doctor on it, but there's some on the cruisers and destroyers. Two rescue boats also have doctors aboard, but they don't figure to put one aboard us now. Too tricky to make a transfer in case the Germans come back. We'll be in port in a few hours and they promise a doctor from one of the Royal Navy ships when we get there."

Third Mate Stevens, now acting captain by a perverse stroke of luck, sighed audibly.

"Tell them 'Thanks.' That's all. 'Thanks.' "

"The rescue vessel's on our port side," the signalman continued. "They also want to know if we need help."

The mate sighed again. He looked at the two damaged guntubs, their 20-millimeters hanging helplessly over the gunwales.

"Ask them to look for five in the water. With their lifejackets on, our boys may be floating, but they're probably dead by now. If the Germans didn't kill them, that ocean will."

He ordered the helmsman to continue the zig-zag pattern the ship had been steaming before the attack. Thirty-degree angle to starboard, then thirty-degree angle to port, hoping for a slight advantage by not giving the skipper of any lurking submarine enough time to set up a torpedo solution.

The rest of Convoy 37B was out of sight.

1500 HOURS
Murmansk, Russia

The *Nicholson* limped into Murmansk harbor, trailed by the corvette and the rescue vessel. A Russian launch signalled the American Liberty ship to drop anchor near a dozen other ships several hundred yards from the twelve berths. A Royal Navy destroyer dispatched a launch with a medical doctor to examine the wounded. All, except the third assistant engineer, were responding well to the purser's first aid. The bleeding from the third's abdomen and thigh had stopped, but he was still unconscious. The second mate slept soundly in his stateroom, heavily sedated. The boatswain had a small bandage on his left forearm.

The British doctor wanted to send the third engineer and the second mate to a hospital ashore. The Russians were willing to remove the bodies of the dead, but refused to admit the two men to a hospital.

"We must get approval from Moscow," a Russian Army officer told the acting captain.

Slim had the feeling approval would never come.

Finally, the British doctor ordered the third engineer to be taken aboard his ship, promising the man would be returned in two, three days. He left extra medication and explicit instructions for the care of the other wounded. No one knew what to do with the second mate. When he awoke, he hallucinated and the doctor ordered him tied to his bunk. The matter was settled when the United States Counsel, fearing the mate might commit suicide or injure someone else, agreed to take the man to the Consulate temporarily, and to send him on to the U. S. Embassy in Moscow where, it was hoped, a staff psychiatrist would try to heal his mental suffering.

Two Russian Army officers, accompanied by a U. S. Army colonel, came aboard to inspect the ship, but Slim noted they spent more time looking at the damage than at the tanks, tractors and trucks on deck. They did not look into the holds and asked only for a copy of the manifest, saying they would be back in two, three hours.

They didn't show.

15 February 1942

1530 HOURS
Room 419, General Hospital, Wilmington, North Carolina
Boatswain Jim Davis rang for the duty nurse. She took her sweet time getting to his room. He had not seen her before. She was plump, frumpy and totally bored.

"You want somethun?" she asked coldly.

"Any secretaries in this place?"

"Secretaries?"

"That's what I asked for," he said patiently.

The woman scratched her brow.

"Yeah. There's a cuppel'a secretaries in the admin office."

"Please get one of them for me," Jim said earnestly.

"What for?"

"To dictate some letters."

"Look," the nurse said. "They're busy just like we are up here. They can't leave their desks to take letters from patients. They've got enough to do."

Jim contemplated that.

"Wasn't thinking of doing it on hospital time. Ask if one of them will come up after work. I'm union. I'll pay overtime. Double time. Whatever she wants."

He held up both hands, indicating with his eyes there was no way he could write letters himself.

"I want to dictate twenty-seven letters," he said evenly. "It would take too long for me to write them with these bumps on my hands."

"That's for sure," she laughed. "I'll ask, but I can't promise any will do it."

"Try," Jim urged.

1715 HOURS
The Same Hospital Room
A petite woman with brunette hair, cut short, knocked on the open door to Jim's room.

"I hear you want a secretary," she said pleasantly, stepping inside.

"That I do."

"I'm a volunteer, helping out two days a week in the medical office. I was just getting ready to go home when they told me about you. I offered to come up. I don't have much to do at night. I'm not too fast," she excused, sitting on the chair next to the bed, brushing her skirt down over her knees and pulling a secretarial pad from her pocketbook. "I can take about fifty words a minute dictation and do about the same on the typewriter."

"Fifty words a minute?" Jim wondered. "I can't talk that fast."

They chuckled.

"My name's Alexandra Williams," she introduced herself. "People call me Alex."

"My name's . . "

"James Charles Davis. You were on that tanker torpedoed a week or so ago. I'm sorry."

Jim studied the woman. She was about five feet, two inches and, he guessed, weighed about one hundred and five pounds. About forty-five. Attractive in a quiet sort of way. Her mouth seemed to have a perpetual smile. Not a big one. A smile nonetheless.

"That's all right," he said simply.

"You want to write to the families of the twenty-seven men who were killed," she continued.

"How'd you know?" he asked, surprised.

"Women's intuition." Her smile became more generous. "When the floor nurse said you wanted to write twenty-seven letters, I knew just what you wanted to do."

"They'll get a form telegram from the Navy or the Coast Guard," he explained. "It won't say much. *'The Navy Department regrets to inform you that your husband is missing and presumed lost following action in the performance of his duty and in the service of his country. To prevent possible aid to our enemies, please do not divulge the name of his ship.'* God, can you imagine getting a telegram like that? And, me, I told the U-boat captain our ship's name. Now the Navy will tell the mothers and wives to keep the ship's name secret. I feel guilty."

"I'm sure you did what you had to do," Alex said quietly.

"I knew those men, knew them well. Their families

deserve more than a stark message saying they're presumed lost. They'll have hope and there is no hope. They must be told that and they must be told how fine their sons or husbands were. They were good men."

Alex put her hand on his left arm, avoiding the bandage. He could feel her warmth flowing through his body.

"You're a kind man," she said looking into his eyes. "Why don't we get started?"

Her pencil was poised. Jim hesitated.

"Now that you're here, I don't know how to start."

"Do you know the names and addresses of the families?"

"I know the names, at least the last names of the families. We can get the addresses from the shipping company."

"Okay. Let's start with their names. If you'll give me the company's name, I'll call tomorrow and get the addresses."

He gave her all the names and the shipping company's telephone number in New York, telling her to ask for Captain Phillip Weatherby.

"Okay, then," she said businesslike. "Now, let's write our first letter."

The letters were lengthy. Each was different.

Herb was a friend, a good friend to whom I could turn when I felt depressed.

Clayton was always laughing, keeping our spirits up. He could make a joke out of the smallest thing, sort of like Bob Hope.

Johnny saved my life once. We were on deck in a storm. I was hit by a wave washing over the ship. He grabbed me before I could fall overboard. I owe my life to him.

Of all the messmen on the ship, Jamie was the best. He knew exactly how I liked my coffee -- how each member of the crew liked his coffee -- and he made sure the cook prepared eggs just the way each of us liked them.

There was one thing about Henry that all of us admired. That was his infectious courage.

And, so, the letters went, describing intimate details about each of his dead shipmates, consoling, giving each family an extraordinary word picture of their husbands, or sons, or brothers, as one shipmate remembered them.

Jim closed his eyes momentarily.

"Thanks, Alex. Thanks very much. I had to get those letters done tonight. I'm going home tomorrow."

"Tomorrow?"

"Yes, Dr. Shaw is taking off these hornet's nests and says he'll just wrap the fingers lightly. I'll be able to use them."

"What time will you leave?"

"The doc said about ten."

"I'll try to have the letters typed by then."

"Oh," he said thoughtfully. "I wasn't thinking straight a minute ago. I don't have to leave until noon, even a little later. My train leaves at two-oh-five."

"They'll be finished in time for you."

She looked out the window, then back at him.

"Gosh, Jim, I'm sorry you have to leave so soon. We just met and I have a feeling already that I'll miss you."

"I've called my daughter-in-law in Maryland. She expects to meet me on the evening train."

Alex sat on the edge of the bed.

"I know I'll miss you."

He took her hand.

"We don't know each other."

"I've been with you long enough tonight to know you are a very good man," she said. "Sensitive. Caring. I wish I had a chance to know you better."

He studied her quivering lips.

"Look, I'll call and tell her I'll be delayed one day. Doctor's orders. We'll go to dinner tomorrow night."

"I'll cook dinner for you," she smiled.

16 February 1942

0430 HOURS
In the Pacific

Ordinary Seaman Tony Durante, standing at the helm on the four to eight watch, was the first to see the white bird land atop the number one mast of the *S. S. Andrew Bennett*. The Liberty was loaded to her tropical marks, fully laden, with just enough reserve buoyancy to keep her afloat.

"Look at that big bird!" he called excitedly to Second Mate Turner. "What kind is it?"

The second mate looked, his eyes at first disbelieving.

"Keep your voice down" he cautioned. "That's an albatross! My God, an albatross has landed on the foremast! That means good luck."

"Good luck? I'da thought it means bad luck, sir," the seaman said. "I mean, isn't there a saying that someone with a problem has an albatross around his neck?"

"That's also true," Turner replied knowingly.

"How can that be?"

"You ever read the *Rime of the Ancient Mariner*?" the second mate asked.

"No," Tony replied.

"I know most of it by heart." Turner cleared his throat, stood erect like a schoolboy at a recital and began:

"The ice was here, the ice was there,
The ice was all around;
It cracked and growled and roared and howled,
Like noises in a swound!

"'At length did come an Albatross,
Through the fog it came;
As if it had been a Christian soul,
We hailed it in God's name.

"'And a good . .' No, no, that's not right. I'm getting ahead of myself."

He rubbed his chin, deep in thought.

"Okay, got it."

"'It ate the food it ne'er had eat,
And round and round it flew.
The ice did split with a thunder fit;
The helmsman steered us through.

"'And a good south wind sprung up behind;
The Albatross did follow,
And every day, for food or play,
Came to the mariner's hollo!'"

The second mate bowed as if expecting applause.

"That the whole poem?" Durante asked, wondering.

"No," the second said. "Just a few verses out of more than a hundred."

"It sounds like the ship was in trouble and the albatross saved it," Tony ventured.

"You got the gist. The poem was written in the late eighteenth century about a ship that was driven by storms toward the South Pole. There it was locked in ice and surrounded by fog. Everything seemed hopeless for the seamen until the albatross landed on the ship. The crew fed it and the bird kept flying around and around, landing every hour or so for more food, day after day. Finally, good weather came, some of the ice melted and the ship was set free. It made its way to the tropical latitudes of the Equator. The seabird stayed with it all the time."

"That explains the good luck. What about the bad?"

"Well, one of the seamen killed the albatross with a crossbow."

"Holy Mother of Jesus!" Tony exclaimed, shaken by the mate's words. "Why would anyone kill the bird?"

"I don't know. The poem doesn't give a reason."

The mate stood silent for a moment, his eyes closed.

"Ah, yes," he remembered. "This is what happened after the bird was killed:

*"'Day after day, day after day,
We stuck, nor breath nor motion;
As idle as a painted ship
Upon a painted ocean.*

*"'Water, water, every where,
And all the boards did shrink;
Water, water, every where,
Nor any drop to drink.'"*

"I've heard that before," Tony said knowingly. "'Water, water, everywhere, and not a drop to drink.'"

"Well, that's a spinoff from the original line, but it's close enough. Those last two verses tell us the ship fell on bad times again after the bird was killed. The seaman's shipmates, in their anger, put the whole blame on the man who did it. They hung the dead bird around his neck. That's why people down on their luck are said to have an albatross around their neck."

"Now I understand that expression," the seaman said.

"The rhyme also describes many strange things that happened to the ship and the seaman after that. He was the ancient mariner and admitted his guilt by writing the poem many years later."

"Geez, that's some story!"

"Yes, a good one. You should read it some time."

"Heck," Tony frowned. "I wouldn't kill any bird."

"Nor would most seaman. Older seafarers like me think an albatross landing and hanging around a ship brings good luck. The longer it stays, the better the luck."

Turner was fifty-four and had been a merchant seaman for thirty-seven years.

"Hey, that's great, Mister! This trip's gotta be a lucky one. I'm gonna get married when we get back."

Tony was still miffed that Marilyn Littman had refused sex with him before he sailed, but he consoled himself with the thought she wanted to keep her virginity just for him, for their wedding night. Virginity was as precious as gold to some women. The second mate's promise of good luck meant Tony would get home safely, marry Marilyn and finally find out what sex was all about. He often had wet dreams at night, thinking of making love to Marilyn.

"Well, I don't know that getting married brings good luck," the second mate said sourly. "I tried it twice and was miserable both times. Guess I was lucky though."

"How?" Durante asked.

"I got out of both without paying alimony!"

"That won't happen with Marilyn and me," Tony said positively. "We were made for each other."

He looked back at the bird. Even in the semi-dawn, he could see it was white with a long beak. The wings were laced with tiny brush strokes of black.

"Sure is big," he said.

"I've seen bigger. Some have a wing-span of sixteen feet, maybe more. This one doesn't look that big."

They heard a pinglike sound and the startled albatross raised its wings, stretched them out about twelve feet and flew quietly in the direction of the rising sun.

"Damn!" the mate said. "He's flown off too soon!"

"Something scared it off," Tony complained.

"Yeah, sounded like something flapped and hit the mast. Maybe a loose cable."

"Maybe he'll come back and stay with us a few days, like in the poem."

"Maybe." The mate's tone wasn't encouraging.

"Well, maybe his just landing for a few minutes will bring us some luck."

Durante was hopeful but disappointed. If what the second mate said was true, they would have more luck if the albatross had stayed longer.

On the main deck, Able-Bodied Seaman Howard Robinson put the handmade slingshot in his hip pocket.

"Damnit, I missed!" he groaned.

"Yeah, Howie, but not by much. That lead pellet must'a hit the mast just inches from him," Able-Bodied Seaman Stanley Gruen encouraged. "That bird really took off. You scared the living shit out of him."

"Wouldn'ta missed if I'da used a thirty-eight 'stead of this pissy-ass rubber band. But they'd get me for violating parole if I brought one aboard. I'da like to got that bird. We'da had a feast."

"What kind of bird was it?" Gruen asked.

"Don't know and don't give a good damn. Cooked right, all birds taste great! Best I ever had was one-inch rice birds dipped in brown sugar sauce and burned on a spit in Mozambique."

"That don't sound appetizing or even much to eat," Gruen said.

"Hell, man, it was a delicacy! If I'da killed that bird, I'da had Bib cook it just the way those African niggers did. Brown sugar and all!"

He smacked his lips.

1400 HOURS
In the Armed Guard Mess
At twenty-three, Gunner's Mate First Class Charlie Hunt was the oldest man in the Armed Guard contingent on the S. S. Andrew Bennett, a year older than the gunnery officer. He wasn't the oldest man on the ship. The merchant crew was made up of seamen mostly in their thirties and forties, with a few older and an even smaller number in their teens or early twenties. The other nineteen in the Navy enlisted crew were fresh out of high school and boot camp, seventeen to nineteen years old. Charlie had been in the Navy three years and that made him an "old salt." The kids sought his advice whenever they had a chance and whenever Charlie would sit down long enough to answer their questions. This was one of those times.

"You were good today," Seaman First Class George Cookman told Charlie as four of the Navy gunners sat drinking coffee in the Armed Guard mess. "Christ, you're a crack shot with that twenty!"

Charlie acknowledged with a shrug.

The Armed Guard had another target practice off the stern a half-hour earlier and, while the other 20-millimeter gunners had completely missed the bobbing orange balloon fifteen hundred yards astern after firing two magazines each. Charlie used a five-second burst to deflate the colorful bubble.

Lieutenant (j.g.) Harold Hamilton had not seen any of it. He stayed in his cabin.

"You seen any action?" Cookie asked Charlie.

"Some."

"Where?"

"Around."

Charlie wasn't known for talking in long sentences.

"Around where?" pressed Gunner's Mate Third Class Stephen "Rabbit" Ellard, lead man on the forward three-inch fifty.

"Malta."

"Malta? Christ, Charlie, that's in the Mediterranean!" Cookie exclaimed. "What were you doing there?"

"Delivering food."

Food was a commodity as important as ammunition on that British stronghold in the middle of a sea that separates Southern Europe from North Africa. Ever since the Italians had suffered an ignominious defeat by the British in Africa, wresting from Benito Mussolini his dream of establishing a new Roman Empire, and ever since the Germans had moved in to rescue the embattled Italians in late 1941, the flyspeck of an island was the keystone of the British defense of North Africa. As long as its airfields and docks remained open, the British were in a position to destroy German shipping heading for the ports they held in Africa. Yet, the island, only seventy miles from the German airfields of Sicily, was pummeled six to eight times a day by Luftwaffe bombers. So strategic was its position that German Reich Marshall Herman Goring ordered it to be "Coventrated," to be completely destroyed from the air in the way the Luftwaffe had destroyed the English city of Coventry in 1940. The bombings got heavier. The 280,000 native Maltese and Royal Air Force crews refused to give up. They repaired the damaged airfields daily, sending fighters up to battle the Germans, and rebuilt the docks over and over again. So devastating were those bombings, and the attacks on British convoys headed to the island, that few ships got through to deliver much-needed food and ammunition. Hunt's ship, a Liberty, was one of the few. While being unloaded in a period of two days, the ship was attacked eleven times and was credited with downing six planes. Hunt personally got four of them.

"That where you got the Bronze Star and the Purple Heart?" Rabbit asked.

Charlie looked at the man, expressionless, then nodded.

"Hey!" Cookie shouted, his nicotine-brown eyes lighting up. "No wonder the Germans can't take that island! Hunt was there!"

Everyone laughed but Charlie.

"What was it like, Charlie?" Cookie asked. "I mean, the fighting? Must have been a lot of action."

"There was."

"How many did *you* shoot down?"

Charlie didn't answer.

"Man!" Cookie said excitedly. "I can't wait to see some real action!"

"You ain't gonna like it," Charlie warned, getting up and walking out of the mess.

"Christ, he's a cold one," Rabbit said.

"Maybe you get that way after you've been shot at," Cookie pointed out. "I hear it bends your mind."

"Killing Japs or Germans won't bother me," Rabbit said. "I'd brag about it."

"Yeah, Rabbit, but you'll have to be as sharp as Charlie is. No question, he's sharper than the rest of us. He's ready to fire before any of us even get the shrouds off and he doesn't have a merchant seaman to help him."

"How's he do it so fast?" the other seaman asked.

"Wish I could tell you, but I'm not sure. I'm at the number seven gun and I've tried to watch him across the deck while trying to get my own gun ready. Even with a seaman helping me, keeping an eye on Charlie slows me up. What I see, when he gets into the tub, he jumps on the gun shield to pull the cover off with one hand, at the same time grabbing the top of the barrel with the other. He puts his feet on the parallel bars and thrusts downward to depress the recoil springs. Then he jumps down and pulls the pin."

Cookie made a hand motion as if he were pulling a pin himself.

"He looks like a monkey swinging on a tree limb," he snickered, "but, hell, his gun's cocked and all he has to do is throw on the magazine and begin firing. Fastest man I've ever seen with a twenty."

"He'll get a seaman assigned, though," Rabbit said. "He can't load, sight and fire at the same time. Not with the other guy shooting at him. He'll need some help if they can find a qualified loader. Meantime, I wish he'd take the time to teach us now, before we see any action."

"He's already started," Cookie said. "Seems like he's telling us that talking about it doesn't make us good gunners."

1430 HOURS
In the Captain's Quarters
Captain Davis sent word to the gunnery officer to report to him. *Immediately.* It took Lieutenant Hamilton ten minutes to make it. His khaki uniform was rumpled, as if he had been sleeping in it. His hair was disheveled, although the lieutenant had made an effort to smooth it with his hands. His face was ashen and his pale blue eyes were bloodshot.

"Coffee?" Frank asked, pointing to a pot warming on a hot plate.

"No, thanks," the lieutenant said meekly. "Makes me gag."

"What gives?" the captain asked, motioning the lieutenant to the other chair in the office. "You been drinking? You look like a hangover."

"No . . no, sir," Hamilton sputtered as he sat down. "I don't like alcohol."

"Then, what is it, man? We've been at sea eight days and I've hardly seen you. You weren't on deck for target practice today. You've only been out for two others. Suppose today had been the real thing, not a drill. You'd be a goner. You expect the gunners to do their job without leadership?"

The lieutenant didn't answer. His eyes focused on the deck.

"I haven't seen you in the officers' saloon. Don't you eat? Or don't you like the company of merchant seamen?"

Hamilton pondered a way to avoid answering those questions, to get out of the conversation, to get out the of cabin altogether. There was no answer short of discourteously getting up and walking out. He knew he couldn't do that.

"I don't have a big appetite," he said apologetically.

"From the looks of you, Lieutenant, you're starving to death. Something wrong with your health? If there is, why'd the Navy assign you to this ship? I heard you hardly came out of your cabin last trip. Why'd they send you out again?"

"Wasn't my idea, Captain. I asked to be relieved, to go on shore duty."

Frank studied the man. There was more to it than a small appetite. He could not read cowardice in the man's eyes. It had to be something else.

"Why?" he asked again.

The lieutenant's eyes roved from the deck, to the ceiling, to the outside bulkhead, through the door leading to the captain's stateroom, to Lynne's photograph on the bulkhead at the foot of Frank's bunk. They remained there.

"That your wife?" he asked.

"Yes."

"Her eyes . . I think she'd understand."

Frank wasn't sure what that meant.

"Try me. I learned understanding from her."

The lieutenant turned his eyes away from the photograph and looked at the captain, tiredly.

"To be honest, sir, I can't hold down food. I'm seasick all the time. Every minute almost. I don't know why."

"It'll pass," Frank tried to soothe. "Happens to a lot of guys."

"No, Captain. I was sick all last trip. I tried all the tricks the last purser gave me. I avoided liquids and chewed on cracked ice. I put hot water bags, mustard plaster and turpentine stupes on my stomach. Didn't do a bit of good. Aspirin didn't help. Nor phenobarbital tablets. They're not working this trip either. I feel worse."

He wiped his brow. His khaki shirt was covered with sweat. Frank could see perspiration flooding from the pores on the man's forearms and face.

"When we were in 'Frisco, I didn't eat greasy foods," the lieutenant added. "No eggs. No bacon. Nothing with fat. I still threw up, even there. Now I eat soda crackers, toast and dry bread. I have them and dry cereal in my cabin. I take it all without milk or any liquid. Those dry things help a bit, but I still vomit eight, ten times a day. Nights are worse, lying down, trying to sleep. I can't."

Frank had heard about men with a condition like this. Seasickness seldom lasts more than a couple of hours, perhaps a day or two. It soon passes, particularly if the patient is kept quiet, warm and given a little dry food with an occasional walk in fresh air. Frank remembered an instructor at the New York Maritime Academy saying there have been reported cases of death from seasickness. It was rare. Very rare, but it did happen.

Perhaps, God forbid, I'm looking at one of those cases right now. I can't tell him that his condition might be life-threatening.

"You tell this to your superiors?" he asked.

"Yes, but they wouldn't listen. They thought I was making it up to get out of sea duty. But I'm not, Captain. I'm not."

"From the looks of you, I have to believe that," Frank said kindly. "Anything else?"

The lieutenant started to say something, but put a hand to his mouth.

"Come on, Hamilton, open up. I'm your friend. I want to help you."

Pain filled the lieutenant's face.

"I've asked to resign my commission," he said ashamed, not looking at the captain.

"When?"

"Two days before we sailed. They wouldn't accept it. Said it would have to go through channels. They sent me back aboard."

He closed his eyes, expecting a harangue from the merchant captain like the harassment he got from Navy Commander Roosevelt. It didn't come. Frank was quiet a long time.

"If I had only known," Captain Davis started.

He focused his own eyes on Lynne's photograph. Her smile gave him strength.

"If. That's a big word, Lieutenant, but it's too late for if's now. We're at sea. It's obvious you're a sick man. Very sick. It's also obvious that leading your Armed Guard crew is impossible in your condition."

He thought another moment.

"You're going into sickbay. It may help. Mr. Tanner, the purser, has had some pre-med training. He's a gentle young man. Also understanding. He'll try to make you comfortable. That's the least we can do."

"I don't want to be a bother," the lieutenant protested.

"I can stay in my cabin. I don't want my gunners to know."

"That's foolish, Hamilton," Captain Davis rebuked. "Things are worse the way they are now. Your men already think you're chicken, that you're scared you might get hurt if we see any combat. At least, if you're in sickbay, and we tell them the truth, we'll dispel that scuttlebutt. Some of them have been seasick. They know how it feels. Some wanted to die, they felt that bad. Believe me, Lieutenant, they'll understand."

"If you say so, sir," Hamilton said quietly.

"We'll have to put someone in charge of your gunners," Frank said. "Any recommendation?"

"I don't know any of them well," the lieutenant admitted, "but I have read their records. The most senior is a new man, assigned to take place of . . to take the . . "

"I know," Frank said gently, not wanting the lieutenant to become more upset by talking about the suicide of one of his gunners.

"This new man is a Gunner's Mate First Class. Name's Hunt. His record shows he won the Bronze Star for shooting down four planes in a single day's attack on his ship. That was *after* he took more than ten fifty-calibers in his left leg. He could hardly stand but stayed at his gun and kept firing. Got the Purple Heart, of course."

A strange, gurgling sound came from the lieutenant's mouth.

"He's assigned the number eight twenty-millimeter, but he doesn't have a merchant seaman ammunition loader."

"That the short, skinny fellow with a limp?" Captain Davis asked.

"Yes."

The lieutenant grabbed at his stomach.

"May I use your head, sir?" he asked.

"Of course."

Hamilton vomited before he reached the toilet.

Captain Davis helped the man to the bunk, lifted him to it, then washed his face with a towel soaked in cold water. He took another cold towel and placed it on the man's forehead. Then he called Purser Tanner to his quarters, explained the situation and ordered the Navy lieutenant to sickbay.

"We'll get a replacement for you in Noumea," he

promised the lieutenant as the two men left the cabin.

He called for A.B. Wilson and Gunner's Mate Hunt to meet with him.

"You've got additional duty," he told Wilson. "I understand you've had some combat experience. I'm assigning you to load ammunition for Hunt's number eight gun."

"Yes, sir," Wilson answered crisply.

"Although I don't usually give orders to the Armed Guard, what I tell you now comes from Lieutenant Hamilton," he told Hunt. "You've got additional duty, too. The lieutenant's in sickbay. He's a sick man. Very sick. Serious abdominal problems. Began with seasickness and has developed into other problems. A rare complication."

He looked the Navy man squarely in the eyes.

"The lieutenant could die, seaman," he said. "He might not make it to our next port. We'll do the best we can for him, but you know we don't have a real doctor aboard this ship. We can't radio anyone to get a doctor's advice. We're on our own with this thing."

Hunt nodded, not sure what to say.

"Lieutenant Hamilton should have been hospitalized in San Francisco," Captain Davis continued.

He wanted his words to sink in so the two would spread the story correctly to the rest of the crew and the Armed Guard.

"Frankly, I hope he'll make it to Noumea. If he does, we'll get him to a hospital there. Maybe their doctors can help. Meantime, Hunt, you're in charge of the Armed Guard 'til we get a replacement. Any questions?"

Hunt swallowed hard and shook his head. It was the last thing he wanted. He hated giving orders.

Wilson and Hunt walked out of the cabin. Frank got up, closed the door and walked back to his desk. He sat and sipped absently on a cold cup of coffee.

"Damnit," he said angrily. "I never bought that old seaman's tale that an albatross brings good luck to a ship. That damn albatross that landed this morning has brought us more but bad luck."

He looked again at Lynne's photograph.

"All right, all right. Maybe that bird didn't have anything to do with this. But, Lynne, there's something wrong on this ship. I hope it's not me."

Lynne's face kept smiling.

"Okay, honey," Frank said. "You win. I'll stop feeling sorry for myself."

He was tempted to cross his fingers, but didn't.

2200 HOURS
In the Chartroom
Captain Davis stood in the chartroom with Third Mate Franklin. The third would take over the bridge in an hour and was working on the route he would be taking. Frank pointed to the sextant resting on the chart table.

"I've noticed you're pretty good with that." He had been watching Franklin for days and thought that, for a young man only a few months out of a maritime academy, the third mate was extremely capable. "Your navigation plotting is almost perfect."

"Well, thank you, sir," the third smiled, standing straighter. "I'm trying."

"Have you studied our position?" Frank asked.

"Oh, yes, Captain, we're at Latitude Zero Degrees, seven minutes North and Longitude one hundred seventy nine degrees, fifty-three minutes west."

"Where's that close to?"

"You're kidding, Captain. You know as well as I do we're not far from the Equator. We'll cross it in about two hours, give or take a few minutes."

"True. But there's something else," the captain said seriously. "Look at the chart again."

Franklin studied the chart, not sure what the captain was talking about. He shrugged and put his right index finger at the ship's approximate location.

"Let's see," he said. "We're here, the Equator's there and . . Hey, wait a minute! We're almost at the International Date Line!"

"The student gets an A!" Frank said.

"Gee, that's something! I was so involved planning our Equator crossing I didn't notice the Date Line. You know, Captain, when we cross that line it's not the same as crossing the imaginary line that separates the top half from the bottom half of the world. We'll actually lose a day on the calendar."

"Right again."

The young California Maritime Academy graduate peered more closely at the chart.

"Hey, Skipper!" he said excitedly. "We could cross the Equator and the Date Line at the same moment."

"We could," Frank said steadily. "But only if you're on

the right course. Think you can set it?"

"Man! What a challenge! Sure, sir, sure, I can do it. I think. My gosh, that'll be a real first for navigation and imagine me doing it!"

"Wrong," Captain Davis said. "It's been done before, many times, by smart navigators and by accident by others."

The third slumped, dejected.

"Don't take it personally," Frank said. "Men have been navigating on this ocean for centuries. Perhaps for thousands of years. Even natives in their outrigger canoes have followed the stars to go from one island to another and they didn't have sextants, compasses and other modern navigation aids. They probably crossed both lines at the same time, but didn't know it."

"I would like to have been the first," the third said, biting his lip.

"Look, it takes a smart navigator to do it even with charts and modern equipment," Frank consoled. "It's not easy. It takes proper planning. You ever hear about the record set by the *S. S. Warrimoo*?"

"The *Warrimoo*? No, sir, never heard of that ship."

"She was a passenger liner and she pulled off the neatest of navigation tricks back on December thirtieth, eighteen ninety-nine. She set a record that may never happen again."

"What was that?"

"Remember, it was December thirty. Still another day left on the eighteen-ninety-nine calendar. At precisely midnight, local time, she was exactly at the Equator at exactly the point it crosses the International Date Line. Just where you want to be in two hours. Now, if you think about it, the date on the stern of the *Warrimoo* was December thirty, eighteen-ninety-nine, and the date on the bow was January first, nineteen-hundred. The ship skipped December thirty-one. So . . "

"So, the ship was in two different days, two different months and two different years," the third said .

"And in two different centuries -- half of it in eighteen-ninety-nine and half in nineteen-hundred."

"Geez, that was something!" Franklin exclaimed.

"The passengers got cheated out of a New Year's Eve celebration."

"Oh, come on, Skipper. I bet that captain didn't let that happen."

"You're right, Mister, he didn't. While the ship completely lost December thirty-first, the captain put on a whale of a party for the passengers."

The third mate was visibly thrilled.

"If I figure things out, Captain, we can put the *Bennett* right at that intersection. I'd love it."

"Start figuring," Captain Davis urged, looking at his watch. "You'll have to do it fast. I'll ask the second mate to stay on the bridge if you need more time to get it all planned. If necessary, we'll get the engine room to adjust speed. We'll even stop engines if we have to. But not for long. Get to work!"

The third did, feverishly, bending over and examining the chart. Word spread quickly among the crew what the captain and third were planning. So many men ran into the charthouse to encourage the young mate or to ask questions that Captain Davis finally posted a seaman at the chartroom door.

"No one gets in there until Mister Franklin is ready to tell us our course."

The third mate drew a Rhumb line, a direct shot, from San Francisco to Noumea, showing a true course of 225 degrees. That would have taken the *Bennett* right through the Hawaiian Islands.

"Glad we didn't come that way," he laughed aloud. "We'd have tied up traffic on Honolulu's narrow streets."

He concentrated on where the Rhumb line intersected the Equator and the Date Line. He began talking to himself as he traced other lines on the chart. *At the Equator*, he remembered from navigation class, *a degree of longitude is equal to one nautical mile, the same as a degree of latitude.*

He looked at his watch. Exactly 2207 and ticking.

We were at zero degrees, oh seven minutes north, one hundred seventy-nine degrees west exactly seven minutes ago. So, if we travel in a straight line, no more zigzagging, at exactly ten knots, we'll cross both lines in one hour, fifty-three minutes.

He ran to the wheelhouse to tell the captain.

2359 HOURS
In the Wheelhouse
Captain Davis told the excited third mate to signal two short blasts on the ship's foghorn in exactly one minute

to announce their precise position to an unusually large crowd of seamen eagerly crowding the wheelhouse.

The second hand on the clock ticked slowly. Franklin held his breath momentarily.

"At this second," Franklin shouted as he signalled the two blasts, "this is February sixteen to all men aft. It's February eighteen to all men forward. I don't know where that leaves those of us midships."

28 February 1942

1100 HOURS
In the South Pacific
Able-Bodied Seaman Jones and Donkeyman Phipps were leaning against the starboard rail when New Caledonia island came into sight. The sun had already made a griddle out of the steel railing of the *S. S. Andrew Bennett* and their forearms rested on cleaning rags.

"That's a garden spot in this lonely ocean," Jones said.

"You been here before?" Phipps asked.

"Yeah, three, four years ago," Jones allowed. "It's not as good as ports in Australia, but one can get quite a few good things here. Know what I mean?"

His hands moved downward simultaneously to form the shape of a woman.

"You mean nigger natives?"

"There's plenty of those, too, but I mean good white meat. This island belongs to the French and I remember one girl . . Mary . . no, Margot. She's got a plush place right in Noumea. Wonder if she's still at it?"

He looked at the island looming closer, its silhouette turning from brown to green.

"Hell, her place is a hundred times better than those government-run whorehouses in Honolulu, particularly those on River Street. This one has class. Those in Honolulu are just cheap, ripoff joints."

"Whaddaya mean?" Phipps asked.

"All those red light places are the same. Most have names tied to the sea. The Rex. The Anchor. The Mermaid. The Mermaid! Hell! Most the girls are old, over thirty at least. And fat! All those whorehouses have the same small white signs and the same black letters. You can't miss one."

"Are they legal?"

"Oh, yeah."

"Is there much V. D. there?" Phipps asked.

"Shucks, no! Where prostitution is legal, like in France, the girls are real clean. They have to be checked by a doctor every week."

"I've never been to Hawaii," Phipps said.

"You ain't missed anything. We call getting laid there the 'four threes.' You stand in lines three blocks long, for three hours to get three minutes with a whore for three bucks. Three minutes is all you get. Each girl has two rooms with a bathroom in between. She walks naked from one bedroom, squirts water between her legs and walks to the next room. If you ain't ready, in bed with a hard on, you won't have time to get it off. The worst is, you pay the three lousy bucks downstairs so, if you don't make it, you lose your money."

He snorted.

"Now Margot's place is different! She's a doll herself. Well built. Redhead. Particular. She selects only the best for herself. Gives the other guys to her girls. I had her a couple of times," he boasted. "She don't do it like in Pearl. Her girls don't either. Everyone gets a drink and sits around talking. Sooner or later, one of the girls walks up and asks if you'd like to spend some time with her. She gives you a half hour, more if you need it."

Phipps already had an erection.

"Sounds fantastic? Do we go?" he asked.

"Sure. Hope her place is still there."

"Can we take someone with us?"

"Who?"

"Well," Phipps said knowingly. "Durante has never had a piece."

"You're kidding?"

"No. He told me his girlfriend is a virgin and he wants to be one when they get married."

"Damn!" Jones exploded. "We'll have to change that."

1400 HOURS
Noumea Harbor
Two destroyers patrolled the mouth of the harbor at Noumea when the *Bennett* entered. More than a dozen ships lay at anchor and others were being unloaded at the docks. Navy launches skirted between the anchored ships. The water in the harbor was calm and the hu-

midity oppressive. A Navy launch headed their way, a signalman waving flags, ordering the ship to anchor and prepare for an official boarding. The anchor was played out, noisily. A Jacob's ladder was slung over the side. The launch came alongside, a sailor grabbed the rope ladder and a Navy lieutenant and an Army major scrambled deckward.

"Permission to board," the Navy officer said after he saluted aft.

"Permission granted, sir," Ordinary Seaman Durante said, standing straight as an arrow.

The major did not salute the colors nor ask permission to board. Tony thought the officer hadn't been trained properly.

"May we see your captain?" the Navy man asked.

"Yes, sir. He's in the saloon."

"The saloon?" the major asked incredulously. "There's a saloon on this ship?"

"Yes, sir, but they're not serving now," Tony said with a straight face. "Through that passageway. Walk forward. You'll run right into it."

The major huffed, walked, almost ran, with the lieutenant following. He introduced himself to the captain. He did not salute.

"Major William Yardley, U. S. Army, Quartermaster's Office," he said formally.

"Welcome. I'm Captain Davis," Frank said. "This is my chief mate, Mister Speer. At the next table is Mister Tanner, our purser. Sit down, won't you?"

Before they did, the major introduced the lieutenant as Albert Scott, U. S. Navy.

"What's the name of your ship?" the major asked.

The name had been painted over on both sides of the bow and on the stern. No ships carry a name on the hull in wartime. Only a brass plate in the saloon identifies the vessel, where it was built and the date of delivery to the U. S. Maritime Commission.

"*S. S. Andrew Bennett*," Davis replied. "We're out of San Francisco."

The major studied a list on his clipboard.

"We have no *Andrew Bennett* due today," he said matter of factly.

"We're ahead of schedule," Captain Davis replied. "Good winds, calm sea, no trouble."

The major flipped a page. "No *Bennett* due tomorrow."

He turned another page. "Or the next day."

The five officers looked at each other, puzzled.

"That's ridiculous!" Captain Davis finally blustered. "Our orders are for Noumea. Here, look for yourself."

He handed the major a sheath of papers.

"See. Noumea. It's right here. In code."

He pointed with a finger to a square near the top of the first page. The major studied the orders.

"That's what it says all right. Must be some kind of snafu," he offered, recognizing the code for his port. "No one advised us. Let me take your manifest and go back to my headquarters. Perhaps we've missed something. The clerks we have today are only young kids and they sometimes make mistakes. Oh, how they do make mistakes!"

"I understand," Davis said, relieved. "We all do."

"Look," the major said pleasantly. "You catch a launch tomorrow morning and come to my headquarters. One of our drivers will meet you with a jeep. We'll have it straightened out by then. Okay?"

"Sure. I'll be there."

When the two military officers left, the three merchant seamen looked at each other, baffled.

"You ever heard anything like this?" Frank finally broke the silence. "What do you think, Mister Tanner?"

"I don't know, sir. I'm new at this. I have a funny feeling, though, he wasn't happy about seeing us."

"And you, Mister Mate?"

The chief mate threw up his hands.

"Typical Army paper screwup!" Speer said sourly. "Can't keep their papers in the right file. Or maybe Bib's ghost fouled things up!"

1700 HOURS
Navy Hospital Ashore
The Navy doctor, a two-stripe lieutenant, laughed when Purser Tanner described the symptoms that brought him and Lieutenant Hamilton to the port hospital.

"Seasickness?" he asked. "We don't hospitalize for that."

"You will this one," Tanner said emphatically. "This man's been seasick since we left 'Frisco, without relief, and was sick his first voyage to Pango Pango and back. His condition, doctor, is rare. I'm sure if you look it up in your medical books you'll find I'm right."

"You a physician?" the Navy lieutenant asked sharply.

"Close to one as you'll ever find on a merchant ship," Tanner answered crisply.

The lieutenant took a closer look at Hamilton. What he saw was a man of about twenty-two who was so gaunt, pinch-faced and ill-appearing he looked fifty. Hamilton's face was drained of all color and the cheek bones almost pierced the skin.

"You that sick?" he asked.

"Yes, sir."

"Well, we'll admit you and try to find out what's wrong. Frankly, I have no idea. Maybe there's a twist in your intestines."

The doctor turned to Tanner.

"We'll have a good look at him. I just hope this isn't another case of a slacker wanting to go home to mother."

1 March 1942

0800 HOURS
Army Quartermaster's Office
Major Yardley came out of the General's office, walked to the desk where Captain Davis sat, waiting impatiently for more than an hour, and lifted a book from the middle drawer. He sat down, leafed through the book's pages, finally finding the one he wanted and then compared the code names with those on the *S. S. Andrew Bennett*'s manifest. His eyes moved back and forth between the documents and, when Frank was ready to explode, said crisply:

"There's a problem, Captain."

"I know that," Frank said, miffed. "What kind?"

The major scratched his forehead, then picked his nose. "Well, I don't know how to explain it. Your cargo isn't consigned to this T. O."

"To what?"

"T. O. Theatre of Operations."

"Not consigned here? Then where?"

The major looked into the captain's eyes, then shifted his gaze to the only window in the room. "You were supposed to go to Loch Ewe," he said casually.

Captain Davis jumped up from his chair, toppling it over. He spread his hands eaglelike on the desk.

"Loch Ewe? Good God, Major, that's in Scotland! What am I doing in New Caledonia?"

"I . . I don't know, Captain."

"Our orders explicitly state Noumea, New Caledonia. What kind of a mistake is this?"

The major shifted his position to avoid looking at the ship's captain.

"We don't have any need in this T. O., at least not yet, for heavy Sherman tanks," he said evenly. "Those babies aren't exactly designed for island fighting. What can we do with sixty-seven of them?"

"Seems to me that's your problem," Frank spat. "We've come all the way from 'Frisco. Our orders clearly call for this cargo to be delivered right here to your headquarters. We've done that."

"Yes, you have," Major Yardley said smoothly. "But those tanks belong to another Army outfit. They were to be delivered to Loch Ewe. That's one of the assembly points."

"Assembly points? For what?"

"It's top secret, supposedly, but there's talk about a joint Anglo-American invasion of North Africa. Some time this year. They're already stocking up for it."

The last thing Frank had expected to hear was a secret plan about an African invasion. He had read in the newspapers at home, over the past year, that a large but poorly trained, poorly equipped Italian Army had reached for the glory of the old Roman Empire. Italy already occupied Libya in the North and Eitrea and Italian Somaliland in the southeast. In 1936, it had quickly conquered Ethiopia. Benito Mussolini, jealous of Hitler's early successes in Europe, had wanted to take Egypt and the Suez Canal from the British, but his troops were roundly defeated, tens of thousands of his soldiers taken prisoners of war. In response, Hitler had sent his most daring and audacious general to Africa to rescue the beleaguered Italians and to regain the ground lost by them. In a few short months. Lieutenant General Erwin Rommel, whose exploits earned him the nickname, "Desert Fox," had taken back most of the land lost by the Italians and then some. It was as obvious to Frank, a merchant ship captain, as it was to high-ranking Allied political and military leaders, that Rommel would have to be stopped.

"Okay, okay, Major," Frank said, picking up his chair

and sitting down, trying to make some sense out of the situation. "I understand the need to invade North Africa. I understand men and equipment must be assembled at various points for the invasion. But, for Christ's sake, Noumea isn't anywhere near Africa! Or Scotland. How can we have been sent here? And why were the tanks loaded in San Francisco when it would have been better to send them by train to the East Coast? They'd be in Scotland now."

He was red-faced with anger.

"I can't answer your questions, Captain," Major Yardley said placidly. "Somehow, I don't think you realize this is a real World War, a helluva bigger war than the last one. That was a puny war, fought only in a small part of Europe, mostly France. This is a big war, with fighting on four continents and islands here in the Pacific. Who knows? It may spread to every continent, even to the United States. With something so big, I suggest you stop feeling sorry for yourself about getting wrong orders. It's not the first and it won't be the last time this'll happen. You can bet your life on that."

"They sank merchant ships in that war, too," Frank challenged.

"Yeah, and Eddie Rickenbacker became an ace flying in a canvas-covered airplane. Hell, Captain, one of our planes fires more ammunition in a single run today than all the planes did in that war!"

"Weapons have changed," Frank said.

"Men haven't!" the major shot back. "They're human and humans make mistakes. So, if you'll calm down, maybe we can work things out. The general says we can take some of the cargo off your hands. We sure can use all the jeeps and trucks. We can also use the radio equipment. Especially the radio equipment. We need that badly. Then there are those cases of whiskey and beer . . "

"Wait just a minute!" Frank cut in. "You mean I'm supposed to deliver all of this cargo to Scotland but, before we go, you'll handpick what you want?"

"There's a war on over here, too, you know."

Davis pushed his head forward, staring hard into the major's eyes.

"And you need the whiskey?"

"Our soldiers can use it as well as the next guy," the major said flippantly. "The general says to offload what we want, then send you with the rest of your cargo to

Scotland. You'll like it there. Pretty country."

"That's stealing!" Davis yelled, poking his jaw almost in the major's face.

"Not really, Captain. We're just appropriating what we can use."

"Not from my ship, you won't!"

"Be reasonable, Captain," the major intoned in a soft voice. "You're here. You have some equipment we need. Desperately. You wouldn't want some Americans to die because you refused to give us those jeeps and trucks and radio equipment, would you?"

"I suppose the whiskey will save their lives, too?"

"Well, sir, it'll sure make some of them happy before they go into combat."

Frank shook his head.

What a helluva way to fight a war, he thought.

"I'll think about it," he said.

"You'll have to hurry. The general said if I couldn't work things out with you he'd want to see you in his office."

1100 HOURS
Aboard the S. S. Andrew Bennett

"It's the worst snafu I've seen yet and I've seen a few," Captain Davis shot at his chief mate in the saloon aboard the *Bennett*. The two men were having iced tea.

"There's something else you can do," Speer said.

"What?"

"Let them have all the cargo. Every piece. Sherman tanks. The lot. Just drop it off then head back home."

"We can't do that, damnit. Those tanks are going to be needed in North Africa if there's going to be an invasion there. So will the jeeps and trucks."

"Don't forget the whiskey!"

The mate took his empty glass, walked over to a cupboard, and poured a stiff belt of Dewar's Scotch.

"Look, Frank," he said. "Why sweat it? We were ordered to Noumea. We came here. We've done our duty. The Army here wants some of the cargo. Tell them they must take it all. Let them figure out what to do with what they don't want. We can go back home and get another load. Hell, I heard of a captain right after Pearl who dropped all his cargo on the beach at Pango Pango when they told him it wasn't supposed to be delivered there.

Last trip I took a look. The stuff is still sitting on the beach. Rusting."

He took another swallow of Scotch.

"This won't be the last time a cargo is sent to the wrong place. I say you tell the Army they can have it all, lock, stock, barrel, tanks and whiskey."

He raised his glass, then drained it.

Who cares who drinks the stuff?" the mate said scornfully. "Everybody gets drunk with it."

"I don't know, John, I don't know. Suppose American lives in North Africa depend on our entire cargo?"

1200 HOURS
In the Bennett's Saloon
"Ah tole yo' so, suh!" the second cook and baker boasted to the second mate after the officers had finished their meeting.

"You told me what, Bib?" Mr. Turner asked.

"That he warned us, fo' sure he did!"

"Stop horsing around, Bib. Who warned us about what?"

"Yo' knows, suh. The major!"

Oh, Lord, the ghost again!

"Yo' rememba, he tole us to turn 'round an' go back. Now we knows why."

"Oh, yes, Major Bennett," the mate chortled underneath a napkin hastily raised to his lips. "Good man, that major. He was trying to tell you we should have headed to Scotland."

"Tha's right, suh!" Bib beamed, proud that in a way he knew before anyone else the *Bennett* was making for the wrong port a couple of weeks ago.

"We'll have to pay more attention to your friend in the future, Bib," Mr. Turner said with a straight face. "He sure tried to help you -- help the ship last time you saw him."

Bib was pleased. The second mate, who earlier denied that ghosts exist, now acknowledged the ghost of Major Bennett was perhaps the ship's best protector.

"Ah'll sure keep on good terms wit' 'im!" he promised.

1300 HOURS
Noumea
Able-Bodied Seaman Jones and Donkeyman Phipps had

no trouble coaxing Ordinary Seaman Durante to go ashore with them. The young seaman wanted to see the sights of Noumea and he put a few dollar bills in his pocket to buy souvenirs. They took the afternoon launch to the dock and the teeming tropical port city. It took only a minute for Jones to hail a taxi.

Margot's place," he said confidently.

"Sure, Joe, sure," the black driver smiled, flashing a display of sparkling white teeth. He took off before Phipps closed the door.

"What's Margot's place?" Durante asked.

"A quiet, private lounge," Jones winked at Phipps. "They don't soak you for drinks like some places here. Best of all, there's beautiful girls. Lots of them."

"Oh," Tony said quietly. It was hot. He wanted a cold beer.

The taxi stopped, brakes screeching in front of a three-story house, surrounded on all sides by tall palm trees. A brown dog drowsed lazily on the orange-tiled veranda, lifting only its eyes to look at the three men walking to the front door. Jones didn't knock. He opened the door and walked in, the others following. They entered a huge carpeted living room, with four sofas, six side chairs, several small end tables, two large mirrors and a cozy bar with four stools in one corner. A bartender was wiping off a glass. Six young women sat leisurely on the sofas and chairs, some of them holding glasses, all of them holding conversations. Each wore a red dress. All of them, Tony had to admit, were beautiful.

"Margot here?" Jones asked.

"In the kitchen," one of the girls said. **"Mar . . go!"**

A woman walked into the room and Tony was awestruck. Flaming red hair down to her shoulders. Green eyes. Greener than any he had ever seen. Satin face. Small mouth frozen in a perpetual smile. Bright red lipstick. Tall, lithe body, wrapped in a tight, gleaming white dress, slit up the left side to show a full leg, top thigh to ankle. Her breasts were enormous. She glided across the floor like a movie actress.

"Margot!" Jones said, rushing to her.

"Well, I'll be darned. The old sailor boy himself."

"Not so old I can't handle you, baby," he said, grabbing her around the slim waist and pulling her to him.

"Uh, uh. Don't touch the merchandise. Not yet. Aloysius, isn't it?" she asked coyly.

"Come on, Margot. That's my middle name. I'm Joe. Remember?"

"Sure do, Aloysius." She looked at Phipps and Durante. "Friends of yours?"

"Shipmates."

"Good. Bill," she called to the bartender. "Be a good boy and give those fellas whatever they want. Aloysius will pay. Won't you, darling?"

"Joe, Margot, Joe. Call me Joe."

"You're paying, aren't you?"

"Yeah. For the first drink."

"Okay, Aloysius."

She kissed him flush on the mouth and teased him with her tongue. He gently pulled her to the side of the room.

"Got to talk to you quietly, Margot," he whispered. "Need a favor. See that young boy with the real short hair?"

"Yes. What about him?"

"He's a virgin, Margot. A real virgin."

The woman looked at Tony, sizing him up. About seventeen, maybe eighteen, she guessed. Good build. Not handsome, but good looking.

"For real?"

"For real. Which girl you want to give him?"

Margot looked at Tony again. She toyed with her hair.

"I think I'll take him myself."

"But I was counting on us," Jones protested.

"A virgin you ain't, Aloysius. I haven't had one of those in years. Should be fun."

"Okay, Margot, okay. But the deal is, baby, the other guy and I get to watch."

She thought for a moment about that.

"Why not? Should be more fun."

"I don't think he'll just go up to the room with you," Jones said. "He says he wants to be a virgin when he gets married after this trip. We had to talk him into coming here for a drink. Told him it was a private lounge. He has more'n a few dollars. Any ideas?"

"You gotta shock his kind. First of all, I won't take any money. I want to enjoy this. Second, I'll go up now and get undressed. You have a drink with him. Make sure he has two, maybe three. Then say you want to show him this old house. You know where my bedroom is?"

"Sure. Second floor. Last one down the left hall."

"Once he sees me on the bed, he'll bite."

Flashing a signal to the girls, she went upstairs.

"You bet he will," Jones laughed.

He sauntered over to the bar.

"Bill, give me a gin and tonic. With lime. Give my friends here another."

"Two green G and T's coming up," the bartender said happily.

"How're the drinks, guys?" Jones asked, putting a hand on Tony's shoulders.

"Good," Phipps answered.

"Strong," Tony said, swallowing what was left in his first glass. He had wanted a beer, but the bartender told him the mixed drink would be more cooling.

"Nice place, don't you think, Tony?"

"Yeah," Tony said, looking around. "Sure is well furnished. This Margot friend of yours must have lots of money. Are all these girls her sisters?"

"Well, you might say that," Jones answered slyly.

"They're all so . . so pretty," Tony said.

The shipmates talked about each girl, giving their own descriptions of what they considered beautiful. It was funny how the girl that seemed the prettiest to Tony seemed the ugliest to Jones. They had another drink. None of the girls moved. They were involved in their own conversations.

"Say, guys, how'd you like to see the rest of this house?" Jones asked, nudging Phipps slightly. The donkeyman returned the signal, letting him know he understood. "This place was built back around eighteen seventy, maybe earlier, and it's as beautiful today as it was then."

"Sure," Phipps said. "You were here then!"

Tony stood up slowly. The gin had already gone to his head.

"Why not?" he said. "I like old houses."

Upstairs, on the second floor, they poked their heads in and out of bedrooms, each decorated in a different style, each full of color, each with fresh flowers on tables near the windows. Each with the soft aroma of a different perfume.

"Beautiful place," Tony said.

Jones opened the door to Margot's bedroom.

"Take a look at this, Tony," he prodded, pushing the boy in front of him.

Tony's eyes bulged at the nude woman lying on the sparkling white sheets of the canopy bed.

"Beautiful," he sputtered.

His mouth opened wide. It was the first time he had seen a naked woman. He wanted to turn and walk out, but his feet were riveted to the floor. He just stared and he felt a rising in his groin.

"Come over to me, Tony," Margot said in a voice just above a whisper. She patted the sheet with her right hand. "Come join me."

Tony started to climb on the bed.

"Silly boy," she scolded. "Take your clothes off."

"But . . " he began to protest. Then he took off his shirt.

"Your pants, too," she cajoled.

He took them off and his erection made the front of his undershorts stand out like a tent.

"Look, he does have a rod!" Jones exclaimed.

Tony gingerly removed his shorts, lay down on the bed and Margot immediately covered his chest and stomach with kisses, clasping his penis in her right hand. She kissed its head.

"My, my," she said. "It smells so clean."

"Do him around the world, Margot!" Jones urged.

She did.

Turning Tony on his side, she stuck her tongue between his lower cheeks, briefly nicking his rectal orifice. She rolled him on his back again. Slowly, with her tongue, she licked his navel, belly, thighs, then his pubic hair. His body quivered with each touch and he grabbed her red hair, holding tight. He was breathing heavily and fast.

Then she stopped suddenly.

"Why don't you give it to me? Now!"

"I . . I don't know how," Tony stammered.

"It's easy," she said, turning on her back and guiding him atop her. "Just push it into me. Right here."

He did.

"Now," she squealed. "Ride me! Push in and out."

"Push, man, push!" his shipmates shouted, slapping their thighs. "You gotta push all the way in!"

He did.

"Now, out!"

He did and pulled out of her.

"Not that far, stupid! Put it back in!"

Tony tried but felt a tightening in his groin, then a quick release. And another. Three, four times, his body jerked as he shouted "My God!" over and over again.

He stopped moving, exhausted. Margot kissed him on the forehead.

"You'll last longer next time, honey," she said, disappointed.

She had forgotten how quickly male virgins ejaculate. Sometimes before they even entered a woman.

"It takes experience to hold it. Once you've used it a few times, you can hold back five, ten minutes, even longer. Then that girl you're gonna marry will know she's been laid."

She got up quickly and went into the bathroom.

Tony lay there a moment, not sure what to do. He looked at his shipmates, embarrassed. They were laughing. He jumped up, threw on his clothes, ran down the stairs, out of the house and raced to the dock, getting there seconds before a launch pulled away.

On the ship, he took the gangway steps two at a time, ran to his cabin, grabbed a towel, hurried to the shower and threw his clothes in a heap outside the stall. The cold water felt good and he lathered and cleansed, soaped and scrubbed a full fifteen minutes, trying to wash the experience away.

Still naked, he climbed onto his bunk and began to worry.

Suppose she has clap and now I have it? he asked himself. *Or syphilis?*

He had heard about those awful diseases.

My God, I could never marry Marilyn!

He sobbed and tears rolled down his face.

I'm not a virgin any more and I promised Marilyn.

He took deeper breaths, trying to control himself. Thoughtfully, quietly, he remembered the feel of himself inside the girl. It calmed him and he smiled, feeling satisfied.

It was not bad. Not bad at all. Felt pretty good.

When he ejaculated, he had the feeling of tremendous relief, as though he had soared someplace way up in Heaven.

So that's what it's like? Good! Great! Maybe I'll try it again. The girl said it lasts longer if you use it more. I bet Marilyn will like it if I last longer.

He vowed to go back to Margot's place tomorrow.

1300 HOURS
In the Captain's Quarters
"Good news or bad news, depending on your viewpoint," Captain Davis told Gunner's Mate First Class Hunt. He had called the sailor to his quarters again after talking with a Navy personnel officer ashore following his morning meeting with Major Yardley.

"What's that, sir?" Hunt asked cautiously.

"There's no qualified officer on this God forsaken island to replace Lieutenant Hamilton," the captain said bluntly. "Not even an unqualified one. You'll have to take charge of the Armed Guard 'til we get to a port where we can find one."

Hunt didn't say anything. He stared at the merchant captain, perturbed.

"We'll move you up to the lieutenant's quarters," Davis continued. "You'll have your own cabin and . . "

"I'd rather not," Hunt said quickly.

"No? Why not?"

"That would put me out of touch with the men, sir."

Captain Davis looked askance at the seaman only one year younger than himself. *One would think an enlisted sailor would relish having his own cabin and be out of a crowded foc'sle. It would be more comfortable.*

"You wouldn't be out of touch, Hunt," he finally said. "I want you to continue daily gunnery drills when we leave here. We'll relieve you from your gun station and you'll have time to work with each gunner at his post. Besides, you'll have to keep the Guard's daily log and a quieter room would be a better place for that."

"If you don't mind, sir, I'm a gunner's mate, not an officer," Hunt said, emphasizing the last words. "I belong with my fellow enlisted men. I'd be more comfortable with them, not trying to put on any airs that I'm in command."

"But you will be."

"I can help the men with gunnery drills, Captain," he said. "I can write in the log right on my bunk and I can report to you daily on any matters to be brought to your attention. I don't need the lieutenant's quarters to do that."

Frank admired the man. Hunt could have more comforts, but wanted to be with his own kind. He obviously wasn't a man seeking power over other men. There are some Army generals, Frank had heard, who prefer roughing it with their foot soldiers and leading them in battle. Perhaps this seaman has the same type of temperament.

"Besides, sir, when there is a real G. Q., I want to be at my own gun," Hunt put in.

That was probably the key. The sailor needed his hands on a gun.

"Okay," Davis said. "Have it your way. Just keep me posted. If you need anything, let me know."

"Yes, sir."

Hunt did a stiff about face, took one step and suddenly turned back to the captain.

"Mind if I say something, sir?"

"Please do. Why don't you sit down first. In that chair."

"No, sir, but may I stand at parade rest?"

"Hunt, you look like a first year cadet at the Naval Academy. Chest out, stomach in, chin tucked. Why don't you get comfortable? Slouch if you want."

The sailor took a parade rest position.

"Is it true, sir, we're being sent to Scotland?"

"Scuttlebutt does travel fast," Captain Davis marvelled. "Frankly, I'm not yet sure, Hunt. We may unload some of our cargo here and head back to the States, pick up more and join a convoy headed for Scotland. But we may get orders to head through the Indian Ocean and up the Suez Canal to the Mediterranean and Alexandria, Egypt where, I'm sure, our load of tanks can be put to good use for invasions further up the African coast. Personally, I'd prefer the route to Egypt. It'd be safer."

Hunt shuffled his feet uneasily.

"I've been in the Med before, Captain. Nothing like it. Calm water, just like a big lake. Good weather. But dangerous."

Captain Davis listened quietly as the gunner talked about the sea war in the Mediterranean, beginning with the sinking of French warships in African harbors by the British fleet shortly after France surrendered, to assure the ships wouldn't be used by the Germans. Hunt described the Mediterranean, stretching no more than 850 miles at any point from the southern coast of Europe to the northern coast of Africa, as a huge pond in which merchant shipping is mercilessly attacked from the air and from above and below the surface. He told the captain about the large number of German and Italian aircraft that daily attack naval and merchant ships from airfields at

Catania Comiso, Trapani, Palermo and Reggio Calabria in Italy. He said the Italian Navy has a huge fleet of submarines, supplemented by German U-boats based at La Spezia. That there are more German subs based at Salamis in occupied Greece. He expressed concern about the explosive-laden Italian E-boats, some of which are flimsy nineteen-foot craft steered by one man who abandons it just before the boat hit its target.

"The man sometimes doesn't get off in time," Hunt continued. "There are also two-man assault boats, some forty-eight feet long, capable of doing forty-two knots, and carrying depth charges, torpedoes and machine guns. Those explosive boats cause devastating damage. The Italians also have two-man submarines that are sinking a lot of ships. You don't hear much about it, but the Med's not a real safe place. We go there, we've got to be on our toes."

"I appreciate your concern, Hunt," the captain said. "I don't yet know where we'll be sent. We'll just have to wait and see."

"I understand, sir."

"Meantime, Hunt, keep your gun crew happy with shore liberty today. They'll have enough to worry about when we leave port tomorrow night or the next day, no matter which way we head."

"I'll do my best, sir," Hunt said, saluting.

He wasn't happy. He still didn't like giving orders.

1400 HOURS
At the Military Stockade
Third Mate Franklin knocked loudly on the door to the captain's cabin.

"Captain!" he called. "They want you ashore!"

"What's this all about, Mister?" Captain Davis snapped, opening the door and showing his annoyance. He was shirtless.

"Sir, the Army wants you ashore right now. There's a launch here and the Army's got a jeep waiting at the dock."

"That's ridiculous! I left the quartermaster's office this morning and told them I'd be back tomorrow. I don't intend going back until then."

He turned back into his cabin.

"But it's the Military Police, Captain," the young mate

protested. "There's some kind of trouble."

"Trouble?"

"Yes, sir. They've locked up Jones and Robinson. They said something about inciting a riot."

"A riot?" Davis shouted, reaching for his shirt. "What in hell have they done now?"

"I don't know, Captain, and that's the truth. All the driver told me was they broke a window, started a riot and are locked up in the stockade. They want to see you there."

Goddamnit, Frank swore under his breath.

"Okay, let's get going."

In the Army stockade, Captain Davis looked sternly at his fist-swinging able-bodied seaman.

"What happened, Jones?"

Jones flashed a quick, nervous smile.

"Well, sir, it was like this. Me and Phipps walked around town a bit, visited a quiet lounge I know, joined up with Robinson in a bar, had a couple of drinks and then Robinson and me started walking around town again, minding our own business. Phipps went off on his own. Well, Captain, you wouldn't believe what was in that storefront."

"What storefront?"

"Where the Red Cross has its canteen, sir."

"So?"

"So they had this big sign right in the window. I didn't like it."

"What sign?"

"'No Merchant Marine Allowed' it said. That made me mad."

Captain Davis sighed.

"Jones, for God's sake! You know the rules. The Red Cross and U. S. O. don't let merchant seamen in their canteens. They're for men in the military."

"Military? Military be damned, sir, and pardon me. What do they think we are? The enemy? We're Americans. We deliver the goods to these fucking Army guys, even the stuff they drink in there, and the Red Cross tells us we ain't fit to have a soda with them. Pisses me off."

"What did you do?" the captain asked, really not sure he wanted an answer.

"Well, me . . I picked up this rock, see, and threw it into the store window. You shoulda seen the whole damn thing break up. It was smashing!"

"Oh, God!" Davis said. "Then what happened?"

"Well, sir, a bunch of GIs came out, along with a couple of Red Cross ladies, and we tried to be nice on account of the ladies, you see. I tried to explain my feelings, but those Army guys wouldn't listen. They started punching me first. Then they jumped on Robinson. Five against two, it was."

He worked his face into a crafty smile.

"We had 'em beat a mile when the M.P.s came. So here I am. Robinson is here too. But he didn't do nothing except try to protect me."

He looked innocently at the captain, his eyes focusing between the bars.

"Can you get us out, sir?"

"I should let you rot here!" Captain Davis steamed as he stalked into the M.P. headquarters building.

"Major," he spoke to the M.P. commander. "Looks like we've got ourselves a handful of trouble."

"A bucket's more like it," the major retorted.

He pointed to a man in khaki with Red Cross buttons on the two tips of his shirt collar.

"This is Dudley Harrison. He's the Red Cross director here. Tell the captain what his men did, Dudley."

Captain Davis raised his hand.

"Don't. I already know. Bad. No doubt about it. Bad. Not sure I can excuse their behavior -- I'll deal with that on the ship -- but you should know my officers and crew are pretty frustrated here."

"Frustrated?" Mr. Harrison asked.

"Yes, frustrated. More than frustrated. Angry. We travel all the way from San Francisco with a cargo consigned to Noumea and, when we get here, the Army tells us they made a mistake. We should have been sent to Scotland."

"Scotland?" the major echoed.

"Yes. The crew's real uptight. Some want to dump everything right on the docks here and go home. Others think we must take our cargo to Scotland. My men have been spoiling for a fight and looks like a couple got into one. I'm sorry."

He was seeking sympathy for the two men.

"I didn't know," the major said.

"I can understand," the Red Cross man said symphathetically. "Snafus like that are tough to deal with."

"Still," Captain Davis said, "it's no excuse for breaking

the window. I'll pay for the damages. How much?"

"Gosh, I don't know, Captain. I've no idea when or where we can get another big glass plate like that. We're rigging up a temporary awning."

"Suppose I give you fifty dollars? That should cover it, don't you think?"

"Oh, that's too much, Captain," Mr. Harrison protested. "I think twenty dollars would be enough, don't you, Major?"

"Hell, Dudley. You won't get any glass 'til the end of this war anyway. You can use the fifty bucks for something else you need."

He focused his eyes on Captain Davis.

"You will punish these men, won't you, Captain?"

"You bet, Major. They'll get extra duty scrubbing down the deck when we're back at sea."

He didn't tell the Army man he might have to pay overtime for that. Union rules.

"Good. Sergeant, let those seamen out. They can go back to the ship with their captain."

Frank handed the money to Mr. Harrison.

The major stood up and saluted Captain Davis. It was the first time a military man had saluted Frank and he was unsure what to do. He was a civilian even if he wore a Merchant Marine captain's uniform. He returned the salute.

"Thank you, Major."

"When are you sailing, Captain?" the Red Cross man asked.

"Not sure, Mr. Harrison. We're trying to settle things here. The Army wants some of our cargo, but I think we're duty bound to take all of it to Scotland where it's supposed to be. We should settle the matter tomorrow."

"Good, then. Please tell your crew our canteen will be open to them tonight. It may be against policy, but I wouldn't want them to think the Red Cross doesn't care about all Americans out here."

1600 HOURS
Mail Call
Purser Tanner returned to the ship on a late afternoon launch and carried a small sack of mail. It was a wonderment to him that, with millions in the military forces spread throughout the world, any mail would find

itself to a little merchant ship like the *Bennett*. Tanner didn't know that a couple of months ago, letters were not sent to any merchant ship. Its next port of call was in sealed orders, not opened until the vessel left port. A smart officer, or enlisted man, in the Navy Postal Office figured that, since there were Navy Armed Guard aboard, *someone* ashore had to know where the ship was headed. It was a simple matter to get that information and forward a mail pouch to all ships destined to a particular port where it could be sorted and delivered. The pouch sometimes arrived after the ship had left and the military postmasters there went through the same process, hoping it would arrive at the next port in time.

The merchant seamen and the Armed Guard eagerly grabbed for an envelope or box when their names were called.

Dear Tony,
It was only yesterday that we had a picnic together and today you are gone, someplace out on that big Pacific Ocean. For a while last night, lying in bed, I had some second thoughts. Maybe we should have done "it" yesterday. I wanted to just as much as you. I touched myself down there and wondered what "it" would be like. They say "it" sometimes hurts at first, but then becomes enjoyable.
I almost wish we had tried, but when Sis took me to the bridal shop today and I looked at so many beautiful white gowns, I knew we were right. We've saved something special for our wedding night.
You'll be home soon and I've decided, wickedly, not to wear any panties under the gown when we get married. That way, if you want, we can do "it" without undressing. Won't that be grand?
Please come home quickly. I have "it" waiting for you.
Love and kisses,
Marilyn

Dearest Frank,
Do you have any women on your ship? One woman? More?
I've got to know.
Captain Weatherby at the shipping company told me today a woman was on an American ship torpedoed in the Pacific a few days ago . He says she was part of the crew.

He also says that women are on merchant ships of many countries, Russia, Norway, Sweden. I just didn't know women are on ships like yours. Are you friendly with any of them?
Yes, damnit, I'm jealous!
I've been working on a surprise for you and I don't want to think I have competition with a woman who's there with you and I'm not. I won't tell you about the surprise yet, particularly if you have a woman on your ship.
As I told you yesterday when you called from San Francisco, I haven't heard from Dad. His ship has not come into Baltimore and I'm worried. I'm hoping he was sent to another port and will call soon. I haven't heard a word from Billy.
I miss you. Be sure to stay away from women, any women. I need you here.
Love ya,
Lynne

Dear Hank,
I'm not much good at writing letters. Mother always does that. Trouble is, she's sick now. Real sick. The doctors say she has Hodgkins Disease. That's a type of cancer, but they're not telling me much. They don't give me much hope. They say she'll have maybe a couple of months. They're keeping her comfortable in the Mount Kisco Hospital.
I know you'd like to be home, but this war has to come first. Someone's got to stop that maniac Hitler and those sneaky Japs. You can be that someone. I'm proud of you, son. So is mother. Being a ship's boatswain is an important job. Mother asked me to send her love and tell you not to worry. That's her, always thinking of someone else.
Take care of yourself and come home when you can.
Dad

2100 HOURS
In the Captain's Quarters
Captain Davis lay on his bunk, staring at the ceiling. *Funny how the sounds of a ship are magnified at night,* he thought. He could hear the decks creak as the *Bennett* gently tugged at her anchor. Water sloshed in the cistern over the toilet in his private head. Someone was

humming in the wheelhouse. Or was it the flying bridge? From down below, he could hear the movement of pots and pans being cleaned in the galley. He was still struggling with his conscience. At his meeting with the Army that morning, General Alan Slewsbury had tried to persuade the captain to unload the jeeps, trucks and radio equipment, ignoring the issue of the whiskey. Major Yardley had stood near the general's desk, anxious to bring up the issue, but changed his mind when Slewsbury said the vehicles and radio equipment "are all we want."

"We really need that stuff," the general said. "Noumea is a major port in the Southwest Pacific. We pile up material here and send it on to where it's needed, when it's needed. We're still on the defensive in this theatre. The Japs are running amuck all over the Pacific. They moved into the Solomon Islands just a few weeks ago, taking the port of Rabaul in New Britain and they're building a huge air-and-sea base there. Their bombers have been hitting hard at Port Moresby, New Guinea, a large Australian naval station on the southeastern coast. They've made landings at Lae and Salamaua on the northeastern New Guinea coast and they may soon take all of that strategic island."

He paused, wanting to find something to say to hit hard at the captain's patriotism, at his sense of wanting to be a part of winning this war.

"Moresby is only spitting distance from Australia," he continued. "The threat to Australia is serious, Captain. Without American planes, arms and troops, the Aussies won't be able to hold. That's not only a problem for them but for us. We've got to stop them and we need all the equipment we can get."

He looked directly into Frank's eyes.

"Look, Captain, you're under Navy command in this port. I could ask Admiral Staire to order you to unload what we want. I'd rather not go that far. I'd rather you do it willingly. You give us what we can use, then head back to the States with those tanks and pick up some more materials. They'll send you on to Loch Ewe or perhaps another port where they're stockpiling material for the North Africa invasion."

The general was right. The Navy admiral could give such an order. Frank had said he would give his answer tomorrow.

Lying on his bunk, Frank debated whether to give the equipment to the general or to pull up the hook immediately and take his entire cargo to Scotland. General Slewsbury had been convincing. Things didn't look good for the Allies in the Southwest Pacific.

On the other hand, Frank argued with himself, *things don't look good in Africa either. Rommel's tearing up the place. That's where our Sherman tanks are ultimately destined. If we take the ship out during the darkness,* he figured, *we won't be missed until morning.* By then the *Bennett* would have started a solo run through the Indian Ocean, up the Red Sea and through the Suez Canal to Alexandria where he was sure the Allies would welcome the tanks.

There would be Japanese and German submarines all the way. If, however, he let General Slewsbury have the jeeps, trucks and radio equipment, it might help secure the Southwest Pacific and Australia. He could head eastward to the States with his cargo of tanks and then join a convoy to Scotland.

Either way, he thought, *we'd face the same enemy submarines.*

He got up and went to the chartroom.

2300 HOURS
In the Bennett's Engine Room
No one heard a sound when Chief Engineer Huben fell down the last six steps of the ladder to the engine room. He lay there for five minutes, maybe more, before Oiler Otto Blakeslee spotted the man sprawled on the steel deck, face down. Huben was unconscious.

"Holy hell!" Blakeslee shouted, quickly squatting and feeling for the chief's pulse. "Hey, Benny!" he called to a wiper. "The chief's hurt. Come over here quick!"

Wiper Benny Thurmond ran to his shipmate's side. "Is he dead?"

"No. I can feel some pulse. Quick! Get topside and find the purser!"

Benny raced up the ladder two steps at a time and, as he hit the bridge deck, began calling for Mr. Tanner. He found the officer in the chartroom, pouring over maps with Captain Davis and Chief Mate Speer.

"Sir," Thurmond said loudly. "The chief engineer's hurt bad. He's unconscious."

The three officers turned quickly, the captain and mate dropping the papers held in their hands. They had been charting a course through the Indian Ocean and were pondering the need for additional provisions for such a long journey. They had just about reached the conclusion that a furtive sailing from Noumea might not be the wisest choice.

"Where?" Captain Davis asked.

"In the engine room. At the bottom of the ladder."

"Let's go!" Tanner called, already running out the chartroom door.

At the bottom of the engine room ladder, the fallen chief was conscious and swearing at Blakeslee.

"Damn you, man! Help me up!" the chief demanded.

"But, sir," Blakeslee protested. "I told you I think your right leg's broken. I don't want to move you without help and.."

"You've got it," Tanner said, reaching the chief's side and kneeling down to examine him.

"Not a goddamn thing wrong with me!" Huben swore. "Just slipped and fell."

"Take it easy, Chief," Captain Davis said. "Give Tanner a chance to find out what's wrong."

"Nothing wrong that a good shot of bourbon won't cure," the chief pouted.

Tanner stood up and turned to the captain.

"His right leg is broken, sir. He's got quite a lump on the back of his head and may have a concussion. There are bruises on both arms."

"Can we get him topside?" the captain asked.

"Yes. We've a stretcher in the sick bay."

Tanner looked at Blakeslee and Thurmond.

"These men are strong enough to carry him up there."

He kneeled and examined the leg again.

"Not good. Compound fractures of the tibia and fibula. We should get him ashore to the hospital. They can set them there."

The chief engineer spit.

"You ain't taking me to no damn hospital!" he swore vehemently. "You fix me up on the ship."

Tanner looked at the captain, then turned to the chief.

"I've never set a broken leg before. It should be done by a real doctor. He'll do it right and it won't take long. You're lucky we're in port."

"I won't go!" Huben insisted.

"You will," Captain Davis said calmly, knowing his stubborn chief engineer would fight in every way against staying in a hospital. "I'll get you that shot of bourbon and, if the doctor agrees, we'll bring you back on board."

The chief eyed the captain suspiciously.

"You will?"

"I promise," Frank said.

"The captain is a man of his word," Speer said.

"Okay," Huben said through a clog of phlegm in his throat. "But I want back on board soon's they fix it. I ain't staying in no hospital. Not even tonight!"

Tanner was relieved.

"Get the stretcher from sick bay," he instructed Blakeslee. "It's stored beneath one of the lower bunks."

Then to Thurmond: "Find Sparks. Tell him to radio the Navy for a launch to take an injured officer to the hospital."

Both men raced up the ladder.

Captain Davis looked down at his chief engineer. The Dutchman was seventy-one, stood only five feet, four inches and weighed about one hundred thirty pounds. He was gnarled and wrinkled, with flecks of grey in his wiry brown hair and, although he was hurt, there were no outward signs he felt any pain. Instead, there was a sparkle in his eyes and a firm jaw set that exuded personal confidence that he would be okay.

Frank knew it would be a long time before the man could return to duty. He also knew it would be a big loss. Huben could take the ship's whole reciprocating steam engine apart and put it back together again. Blindfolded. *Losing the chief will hurt us*, he thought.

"Your home's in Mississippi, right, Chief?"

"Yeah. Got a small house in Orange Grove."

"Well, this makes up my mind," Frank said, speaking to Mister Speer. "We'll let the Army take the jeeps, trucks and radio equipment and head back to the States."

He turned to his chief engineer.

"We'll go through the Panama Canal to New Orleans. That'll get you pretty close to home. They'll tell us there what to do with the tanks. Either unload them for another ship to carry or take them ourselves to Scotland or any port they want."

"You don't have to do that for me," Huben said.

"I'm not doing it just for you. This helps solve a couple of problems. The Army gets what it wants here. We get you home. We can get our cargo of tanks to where they're needed. Everybody's happy."

"Captain," the chief engineer said. "I can't just sit around home. I know it was foolish of me to come back and bring you this trouble. My arthritis has been killing me for more than ten years. I quit shipping out because of the pain and I should not have signed on again. Felt I had to. I didn't know what else to do."

"I understand," Frank said.

"No, you don't!" Huben snapped. "It wasn't just Pearl Harbor. My wife died a year ago and I was lonely. No kids. No grandkids. Just a sister in Biloxi. She's sixty-seven and widowed."

He rubbed the lump on the back of his head and looked own at his leg.

"I felt useless then. I feel worthless now."

"Come on, Chief," Frank chided. "Stop feeling sorry for yourself. That doesn't do any good. You're a good engineer."

"I know I can't come back down here again," Huben countered sadly. "I want to help win this war, but now there's very little I can do."

Frank put a knee on the deck and reached over to tap the chief's chest.

"You know, Klaus," he said kindly, "a wise man, he may have been a Dutchman like you, I don't know, once said: 'Nobody makes a greater mistake in life than he who did nothing because he could only do a little.' Think about those words. It's easy to let your condition overwhelm you, if you let it, to think there's little if anything you can do to help the war effort. You've gone to sea so long you think that's the only way you can help. It's not. Trust me, Chief, you can do a little thing every day that will make a big difference in this war. A big difference."

"How?" Huben was skeptical.

"Well, for one thing, you can teach other men to be engineers. Engineers as good as you. You could go to one of the maritime schools and teach a class. They'd be learning from the best. The cadet officer school at Pass Christian isn't far from your home. I bet they'd even put you up there."

"You think so?"

"Bet half my pay on it," Frank said confidently. "I know the superintendent."

"I don't want any favors," Huben protested.

"Oh, come off your stubborn high horse, Klaus! You know damn well the Merchant Marine needs good engine room officers and crews. With your knowledge, you could train hundreds and you'd be helping the war effort more than sitting around your house or an old folk's home feeling sorry for yourself."

"I'll think about it," Huben said, turning on his side and closing his eyes.

As far as he was concerned, the lecture from the young captain was over. Still, the idea of teaching maritime cadets intrigued him. Maybe he could help.

Just a little.

2 March 1942

0100 HOURS
In the Captain's Quarters
Captain Davis was in his bunk again, unable to sleep. He had dispatched the chief mate minutes ago to General Slewsbury's headquarters to tell the Army he would permit unloading the cargo needed in Noumea. He wanted to get out of this port as soon as possible.

What else can go wrong with this ship? he asked himself. *Do all captains have as much trouble? Or is it because I'm too young to be a good captain?*

The last question troubled him.

He tried to reassure himself that his age played no part in the issuance of the orders to the wrong port or the sickness of the Navy gunnery officer. That his youth had nothing to do with the near riot at the Red Cross Canteen. That, certainly, his age wasn't to blame for the fall of the chief engineer. Still, he could not console himself. There was either something wrong with him or the ship was jinxed from the day its keel was laid.

He began to wonder if there was some truth to the ghost of Major Andrew Bennett prowling the ship.

"Lynne," he said to the photo of his wife at the foot of his bunk. "Pray for me and this ship."

0700 HOURS
A Noumea Dock
The chief engineer was back on board, resting comfortably in his own cabin, his right leg encased in a

plaster of paris cast. The *Bennett* moved to a dock and Army longshoremen began unloading the requested cargo. Approval was granted for the jeeps, trucks and radio equipment to be unloaded in Noumea. The whiskey was taken off as well and, somehow, it didn't bother Frank. After unloading, the ship would proceed to New Orleans where a decision would be made whether to continue to Scotland with the tanks or to another assembly point.

4 March 1942

1130 HOURS
In the Southwest Pacific
The island of New Caledonia was still in sight when Tokyo Rose, in her silky voice, spoke on shortwave radio to the thousands of American troops who regularly tuned into her broadcasts.

"This next song is for all you unfortunate boys on the *Andrew Bennett*," she said, putting the needle on the record, *Night and Day*. After a few seconds, the sound was turned down to background music. "I can't believe what happened to you fellows. You sailed your Liberty ship all the way from San Francisco to New Caledonia with a cargo of large Sherman tanks that was supposed to go to Scotland. Can you believe it? Some snafu!"

The music was turned up briefly, then down.

"Sad. My, how mixed up your government is. Now you must sail back, go through the Panama Canal and face those awful German submarines on your way across the Caribbean to New Orleans. That's a dangerous journey for merchant ships. Then you'll cross the Atlantic to -- oh, where will you go? Loch Ewe, Scotland? Or Alexandria, Egypt?"

Music up.

"How'd she know where we're going?" Ordinary Seaman Durante bellowed. "The captain hasn't even told us yet."

Music down again.

"And, what's all this about Ordinary Seaman Tony Durante? Tony, oh, Tony! You lost your virginity in Noumea. Naughty boy. Margot has a good reputation . . in bed! How'd you like her, Tony?"

"Goddamnit!" exploded Durante. "How'd she know about that?"

"Spies, man, spies," Donkeyman Phipps said. "That island is crawling with them."

"Maybe Margot's one," Durante sputtered. "Damn! Suppose Marilyn finds out? I'll be dead!""

5 March 1942

0800 HOURS
Murmansk, Russia

Murmansk was no safe haven for the *S. S. Elihu Nicholson*. German planes came in at dusk and continued to drop their lethal loads on the city, the docks and the anchored ships until dawn, almost without interruption. Russian ack-ack guns on land, and the antiaircraft guns on the naval and merchant ships, fired away in one continuous rumble, their shells sometimes hitting other ships rather than their intended targets. It seemed the Germans, having hit the convoy just outside the port and having harassed other convoys all the way from Iceland, were not ready to forget any of the ships in Murmansk.

The crew of the *Nicholson* wondered if they would be sunk in the harbor before the Russians got their hands on the cargo the seamen risked their lives to deliver. There were only twelve berths for merchantmen and, when a ship left one of the piers, the captains of all the ships at anchorage prayed their vessel would be the next called for berthing and unloading. The *Nicholson* remained at anchorage. Acting Captain Slim Stevens had gone ashore every morning for the past week on a launch that moved from ship to ship, picking up captains and taking them to the harbormaster's office where they met with Russian officers and the U. S. Army colonel, hoping for orders to dock and unload.

He came back from every trip frustrated and dejected.

"I don't understand," he told Billy. "The Russians say they need our cargo, especially the tanks and trucks. The U. S. Army colonel says the Russians need our cargo. He points out they only have twelve piers and not too much in the way of cranes to offload. I know their longshoremen are ill-equipped for the job. Most are women. There are a few wounded soldiers and some half-starved political prisoners. But, damn it, ships that came in after us have already been docked, unloaded and gone home. Here we sit. It makes no sense."

"Wars make no sense," Billy answered.

6 March 1942

0730 HOURS
At the Same Anchorage
Looking at the same ships day after day, it became clear to Acting Captain Stevens that the ships still at anchor, including his, were damaged, some more severely than others. His had probably suffered the most damage. He wondered why none of the damaged ships were taken to the docks to have their cargoes unloaded. There were an even dozen.

He began to smell an answer when he saw the entire crew leave the Hog Islander on several launches, carrying seabags, suitcases and boxes.

Where are they going? he asked himself, puzzled. *Home? On another ship? Something smells and it's not just the water in the harbor.*

That gave him an idea. Dressed in his best uniform, even the tie, he walked with a determined gait to the Jacob's ladder that led to the daily launch ride ashore. The crew's collective eyebrows raised.

When the launch returned, it was followed by a tugboat. The acting captain quickly climbed the ladder, jumped over the railing, called to the boatswain and the carpenter to follow and strode with long, quick steps to the saloon. A messboy raced in with a pot of coffee, then hid himself in the passageway just outside the door, listening.

"Chips," Stevens said to the carpenter. "Can you build a wooden superstructure on the starboard side of the wheelhouse?"

"Yes, sir!" the carpenter said with confidence.

"How will you do it?"

"We can use wood from some of the large cargo crates. Most of it's an inch thick or more and there are some four by fours."

"Bulkheads and a deck that can withstand a North Atlantic storm?"

"Can't guarantee that, sir," the carpenter answered.

He wore thick glasses and a dozen or so scraggly whiskers marred an otherwise mild countenance. He was still trying to grow a beard, with little success, and he looked more like a college student than a ship's carpenter.

"Those storms can damage steel, much less wood, sir. But we can build a superstructure, one that will hold unless we're tossed on our side. That's not likely to happen, Skipper, not with a Liberty."

"What do you have in mind, Captain?" Billy asked.

He had entered the saloon just seconds after the carpenter got there. Stevens ignored the question.

"Is the tugboat coming alongside?" he asked the boatswain.

Boats looked out a porthole.

"Not yet. Looks like she's standing off about one hundred yards. Some guy is on the foredeck, looking at us with binoculars."

"Okay," the acting captain said calmly. "Here's the plan. Chips, you and Boats get a crew up to the wheelhouse and build bulkheads with a deck where the flying bridge is missing. Have some others break up cargo crates on the deck. Turn every man to. Make a lot of noise. I want that tug captain to see what you're doing so make a big display of it, will you?"

"Right, sir!"

The carpenter and boatswain nearly collided running from the saloon.

"What's behind the plan, Slim?" Billy asked again.

Slim flashed a quick smile, pulled a Chesterfield from his breast pocket and lit it.

"Billy," he said, slowly exhaling. "I think those damn Ruskies have been playing chess with us. They've calculated we'd get tired of air raids and sitting around. They figured, because our captain and chief mate are gone and our ship is hurt, we'd sooner or later decide it'd be safer to ask for a transfer to any of the other ships heading home. That's what happened to the Hog Islander. They quit the ship this morning. The officers. The crew. The Armed Guard. And now they're on six, seven other ships, getting ready to go home. I wondered what was happening when I saw so many leave it."

He paused, took another drag on the cigarette and looked out a forward porthole. He could hear the sounds of hammering and the tearing of wood from crates.

"I didn't like what happened to the Hog. Those damn Commie bastards are taking it over. They'll keep it for their own. Smart trick. They just waited that crew out and now they have a ship they can fix up for their own fleet. Without paying a dime for it." He pointed a finger at the chief engineer. "Some Allies they are! But I won't let them have this ship! Told them an hour ago. Told that friggin' U. S. Army colonel the same thing. Gave them an ultimatum. Either this ship gets to a dock today, and unloading begins within an hour of tying up, or I'm taking us out of the harbor, deep-sixing the cargo and making a beeline for New York."

He grinned spaciously.

"I think they bought it, though they questioned how we could sail with half our wheelhouse gone. Told them that's my problem. At any rate, they promised to move another ship from a pier, still half-loaded, to make room for us. Said it would take six hours. I gave them four. If they don't, I'm pulling up anchor, moving into the channel and deep-sixing everything we can toss overboard with our own booms. Then I'm taking us home, with or without escort. You with me?"

Billy's mouth was open but no words came for a moment. It was the most magnificent display of authority, leadership and courage he had seen in his eleven years of going to sea. What the acting captain had done took nerves of steel.

"My God, Slim, you know I am! So's every man on this ship!" His voice was full of pride and assurance. "Unload here or in Davy Jones' locker. Jesus, you've got guts!"

"Come with me," Slim invited as he headed to the ladder leading to the flying bridge, port side.

Standing tall and erect in his uniform, he waved to the tugboat captain, then walked to starboard, as far as he could go, to where the carpenter and boatswain, with every available deckhand, already had wooden stanchions running from the wheelhouse deck to the flying bridge deck. He called encouragement to the men, then waved again to the tugboat captain.

"You sonofabitch!" he shouted, waving both arms in a signal to move the tug alongside. "We're going one way or another! If you want what we got, you'll begin moving up to us!"

The tug captain probably could not hear the words or, if he did, probably did not understand them. But he got the message. The tug suddenly picked up steam and headed for the *Nicholson*'s port side.

Word about what the acting captain had threatened,

and was planning to do, spread through the ship quickly. Men from the engine room and the steward's department, as well as the Armed Guard, gathered on the main deck and cheered the man who told the Russians to shove it up their collective ass. Acting Captain Stevens knew then he was a hero to his crew.

1030 HOURS
At a Murmansk Dock
The *Nicholson* was tied to a pier and Russian stevedores boarded. Most were women. The unloading was difficult, with ice coating much of the deck and cargo. The rusted pier cranes seemed to bend with every load as the damaged tanks went over the gunwales to the pier below. Undamaged tanks, tractors, trucks, crates followed. The longshoremen seemed to be in a frenzied hurry. They stopped only when six German planes came in, strafing and bombing, taking cover in the passageways of the ship.

When the attack ended, the U. S. Army colonel came aboard with a man in a pinstripe suit, obviously a diplomat. He didn't identify himself. The officer approached the acting captain in the wheelhouse with a quick, nervous smile.

"So, you're going through with it?" he asked.

Slim looked at Billy, then fixed his eyes on the colonel's, unblinking.

"You're seeing it. We'll pull out the moment we're unloaded. I don't trust these Russians as far as I can throw a tractor!"

The sounds of sawing and hammering provided background music for the conversation. The wooden superstructure took on more shape.

"I've come with a message from the United States ambassador," the civilian said tersely. "He wants you to know, whether you realize it or not, you're in a war zone, in the port of a friendly nation. He's upset you've threatened to dump your cargo at the mouth of the harbor. Under the Articles of War, you can be tried for treason."

"You -- "

"Let me finish, Captain," the civilian continued. "He doesn't want it to come to that. The Russians don't either. They want you to stay here, to repair the damage to your ship as soon as they get a drydock open for repairs. Then you can go home. Or, you can get on another ship and go home now . . if you want. Others have done it. The ambassador wants you to reconsider."

Weaselmouth bastard! Threatening me with treason! Slim looked hard at the civilian and decided the man had a face he couldn't trust. Dark hair, swarthy complexion, black eyes and huge grooves on either side of his mouth that looked like parentheses. *Sonofabitch should be tried for treason himself, working in collusion with these Commies to give them ships for free!*

"No deal!" he said to the parentheses. "Does the ambassador know you give these Russians our merchant ships without a Lend-Lease clause? I'll bet he doesn't! Well, they'll never get this ship! Not like they got the Hog. You want to try me for treason? Try it. I defy you to make the charge stick!"

"We can stop you from leaving the dock, Captain," the civilian said sarcastically.

"Well, I've thought about that. We have another option, you know."

"What?"

"Understand this, Mr. Ambassador's Man! You, too, Colonel! I'll say it slowly and clearly. I'm taking this ship out as soon as we're unloaded and I'll give the Russians just two days to do it. Forty-eight hours. If they haven't finished by then, I'm pulling away. Any interference before then, or trying to stop us leaving . . " He paused for effect . . "I'll scuttle her right here!"

"Checkmate," Billy applauded loudly. "I'll pull the plug myself, Captain."

The eyes and mouths of the two men were wide open, the civilian's parentheses stretched to oversized exclamation marks. They looked at each other, then at the captain, and said nothing. Billy bowed low, motioning with his right hand to the door.

"Why don't you be nice boys and trundle back on dock. Sing the *Volga Boatman Song* to keep those stevedores working."

He had no idea how the song went, but he hummed a few notes, smiled and again pointed to the door. The two hastily retreated.

"Nice going, Slim." Billy said. "You really stuck it to those guys. Goddamnit, you're something!"

Slim brushed him off.

"We've a lot to do."

"Right!"

"Tell the chief gunner's mate I want every gun station manned 'round-the-clock and ready to shoot at the slightest hint of interference . . from anyone."

"Right!"

"And tell the boatswain I want double twenty-four hour lookouts fore, aft and midships!"

"Right!"

"Both sides, in case they try to sneak up on us from the water."

"Right!"

Slim sat down in the captain's chair and lit a cigarette.

"What kind of a mess have I gotten us into?" he asked tiredly.

"Hey, don't back off now, Slim!" Billy encouraged. "You're doing great! Wish I could be as calm as you, telling them off like that!"

"I'm not calm. Christ, my insides are shaking!"

"You're okay, Skipper, okay. Talk about something else. It'll help get your mind off those guys."

"Like what?"

"Like . . how're you fixing the watches? You're three officers short on deck."

Slim didn't hesitate.

"I'm moving A. B. Seltzer to the second mate's watch. He's got twelve years. And A. B. Hardebaugh to my old watch. He's got eight. Both have the ability to make decisions. Both have guts. They'll do six hours on, six off and I'll spend time with each of them. I'll also sleep here. They'll get an on-the-job course in using the sextant and in keeping the log. I don't know about Hardebaugh. He's a bit rough on the edges, but Seltzer will make a good mate some day."

Billy nodded agreement. He knew the men.

"How about your black gang?" Slim asked.

"We're in good shape. The third assistant is back on board. He may have some problems navigating the ladders, but I think he'll do okay. If it's too much trouble for him, I'll do the same as you. Put the first and second on six-hour watches. I'll go eight hours on, four off, if I have to. Won't sleep in the engine room 'tho. Too hot. We'll make it."

The man's confidence reassured the acting captain. Billy had a self-assurance that was infectious. At five feet nine and 165 pounds, he was a large bantam rooster, four inches shorter than his younger brother but, like Frank, had solid muscles kept in shape by lifting weights, doing one hundred pushups daily and hitting a small punching bag hung from the ceiling in his stateroom. The bag was in the corner, out of the way, but anyone who visited there could see it, the mark of a man who kept his body in good form. He allowed himself one exercise on deck, a brisk walk fore and aft each day, weather permitting. In bad weather, he circled the passageways from the galley to the crew's mess, past the Armed Guard mess, around the saloon and down the starboard side past the deck crew's quarters several times. Although he was shorter than Frank, the two had facial features that were virtual images of one another. Both had light brown hair, hazel eyes, straight noses and firm jaw sets with deep dimples in the center of the chin. Yet, the two had opposite personalities. Where Frank was gregarious, Billy kept to himself. He read when he was off watch. Books about ship's engines and books on American history. He was a Civil War buff. In the engine room he was a taskmaster, claiming that anyone who says a job can't be done is a shirker and then doing the job himself.

"Yes, Billy," Slim said, "we can make it."

1300 HOURS
At the Nicholson's Gangway
"Look what I've found, Skipper!" the carpenter shouted, holding up two five-gallon cans of paint for Acting Captain Stevens to see.

"What's that?" Slim asked.

"Paint. White paint."

"What's it for, Chips?"

"Why, sir, to paint the ship, of course."

"The whole ship? With that?"

Chips set down the cans, rubbing his palms to erase the indentations from the wire handles.

"With this. There's a shed full of it not far from the gangway. The building's heated and the paint is okay."

Stevens looked down and the carpenter pointed a finger at the dismal-looking shed.

"You can't steal that!" the captain protested.

"Wanna bet, Skipper!" Chips boasted more than asked. "We've already got sixty-two cans aboard and we're bringing up more. Look."

He pointed to a woman carrying two of the cans, balancing them carefully. As she approached topside, the captain could hear her puffing. She smiled warmly at Chips as she passed, heading for the aft paint locker. The carpenter followed and the captain could see the man deftly pour something from a paper bag into the pockets of her jacket. She quickly turned, crossed the deck and headed back down the gangway. The carpenter rejoined the acting captain.

"Doesn't look as suspicious with them carrying this stuff aboard," the carpenter explained. "Each trip up, I give them some coffee. They can't take it off in our five-pound tins -- someone might see them and think they're stealing from us -- so I fill the pockets of their jackets and they empty the grounds in a box in that shed. Pretty fair trade, I'd say."

"You're going to paint the whole ship with it?"

"Yep. Bow to stern. From the tops of the masts to the waterline."

"Why in heaven would we do that?"

"Simple, Skipper. On our way back, the warming seas will break icebergs loose. Ever see one?"

"No."

"I have. Some higher than this ship's flying bridge. We'll be cruising past them, hundreds of them, and U-boats won't be able to see us. We'll blend against the background."

He covered his face with his hands momentarily, as if to hide it.

"Good idea, don't you think, Captain?"

Stevens was astonished. He hadn't thought about camouflaging the Liberty, but the carpenter's idea made sense. On the way to Murmansk it was winter and the days were shorter. The longer hours of darkness and the bad weather had favored Convoy 37B during most of that trip. On the return leg, the days would became longer and longer in this northern part of the world, until the sun was suspended low on the horizon for twenty-four hours a day. Perpetual daylight. It would be easy for lurking submarines to spot a ship traveling alone. It would still be cold, with temperatures hovering above and below the freezing mark, but the warming weather would loosen ice packs causing them to drift southward toward the *Nicholson*'s return route. A merchantman painted white would be harder to see, from a periscope or from the bridge of a surfaced sub. Even from a dive bomber.

"Good thinking, Chips," he complimented, warming to the idea. "Tell the bo's'n to turn the men to. I'll ask the chief engineer to get the black gang to help. And give me a brush. We'll want to look like an iceberg before we sail."

8 March 1942

0815 HOURS
Murmansk, Russia
With the removal of the last of the cargo, Acting Captain Stevens called for steam in the engines. The entire hull and bridgehouse of the *Nicholson* glistened white. All that remained to be painted were the guntubs. That would be done as the ship moved out of the harbor and into the open sea. There was no sign of the Army colonel or the Ambassador's Man.

"Fore and aft, bo's'n, all hands," he ordered.

The gangway was raised and the hawsers set free. Stevens reached for the engine room telegraph and rang up "Slow Ahead."

The *Nicholson* moved away from the pier, a non-English speaking Russian pilot motioning with his hands to the clearest path through the harbor. When the pilot left on a launch, Stevens ordered "Full Ahead" and set a course for New York.

He opted not to wait for a convoy. They would make this trip alone.

1000 HOURS
Five Nautical Miles off the Coast of Massachusetts
Lieutenant Commander Reinhard Barnschmidt stood on the cigarette bridge of U-84-B, staring at the black water of the Atlantic Ocean, now seeming to turn blue as the sun rose higher in the sky. He, like the rest of his crew, was jubilant after a night in which the submarine had torpedoed two U. S. merchant ships, sinking both, and now the boat was on the surface, exposing itself to possible detection by men on other ships or low-flying aircraft. Barnschmidt didn't care. He felt indestructible and was willing to take chances.

"Four ships in seven days!" he said jubilantly to his executive officer.

"We're blasting them out of the water!" the lieutenant

said happily.

"Under the water!" the captain thundered. "We should sink one more before we head south to our milch cow to reload torpedoes. The Americans don't know what's hitting them."

"True, Mein Capitan, but doesn't it bother you that there were no survivors from the last ship?"

"Why should it?" Barnschmidt answered. "This is war." He was gloating over his success in expending only three torpedoes to sink two more ships, the last one obviously carrying munitions. It blew up in a thunderous explosion, sinking in little more than a minute.

"But, as usual, they had no warning," the exec argued. "I thought Germany was a signator to the Nineteen Thirty-Six Submarine Protocol."

He was referring to the treaty, signed at a London conference, that outlawed the sinking of an unescorted merchant ship without warning. It also forbade the sinking of a ship without first searching it to discover if any contraband was aboard and it called for assuring the crew of any merchant ship a safe means of reaching shore, their own lifeboats being deemed insufficient unless land was near. That meant taking the merchant crew aboard the submarine and taking the men to the safety of a neutral port. In the first month of the war, Barnschmidt and other German U-boat commanders did honor the Protocol and the Hague Convention which prohibited attacks without warning on enemy passenger ships as well.

"You haven't given a warning to any of the ships we've sunk," the exec said somewhat accusingly.

"That treaty was naive," Barnschmidt said. "No one can win a war that way. Can you imagine us taking aboard the survivors of the first ship last night and heading for a port in South America? We wouldn't have gotten the second one."

He explained that he attended the London conference, assigned as an aide to an admiral, and he knew then that if he ever had command of a sub, he'd ignore the Protocol, shoot first and, with some thoughts of compassion, help the survivors, if any, on a lifeboat or raft. That last was a concession to his inner feeling of humanity.

He recounted how respect for the treaty, for international law, changed after his friend, Lieutenant Commander Gunther Prien, on the evening of 13 October 1939, had brilliantly and audaciously taken his boat, U-27, into the virtually impregnable harbor at Scapa Flow, a deepwater, almost landlocked basin in England's Orkney Islands. Within hours, this daring German officer, only recently assigned to his first submarine command, had sunk the British battleship, *Royal Oak*. Despite depth charge chases from destroyers, Prien escaped.

That was the beginning of the battle for control of the Atlantic Ocean. The orders that came down three days later from Grand Admiral Erich Raeder, commander-in-chief of the German Navy, changed the nature of how that battle would be fought. "

All merchant ships definitely identified as enemy (British and French) can be torpedoed without warning.

Ever since the United States entered the war, that meant American merchant ships as well.

Barnschmidt turned to his executive officer.

"My only regret is there were no survivors on that ship to report it was sunk by my boat."

"The Americans should know you did it, sir. You sank the other freighter less than two hours before in the same waters. I think everyone on that ship survived and you let them know you were responsible. I'm still --- "

He hesitated, again not sure that it was good military procedure to warn his captain about his behavior.

"You're still what, Lieutenant? Scared?"

"No, sir. I'm still worried about your giving your name and boat number to them. I fear that will backfire on you. On this boat."

"Why? I show the survivors mercy," Barnschmidt said proudly. "They'll tell that to their president. I sink his ships and some seamen may die when the torpedoes hit, but I don't kill his unarmed citizens in lifeboats as some other captains do. He'll respect me for that."

"He may," the lieutenant said. "It's those citizens I worry about."

11 March 1942

0900 HOURS
Balboa, Panama
"This canal is something else!" Seaman First Class "Cookie" Cookman exclaimed to his friend, Ordinary Sea-

man Gary Benson, as the Liberty ship, at Balboa, entered the first in a series of locks on the fifty-one mile waterway that sliced through a country that once had been largely jungle. The two had just finished breakfast and were standing on the *Bennett*'s bow, taking in the sights of the Panama Canal.

"Something else?" Gary countered. "It's an engineering marvel! It took genius to design and build it thirty years ago. This is actually a water bridge that will take us up to, let's see, eighty, no, eighty-five feet above sea level and lower us again when we get to the Atlantic side. That'll be about ten, eleven hours from now. We'll go through six locks exactly like this one. Each is one thousand feet long and one hundred and ten feet wide."

"If they're only one thousand feet each, and there are only six of them, that's a little more than a mile," Cookie said. "Why will it take ten hours?"

"Well, in the first place, it takes about a half hour to go through each lock. That's three hours right there. Then there are lakes and other stretches in between."

He pointed to the rising water.

"The first two are going to raise us to fifty-five feet above sea level. I think that's right. Fifty-five feet. Yeah."

"You've been through this Canal before?"

"No," Gary said, "but I remember a lot from a history teacher and, you know, Buddy, how much I fill this sponge brain of mine with useless facts."

"Geez, Gary," Cookie said admiringly. "You're a walking encyclopedia."

"Naw," Gary said modestly. "I just have a good memory. Here's some more. Most people think the United States built the canal as a shortcut between the two oceans for merchant ships. There may have been some truth to that, but the real reason was that, after the French failed in two attempts to build the canal, President Theodore Roosevelt wanted us to finish it as a standby war plan."

"A war plan? For what war?"

"The story goes that some Americans were sure Japan would some day want to take over the Philippines and those Americans began developing what they called 'Plan Orange,'" Gary said with confidence. "That was over forty years ago and those people were right. Japan did attack the Philippines. Except they waited forty years!"

"I never heard about Plan Orange. What was it?"

Gary explained that Plan Orange called for the U. S.

Army garrison in the Philippines to fight a holding action while American warships and troopships rushed from Pacific Coast ports while ships on the Atlantic and Gulf coasts would transit the Canal to go to the small garrison's rescue.

"The war we're in started almost exactly the way those planners predicted," he went on. "Except we didn't have enough ships in the Gulf or Atlantic to rush over there when this war started. We needed them in Europe. Besides, the planners didn't figure on the airplane. Still, it was to be a shortcut. A shortcut to war."

"Well, it's still a shortcut for ships."

"True. You know, Cookie, even with all that planning, this canal wouldn't have been built if it weren't for American veterinarians."

"Now, that's bullshit! What would horse doctors know about building something like this?"

"Good question," Gary smiled paternally. "Now let me tell you."

The young merchant seaman relished in providing trivia to his shipmates, little known facts he had picked up by sitting in on conversations between his father, a high school math teacher, and a fellow teacher at the same school, a widowed history teacher who had two or three dinners at the Benson family's table each week. Gary found out at a young age that he could learn more in an hour-long after-dinner discussion than he could in two weeks of history classes at school. The two men talked about everything from the ancient dinosaurs to the economic and political reasons for the rise of Hitler to power in Germany.

"You see," he said smugly, "France had failed twice in attempts to dig an Atlantic-Pacific shortcut route. It wasn't because their engineers were dumb. I mean, after all, the Suez Canal was designed and built by the French in 1869. So the French knew what to do and they had a good design. Problem was, hundreds, no thousands, of workmen died of a terrible fever down here. Yellow fever."

"Yellow fever?"

"Yes. The French thought it came from a yellowish tinge on many of the trees in the region. They cut down the trees, but the workmen kept dying. Some of them also died of malaria. The French doctors didn't know why. So their government stopped work on the canal."

"I know about malaria," the Navy man said. "You, too.

We take atabrine so we don't get it. Look, my skin's yellowed. So's yours."

"That's right. That pill gives us the same skin color as the Japs. But you see, Cookie, it was a couple of American veterinarians who discovered that ticks are the cause of another sickness called Texas Fever, a fever that killed thousands of cattle in the South and Southwest. Those vets found a way to prevent that disease and their research discovered that a mosquito caused yellow fever. A special mosquito. Other types of mosquitoes caused malaria and sleeping sickness and all kinds of other diseases. All the United States had to do was develop mosquito control programs down here. It didn't take us long to do that and, with Teddy Roosevelt's war plan, we finished the canal in 1912."

He sounded like a history teacher in a high school classroom.

"I didn't know that," Cookie admitted.

"Most Americans don't," Gary said. "References to the canal in high school history books tell only part of the story. You'd have to read dozens of books to get the full story about how and why this canal was built. Part of the story is that, in 1903, after the French failed, the United States, with Plan Orange in mind, and Colombia negotiated a treaty to let us build the canal on a thirty-mile wide strip of land. That treaty gave Colombia sovereignty over the canal, but gave us police control."

"But this canal isn't cutting through Colombia," Cookie protested. "We're going through Panama."

"You did learn something in geography class, my friend. I'm not exactly sure how it started but, right after the treaty was signed, the people who lived here, people who called themselves Panamanians, wanted independence from Colombia and they staged a coup. They occupied some of the buildings near the canal."

"Geez, was it bloody?"

"No. There were American workmen here and a few Panamanian rebels. The Colmbian army was some miles away and its soldiers got on a train going to the canal site, but the engineer was a Panamanian. He slowed the train. Hearing of the army movement, the captain of a U. S. Navy ship ordered forty-two Marines ashore to protect the workmen."

"Only forty-two Marines?"

"Only forty-two," Gary reaffirmed. "They were outnumbered ten to one by the Colombian soldiers who finally arrived on the train. Those soldiers backed down when they saw the Marines and left the area. Panama immediately declared its independence and the United States recognized the new country."

"Damn, Gary, you're a smart guy," Cookie said admiringly. "I still can't figure how come you weren't picked up by the Army or the Navy to be an officer. With what you know, you'd be a general or an admiral in no time."

Gary sloughed off the compliment.

"Flat feet, remember?" he reminded his friend.

"Hell, generals and admirals can have flat feet," Cookie said. "They don't do much more than sit at desks."

"Yeah, but the Army needs foot soldiers, not history buffs."

13 March 1942

2000 HOURS
Off the Coast of Newfoundland
U-84-B lounged effortlessly, its engines silent. Banks of fog rolled lazily, shrouding vision on all sides, opening up now and then to allow a line of sight for a couple thousand yards, then closing tightly.

"Hunting won't be good tonight," Lieutenant Commander Barnschmidt complained. "Too much fog."

His executive officer nodded agreement.

"I've told the crew to relax. They're already watching an American movie. Lon Chaney in *The Wolf Man.*"

"Relaxation? You call those cheap horror melodramas relaxation?"

"I don't, but the men love them. Their favorite is Boris Karloff and Bela Lugosi in *The Raven*. It's about a mad doctor who specializes in horror devices. They've shown it four times this patrol. You must admit, sir, it sharpens their killer instinct. They've been doing a fine job."

He lit a cigarette, not bothering to cup his hands to conceal the flame or protect against the foggy dew.

"Put out that match!" Barnschmidt warned sharply. "Now!"

"Why?" The exec threw the match overboard.

"Look! To starboard. That's a ship! Between those two banks of fog. By God, she's painted white!"

"A hospital ship?"

"Maybe," Barnschmidt murmured, peering through binoculars. "No. I don't think so. There's no red cross. Strange. A ship painted white. Why?"

The white ship melted into one of the banks and disappeared from view.

"Are we going after it?" the exec asked anxiously.

"Of course!"

"But we can't see it now."

"We know the direction it's running. That's enough. We'll just follow until the fog opens enough for us to get in a shot."

"Are we staying on the surface?" the exec asked.

"Yes. The fog will hide us as much as it hides them. Look! There it is!"

Before the exec could get another glimpse, the fog shrouded the ship again.

2137 HOURS
Aboard the S. S. Elihu Nicholson

The lookout in the *Nicholson*'s crow's nest was cold, tired and bored. He rubbed his gloved hands to increase the circulation, wishing he had a cup of coffee. *There ought to be a way to send coffee up here,* he thought. *Two hours standing in a small waist-high cage, thirty feet above the deck, is too long for anyone without something hot to drink.* He'd even take cocoa now, much as he disliked the stuff. He always thought it was for kids and sissies.

The ship had made good progress on its return leg from Murmansk, encountering no storms and blending with the icebergs and floes as it moved across the Arctic Ocean and then into the Atlantic. There had been no sign of the enemy, not even a friendly ship or plane, and the safety of New York was only a few days away. The lookout could not see very far, perhaps two hundred yards most of the time and two or three thousand yards when the fog occasionally split in two. He looked at his watch. He'd be relieved in another twenty-three minutes. A cup of coffee would taste like a million dollars.

A movement in the water far to port caught his eye. He wasn't sure as he stared into the fifty-yard wide tunnel between two misty blankets. He raised his binoculars.

"Submarine!" he shouted to the bridge.

"Where away?" Acting Captain Stevens called from the bridge.

"Four miles off the port beam! She's on the surface!"

"You sure?" Stevens called, trying to find the U-boat with his binoculars. "I can't see anything."

"She's there all right, Captain!" the lookout shouted. "The fog is obscuring part of her, but she's there. You'll see her."

"I do now!" Captain Stevens said.

He pointed to the submarine.

"See her?" he asked the helmsman.

"Sure do, Captain. Damn! I thought we were home free!"

"We will be," came the captain's assurance. "We get inside that large bank to starboard, they won't be able to see us. That looks like a thick one. Hard right!"

The seaman turned the wheel and the *Nicholson* swung quickly. Fog soon surrounded them and Slim could not see the ship's bow. Nor the crow's nest. It was as if everything ten feet from him had disappeared.

"Keep your rudder right until we've turned one hundred and eighty degrees!" he commanded. "Then steady her up."

"We going back?"

"In a way. If she's spotted us, she knows our direction. I want her captain to think we're still heading southeast, but maybe our heading back for a while will fool him. We'll turn around again."

"Yes, sir," the seaman said smiling.

The crew should be at their battle stations, Slim told himself, *but I don't want to sound the general quarters alarm. The clanging bell will give away our position and we're supposed to be hiding.*

He called for the boatswain.

"Pass the word," he told the man. "A submarine is tracking us. I want everyone at their battle stations. But do it quietly. No noise."

"Yes, sir."

The boatswain ran below.

2147 HOURS
Aboard the U-84-B

"We haven't seen her for ten minutes," the exec said. "Do you think she got away?"

"Not in ten minutes!" Barnschmidt thundered. "They probably spotted us and they're hiding in the fog. It'll open up again soon and we'll spot her. Keep a sharp lookout!"

2148 HOURS
Aboard the S. S. Elihu Nicholson
"What's up, Slim?" Billy asked when he reached the bridge.
 "Submarine's following us," Acting Captain Stevens said. "The lookout in the crow's nest spotted her ten minutes ago. We're hiding in this fog. I've turned the ship around. Between the two, maybe she won't find us."
 "Good hiding place," the chief engineer agreed. "I can't see a damn thing. She probably can't see us either."
 "I'm counting on that." Slim lit a Chesterfield. "We'll head back in the direction we came for a couple of hours, if this fog holds. Then I'll bring her about again. In the meantime, I've put the crew on general quarters and asked for quiet. I don't want the guys on that sub to hear us."
 "Hell, they can hear the engines. If you want things quiet aboard, we should shut them down," Billy suggested.
 "Not a bad idea, Chief. Okay. Shut everything down. We'll sit it out here. If they can't hear us with their sound equipment, they may think we've gotten out of their range. Maybe her skipper will get tired and pull away before the fog lifts."
 "That's hoping for a lot, Slim," Billy said.

2204 HOURS
Aboard the U-84-B
A submariner scrambled up the ladder, held himself steady with his arms at the hatch opening and called to the captain.
 "Sir, we've lost all sound from the ship!"
 "What?" Barnschmidt asked incredulously.
 "It's true, Capitan! We can't pick up her screw!"
 "It can't be!" Barnschmidt turned, dropped down the hatch and walked quickly to U-84-B's listening room. He grabbed the phones from the hydrophone operator and pulled them over his ears, his face intent.
 "Silence!"
 He heard nothing.
 "Vonderbar!" he roared. "Shut down our engines!"

Valves were turned quickly. There was an erie silence. Barnschmidt pressed the phones to each ear. Still no sound.

"Dummkopfs!" he shouted, throwing the earphones to the deck. "Keep listening! We must pick her up again!"

14 March 1942

0815 HOURS
Aboard the S. S. Elihu Nicholson
The fog had cleared.

"The sub's nowhere in sight!" the lookout called from the crow's nest.

"Then we've lost her," Captain Stevens said happily, his voice more raspy now that he had resumed smoking three packs of cigarettes a day. He ordered the helmsman to turn back to the *Nicholson*'s original heading.

"New York, here we come!" he shouted at Billy, still in the wheelhouse.

"You know, Billy, I love this ship as though I'm tied to her with an umbilical cord," he said motherly. "I'm going to stay aboard and take her out again. She's mine 'tho they'll put me back to mate. I won't mind. What'll you do when we get to New York? Stay on or get another ship?"

Billy thought for a moment.

"Well, this ship will be in drydock three weeks to a month, for sure. I'd like to go out with her again. If the company'll let me, I'll take most of that time and head for my brother's home in Baltimore. Maybe he'll be there. And my father. They're both merchant seamen, you know. It would be great to see them again."

0820 HOURS
Aboard the U-84-B
"We've lost her!" Barnschmidt shouted at his executive officer, disappointed. "How could this happen?"

"Too much fog last night," the exec said.

"Fog, hell! Our sonar operators didn't do their job!"

"You can't blame them, sir. That ship's captain must have stopped her engines. Besides, the men are tired. It's been a long patrol."

"I'm tired, too," the sub captain said. "And fed up! We've only two torpedoes left anyway so I'm heading for our milch cow. Won't do us much good to sit around here."

"You've done a good job on this patrol, sir," the lieutenant patronized. "Don't feel bad about losing sight of one ship. There'll be many more when we get back."

"That's the problem."

"What?"

"I don't like wasting time to go all the way to the coast of Brazil and back," the captain said ruefully. "I wish the milch cow was in these waters. We'll miss out on more ships while we're gone."

15 March 1942

0600 HOURS
In the Gulf of Mexico
"Ah saw 'im again," the second cook and baker told Second Mate Turner.

"Who?"

"The ghost of Major Bennett, suh. Ah tried to talk to 'im nicely, but he jus' stared at me, blank like, an' ah asked 'im what's wrong. Ah had a feelin' we's in fo' some more bad news. He jus' wrung his hands. It seemed like he didn' want to tell me. So ah picked up a butcha's knife an' shoosed 'im out of the galley. Ah told 'im not to come back."

"Good, Bib, good!" the mate said, but he was worried.

It was the second time the cook reported sighting the ghost of the *Bennett's* namesake. *Bib is either seeing things in a disturbed mind or the ghost is real.*

He hoped neither was true.

0850 HOURS
In the Bennett's Wheelhouse
Boatswain Hank Burleson quietly entered the wheelhouse and stood a full minute before he spoke.

"Permission to speak to the captain," he said softly.

Captain Davis turned to look at the voice and saw torment in Burleson's eyes.

"Come in, Boats," he said. "Why so glum?"

"May we speak privately, sir?"

"Of course, of course." Frank walked to the captain's chair in the corner. "I can't leave the bridge now. We can talk privately here." He motioned to the chair. "Sit down, Burleson. You look troubled."

"Thank you, Captain, but I'll stand," Burleson said. He twisted his hands nervously, looking first at the captain, then at the deck.

"What's up, Boats?"

"I don't want to do it, Captain. I like this ship and you're a good captain. The best."

"What don't you want to do?"

"Sign off, sir."

Frank was startled. Burleson was a good boatswain. Pushing the deckhands when they needed it, patting them on their backs when jobs were well done. He had a way about him that made his subordinates want to do their best, to please him and, in so doing, make themselves better seamen.

"In New Orleans?" Captain Davis asked. "I thought your home was in upstate New York?"

"It is, Captain," Burleson said, lifting his eyes from the deck. "Pleasantville. I must go there."

"Something wrong?"

Burleson looked at the overhead beams, turned to stare out one of the portholes and then focused his eyes on the captain. He was silent a long time, breathing heavily.

"I've been meaning to talk to you for some time, Skipper," he finally said. "I got a letter from my father when we got to Noumea."

He stopped, ran his tongue across his lips.

"It's my mother. She's dying." Tears began rolling from his thirty-two-year-old eyes. "Of Hodgkins Disease."

Frank put an arm around Burleson's shoulder and gently pushed him down into the chair.

"I'm sorry, Boats. I didn't know."

He kept a hand on the boatswain's shoulders until the sobbing stopped.

"I haven't seen her in more'n five years," Burleson said softly. "My father said she might have a couple of months. Maybe she's already gone."

"Of course you've got to go home," Captain Davis consoled. "We'll get you off the ship as soon as we dock in New Orleans."

"Thank you, sir," the bo's'n said gratefully, standing up and reaching out to shake the captain's hand. He changed his mind and saluted hurriedly.

Frank returned the salute, then sat down in the chair, suddenly tired. He didn't know how many other seamen would sign off when the ship docked. A few always left for one reason or another, mostly to find a woman if they didn't already know one in the port and to get drunk until their pay ran out. There would be a call to the union halls for replacements. He knew for sure he would be losing two good men. A chief engineer who knew more about ship's engines than any other below-decks mariner and a boatswain who was a spit and polish deck foreman. He hoped Chief Mate Speer would remain aboard.

He also hoped Bib's ghost would sign off.

22 March 1942

1500 HOURS
New Orleans, Louisiana
Captain Davis broke a promise he had made to himself a couple of months ago. He put on the white uniform. He had called his wife two days ago, shortly after his ship docked in New Orleans and learned that his father had been at his home for nearly two weeks and Billy had arrived just the day before.

"Why don't all of you fly down here?" he asked Lynne. "God, it would be great family reunion!"

"I can't fly!" Lynne protested. "I'm afraid of planes."

"You can if you want to see me."

"Oh, I do, Frank, I do! I've so much to tell you."

"Well, take a drink before you board the plane," Frank had said. "You won't know you're on it and you'll be here before you know it."

The three did take a plane and arrived this morning, checking into the Regency Hotel. Frank dressed for the reunion, in the white uniform, but he packed civilian clothes in the brown suitcase with the four encircling blue bands.

"Lynne will be pleased," he said happily as he went out on deck.

"I'll see you day after tomorrow," he told Chief Mate Speer at the head of the gangway. "I'm taking tomorrow off."

"Good thing," Speer said. "I wouldn't want you moping about this ship when you can have a better time with your wife."

1530 HOURS
At the Regency Hotel
The taxi ride to the hotel took more than an hour.

"Traffic's always heavy this time of the afternoon and I'm taking a few short cuts to avoid getting into a real jam," the driver explained, but Frank had the feeling he was being taken the long way to build up the meter fare.

"People must be getting a lot more gas than the news reports tell us," Frank said casually. "Maybe all this talk about gas rationing is just to fool Hitler."

The cabbie wouldn't touch that one. He kept quiet.

As Frank got out of the cab in front of the hotel, another taxi pulled up behind and a lady stepped out onto the curb. She reached into her pocketbook and handed the driver a bill, saying "Keep the change." She headed toward the hotel door, her heels clicking on the sidewalk.

"Looking for some company, lady?" Frank called, taking off his hat and bowing.

Lynne turned around and looked at her husband.

"You got something special in mind, sailor boy?" she said with a sly smile.

"Like to take you on my ship, baby," he grinned. "To show you my art collection."

"A sailor with an art collection?"

"Well, some real jazzy tattoos I picked up in Hong Kong and Singapore. I keep them hidden in a special place."

He patted his rump.

"Sounds mighty interesting, sailor boy."

"Problem is," he moaned, "my ship's off limits to ladies."

"Know a good hotel close by?" Lynne whispered.

Frank surveyed the hotel's facade.

"Well, this one ain't the best in town, but it looks clean. We could book a suite and have dinner sent up by room service. Lobster. Champagne. The works."

"Sounds inviting, but I warn you, I'm very expensive."

"Money's no object, lady!" he said, reaching into a pocket and jingling some coins.

"You sure?"

"This sure," he said, sliding both arms around her waist and pulling her to him. "My God! I've missed you!"

They kissed long and hard. The doorman and taxi drivers whistled.

"But what have you been doing? Shopping?" he

demanded, stepping back just a bit, one arm still around her waist.

"We've got better things to talk about and do right now," she smiled.

"You're right," he said, pressing his body against her. "I'm bursting."

She could feel his bulge against her thigh.

"Patience, Captain, patience," she said coolly. "Good things come to those who wait. And I'm *good*."

She kissed him again.

"But, for heaven's sake, Frank, let's go. I can't wait any longer!" she said, pulling him toward the hotel door.

At the front desk, they switched Lynne's room on the third floor to the bridal suite on the top floor. Frank also arranged for the double-double shared by his father and Billy to be changed to an adjacent suite.

"We're on our honeymoon," Frank assured the desk clerk. "My father and brother are playing chaperons, but I'm locking the connecting doors."

1635 HOURS
In the Suite's Bedroom

"Oh, that was wonderful!" Lynne moaned, letting one arm drop to the sheet and keeping the other around Frank's chest. "Just wonderful. You sure know how to make me happy."

Frank kissed her softly.

"Still jealous about other women?" he asked.

"Oh, that," she said, turning her face away for a moment. "That was silly of me. I was wrong to write you about that. I found out there are only a few women on merchant ships, none on the *Bennett*, and that the government is talking about not letting them go out any more. Roosevelt's afraid women might be killed."

She turned back to face him and cupped his chin with her hands. She lifted his head and kissed him.

"I'm sorry, Frank."

"Apology accepted, lady," he said gladly. "Now, what about that secret you wouldn't tell me in your letter?"

Lynne reached for her purse on the night table, pulled out a large brown envelope and handed it to Frank.

"What's this?" he asked.

"Look and you'll find out."

He opened the flap and fished out a color photograph

of Frank, Junior, dressed in a white sailor suit and holding an American flag.

"Fantastic!" he said grinning broadly. "Looks just like him. I'll hang it up next to my favorite pinup girl."

"Only pinup girl," Lynne corrected.

"Only."

Lynne smiled and touched a finger to his chest.

"You may have another to pin up alongside him."

"What do you mean?"

"I'm pregnant."

Frank sat up quickly and stared at the naked body of his wife, particularly at her stomach. It didn't seem bloated. It was still daylight and, although the window drapes were closed, he could see her clearly. He pulled her to him, holding her close.

"Pregnant? Should we have . . should we have done what we just . . ?"

"Silly man," she interrupted. "Of course we should. I'm not two months gone. We can have sex through the eighth month-- if you'd stay home more!"

He kissed her several times happily.

"It must have happened . . "

"Yes, Frank, I'm guessing it was the night you got your captain's license. I'm so happy."

"I am too," he said. "Is that why you . . ?"

He stopped and didn't finish the question. Lynne understood.

"Yes," she said. "I wanted another baby, but I felt guilty forcing you to make love to me every night. I wanted to be sure it would happen."

"You weren't forcing me," he protested. "I wanted it as much as you, but I did wonder why you suddenly got so oversexed."

"Jealous?"

"Yes."

"Good," Lynne said smugly. "Stay that way. You'll get home more often."

They kissed again.

"What do you want? A boy or a girl?" Frank asked.

"A girl. Then, when she grows up, I won't have to worry about her going off to sea. Junior already likes to wear sailor suits and pretend he's captain of a ship. Just like you!"

2000 HOURS
In the Suite's Parlor
"What's our next move?" Frank asked as his family sat drinking gin and tonic in the honeymoon suite.

"Now that you've had a couple of hours to get intimate with your wife, we go back to war," Billy said half-seriously.

"I'm ready," their father said, holding up his still-bandaged hands. "My hands aren't."

Lynne stood up and, with her blue eyes, surveyed her husband, father-in-law and brother-in-law.

"Can't we have a few days without talk about the war?" she asked, her hands on her hips. "Can't we just enjoy ourselves? Frank has six days before he puts to sea again. Neither Billy nor you, Dad, have a ship."

"I have," Billy objected. "I can go back to New York and sail out with the *Nicholson*."

"Don't get technical," Lynne said. "Why don't we spend what time we have together seeing the sights of New Orleans? The four of us can have lots of laughs before Frank has to go."

"Lynne's right," Jim said. "We'll have dinner tonight at Arthur's. My treat."

Frank and Billy nodded agreement.

"It's your money, Dad," Frank said amiably. "We'll order the top of the menu."

"Okay with me," Jim replied.

"Before we go, though," Frank said, "I'd like to ask you guys something. It's important to me."

Jim and Billy looked quizzically.

"Shoot," Jim said.

"We've got some vacancies on the *Bennett*," Frank said seriously. "We've lost our chief engineer. He broke a leg in Noumea and he's already signed off. Even when his leg's healed, he won't go back to sea. His arthritis has crippled him, but he's got a fine-tuned mind. I'm fixing him up with a teaching job at the cadet officer school in Pass Christian. He'll be a good teacher and he'll be happy there."

"Well done," Billy said, getting up to pour another drink and already sensing what his kid brother had in mind. "Anyone want another?"

Lynne demurred.

"Not yet," Frank said looking at his half-filled glass.

"Make mine weak, Billy," Jim said. "That last one had

the punch of a howitzer."

"Anyway, Billy," Frank continued, "we both work for the same shipping company. I've already talked to Captain Weatherby. If you're willing, he'll release you from the *Nicholson* and assign you to the *Bennett.* So will the engineers' union."

Billy set his glass down angrily.

"Jesus, brother, you had a helluva nerve to do that!" he railed. "You should have asked me first."

"When we were kids," Frank explained, ignoring his brother's outburst, "we always went to the docks and talked about going to sea together. Remember?"

Billy didn't answer.

"Remember?" Frank demanded.

"Okay, I remember," Billy said, harassed.

"Well, we haven't had the chance 'til now," Frank said enthusiastically. "It would be our kid dream come true."

"I'm your older brother," Billy said.

"So what? That doesn't change the dreams we had on those docks in Canton. You afraid to serve in your kid brother's command?"

Billy flinched.

"I'm not afraid of anything. Including you."

"Good, then," Frank said. "I take it you'll sign on."

"Damn you, kid brother, you've trapped me!"

"Learned that trick from you, big brother," Frank smiled. "But I'll give you a break. You don't have to call me 'sir.' That's probably too stiff for you. Just 'Captain.'"

He put out a hand. Billy hesitated, then put out his. They shook.

"Deal, *sir,*" Billy said, emphasizing the salutation to a senior officer.

"I'm not finished yet," Frank said, turning to his father. "We've also lost our bo's'n."

Jim held up a hand to stop his son's words.

"Don't bother. I'm not as weak-minded as my first born."

He winked at Billy.

"No, seriously, Dad," Frank went on. "My bo's'n had to sign off. His mother is dying of Hodgkins Disease. I've talked to the union and they've agreed to let you sign on."

"Won't do it," Jim said firmly.

"Why not?"

"Superstitious," Jim said. "Bad luck runs in threes and there'd be three of us. Besides, my hands won't be fully healed for another couple of weeks."

Frank pointed a finger at his father.

"That's just an excuse, Dad. A bo's'n doesn't have to pull hawsers or chip paint. He just has to see the deckhands do a good job. Your hands will heal and, for sure, you'll use them again."

"The answer's still no," Jim said firmly.

"You afraid the crew will look down on you, laugh at you, if you're the bo's'n on a ship your son commands?" Frank challenged.

"Not afraid, Frank," Jim said. "Don't try to embarrass me like you did Billy. You're a good captain. Doesn't surprise me. After all, you're a Davis and we have sea water in our veins, don't you know?"

He chuckled.

"Like I said, son, I don't believe in three's. And the three of us on the same ship would be a crowd."

"Look, Dad, I can't believe you're that superstitious. Besides, when we were kids you talked about letting us go with you to sea."

"That was in peacetime."

"Billy and I often pretended we were on a ship with you," Frank said, ignoring his father's excuses. "Right, Billy?"

"Yeah," Billy agreed.

"We thought it would be fun," Frank went on. "It still could be even in this war. Why don't you ship out with us? We'd all be together every day for a change."

"The answer's still no. I'm going up to Wilmington."

Lynne jumped up, raced to her father-in-law's chair and put an arm around his shoulder.

"It's getting serious, isn't it, Dad?"

"Don't know yet. I sure am fond of Alex."

Lynne turned to her husband.

"Frank, it looks like you've lost a bo's'n, but I think I'm gaining a mother-in-law!"

LOG BOOK TWO
24 October 1942 - 29 November 1943

Never trust her at any time, when the calm sea shows her false, alluring smile.
- Lucretius

24 October 1942

1100 HOURS
A Dock in New York
"There's no doubt about where we're headed this trip," Ordinary Seaman Gary Benson told Seaman Third Class George "Cookie" Cookman as the two watched the loading of heavy Sherman tanks into the holds of the *S. S. Andrew Bennett*. It was the Liberty ship's second stop in New York after the snafu in February when another cargo of the 36-ton tanks was sent to Noumea, New Caledonia, instead of Loch Ewe, Scotland. The ship eventually made it to the Scottish port, via the Panama Canal, New Orleans, Boston and Reykjavik. After unloading there, the *Bennett*, in two heavily protected convoys, carried ammunition in the holds and P-40 pursuit planes chained to the deck, from Portland, Maine and New York to Southampton, England. She had returned to New York yesterday and the loading of the tanks had begun just after dawn this morning. The American war industry was tooling up faster than even President Roosevelt had imagined and the planes, tank and ammunition were rolling out in seemingly endless streams from factories twenty-four hours a day, seven days a week.

"Where are we going?" Cookie asked.

"To the Mediterranean and Africa," Benson said knowingly.

"How do you know that?"

"It's obvious. The morning newspapers say the British Eighth Army, led by General Montgomery, went on the offensive last night from its headquarters at El Alamein. I bet that spells the beginning of the end for the Desert Fox -- that's what they call General Rommel, who heads the German forces -- and the American invasion of North Africa will begin soon. We're gonna be in on it."

There had been talk for months about an invasion of North Africa where the desert war had been fought savagely for two years. The Allies had for too long been overpowered by the Axis powers, but since summer the tide had begun to turn with the arrival of the 54-year-old

Montgomery, an eager, ruthless and unconventional general in his first major command. He knew about the disillusionment of the men in the Eighth Army following their crushing reverses in the face of Rommel's Panzer division's onslaughts and he issued an ultimatum to them:

"*From now on the Eighth Army will not yield a yard of ground to the enemy. Troops will fight and die where they stand. Your job is to kill Germans, even the padres, one per weekday and two on Sundays.*"

With his black Tank Corps beret and his cocksureness, Montgomery was convincing and there was a new mood of confidence among the British troops.

Meanwhile, the growing American army prepared itself for the impending invasion, originally under the code name *Super Gymnast* but now dubbed *Operation Torch*. England's Prime Minister Winston Churchill suggested the new code name to Lieutenant General Dwight D. Eisenhower, the American commander, because he thought it was more lyrical. Eisenhower conceded although, like his leadership counterparts in the British army, he objected to the interference from a fat, pompous politician who pictured himself a master military strategist. Almost everyone expected the invasion. Except the Russians. Stalin pleaded for a second front in Europe, but the Allied command figured North Africa would be easier. From there, the Allies could strike at Italy and Hitler would have to divert divisions from the Russian front. Most of the Allied leaders agreed the Italians had not been much good at war since the Roman Empire was destroyed.

Ordinary Seaman Benson didn't know it, but *Operation Torch* was set for 8 November.

1230 HOURS
Aboard the S. S. Andrew Bennett
Two men in black uniforms, both about seventeen and with seabags slung over their shoulders, eagerly climbed the *Bennett*'s gangway. Their sailor hats were black, not white.

"Who are those guys?" Able-Bodied Seaman Joseph Aloysius Jones asked.

"Look like Armed Guard, but there's something funny about their uniforms," Navy Seaman First Class Edward "Rabbit" Ellard said. "I wonder if the Navy is changing what we wear. Same kind of blouse and kerchief. They've got Navy hats, but would you believe, they're black! Black hats! I don't like that!"

Ellard was not in uniform. He was wearing standard Navy shipboard dungarees, a blue shirt and white hat.

"Look, the flap on the back of the blouse doesn't have white strips and stars like your dress uniform," Jones said. "There's a red insignia in each corner. Looks like crossed anchors."

They studied the uniforms closer as the two men approached the halfway point.

"Geez," Rabbit said, "the Navy's done away with bell bottoms! I don't believe it! And they must have zippers on their flies. They don't have buttons like on mine. Weird."

"Maybe they're from another country," Jones suggested. "I've heard they may put foreign seamen on our ships."

"We'll know in a few seconds," Rabbit said as the young men stepped on the top of the gangway platform, saluted aft and asked for permission to board.

"You supposed to be on this ship?" Jones asked.

"This is the *Bennett*, isn't it?" one answered with another question.

"Yeah."

"Then it's our ship," the other man said assuredly.

"Are those new Navy uniforms?" Rabbit asked.

The two men looked at each other and laughed. They dropped their seabags on the deck.

"No, Merchant Marine," the taller of the two said.

He offered his hand to Rabbit.

"Name's Henderson. Travis Henderson, ordinary seaman. This fellow's Russell Wunderlich, engine room wiper."

The four men shook hands, Jones and Ellard giving their names and rates.

"But why those uniforms?" Jones asked. "Merchant seamen don't wear uniforms. Except officers."

Henderson stroked his kerchief and took off his black hat. His hair was crew cut.

"Kinda neat, ain't they?" he posed. "We also have whites. Even a white hat. We came straight over from Sheepshead Bay."

"After a stop at the union hall," Wunderlich put in.

"Sheepshead Bay?" Jones asked. "Where's that?"

"In Brooklyn. A couple of miles from here. We just

got out of boot camp."

"What boot camp?" Rabbit challenged.

"Just told you," Henderson said. "The new boot camp for merchant seamen at Sheepshead Bay. Had four weeks of training. They've opened other boots in St. Pete, Florida, and Catalina Island, California."

"Like Navy boot camp?" Rabbit asked.

"I dunno. Never been in a Navy one. A lot of chickenshit stuff, though."

"Yeah, like squaring our beds," Wunderlich complained. "We gotta do that on this ship?"

"I don't know what you mean by 'squaring,'" Jones answered, "but I can tell you if you don't keep a clean bed and a clean foc'sle, your mates will make you wish you were someplace else. A dirty foc'sle is the sign of a stupid guy who doesn't care about himself or his shipmates. It won't take long for that kind of guy to have his ass cleaned in a special way by his foc'sle buddies."

He winked at Rabbit.

"Yeah," the Navy man said. "Alcohol burns a helluva lot."

"Jesus!" Henderson swore. "I thought we had it bad when we had to go through an obstacle course with live machine gun bullets fired three feet over our heads. We ain't gonna have those kind of obstacles on this ship, are we?"

"You'd be surprised what obstacles you're gonna face," Rabbit said. "Being on a Liberty is no piece of cake."

Jones touched the red insignia on Henderson's upper sleeve.

"What's that U. S. M. S. mean?" he asked, curious. "That ain't the initials for Merchant Marine."

"United States Maritime Service," Henderson said proudly.

Jones huffed. "Merchant seamen don't like uniforms," he said. "You look military and we're civilians."

"Us too," Henderson said. "We don't have to wear these if we don't want. We can wear civvies, but let me tell you, Jones, this uniform really attracts girls!"

"All uniforms do," Rabbit said.

"Yeah, but these draw them faster."

"How come?"

Henderson thought for a moment.

"Better we show you. Can we get off the ship tonight?"

"Sure," Jones said. "The watch is set. Both of us are off at four."

"Good," Henderson said.

He looked at Jones.

"Those dungarees are okay. You got a black turtleneck?"

"Sure."

Henderson handed his black sailor hat to Jones.

"Try this on."

Jones did and it fit.

"Good," the newcomer said. "You can wear that one. I've got another." He turned to Ellard. "You'll wear your Navy whites?"

"It's October but it's warm enough to wear them. Sure."

"Okay, then. We'll wear ours too. Let's leave early. Say about five o'clock. We want to ride into town on a bus. A crowded bus. You guys are in for a treat." He pointed to the two crossed anchors and the initials "U. S. M. S." "You'll *really* find out what these initials mean," he crowed, picking up his seabag. "Now, do we have permission to board?"

"Oh, yeah, sure," Jones said, still feeling wonderment at the sight of the strange uniforms. "Hey, Rabbit, show these guys where to dump their gear. We'll be off watch in a couple of hours. Then, wham, we go ashore and see what these dudes are bragging about. I think they're full of bullcrap."

1300 HOURS
In the Bennett's Saloon
Boatswain Terry Campbell, who had succeeded Hank Burleson as head of the deck crew seven months ago, met with the captain and chief mate in the *Bennett*'s saloon, comparing notes about the condition of the ship and the deck crew. Captain Davis had just returned from a meeting with Captain Weatherby in the shipping company's office.

"Full complement of deckhands assigned?" he asked the boatswain.

"Yes, sir," Campbell answered. "Most of the old crew's stayed on. We've one new A. B. and two new ordinaries on deck. I'm sure not happy that Robinson is still with us. He's the guy out of San Quentin, you know."

"He's paroled to this ship and, so far, he hasn't done anything serious enough to turn him back to the federal authorities," Captain Davis said. "A few minor incidents, including getting busted with Jones in New Caledonia for breaking the window of a Red Cross canteen."

"We've had some problems with him I haven't reported to you, sir," the boatswain admitted with a tinge of guilt. "We had another incident last night. The sneaky scum stole off the ship after I told him he'd have gangway watch from eight to twelve. He told Durante to take his place. The stupid kid did. Afraid, I guess. It's not just those incidents though. Robinson has an attitude, a mean one to the crew and the officers. He's always sassing the officers back. You know that, sir, and he threatens the crew repeatedly. I worry that one day he'll make good on one of those threats."

"You're right, bo's'n, but speaking of last night he did get someone to fill in for him," Chief Mate Speer offered. "That's acceptable by the union."

"Yeah, but he didn't tell me."

"He should have, but I don't think our worry over his attitude is enough to send him back to prison," Captain Davis said. "Keep your eye on him, though."

"Don't worry," Campbell said. "I will."

Lieutenant (j.g.) Craig Spencer Taylor, who had replaced Lieutenant Hamilton as the gunnery officer months ago, hurried into the saloon.

"Good news, Captain!" he shouted.

"What's the good news?" Frank asked.

"We've been selected for the new Mark Twenty-Nine!" the lieutenant beamed.

"The what?"

"The Mark Twenty-Nine! It's a special gear designed to stop torpedoes from hitting the ship!"

The lieutenant was obviously thrilled.

"How the hell does it do that?" Frank asked. "Some robot hand reaches out from the bridge and grabs a torpedo before it hits? Sounds like something out of Buck Rogers."

"Something like that but real, not science fiction."

Frank had heard all kinds of rumors about new German weapons of war. Suction torpedoes that didn't explode on impact, but fastened themselves to the ship's hull and exploded a day or two later when the crew felt safe. Kangaroo planes that reportedly were pilotless robots released from bombers miles away and streaked toward an unsuspecting ship with hardly a sound. He was not quite prepared, however, to accept that the United

States, or any country, had developed a way to stop a hurtling torpedo from hitting a ship.

"This some kind of joke?" he asked, taking a hard look at the lieutenant.

The man was about twenty-three. Tall, almost six feet. Slim. Trim. His short sleeve white shirt revealed well-developed muscles. Red hair. High forehead. Blue eyes. A facial expression that said "smile" whether he was talking or not.

"No joke, Captain," Taylor said. "Workmen already have begun welding a pair of frames above the gunwales on both sides of the bow. Look, you can see them through the porthole."

"Sorry, Captain, I didn't get a chance to tell you," the chief mate apologized. "They came aboard with a Navy captain just after you left for the conference. He had a set of orders. I checked them and okayed their going to work."

Frank looked quizzically at the mate, then got up from his chair and peered through the porthole. He saw wierd-looking frames on either side of the bow and enormous reels were being welded to both sides of the forward deck. Wires ran everywhere.

"What in hell?" the captain fumed.

"Let's go forward so you can take a closer look," the lieutenant said enthusiastically.

The three walked to the bow. Two paravanes, looking very much like torpedoes themselves, were suspended from the frames and four-inch diameter rubberized cables were wound around and around the big reels.

"The way this thing works," Taylor said, "is that in the open sea these paravanes are launched straight out from both sides of the bow, at right angles to the ship, tethered by these wire cables. Now, these big rubber cables are then run out with one end fast to the tether holding each paravane. We'll have four cables on each side, streaming the full length of the ship."

"So, what good are rubber cables?" Frank asked. "The torpedoes will go right through them."

"Wrong," Taylor said. "You see, Captain, the outer cables on each side are equipped with microphones. Sensitive microphones. The next two rows of cables are loaded with high explosives. The cables closest the ship act as stabilizers to keep the other cables at a depth we preset."

"That's ridiculous. Those cables will cause a drag that'll slow us down and unstabilize the ship."

"Not so, Captain," the gunnery officer responded. "Libertys, you know, have double hulls, or double bottoms, as some call them. That's for the storage of bunker oil when the ships come back empty. The double hull places the ship's center of gravity very low, making her very stiff and giving her tremendous righting ability."

"That's true," Frank said, giving "Guns" credit for knowing something about the design and construction of the ship. "A Liberty can roll thirty-five degrees with little or no danger. The low center of gravity snaps it back upright. This feature makes the Liberty a good ship in heavy seas, 'tho it's damn uncomfortable for the crew."

He studied the rubberized cables more closely.

"How are the explosives set off?" he asked.

The lieutenant smiled, warming to the subject.

"When the torpedo approaches the outer cable, the microphones hear it and cock the triggers on the next two cables. When it approaches them, they explode, blowing up the torpedo and saving the ship."

Frank was momentarily speechless.

"Who dreamt up this crazy idea, Guns?" he finally asked.

"Isn't crazy, sir. The Navy's already tested it with models and dummy torpedoes."

"In a bathtub, I bet," Frank said sarcastically.

"Sir, the Navy's done a lot of research on this and I'm assured it works."

"Even if it does, what's to stop a second torpedo coming in? The cables have blown up!"

"We reel out more cable, sir," Guns answered.

"Quickly, I hope," the boatswain said.

"We're the first ship to be armed with the Mark Twenty-Nine," the lieutenant went on. "I understand two factories have more gear in production. It'll save a lot of merchant ships. You'll see."

"Agreed the Navy is trying to help us," Frank said airily, "but I have my doubts. I just don't see how these cables are going to blow up torpedoes before they hit us. Even the explosions of the torpedoes a few feet from the hull could cause serious damage."

He thought again about the German suction torpedoes.

"But, then, Guns, I guess anything's possible. Have you been trained to work this contraption?"

"No, sir, but I've been given a manual and the Navy's sending two ratings aboard who were in on the field testing. They'll go with us. We'll be ready to stream out the cables soon as we get into position in the convoy. Don't be a worry wart, Captain. This Mark Twenty-Nine will work and every merchant ship will soon be equipped with it. The idea came from a German scientist who fled before the war and, with his technology and our mass production methods, we've come up with a way to beat the Nazis at their own game," he said proudly.

"We'll see," Frank said, still skeptical.

1715 HOURS
On a New York Bus
Ordinary Seaman Travis Henderson, in his white uniform with red insignias, waited for five passengers to board the bus. Then he climbed aboard, reaching into a pocket for a nickel.

"No," the driver said quickly, pushing Henderson's hand from the coin box. "Servicemen ride free."

"Thanks," Henderson said smiling.

The driver didn't know merchant seamen are not servicemen.

Engine Room Wiper Russell Wunderlich and Navy Seaman First Class Edward "Rabbit" Ellard, also in uniform, walked by the box without dropping coins.

"You in the service?" the driver asked Able-Bodied Seaman Joseph Aloysius Jones.

"Sure," Jones answered, showing his borrowed hat.

"Ain't never seen a hat like that," the driver said. "Besides, you're not wearing a uniform. You have to pay."

Jones shrugged and dropped a nickel into the box.

The bus was three-quarters full. Henderson slowly walked the aisle, eyeing each passenger on both sides, and stopped when he came abreast two girls, blondes, sitting next to each other. He reached for the overhead bar to steady himself, facing their direction, but looking out a window. His shipmates did the same.

"You're gonna love New York," he said to Wunderlich in a voice loud enough for the girls to hear. "It's a beautiful city and there's a helluva lot to do in Times Square."

"I'm looking forward to it," the wiper said eagerly.

They kept their eyes on the passing buildings and vehicles going in the other direction. Henderson turned his body slightly so the two girls could see the red insignia on his upper left sleeve, at the point of the shoulder.

"You in the Navy?" one of the girls asked.

Henderson looked down at her.

"No, ma'am," he said politely and turned his eyes to look out the window again, as if ignoring her.

"Well, you look Navy," the girl insisted, testily. "What's that U. S. M. S. mean?"

Henderson bent down, turning his head to examine the red insignia.

"Well, ma'am," he said slowly. "That stands for 'Under Sea Minesweeper Service.'"

Jones coughed. Rabbit raised his eyebrows.

"Never heard of it," the girl said flatly. "Come on, you're in the Navy."

"Well, ma'am, we're sort of Navy, but separate, like the Marines. 'Cept the Under Sea Minesweeper Service don't get a lot of publicity counta we go on secret missions," Henderson said casually.

He focused his eyes on the other girl. The two looked alike and he figured they were sisters, maybe even twins.

"What kind of missions?" the second girl asked.

The bus stopped and the passengers in front of the girls got off. Henderson motioned to Wunderlich to take the inside seat. He sat on the outside and turned his head to face both girls. Jones and Ellard moved closer, still standing, dumbfounded at what they were hearing.

Under Sea Minesweeper Service! Jones mumbled to himself. *Jesus H. Christ! This guy's full of crap!*

"What kind of missions?" the girl repeated.

"Well, Russ and me -- I'm Tyler -- we're the crew of a specially-equipped two-man submarine," Henderson confided.

"My heavens!" the girl on the inside seat exclaimed. "Do they have submarines that small?"

Henderson nodded. Jones coughed again.

"What do you do in such small boats?" the other sister asked.

Henderson looked at Wunderlich, then up at Jones and Ellard.

"Okay to tell them?" he asked.

"Yeah, but don't give out any secrets," Wunderlich warned. "You know, about the --- "

"Okay, okay. I won't talk about that."

He looked back at the girls.

"Well, you see, our subs are equipped with special sweepers, sort of like big brooms, you might say, and nets," he said earnestly. "We go into an enemy harbor before our troops invade and we clean out the minefields. You know, those floating balls of explosives that can blow up a troopship."

"Oh, my God!" the girl on the outside said.

"What we do," Henderson continued, pretending not to have heard her, "is sweep mines into our nets, one at a time, very carefully. They could blow up if we don't sweep them just right. After we have six mines, three in each of the nets on both sides, we sneak back out of the harbor to the open sea. Then, using a special procedure I can't talk about, we detonate the mines. BOOM!"

The girls jumped.

"Oh, how dangerous!" one said.

"How exciting!" the other squealed.

"Well, it's both," Henderson said nonchalantly, "but you get used to it after a couple of missions. Russ and I have made four so far. We'll do many more as our Army and Marines continue to make invasions."

He looked out the window as though the conversation was over.

"My name's Kathleen," the inside girl said. "Kathy. This is my twin, Marion."

"I guessed you're twins," Henderson said, looking from one to the other.

"This your first time in New York?" Kathy asked.

He stared into her pale blue eyes.

"Yes," he lied. "I'm from Cleveland and my buddies are all from Atlanta. This is their first time, too."

He pointed to Wunderlich, then to Jones and Ellard. Kathy looked at Ellard in his Navy whites.

"You're in the Navy, 'tho," she said.

"He is," Henderson answered quickly, not wanting Ellard to blow the storyline. "He's on special assignment to our unit. Rabbit -- his real name is Ed, but we call him Rabbit -- is a munitions expert." He patted Rabbit's stomach. "A good munitions expert. Best there is."

Rabbit grinned with newfound pride.

"What about you?" Kathy asked Jones.

Again Henderson hurried an answer, afraid Jones would say he's in the Merchant Marine.

"Joe's a submarine mechanic. A master mechanic. He's the guy that keeps our boats in the water. Tricky machinery, you know."

"Why doesn't he have a uniform?"

"'Cause mechanics are allowed to wear work clothes ashore. Joe was in the Navy for ten years -- right, Joe? -- before he was transferred to our special branch a few months ago. He wears his uniform only when we have a dress parade or special ceremony, like when they gave him the Silver Star four days ago. Right, Joe?"

Flushed, Jones nodded his head weakly, feeling the need to run but having no place to hide. This conversation was almost too much for him.

"He's modest, Kathy," Henderson said. "He's not supposed to ride the boats, but he snuck into one when a sweeper was sick last month. You won't believe it, 'cause he was never in a boat in the water before, but he picked up seventeen mines before the Japs caught onto him. The Nips dropped depth charges, but he and his driver got away."

"I've never heard anything so thrilling!" Kathy said. "Or dangerous! You're real heroes!"

She whispered to her sister. Marion nodded.

"Can we help show you New York? Tonight?"

Henderson casually eyed his shipmates. They were all smiles.

"We ain't doing nothing special," he said, "but there are four of us. Only two of you."

The twins looked at each other. Without a word, both nodded.

"We've a neighbor, Pauline," Kathy said excitedly. "She's single and seventeen. I'm sure she'll go with us." She looked at Jones. "You're a bit older, but we'll ask mother to join us."

"Your mother?" Jones asked incredulously.

Who ever heard of a daughter making a date for her mother? Twin daughters, no less.

"Sure. Our Mother. Dad died two years ago and she just started dating a few months back. No serious boyfriend, though. I'm sure she'll go with us."

"If she's as pretty as you two," Henderson put in, "she'll be just right for Joe." He winked at the older seamen.

"Oh, she's prettier," Kathy said, writing a number and street name on a piece of paper she pulled from her purse. "Here's our address. It's only two blocks off the bus line. Our stop's just two more."

"What time?" Henderson asked pleasantly.

"How about seven-thirty? That'll give us time to wash up and change into something better than these clothes. Mom and Pauline will want to dress up too."

Henderson took the scrap of paper and stuffed it in his blouse pocket.

"Our pleasure, ladies," he smiled graciously. "Seven-thirty. On the dot."

The girls got off at their stop and Jones started to follow. Henderson pulled him back.

"No, man, don't do that," he objected. "Too obvious. We'll get off at the next stop, get something to drink, then go to their house later."

He flicked his eyes at Jones and Ellard.

"Well? What did I tell you?"

"Under Sea Minesweeper Service!" Jones grunted. "I never heard such crap!"

"Right," Henderson agreed smugly. "It's crap, but you see how this uniform works! Like magic! Are you convinced?"

"Hell, yes," Jones grudgingly admitted. "Wish I could wear one."

25 October 1942

0930 HOURS
New York

Gilbert Thomas Mitzell looked up at the huge grey hull of the *S. S. Andrew Bennett* and had second thoughts about running away from home to join the Merchant Marine. He had hitchhiked from Montpelier, Ohio, to New York, making the trip in three days and, with no questions asked, was issued seaman's papers as a utility messman. He paid his National Maritime Union dues and ten minutes later showed his union card when the call came for a utility messman on this shop.

He was not as eager now.

Dressed in a checkered red and black shirt and blue dungarees, seabag slung over his right shoulder, he nervously climbed the gangway and thought about why he was here. It wasn't because he was especially patriotic. He was going to sea because of what his high school principal said when he called Gilbert into his office last week.

"We have to put you back to the sophomore class," Mr.

Ronald Haggerty had told the sixteen-year-old student. "We thought about keeping you back last June, but decided to give you another chance. The problem is you have an F in every class this first period except for music. You are a talented pianist, Gilbert, but you need science, math, history and English if you want to graduate."

He paused to let his words sink in.

"We know you're having problems because of your home life, what with your father drinking all the time, but we think it will be better for you to go back a grade."

Gilbert nodded, shook the principal's hand and hurried out of the office without a word. He walked out of the school, headed for the highway and stuck up his thumb for a ride. He didn't want to go home. He knew he had not been doing well in school, that he had musical talent, but he had to do something to get away from his father, to start a new life. He wanted to play on a piano that wasn't repeatedly hit with a whiskey bottle. At first, he didn't know where he was headed -- just away from home -- but on one of the rides east he read a newspaper article about some kids as young as sixteen serving on merchant ships.

If I can get on a ship, he told himself, *I could read a lot and maybe finish school later.*

He figured he wouldn't find a piano on a ship, but was sure he could find one in various ports he would visit. Besides, the article said, the Merchant Marine needs men. He wanted so much to be a man.

His father always called him a girl.

Now, as he neared the top of the gangway on this Liberty ship, he was not so sure he was ready to become a man. Two pairs of eyes looked down on him.

"Christ! He's the prettiest boy I've ever seen!" Able-Bodied Seaman Howard Robinson exclaimed, feasting over Gilbert's five-foot, six frame topped with a smooth, round cherub face and light blonde hair with little boy curls. "I've got mumbly pegs on him!"

"I didn't know you liked boys, Howie," said Able-Bodied Seaman Stanley Gruen.

"Neither did I until I went to the Big House the first time," Robinson spat, his black eyes gleaming. "I found out they're almost as good as a girl. Maybe better. I had one punk the last time that looked almost like a girl. He kept me warm on cold nights. This kid'll keep me warm this trip!"

He gave Gruen a leering look.

Gilbert reached the platform at the top of the gangway and, after looking around, stepped to the main deck. He appeared confused.

"What are you doing, pretty boy?" Gruen asked.

"I'm a messboy. How do I find my room?"

"Room? Ain't you never been on a ship?"

Gilbert set down his seabag, perplexed.

"Let me handle this," Robinson said helpfully. "This your first time on a ship, boy?"

"Yes . . yes, sir."

"Well, look, boy, we don't call them 'rooms' on a ship. They're foc'sles. I'll take you to yours."

"Yes, sir."

"We don't call anyone 'sir' on a ship except the officers. Stan and me ain't officers. You call him Stan and you call me Howie. I'm going to be your best friend on this here ship."

"I'd like that, sir . . er, Howie."

Robinson winked at Gruen.

"What's your name, boy?"

"Gilbert. Gilbert Thomas Mitzell."

"Gilbert? Hell, that's no name for a seaman. Sounds like a pantywaist librarian or a fart-brain warden."

He snorted.

"How about we call you 'Gill?' Like the gills on a fish, right?"

"Gill? I like that. I've always been called Gilbert."

"Not any more. Not on this bucket. How old you, Gill?"

The boy hesitated.

"Seventeen."

"How old?"

"Well, I'll be seventeen in five months."

I'm going to like this boy, the grinning Robinson told himself.

"You want to be a good seaman, don't you?"

"Yes."

"And a real man?"

"Oh, yes."

"Then stick with me, Gill. I'll teach you how to be both."

He leered again at Gruen.

"Now pick up your seabag and I'll take you to your foc'sle."

A few minutes later, Robinson returned to the gangway where Second Cook and Baker Bib Overall had joined Gruen.

"Your new messboy is unpacking his duds," he told the cook. "He's a really pretty one, a virgin for sure. He'll take good care of me and I'll look after him. He's mine and no one else -- no one -- touches him. Hear me?"

The two men didn't answer.

"Anyone who does goes over the side!" he threatened.

Overall stared hard at Robinson. He knew this man had been paroled from San Quentin back in February to return to his old job at sea, a job he had before killing a man with a knife during an argument in a post office two years ago. Robinson had been serving ten to twenty for second degree murder. He wore the killing, and two previous assault convictions, as badges of honor. But he had not displayed his penchant for boys until now. Overall was aware that a handful of seamen, known as "wolves," enjoyed women in port, but enjoyed young boys even more at sea. Trouble always erupted when two "wolves" vied for the body of the same boy.

The cook didn't know if others in the crew also liked young boys, but he knew this seaman spelled trouble with a capital "T."

He shrugged his shoulders and walked away.

"This ship sho is jinxed," he said aloud. "We's got a ghost an' now a fag!"

No one heard him.

2100 HOURS
Times Square, New York
Ordinary Seaman Tony Durante hung up the phone, feeling guilty. He had lied to Marilyn for the fourth time. Every time the *S. S. Andrew Bennett* returned to the States, Tony called his girlfriend in Oakland, California. Every time he said he couldn't leave the ship to come home and marry her. The war needed him. Every time she told him she was still a virgin, waiting for him. Every time he assured her he was too, but his fingers were crossed.

"Take me to a whorehouse," he asked A. B. Jones. "I need the experience. To last longer, you know. Marilyn will like that when we get married."

"You're getting a lot of experience from what I hear," Jones said. "Laying around with prostitutes in every port we've been in. You should be more careful, boy."

Before he let Tony go upstairs with the prostitute, Jones handed him a Trojan condom.

"This will protect you against V. D.," he warned. "American whores aren't as careful as those in Noumea and England."

"How do I use it?" Tony asked.

"Just give it to the girl. She knows how to put it on you."

26 October 1942

0910 HOURS
Naval District Headquarters, New York City
At the convoy conference, the COMCONVOY told Captain Davis his ship, armed with the new Mark 29, would not be in the middle of the lines of ships where, with its cargo of tanks, it would normally be assigned.

"You'll be on the outside, in the coffin corner," he said bluntly.

Frank pondered that a few seconds. He knew that, in a U-boat attack, his ship would most likely be the first target. This would be a real test for the equipment.

"With all respect, Admiral, we've got a priority cargo," he said. "Tanks. Lots of tanks. Suppose this new-fangled Mark Twenty-Nine gadget doesn't work? We'll lose a valuable cargo."

Another merchant captain spoke up.

"From what we hear, you'll be a helluva lot safer than those of us without that gadget. About time those of us with foodstuffs aren't made the only easy marks."

Frank looked at the man.

"Sorry, Captain," he said. "I was thinking more of the men who will need these tanks than I was about the safety of my ship."

"Those same men need food, too," the other captain said sarcastically. "That's what we're carrying. Remember what Napoleon said. 'An Army travels on its stomach.'"

Laughter filled the room and Frank, shot down, remained silent. It was no small comfort when the other captain's Liberty was assigned to the starboard column, five hundred yards ahead of the *Bennett*. That ship, too, would be an easy mark.

"We'll get steam up at twenty-two hundred hours," the Admiral continued. "We'll move out at midnight and form up in your appointed positions as soon as we clear the harbor. Any questions?"

A third captain raised his hand.

"What's our destination, Admiral?"

"You'll open your sealed orders as soon as we get into position," the Admiral answered. "That's all. I'll see you and your ships tonight. Good luck."

27 October 1942

0200 HOURS
Outside New York Harbor
As the line of ships reached the openess of the Atlantic Ocean, the COMCONVOY destroyer's klaxon horn began burping. Aldis lamps signalled the order to "take up formation." There were fifteen merchant ships and they lined up in four columns of fours, except for the second column, port. The convoy commander's destroyer took first position in that row, with three merchant ships behind. The convoy was spread out less than a mile wide. There were two destroyers and three destroyer escorts further out, but no rescue ships. The *Bennett* was in the starboard "coffin corner."

The lamps signalled another order.

"Maintain a speed of eight knots! Maintain your position!"

With those orders, Frank went to the safe in his cabin, opened it, took out a sealed envelope and walked forward to the chartroom. The chief mate and chief engineer joined him there. Frank opened the envelope and read the ship's orders.

"It's as we guessed," he said calmly. "We're going to the Med. According to these, we'll sail down the East Coast to Hatteras, then shoot across the South Atlantic to Gibraltar where we'll join another convoy to support the landings in French North Africa. We'll stick close to shore on the way down and, with our escort ships, we'll have a good shot at making Hatteras without a sub attack. I doubt there'll be one anyway. Word at the convoy conference was that the Germans have withdrawn their subs from along the east coast. The convoy system is working and the subs, even in wolfpacks, have not been effective."

"It isn't just the convoy system," Billy interjected. "The government has ordered all lights along the East Coast to be completely turned off at night. Finally, a full blackout. Our silhouette can't easily be seen by any lurking subs."

"It's about time we had some luck," Speer said. "But I ain't counting on it too much. This small convoy will be a juicy target, even for a single sub."

28 October 1942

0500 HOURS
In the Bennett's Galley
The shadowy figure in the blue and gold uniform signalled a warning to the second cook and baker. His motions seemed to say: *"Tell the captain this ship is in danger."*

"Are yo' here again?" Zachary "Bib" Overall asked, turning his back on the figure. "Ah thought ah got rid of yo'. 'Sides, yo' don't exist. The captain says so."

He turned away and stirred the vat of oatmeal he was preparing for breakfast.

"Yo' ain't real."

When he looked again, the vision was gone.

"Ah knowed yo' wasn't real," he said, but he wondered if the ghost had really left the ship.

0600 HOURS
One Hundred Nautical Miles East of Hatteras
"We're a good distance off the coast now, Capitan," the exec of U-84-B told Lieutenant Commander Barnschmidt. "Okay to surface?"

"Yes. Take her up."

Slowly, the German submarine headed to the ocean surface. It had been on patrol for more than eight months, except for two brief forays to their milch cow for refueling and to reload torpedoes.

"What are we going to do now?" the exec asked, pointing to the orders lying on the chart table. "We've been ordered away from the East Coast."

"I don't know what's come over Donitz," Barnschmidt said. "The man's obviously lost his nerve. A few of our boats have been sunk by convoy escort vessels. So what? We're still sinking ships."

"Well, we've had some good luck, Capitan. Some of the others have not. I don't think the admiral wants to lose any more boats."

"He's a damn fool! How does he expect the fatherland to win this war if he doesn't take chances? So we lose a few boats! But, with a wolfpack, we can get one out of every four or five ships in a convoy. Those are ships that don't make it across."

"But that's exactly what he wants us to do, sir. Join a wolfpack and operate out of the Caribbean. We're still to go after convoys. I thought, sir, you favored convoys."

"After eight months, I think I like going it alone. It gives me a sense of superiority. I do what I want, go where I want and we sink a lot of ships."

In the eight months, U-84-B had added 18 ships and 60,800 tons to its previous record.

0700 HOURS
Eighty Nautical Miles East of Hatteras
A destroyer escort came alongside the *Bennett* and broke out the laundry. The Navy signalman read the multicolored signal flags ordering the deployment of the Mark 29 equipment. Lieutenant Taylor was as happy as a boy who had caught his first fish.

"Watch this," he told Captain Davis as he ordered the two Navy specialists to play out the reels of rubberized cables. "Those wires will stop any torpedo."

"I hope we never get a chance to find out," Frank said. "We're guinea pigs this trip, put in the coffin corner to attract a U-boat to shoot at us to see if this damn thing works."

"Oh, it'll work," Guns said confidently, looking at his manual.

He shouted new orders. Steam hissed, winches clattered and the paravanes went over the side, followed by the cables, eight in all, four on each side.

Sluggishly, the Liberty plodded ahead, struggling to keep to its assigned position. Within a few minutes, it was one thousand yards, not the assigned five hundred, behind the ship in front. Frank whistled down the tube to his brother on watch in the engine room.

"What's happening down there, Chief?" he asked anxiously. "We're dropping behind the convoy. Get us back to eight knots!"

"Goddamnit, Frank!" Billy shouted, forgetting that he was not to address his brother by his given name. "We are at *full* speed. Seventy-six revolutions! We can't do better than that. What are you doing up there?"

Frank didn't answer. He looked over the port side, studying the cables, flapping on top of the water like long sea serpents. They were not submerged and the drag severely slowed the ship's headway. The *Bennett* was five thousand yards behind its assigned slot.

A destroyer escort sent signals by Aldis lamp.

"Get back in position!" the Navy signalman read to Captain Davis.

"We can't do it, not with this drag," Frank said, agitated. "Tell them that."

The signalman furiously blinked his lamp.

"What can we do, Lieutenant?" Frank asked the gunnery officer. "I thought those cables were to be submerged."

"I'll be damned if I know, Captain," Taylor said. "I've pushed all the buttons and they won't go down to the desired depth. They're just flapping on top of the water. Even the rates who tested this equipment and came with us don't know what do. Nothing is working."

He was frightened.

The DE's klaxon horn burped and more signals were sent.

"Get back into position immediately!"

"Tell them we're dropping out of the convoy . . temporarily," he told the Navy signalman. "We'll catch up after we figure out what to do with the damned cables."

The signalman flicked his lamp. The rest of the convoy was almost out of sight.

"Good luck," the DE signalled back, then took off to catch up with her other charges.

0800 HOURS
Aboard the U-84-B
"Herr Capitan, the hydrophone operator has picked up the sound of ship's screws. Many screws. He thinks it's a convoy."

"How far?" Commander Barnschmidt asked the exec.

"About six miles. Dead ahead."

"Have you seen anything yet?"

"No, sir, but the convoy's speed indicates they're traveling at eight knots."

"We'll stay topside for awhile until we spot them. Then we'll submerge for the attack."

"You're going to attack a convoy, sir? In broad daylight? One boat?" the executive officer asked anxiously. "That's against the admiral's orders. We're to join up with a wolfpack!"

"I wouldn't miss the chance to show Donitz how wrong he is!" Barnschmidt gloated, rubbing his hands happily. "We can get at least two, maybe three. I'll even try for a destroyer."

The exec's eyes opened wide.

0900 HOURS
Aboard the S. S. Andrew Bennett
Captain Davis huddled with Chief Mate Speer. Their situation had become more precarious. The *Bennett* was about fifteen nautical miles behind the convoy and was drifting almost helplessly despite the seventy-six revolutions a minute. He turned to Lieutenant Taylor.

"Any new ideas, Guns?"

"I've tried just about everything in the manual, Captain, except calling the whole thing off and reeling in the cables. We'll try that now, using the steam winches to pull."

"It damn well better work, for your sake. Much longer and we won't be able to catch up with the convoy. I'm not anxious to make the rest of this crossing without escorts."

"It'll work, Captain," the lieutenant said, but his voice was not convincing.

1100 HOURS
Aboard the U-84-B
U-84-B was submerged again. Commander Barnschmidt raised the submarine's periscope for another look. The Liberty ship carrying foodstuffs, now in the coffin corner on the starboard side of the convoy, filled the glass.

"Load torpedoes!" Barnschmidt ordered.

Torpedoes were shoved into the four forward tubes.

"Torpedoes loaded!"

"Range?"

The exec took the measurement.

"Eight thousand yards!"

"Fire one!" Barnschmidt ordered.

"Torpedo los!"

There was a hiss of air pressure and the boat recoiled at the shock of the discharge.

"Fire two!"
The seconds ticked by slowly as the torpedoes ran.

1101 HOURS
Aboard the S. S. Andrew Bennett
The explosions sounded like distant thunder. Intuition told Captain Davis it was not God clapping his hands in the sky, but torpedoes impacting on the hull of a merchant ship. He sounded general quarters and turned to Lieutenant Taylor.
"Cut those cables, Lieutenant! Now!"
"How?"
The Navy lieutenant was more than frightened. He was scared.
"Any goddamn way you can!" the captain shouted. "No, wait a minute! Get Boats for me!"
Word went down to find the boatswain.
"Take wire cutters, cold chisels, anything you can get your hands on, and cut those damn cables!" Frank ordered Boatswain Campbell.
"Right away, skipper!" the deck foreman said and raced to the bow, picking up merchant seamen and tools as he did. In fifteen minutes, all the cables were cut loose and the *Bennett*, its engines still pounding furiously, seemed to lunge ahead.
"That's the end of the Mark Twenty-Nine," Captain Davis told the gunnery officer, telling himself at the same time that bad luck was still plaguing his ship.
"I know," Taylor said sheepishly. "I wish we could radio and report this disaster, Captain. They'll probably put the gear on other ships before we get to Africa. I'll have it on my conscience if some other ship has more trouble than we had. Flailing around like that, those cables could be a real problem in a storm."
"They've already been a helluva problem for us," the captain agreed. "Because of them we have to face a possible submarine attack without a Navy escort."

1103 HOURS
Aboard the U-84-B
The destroyer escort, klaxon horns burping as it raced toward the submarine, loomed large to Commander Barnschmidt's eyes through the periscope.
"Load torpedoes!" he ordered.

"Torpedoes loaded!"
"Range eight thousand yards."
The DE began a turn toward U-84-B.
"Fire three!"
"Torpedo los!"
The submarine shook like a woman trying to lose weight.
"Fire four!"

1105 HOURS
Aboard the S. S. Andrew Bennett
Frank heard two more explosions.
"My God!" he yelled to his chief mate. "Must be a wolfpack!"
On the eastern horizon, dead ahead, he could see two eerie orange glows, close to each other. A series of quick, short explosions raked the humid night air. Brilliant red flashes arched from the flaming balls.
"Looks like two ships have been hit!"
"What do we do?" Speer asked. "Stay here, hoping they don't see us?"
Frank felt like a duck sitting in open water with hunters hiding in duckblinds all around him. He reached for the engine room telegraph.
"All stop!" he rang, agreeing with his chief mate.

1106 HOURS
Aboard the U-84-B
Lieutenant Commander Barnschmidt, peering through the periscope in front of him, was thrilled at the flaming scene. One Liberty ship hit by two torpedoes, forward and 'midships, sinking, men jumping from her decks and swimming toward liferafts. Others lowering lifeboats. One destroyer escort, hit 'midships and aft, burning, blazing missiles from an ammunition locker shooting hundreds of feet into the air.
"The Liberty's going down! " he shouted. "The DE's crippled! Take a look, Lieutenant!"
His executive officer crouched and peered through the scope.
"You're right, Capitan! It's beautiful! But, sir, another destroyer is bearing down on us!"
Barnschmidt didn't look. He sensed the danger.
"Take her down to one hundred feet," he ordered.

1110 HOURS
Aboard the S. S. Andrew Bennett
There were no more explosions.

"Perhaps it was only one sub," Chief Mate Speer ventured.

"I'm not so sure," Frank said cautiously. "We'll sit it out here a while longer."

1112 HOURS
One Hundred Feet Under the Surface
The crew, most of them in their late teens or early twenties, heard the terrifying pinging of sonar. The device, fixed to the bottom of the hull of the American destroyer, transmitted sound impulses that bounced off the steel hull of the submerged boat and returned to a receiver, giving away its position. They had heard its simulation in training classes, but had never faced its warning of danger in actual combat. It frightened them and those in the control room looked anxiously to their captain.

"Take her down to one hundred and fifty feet!" Barnschmidt ordered.

The first pattern of six depth charges exploded close around the lowering boat, bucking and rolling it, and throwing men and objects around.

"To three hundred feet!"

There was a rush of the destroyer's whirring propellers overhead.

"Attacker overhead again!" the hydrophone operator called.

The pinging began again. Then the terrifying wait.

A second pattern of six more depth charges exploded and the boat rocked fiercely. This time the men clung to overhead pipes and stanchions.

"To four hundred feet!"

The boat moved slowly down. A third pattern battered the hull.

"Cut off all electrical equipment except the hydrophones and gyro-compass!" Barnschmidt ordered. "Reduce lighting to a minimum!"

He wanted to save his battery power.

Six more depth charges so scared the crew that some of them began crying. They were afraid. Being crushed by water and steel, four hundred feet below the surface, was not an appealing way to die.

"Stop engines!" Barnschmidt ordered. "Turn off everything! Everything! We'll let them think they got us and we'll sit it out down here for a while."

1150 HOURS
Aboard the S. S. Andrew Bennett
"We haven't heard an explosion for nearly an hour," Chief Mate Speer said hopefully. "Maybe we should try to rejoin the convoy."

Captain Davis still wasn't sure.

"I thought I heard the muffled sounds of depth charges a half hour ago, but I'm not sure. I haven't heard them since. Maybe they got the sub -- or subs."

He scanned the eastern horizon with his binoculars.

"I see only one fire and it's too far away to tell what it is. I wonder what happened to the other fire."

"Maybe they put it out," Speer guessed.

"Or maybe the ship went down."

Frank waived his anxiety, rang "Full Ahead" to the engine room and whistled down the tube.

"Let's push it to eleven knots, Billy. We've got to catch up with the convoy. I have a feeling our escorts are trying to find us. The whole convoy's surely scattered and those destroyers and DE's are probably playing Mother Goose, trying to get her flock back together again."

1431 HOURS
Aboard the U-84-B
The inside of the submarine was hot. Sweaty. Smelly. Quiet. Most of the crew were on their stomachs, their noses close to the decks smelling the foul air.

"I'm sure the destroyer has left," the exec whispered to Commander Barnschmidt optimistically. "There have been no depth charges for more than three hours. We should start the engines, sir. It's stifling and we need fresh air. Much longer down here we'll suffocate."

"Just what I was thinking," Barnschmidt said.

He and the lieutenant were the only ones standing in the control room.

"Start engines! Take her up to thirty feet! We'll surface if things look clear, then head due south! I'd like to get out of this area as quickly as possible! We'll turn around and head north at nightfall."

"Good, Capitan, and good shooting, sir. One merchant

ship down; one destroyer escort crippled. That'll look good in our log."

"Three ships would look better. I hate to run."

"Yes, sir, but the positive side is we're still around to report the two."

1625 HOURS
In the Bennett's Wheelhouse
"Ship about five miles out, off the port bow!" the crow's nest lookout called. "It's one of our destroyers!"

"That's a relief!" sighed Second Mate Turner. "Am I ever glad to see her!"

"All of us are," Captain Davis said, taking a look at the Navy ship and then settling himself in the captain's chair. "God, I'm tired!"

"No wonder!" the second said. "You haven't been to bed since yesterday morning. You've been up more than thirty-four hours, Captain. Why don't you sack out? I've got the bridge now."

Frank shook himself. He felt there were rocks in his head.

"Think I will. But just for a nap. Call me when we meet up with the convoy."

2030 HOURS
In the Captain's Quarters
An ordinary seaman woke Captain Davis.

"We're hooking up with the convoy again, sir. Back in the coffin corner."

"That figures," the captain said, rubbing his eyes. He was fully dressed, his custom when sleeping. "We may have a priority cargo, but they put us there when we were equipped with the Mark Twenty-Nine. Now that the contraption is gone, thank God, the COMCONVOY can't move us to a safer spot, much as he might like to. It would confuse the other captains."

He walked to the wheelhouse. Bib met him with freshly baked doughnuts and Third Mate Franklin held out a steaming mug of his special coffee.

"We've been lucky today, sir," Franklin said. "I know we had trouble with the Mark Twenty-Nine, but we weren't with the convoy when it was attacked."

"Yes, I guess we can call that luck."

"Some others were not so lucky. The destroyer

signalled us that twenty-three seamen and Armed Guard were lost from the Liberty and eighteen sailors died on the destroyer escort. That DE is headed back to the states."

"It'll be a long trip," Frank said.

2115 HOURS
In the Crew's Shower
The chief cook told Messboy Mitzell to leave the cleaning of pots and pans until morning.

"Get some sleep," he told the boy. "You look like you haven't slept for a week."

Gilbert admitted he was tired. He had served three meals, washed dishes and ran up to the wheelhouse two dozen times with fresh coffee after the Mark 29 failed. He went to his foc'sle, picked up a towel and headed for the shower. A. B. Robinson followed quietly. The messboy undressed, stepped into the stall and turned on the faucet. Robinson took off his clothes.

"You sure do look pretty," he said menacingly, walking toward the boy. "I'll bet you feel pretty."

The boy turned around. The naked A. B. reached a hand toward him.

"Yeah," Robinson leered. "I'm going to enjoy this!"

Gilbert screamed. Robinson stepped back.

"Aw, come on, kid. I'm not going to hurt you."

He stepped into the stall.

Gilbert screamed louder.

Walking down the ladder to the main deck after taking more doughnuts to the wheelhouse, Bib heard the muffled screams, stopped, perked his ears and headed for the shower room. He saw Robinson's back and Mitzell's form crowded into the corner of the stall. He lunged and crashed both fists at the back of A. B.'s neck. The cement floor was slippery and Robinson fell over.

"Ah'll kill you!" Bib yelled. "Ah'll kill you!"

He pummeled Robinson's face and kicked him in the groin. Three other seamen ran into the shower room and pulled Bib away.

"Hold it, Bib!" A. B. Wilson urged. "You'll kill him."

"Ah wants to!" Bib shouted, trying to pull himself out of Wilson's grasp. "Ah will kill 'im!"

"You can't!" Wilson shouted. "You'll go to prison. Slow down. The captain's on his way."

As if on cue, Captain Davis entered the crowded room.

"What's going on?" he demanded.

"This fink tried to rape the messboy!" Bib yelled, pointing to Robinson.

"I did not!" Robinson spat back. "I was going to take a shower myself and the kid started screaming. For no reason."

"I don't know how you could do this after what we've been through today," the captain said. "Or any time. There's no place on a ship for a homosexual."

"I'm not a queer!" Robinson protested. "I like women, Captain. I had one in New York the night before we sailed. God, she was good! I don't need boys, sir."

"You're on parole and this was a violation. I could lock you in chains in the number one ammunition locker."

"But I didn't to anything, Captain! Like I said, I was going to take a shower. I walked in here and the boy started screaming."

Captain Davis looked at Gilbert, standing with a towel wrapped around his waist and soapsuds still on his hair and shoulders.

"Gilbert, what happened?"

The boy looked at Robinson. The A. B.'s eyes were fiery, like those of a crazed animal. They also warned the messboy he might be sorry if he told the captain what Robinson had threatened.

"I got scared," he said.

"Why? Did he touch you?"

"No, sir. I saw him coming and thought . . I don't like anyone to see me when I'm naked."

Captain Davis looked at Robinson's blood-smeared face.

"Were you going to touch the boy?"

"Christ, no, Captain! I don't do things like that. It's been a long, sweaty day. You know that, sir, a long, sweaty day and I needed to wash it off. I didn't see the kid until I got in here."

The captain looked at Bib.

"Did you see anything?"

"No. Ah heard 'im screamin' and ran in here."

"Anyone else see anything?"

There was a chorus of "no's.".

"Looks like you made a mistake, Bib. There's no evidence he tried to attack the boy. The boy says that himself."

"Ah knows what Ah knows, Captain," Bib said shakily. "He was goin' after the boy. To rape 'im!"

"Like I said, Bib, no evidence, no crime."

He swung around to Robinson.

"Looks like you get off this time, seaman. But I warn you. Be careful when you want to shower. I don't ever want to hear you came to shower at the same time as this boy. Or anyone else on this ship. You shower alone from now on."

He walked out of the shower room, perturbed.

2130 HOURS
In the Bennett's Saloon
"This is a helluva note," Captain Davis said to his brother and the chief mate as the three sat in the saloon with cups of coffee. "I don't believe that man. I'm sure he was going to try something with the boy, but I can't prove it."

"You never will, Captain," Speer said. "These wolves are slick. Stuff like this has been going on ever since man first went to sea. It gets lonesome for some guys on long trips."

"We've only been out a couple of days!" Frank protested.

"Doesn't matter to men like that. I hear they do a lot of this in prisons. With older men, too. The victims -- and most of them are victims 'tho some enjoy it -- don't report it to the authorities. They're afraid for their lives."

Frank thought Mitzell was afraid for his life.

"Think Robinson will try this again?"

"I doubt it," Billy answered. "He probably learned a lesson tonight."

"I'm not so sure about that," Frank said. "The man's a real troublemaker. The boatswain wants him off the ship. He's caused a number of problems and he has an insolent attitude all the time. That's not good for morale."

Billy nodded.

"You've told me he's a pretty good seaman, John," he said, directing his comment to the mate. "Any chance he can be straightened out?"

"No way!" the mate answered quickly. "He's rotten to the core and I join with Boats. Robinson should be off this ship."

"I don't have enough on him to throw him off," Frank explained. "Other seamen are insolent, too. But I do think he's one of the reasons this ship's jinxed."

"Forget that foolishness about a jinx and a ghost!" the mate argued. "There ain't no such thing on this ship!"

"Bib says he's seen it several times," Frank protested.
"No one else has," Billy said.
"That's the point, you guys," the mate pointed out. "The damn thing's in Bib's mind and only in his mind."
"I wish I knew that were true," the captain said. "Some of the men are scared. Apparently they don't think it's a figment of his imagination."
"Oh, forget all that crap!" The mate stood up. "We've a cargo to deliver. You don't have time to worry about a ghost or spirit that doesn't exist. I'll speak to Boats to keep an eye on Robinson. Any false move, we'll put him in chains."
Frank knew the boatswain would be more watchful. The man had no use for faggots.

5 November 1942

0950 HOURS
Strait of Gibraltar

"Look at that rock, will you!" Navy Seaman First Class "Cookie" Cookman said excitedly to Ordinary Seaman Gary Benson. "I've never seen one as big."
"There are probably bigger rocks in Colorado," Benson said, "but to tell the truth, I've never thought about measuring them. It is big, though. One huge grey limestone mass, overlaimed by dark shales on its western slopes. Its insides are honeycombed with natural caves and man-made tunnels. That mass takes up about two square miles of Gibraltar's two and one-third miles."
"You mean there's more than the rock there?"
"Sure. If you look close enough you'll sit the rock sits on a peninsula that's joined to Spain by that low-lying sandy isthmus over there. See? The entire peninsula is only about three-quarters of a mile wide."
"Joined to Spain?" Cookie asked. "I thought the British own Gibraltar."
"They do. Gibraltar is a British dependency and they use it as a Navy base to guard their interests in the Mediterranean. After all, the North African coast is only fourteen miles to the south."
"You never cease to amaze me," Cookie said admiringly. "Where do you store all that stuff?"
"Same place you do. In my brain."
"Hell, if I carried around all that stuff my brain would

explode."

"No it wouldn't. The human brain is a marvelous piece of machinery. Want to hear about it?"

"Uh, not now, Gary," Cookie said, turning away. "The lieutenant's called an Armed Guard meeting at oh ten hundred. I've gotta go."

Happy to be avoiding another lecture, he headed to the foredeck.

1000 HOURS
The Spanish Coast
The German agent looked down on the convoy cruising through the strait. Eleven merchant ships, three destroyers and two destroyer escorts.

Strange, he thought. *That's the third convoy since dawn. There were other small convoys yesterday and the day before. All of them are assembling into one huge convoy. Something is brewing. Something big!*

He hurried down the slope to his radio transmitter to call Berlin.

1200 HOURS
Berlin
Adolf Hitler didn't want to be bothered with the agent's report. He was worried about other things: The retreat of General Rommel's once-proud Afrika Korps and the Panzer Army Africa from El Alamein to Tunisia, Montgomery's Eighth Army snapping at their heels. German forces on the western front locked in a bloody battle with the Russians at Stalingrad.

"It's nothing more than another convoy to Malta," the Fuhrer knowingly told his war staff. "Tell the Luftwaffe to increase its bombing of that stinking island."

1400 HOURS
Twelve Miles Off the Coast of Algeria
A U. S. Navy patrol boat approached the Liberty ship and a full commander scrambled up a hastily-dropped Jacob's ladder. Jumping over the gunwale to the main deck, he saluted aft.

"Permission to board?" he asked.

"Granted, sir," Ordinary Seaman Durante answered smartly.

"Your captain?"
"He's in the wheelhouse, sir."
"Thank you."
The commander walked quickly across the deck.
Well-trained, Tony thought. *Not like that asshole Army major in Noumea.*
"Your orders, sir," the commander said, handing a single piece of paper to Captain Davis.
Frank read the orders hastily, then a second time more slowly. They advised the *Bennett* was assigned to the invasion's Central Task Force. Objective: Oran, Algeria, French North Africa. Another task force, Eastern, was to hit Algiers, capital city of Algeria, 250 miles to the east. A third, Western, was poised off Casablanca, on Morocco's Atlantic Seaboard. All three would attack at the same time. The *Bennett* would be at the rear of the Central Task Force, behind dozens of troop transports. Its Sherman tanks would be needed after the U. S. Army troops gained a foothold. The convoy would sail east as though headed for Malta. Shortly before zero hour, it would turn south to Oran.
Zero hour: 0100, 8 November.
"You ride it out at anchor tonight until given the signal to move," the commander said.
"Understood," Captain Davis nodded. "What can the landing expect? Will the French put up much resistance?"
"That's a puzzle, Captain. Many of the French have sworn allegiance to the Vichy regime. Vichy is the seat of the government formed to rule that portion of the country not occupied by the Nazis. They're collaborating. Worse, more Frenchmen are still upset about what the British Royal Navy did to their fleet at Mers el Kebir, right near here. You heard about that?"
"No."
"Well, they came, guns pounding, and sank or crippled four French warships. They said they did it to keep the warships out of Hitler's hands after the fall of France. That may have been a good idea, except they killed over twelve hundred French sailors."
"Terrible!" Frank said.
"Terrible is right. Frenchmen all over are damn mad with the British over that. Our agents in French North Africa tell us the French probably would welcome Americans, but they're bound to kill the English. We haven't told them there's more than thirty thousand limeys on

the ships out here. That may not be good for the more than seventy-thousand American GIs set to land."

"Then they may fight?"

"Our agents have tried to talk them out of it, but right now it's anybody's guess, Captain. My opinion is that some of them will put on a show. It might get nasty."

7 November 1942

1400 HOURS
Berlin

The general told Hitler about the massive Allied armada steaming eastward in the Mediterranean.

"This is more than a convoy bound for Malta," he warned. "Our agent in Spain reports dozens of troopships and scores of merchant vessels. American and British. There's more warships in one place than we thought they have. We've no doubt, sir, it's an invasion force."

The Fuhrer studied the wall map.

"Okay. They're going to invade here . . and here."

He stabbed a finger at the Libya ports of Benghazi and Tripoli.

"Tell the commanders at these spots to be ready. We'll give those Americans a welcome filled with their blood."

2300 Hours
In The Bennett's Wheelhouse

"Ah's terrible scared, suh!" Bib cried to the captain.

"We're all scared, Bib," Frank told the cook. "Going into battle is frightening, but it's nothing to be ashamed of."

"Ah's not afraid of the guns, Captain. Ah's scared of Mista Ghost!"

"Don't tell me you've seen that thing again?"

"Yes, ah has, suh. He come into my foc'sle an woke me. Then, when ah turned away an' tried to ignore 'im, he swung at ma back. Ah went back after 'im but he disappeared. Ah don' like it, suh. He's got me troubled."

"I'm troubled, too, Bib," Captain Davis said, "but I've got other worries right now. This ship is part of an invasion force and the shooting's going to start shortly. Now, look, Bib, I've told you before there's no such thing as ghosts. I think you just had a dream, a nightmare, and it woke you."

"If that's what yo' thinks, suh," Bib said, shaking his head and sure the captain didn't believe him. "Ah'll go back to ma foc'sle. Maybe yo's right and he's not there at all."

"He won't be, Bib, I assure you."

8 November 1942

0031 HOURS
Six Miles Off Oran
There was a new moon and the ships of the Central Task Force, including the *Bennett*, rode quietly at anchor. All crews were at general quarters. American soldiers, most of them facing their first test in combat, were quiet, many saying prayers, others blackening the sights of their rifles, sharpening bayonets, writing letters home.

A few reread the communique handed to them when boarding the transports:

To Members of the United States Expeditionary
Forces:
You are a soldier of the United States Army.
You have embarked for distant places where the war is being fought.
Upon the outcome depends the freedom of your lives: the freedom of the lives of those you love -- your fellow citizens -- your people.
Never were the enemies of freedom more tyrannical, more arrogant, more brutal.
Yours is a God-fearing, proud, courageous people, which, throughout its history, has put freedom under God before all other purposes.
We who stay at home have our duties to perform, duties owed in many parts to you. You will be supported by the whole force and power of this nation. The victory you win will be a victory of all the people -- common to them all. You bear with you the hope, the confidence, the gratitude and the prayers of your family, your fellow-citizens, and your president --
Franklin D. Roosevelt

The communique from their commander-in-chief gave

courage to some of the Americans.

British troops, most of them experienced, some of them survivors of the pullback from Dunkirk, laughed and swore as they prepared for another battle with the enemy. Winches squealed as boats were lowered. On orders, the fighting men grappled down rope nets to waiting, bobbing assault craft.

Operation Torch had begun.

0045 HOURS
Aboard the S. S. Andrew Bennett
The men in the number one gun tub listened intently to the Notre Dame-Army football game on shortwave radio.

"There's no score at the half," Seaman First Class Robert "Rabbit" Ellard shouted to the other gunners.

"Who the hell cares?" a voice answered. "The shooting's about to start!"

0105 HOURS
The Port of Oran
Luck was not with the first wave of Americans in their landing crafts. A small French convoy appeared out of nowhere and spotted the troop movement. Signals flashed ashore, sirens sounded throughout the city and lights were turned off. French destroyers fired broadsides at the ships and landing craft. Some GIs ditched in the water and other Frenchmen, in rowboats, rescued them.

The first wave of troops reached the shore, loudspeakers blaring from their landing craft.

"Ne tirez pas! Nous sommes vos amis! Nous sommes Americans!"

It didn't help.

From the city's blackness, French crews began firing 75-millimeter coastal guns.

0200 HOURS
Aboard the S. S. Andrew Bennett
"Notre Dame won it!" Rabbit shouted across the ship. "Thirteen to nothing!"

"Don't let any of the Army guys hear that score," one of the other gunners said. "That won't help their morale in this game!"

0330 HOURS
The Port of Oran
The city's defenders stubbornly resisted the invaders. Most of them. A few scattered units held up white flags, but the ground was being taken in feet, not yards, and it appeared the battle for the city would be a long one.

0600 HOURS
Aboard the S. S. Andrew Bennett
Boatswain Campbell found Bib lying on the main deck, just outside the aft port passageway. Unconscious. Blood flowing from a wound on his back.
 "Man wounded!" he shouted to the bridge.
 Captain Davis ran to help, calling for the purser to join him.
 "What happened? No shells have hit us."
 "I don't know," the boatswain said.
 Purser Tanner kneeled and examined the wound.
 "This is not shrapnel, Captain. Looks like he's been stabbed. With a knife."
 "Oh, God!" Frank moaned.
 He recalled Bib saying the ghost took a swing at his back.

0630 HOURS
The Port of Oran
The commander of a French company greeted the Americans with an unusual request.
 "Can we put up a symbolic resistance?"
 Uncertain and wary, but wanting to get the battle over with, the American officer gave his okay. One French soldier fired his rifle into the air, then handed it to the captain, smiling.

0700 HOURS
In the Bennett's Sickbay
"He's still unconscious but his breathing's erratic," Purser Tanner told Captain Davis. "The knife went into his back, deep, and probably into his right lung. I can't find any other wounds. His blood pressure and pulse are returning to normal. I think he'll make it."
 "Who could have done this?" Captain Davis asked.
 "One guess, Captain," Boatswain Campbell said. "It had

to be Robinson."

"Get him and bring him to my quarters!" the captain ordered.

0710 HOURS
The Captain's Quarters
Captain Davis sat in his cabin, the door open, listening to the explosions coming from the beach. *A helluva time for another personnel problem on this ship*, he told himself. He took a pair of handcuffs from his safe and put them on the desk.

"Here he is, sir," Campbell said, pushing Robinson through the door in front of him.

"What do you want with me, sir?" Robinson asked defensively. "I haven't done anything wrong. I was standing at my fire station when the bo's'n brought me here. Why?"

"Did you knife the cook?" the captain asked bluntly.

"What cook?"

"Overall."

"Hell, no, sir!" Robinson answered quickly. "Is he dead?"

"No, but he's hurt bad. I think you did it."

"Did he say I did?"

"No. He's unconscious."

"Then you have no witnesses. I'm out of here."

He turned to leave.

"Not so fast," Captain Davis said. "You had a motive. Bib went after you when he thought you were trying to make out sexually with the messboy."

"I told you, sir, I wasn't after the boy. I was gonna take a shower and the cook just made a mistake."

"There's apparent bad blood between you two."

"I don't hold any grudges. And I didn't stick him in the back."

"How'd you know he was stabbed in the back?"

Robinson coughed.

"'Cause you said so."

"No. I just asked if you knifed him."

"I ain't falling for that trick. I told you I didn't do it. You can't prove I did."

"What'd you do with the knife?" Campbell asked. "Throw it overboard?"

"Goddamn you!" Robinson shot at the boatswain. "You probably did it! I heard you complain about his eggs a cuppala days ago!"

"That's no motive," Captain Davis said. "Everyone complains about the cook. You had a big reason to go after him."

"No way. Maybe it was the ghost he's always talking about."

"Ghosts don't wield real knives," Captain Davis said.

"Want me to beat it out of you?" Campbell challenged.

Robinson lunged at the boatswain, striking him on the jaw.

"I'll kill you first!"

Captain Davis jumped up from his chair, grabbing the pair of handcuffs in his left hand. He wrapped his right arm around the neck of the seaman and handed the restrainers to the boatswain.

"Put these on him! Quickly!"

The boatswain swung one of the man's arms behind his back. Robinson kicked him. The captain tightened his grip, nearly closing the man's airway.

"Hurry, Boats!"

The boatswain pulled Robinson's other arm behind his back and snapped on the cuffs.

"You can't hold me! I didn't stick a knife in anyone! You ain't got any witnesses! You can't prove it!"

"Maybe I can't, but I can hold you now," Captain Davis said. "You hit the bo's'n. That's a crime on this ship and a violation of your parole. Put him in the number one ammunition locker, Boats."

"Jesus! You can't put me in there!"

"There's some chains in the locker. Chain him. I don't want him interfering with any gunner who may go down there for ammo."

"Yes, sir!"

"I'll turn him over to the Army police when things calm down ashore."

The boatswain pushed Robinson out the door.

0900 HOURS
The Port of Oran
"Damn it, we need tanks here!" the colonel called on his radio. "Our boys can't break through!"

The American GIs were green, weary and a little bit afraid after seven hours on the beach. They weren't moving very fast.

"Whaddya mean there's no tanks?"
He listened impatiently.
"Damn it! Get them off the ship!"

1015 HOURS
Aboard the S. S. Andrew Bennett
The Navy signalman handed Captain Davis a small sheet of paper.
Move into the port quickly. We've secured some docks and need your tanks. Immediately.
Captain Davis handed the note to Chief Mate Speer.
"Let's get a move on with this, Mister," he said.

1200 HOURS
The Port of Oran
"Where in hell are those tanks?" the colonel shouted at his sergeant.
"Navy said they're taking a ship to the docks," the GI answered.
"Does it take all day?"

1305 HOURS
The Docks
Army stevedores began unloading Sherman tanks before the last lines secured the *Bennett* to the dock.
"Looks like they want them in a hurry," Captain Davis said.
"From the sound of that gunfire, they need them," Chief Mate Speer agreed.

1430 HOURS
The City of Oran
The tanks rumbled forward, foot soldiers hiding behind, grateful for the armor protecting them and firing their rifles at everything that moved and some things that didn't. They had advanced one mile in the last hour, more than they had in the previous twelve hours.
"We've got them on the run!" the colonel shouted to his men as he left the cover of the lead tank and ran between buildings, a determined look on his face and a .45 thrust forward in his right hand.
A French sniper's bullet caught him in the throat.

1600 HOURS
In the Bennett's Sickbay
Bib regained consciousness and the purser sent for Captain Davis.

"How do you feel, Bib?" the captain asked.

The cook shook his head up and down.

Frank was surprised the man couldn't talk.

"Is he okay?"

"He's pretty weak, sir," Tanner said. "He lost a lot of blood, but I think he'll come around. Talking's difficult for him right now. He's heavily sedated with morphine. I've talked to the Army about getting him to a hospital. They say they can't. They're still setting up a field hospital on the docks and have their hands full with their own wounded. They're coming in every minute and they don't have time for a knifed merchant seaman."

"You're in good hands," Captain Davis consoled the cook. "Do you know who did this, Bib?"

The cook shook his head side to side, then lapsed back into a deep sleep.

9 November 1942

0600 HOURS
In the Bennett's Forward Ammunition Locker
The crunch-crunch of nearby exploding 75-millimeter shells rocked the *Bennett* at the dock and A. B. Robinson thought some had hit the ship.

"Get me out of here!" he shouted, his voice richochetting off the steel bulkheads of the ammo locker. "Get me out of here!"

No one heard him.

1400 HOURS
The City of Oran
Sporadic sniper fire greeted the Americans as they reached the center of the city. Paratroopers of the U. S. Rangers moved up quickly to join them.

"Where've youse guys been?" one GI called to the newcomers.

In the darkness of the early morning day before yesterday, their planes had flown off course and dropped the airborne soldiers on steep bluffs on the outskirts of the city. They scaled down the hills, meeting token resistance, and finally joined up with their fellow Americans.

"We took the scenic route!" came the rejoinder, airily.

10 November 1942

1600 HOURS
At the Dock
Two Military Police boarded the ship as the last of its cargo was unloaded. Captain Davis told them of the stabbing of the second cook and the assault on Boatswain Campbell.

"We suspect Robinson knifed him, although there are no witnesses," the captain said. "The cook says he doesn't know who did it and I'm not sure we can make the charge stick. I was a witness to the assault on the bo's'n and am willing to give you a signed statement now. As far as I'm concerned, the man has violated his parole and I don't want him on my ship any more. He should be sent back to San Quentin!"

"We'll try to send him back, but knowing criminals I don't think he'll confess to the stabbing," one of the MPs said. "Without witnesses and without the weapon, that'll be tough to prove, sir."

The two walked forward to get their prisoner.

1200 HOURS
The City of Oran
Major General Lloyd R. Fredendall, Commander of the Central Force, solemnly accepted the French surrender.

"It's over here," his aide said. "Now we go after the rest of Africa."

The general nodded. His men had been through hell with the French, supposedly Allies, and he didn't look forward to the battles ahead with the Germans.

1700 HOURS
At the Dock
A Navy launch pulled alongside the *Bennett*.

"Mail pouch!" a yeoman called. "Send down a line."

Ordinary Seaman Durante dropped one end of a piece of rope and, when the plastic covered package was secure, hoisted it up. He took it to Purser Tanner.

"I can't believe mail being delivered here," Purser

Tanner said. "During an invasion operation."
 "Believe it, sir. Any mail there for me?"
 Tanner looked.
 "Here's one." He sniffed the envelope. "Wow! Strong perfume. And lipstick on the back. You're in for it, boy!"

Dear Tony,
I'm confused. You promised to come home months ago so's we could get married, but every time you call you say you're staying on the Bennett. I know there's a war on, but other guys get leave to come home. Why not you? Don't you want to marry me any more?
Upset, but still loving you.
Marilyn

Dear Gilbert,
I can't believe your letter. What have you gone and done? Joined the Merchant Marine! In God's name, why? I know you are not happy with your father. I will leave him if only you will come home. Besides, Mr. Haggerty said he can get a music scholarship for you at that school in Topeka. We can go there together. Somehow we can make it. Please, Gilbert, come home.
Love,
Mother

Dearest Frank:
Do I ever have news for you! You're a father again! Wendy was born yesterday, October 16, and she's beautiful! Brunette hair, green eyes and 7 pounds, 4 ounces. You're going to love her! I can't wait for you to get home to see her. She's a doll and just what the doctor ordered. Or you ordered.
And guess what? Dad got married to Alex yesterday. Isn't that something? Wendy's birthday will be on their anniversary. That's a date we'll never forget. Dad's a boatswain on Billy's old ship, the Elihu Nicholson. It pulled into Philadelphia two days ago. She met him there and they drove to Elkton like we did. They planned to stay in a hotel until the ship sails, but I talked them into going to Uncle Fred's place in Rehobeth Beach. Just like us! Isn't that romantic! Hurry home, husband. You've got to see your little girl.
Your loving wife
Lynne

11 November 1942

0700 HOURS
Aboard the S. S. Andrew Bennett
"New orders, sir." the Navy signalman told Captain Davis.

He handed over a slip of paper, adding: "Looks like we're not going home."

Captain Davis read the orders.

The S. S. Andrew Bennett is ordered to Alexandria, Egypt, for modification to place sleeping racks in holds to carry 304 wounded Australian soldiers to Brisbane, Australia. Passengers also will include 4 doctors and 14 nurses. Depart Oran in six-ship convoy on 12 November 1942 at 2200 hours.

"No, we're not going home," Frank sighed. "I guess it'll be awhile before I see my newborn daughter."

0730 HOURS
Aboard the U-84-B
"New orders, sir," the executive officer told Commander Barnschmidt. He handed over a slip of paper. "Looks like we're going home."

Commander Barnschmidt read the orders:

The U-84-B is to proceed immediately to the Kriegsmarine base in Wilhelmshaven and Lieutenant Commander Reinhard Barnschmidt is ordered to proceed immediately to Berlin. There he is to report to Admiral Donitz without delay.

"Yes, we're going home," the sub captain sighed. "I wonder what else this means. I don't want to see Donitz!"

13 May 1943

1830 HOURS
In the Southwest Pacific
"The war's over in Africa!" the radio operator shouted to Captain Davis and the men on the S. S. Andrew Bennett's monkey bridge. "The Germans and Italians surrendered by the thousands today!" He had heard the news over the ship's shortwave radio and rushed to the bridge to tell everyone.

"The radio says nearly three hundred thousand have given up!"

"Geez, that must be all their army!" Ordinary Seaman Durante said.

"No, only those left in Tunisia," Sparks answered. "The British rolled into Tunis last week and the Germans there were caught by surprise. The radio said some of them ran out of barbershops with lather still on their faces."

"Must have been some scene," Captain Davis said. "Now if only we could wrap things up like that out here, we could get home by Christmas."

His brother, Billy, up from the engine room, added a somber note.

"It took the combined American and British forces six months to clean up Africa after the defeat of Rommel at El Alamein. The British were fighting in the desert for two years before that. They had all their men, ammunition and equipment in one place. We don't. We're just beginning to move here in the Pacific and we've got to move our stuff from island to island. It might be two or more Christmases before things get wrapped up out here."

"What's happened to your optimism?" the captain asked his older brother.

"Six months in this war zone is enough to give anyone pessimism," Billy answered.

The *Bennett* had been in the Southwest Pacific for seven months after leaving North Africa. With its sleeping racks, installed in Alexandria to accommodate wounded Australian soldiers, the Liberty ship had become a modified troop transport, carrying Army and Marine reinforcements to Guadalcanal and to Port Moresby and Milne Bay in New Guinea. It was among the ships that, last December, took elements of a Marine division to Australia for a well-deserved rest. The leathernecks were the first to hit the beaches at Guadalcanal and were exhausted after four months of brave, bitter fighting with the enemy and equally tough battles with the scorching heat, dysentery, malaria and dengue. With scorpions, tree-leeches, spiders, mosquitoes, lizards and jungle ants that picked clean the corpses of friend and foe alike. With the stench of putrefying flesh so overpowering that at times they had to fight in gas masks.

"By the way, Sparks, does the radio say what the Allies plan to do now that they control Africa?" the captain asked.

"It's no secret," the radio operator said. "They're planning to invade Italy."

12 June 1943

1100 HOURS
Berlin

Lieutenant Commander Barnschmidt was relieved. Ever since his recall to Germany last November he had sat uncomfortably at a desk in the Naval Plans Department writing memos to convince Hitler that the Navy needed more submarines. The Fuhrer had slowed their production after last year when 30 U-boats came off the ways each month and the sub fleet totalled more than 300. Germany had only 46 operational submarines at the outbreak of war and Hitler was overjoyed with the production of the undersea machines. He didn't see the need for more of them. What he wanted was more tanks.

Barnschmidt remembered the anger of Admiral Karl Donitz when he reported to the new commander-in-chief of the German Navy. Hitler had appointed Donitz after dismissing Grand Admiral Raeder following the dismal performance of two of his prized naval ships in attacking an Allied convoy off the coast of Norway. Despite the promotion, Donitz was furious. He paced back and forth in his office, spouting obsenities about the "deranged moustached corporal."

"We're losing the battle of the Atlantic!" Admiral Donitz had said. "We had them on the run, sinking hundreds of thousands of tons, millions of tons, of Allied shipping. Our U-boats have sunk eight hundred and eighty-seven of their ships so far this year, with more than four million tons. The United States is building these new Liberty ships faster than we can sink them. With their Navy's new radar that can seek us out on the surface, and with their sonar and asdic that can find us submerged, we're losing twenty and more a month. We can't afford those losses and he's not building them fast enough to keep us even. We need more boats now!"

Hitler scoffed at the idea every time Donitz brought it up earlier in the year. More tanks were needed in Africa and on the Russian front, he said, pointing out that tanks can be built faster than submarines. Besides, Germany would need them for the invasion of England.

"The damn fool can't even see what's happening on the map! We're suffering losses at every turn. We must go back on the attack! We can't let this idiot continue to influence our proud naval operations. Did you know, Barnschmidt, that he wanted glorious battleships and, when he got them, he was afraid to let them go out and do battle with the enemy?"

Barnschmidt nodded.

"One of them, the *Tirpitz*, is holed up in a fjord in Norway and he won't let me take it out! Idiot! Screaming idiot!"

He sat down and looked at his favorite sub commander more calmly.

"Barnschmidt, only one third of our boats are operational at any one time. That means one hundred are always laid up in some port. You and I know that one hundred boats can do more damage than all the battleships and cruisers he could build. With three hundred operational boats, we could completely sever England's lifeline. This war could be over in no time, even with America in it! Your job, Barnschmidt, is to convince him of our need for that extra one hundred right now. He'll listen to you. You're our most capable boat commander with more kills than any other."

Hitler hadn't listened until yesterday. The battle was lost in Africa. His army had been defeated at Stalingrad and things were not going well on the rest of the eastern front. The Allies, he was sure, were planning to invade Italy. He became more and more concerned about the large convoys reaching England and the mounting losses of his once nearly invincible U-boat fleet. That fleet had sunk only three hundred and fourteen ships in the first five months of this year. It had suffered half that many losses.

Hitler gave the order to increase production at the Krupp shipyard in Kiel.

"We'll need to float thirty subs per month, more if possible!" he ordered.

This morning Admiral Donitz gave Barnschmidt three rewards. The Knight's Cross, promotion to full Commander and leader of all wolfpacks in the Atlantic.

"I want to renew my wolfpack strategy to bring England to its knees," he said. "You'll be happy to know I've recalled your old boat, U-Eighty-four-B. It's at its berth in Wilhelmshaven with most of your old crew still aboard."

13 June 1943

0830 HOURS
In the Eastern Atlantic
The Liberty ship ploughed through the eight-foot waves, rolling viciously, twelve hours out of Southampton, England, and headed for Philadelphia. The *S. S. Elihu Nicholson* rode high in the water, her holds empty, bunkers loaded with oil. She was not in convoy and was on her fourth Atlantic crossing following repairs after her nearly disastrous run to Murmansk last year.

Boatswain Jim Davis was on the bridge going over with Second Mate Slim Stevens the work that had to be done en route. Their last cargo, fighter planes chained to the deck with leaking grease forming large puddles under each one, had taken a toll of the deck paint.

"It's seeped through the paint and we've a lot of chipping to do," Jim said.

"From what I've heard about you from your son, Billy, that's something you can get the crew to do in a couple of hours," Slim said.

"Billy always was one to exaggerate," Jim said modestly.

"He spoke a lot about you on our run to Murmansk. That was some trip. I wouldn't want to do another. Did he tell you about it?"

"Not much. He may exaggerate, but he's not a talkative one. From what little he told me, though, I understand you were something of a hero."

Slim blushed.

"Did he call me that?"

"Yes. He said you were a third mate then and you had the guts to tell the Russians to shove a Liberty ship up their butt."

"Well, I didn't quite say that. I wouldn't waste a Liberty on those damn Commies."

"But you did tell them off?"

"Someone had to, Boats. What's Billy doing now?"

"My other son talked him into signing on his ship, the *Andrew Bennett*."

"Talked him into signing on his ship? Your other son a captain?

"He got his master's license a year ago February."

"That's really something! One son a captain, the other a chief engineer. You've got to be proud."

Jim puffed out his chest.

0900 HOURS
Aboard the U-84-B
"We have our first target!" the young exec said excitedly to Commander Barnschmidt. "Look!" He pointed to the stern of the Liberty ship dead ahead.

"Already?" the surprised captain said from the boat's cigarette bridge. "We're but a few hours out of Wilhelmshaven."

"You have luck, sir. I've always said that. We only got two ships in the seven months you've been ashore."

"We may be in a hurry to join the wolfpack off the Azores, but I feel lucky," Barnschmidt said. "We'll stay on the surface, race up to her and fire a couple of torpedoes."

"In broad daylight, sir? Admiral Donitz has instructed that we only attack on the surface at night."

"The admiral isn't here," Barnschmidt chuckled.

"Suppose they spot us?"

"They may, but we'll get our fish off and then submerge."

0945 HOURS
Aboard the S . S. Elihu Nicholson
"Submarine about fifteen thousand yards astern!" the crow's nest lookout called. "She's on the surface!"

General quarters sounded.

Adrenalin pumping, Boatswain Davis ran to his station on the starboard side and removed the canvas cover to the motorized lifeboat.

"Not again!" he said, remembering the terror when the S. S. Terrapin had been torpedoed off America's East Coast.

Navy gunners in the aft gun tub removed the shroud to the five-inch gun.

"Let's go!" one of them shouted. "She's in our range! Let's kick some German butts!"

1015 HOURS
Aboard the U-84-B
The submarine caught up to the Liberty and was parallel to its starboard side.

"Load torpedoes!" Barnschmidt ordered.

"Torpedoes ready!"
"Fire one!"
"Torpedo los!"
Barnschmidt already felt the joy of victory as the torpedo headed for its target.
"Fire two!"

1016 HOURS
Aboard the S. S. Elihu Nicholson
"Bridge! Bridge!" the lookout called. "Two torpedoes off the starboard stern, five o'clock, about nine thousand yards!"

With his binoculars, the second mate could see the fast-running wakes of the metal fish heading at an angle. Their path would hit the *Nicholson* in a little less than a minute.

"Hard right!" Slim ordered.

The helmsman turned the wheel starboard.

Both torpedoes missed, twenty feet off the stern, and would run aimlessly until their motors stopped and they dropped uselessly to the ocean bottom.

"Damn," swore the chief gunner at the aft five-inch gun. "I had her dead in my sights when we made that turn."

He swiveled the gun back toward the sub.

1018 HOURS
Aboard the U-84-B
Commander Barnschmidt saw the belch of flame from the Liberty's aft gun just as he ordered the firing of two more torpedoes. The five-inch shell hit the water only ten feet off the bow, throwing up a huge geyser and rocking the boat.

"Dive! Dive!" he shouted.

His deck crew and exec scrambled toward the hatch. He mounted the railing and took hold of the lanyard, stopping to take a last look at the Liberty. One torpedo exploded near the bow, tearing a hole at the water line. The other missed.

"Damnit!" he shouted.

A second shell whistled in from the *Nicholson*'s aft gun, creasing the sub's bow.

"Hold her on the surface!" he countermanded his earlier order. "We've been hit!"

1019 HOURS
At the Nicholson's Bow
Jim quickly assessed the damage.

"There's a twelve-foot hole at the waterline!" he called to the captain. "We're taking in water, but we can close the watertight doors and start the pumps. She'll hold if we slow down a bit."

1021 HOURS
Aboard the U-84-B
"There's a two-foot opening in her skin, all the way through, five feet from the bow," the exec told Barnschmidt. "Luckily, it's above the waterline, but we can't take her under."

The captain grunted, looked at the Liberty and at the huge hole in her bow. His deck gun didn't have the range to reach her.

"She's hurt, too," he muttered, "but she can finish us off as long as we're in range of her five-inch gun."

Continuing the attack is futile, he thought. *We might be able to get off a torpedo or two, but if we don't sink her there'll be no escape from her guns. We can't submerge.*

"Let's get the hell out of here!"

1023 HOURS
Aboard the S. S. Elihu Nicholson
Jim was the first to see the sub turn tail and pick up speed.

"Look! She's running away!" he shouted to the second mate. "We must have done a lot of damage."

"She apparently can't submerge but, even hurt, she can outrun us on the surface," Slim said. "She's out of range already."

"I wish we could go after her," Jim said. "It's not often a Liberty ship gets a chance to sink a sub."

He didn't know it, but the killer of the *S. S. Terrapin* was getting away.

14 June 1943

0500 HOURS
Aboard the S. S. Elihu Nicholson
Slowly, peacefully, the *Nicholson* limped to Southampton.

The captain had ordered a stop to the erratic zig-zagging to prevent further damage from water pressure. With the gaping twelve-foot hole in the bow, she could make just five knots, top speed. The crew, however, would have gladly rowed the lady all the way to the English port. Mile by mile, they nursed her there, quartering through the soft rolling waves to avoid putting too much strain on the hull. They were becoming more proud of this ship. Although she was slow, she was handling better than the crew had seen since the day she was launched.

"Must know she's hurt," Jim told the second mate as they stood looking out a wheelhouse porthole on the starboard side. "She's taking better care of herself."

0510 HOURS
Aboard the U-84-B
Commander Barnschmidt stood alone on the cigarette bridge, his hands clasped behind his back, his eyes staring blankly at the horizon. He was embarrassed. Depressed.

After his early successes in sinking American and other merchant ships, heading to the port of Brest, in Nazi-occupied France, with a wounded sub was the last thing he expected to be doing on his thirtieth birthday.

1800 HOURS
Southampton, England
"In a way, it's lucky your ship was hit," the Navy commander said, surveying the damage to the *S. S. Elihu Nicholson.*

"Luck?" Boatswain Davis asked curiously.

"Yes, for us. It won't take but a day to patch up that hole and ---"

"That fast?" Second Mate Stevens interrupted.

"Our shipfitters have repairs down to a science," the commander said proudly. "They'll slap on a piece of steel, put some rivets in, paint it and she'll be as good as new. Then, as I told your captain, you're heading to Oran. We're loading up for another invasion and we need every ship."

"Where we hitting this time?" Jim asked.

"Can't say right now, but I'm sure you can guess."

The boatswain thought a moment. He looked questioningly at Slim. The mate pointed to his boots.

"Well, if it's Oran we're sure not going to make the cross-channel invasion everyone's been hollering for," Jim guessed. "I suspect it'll be Italy."

"Close, very close," the commander said, smiling.

"When will we leave?"

"A convoy's going out tomorrow night. I want this ship in it."

"Empty?" Jim asked.

"Empty. You'll load up in Oran."

"We've got another problem, sir."

"What's that?"

"One of our A. B.s has some kind of infection or something," Jim said. "He's been running a fever since we pulled out of here two days ago. One hundred and four degrees. Came on suddenly. The purser can't bring it down so I imagine he's making arrangements to put the lad in a hospital. If we're leaving that soon, he probably won't get back. I hate to go into an invasion with a short deck crew. You got any merchant seamen floating around this port, Commander?"

"I don't know, but I'll have my staff take a look around. If we find one, we'll ship him to you right away."

"Thanks," Jim said. "We'll need a full crew if we're going to be part of an invasion force."

1910 HOURS
Brest, France

"Good thing you came back when you did," the port director told Commander Barnschmidt. "Admiral Donitz has been trying to reach you by radio all night. Haven't you heard any of his calls?"

"No," a surprised Barnschmidt answered. "Our radio's been silent."

"We better take a look at that, too. It'll take only two, three days to patch up that hole and we can check out, can fix your radio in that time."

"Thanks."

The port director suggested gently that the sub commander telephone the admiral at his new headquarters in Paris.

"He's moved there because of the Allied bombings all over Germany," the man explained. "Said he wanted some peace to do his planning. He sure didn't seem peaceful when he was trying to reach you."

2030 HOURS
Paris, France

"Where've you been?" the commander-in-chief of the Germany Navy demanded of Barnschmidt when the two were connected by telephone. "I've radioed you personally five times during the night."

"Something's wrong with our radio," Barnschmidt said. "they're fixing it now."

He said nothing about the shell hole in his boat. That could come later.

"It's just as well," Donitz said more calmly, apparently unconcerned about the radio. "I'm calling you off that patrol."

Barnschmidt was stunned.

"What? You just sent me out two days ago! Have I done something wrong?"

He was afraid the admiral had already heard about his damaging experience with the Liberty ship. The man kept track of every ship and boat in the German navy with colored pins stuck into a huge world map on his office wall. Barnschmidt was sure that map had moved with him to Paris.

"Not with you, Commander. We've intercepted a number of Allied messages and we've received dozens of reports from our agents in Spain and North Africa. Yes, we still have agents there. The British and Americans are cooking up something. Scores of ships have been flooding daily through the Strait of Gibraltar in the last few days. None are coming out. I've dispatched some boats there to cut them off before entering."

So, I'm to take my boat down there to sink ships before they enter the strait, Barnschmidt thought.

"We think they're building up a force to invade Italy, most likely Sicily. For once, the Fuhrer is listening to us. He's sending more planes down there. The Luftwaffe has eight hundred in that theatre already. He's also diverting some divisions from the eastern front."

We're losing there anyway.

"We must build up our forces there," the admiral continued slowly. "We have thirty thousand men on Sicily, including the crack Hermann Goring Division. The Italians have two hundred thousand troops. Hitler has agreed to send twenty thousand paratroops. That should help us. If the Italians fight, we can hold off any invasion."

Don't bet on it.

"I can't do much about our naval presence. We have some surface ships, but the Allies have unquestioned naval superiority. The Italians have a few ships in the Adriatic Sea. Four battleships, six cruisers, about thirty destroyers and some subs. They'll be of help if the Allies do invade Sicily or any place in Italy and if the Italians will come out and fight."

Their army didn't fight much in North Africa.

"The only naval activity we have in the Med is with our U-boats. That's where I'm counting on you, Barnschmidt."

He's coming to the point.

"I'm reassigning you to that fleet, Commander."

Oh, no!

"You're to report to our base at La Spezia. The Luftwaffe will fly you there. Tonight!"

Leave U-Eighty-four-B?

"I'm reading your mind, Barnschmidt. I know you want to stay with your boat, but there's no way to get both of you in there. I need wily and bold men like you for this operation. You're being assigned another boat. The U-Three-Six-One. It has sophisticated listening equipment you'll be happy about. You can, I'm sure, Commander, wreak some havoc on what the Allies are planning."

Havoc? It's suicide.

"It is a difficult assignment, Barnschmidt. Dangerous, in fact, but you've always accepted dangerous tasks. Will you accept this?

It's up to me now?

"Yes, sir," Barnschmidt said, trying to sound enthusiastic.

When they hung up, Barnschmidt collapsed in a chair. He felt he was going into a huge fish bowl. The only way out was blocked by a big rock.

21 June 1943

1400 HOURS
The Port of Oran

Jim eyed the able-bodied seaman warily. The man had been brought to the S. S. *Elihu Nicholson* by two military police to be interviewed for the vacancy in the deck gang. His handcuffs were removed and the M. P.'s left the two alone in the crew mess.

"Let me see your papers," Jim said.

A. B. Howard Robinson reached into his shirt pocket.

"Yes, sir," he said tamely, handing a crumpled piece of paper to the boatswain.

"You got your A. B. ticket in thirty-five?" Jim asked, studying the paper.

"Yes, sir. I first sailed in thirty-two."

Jim handed back the paper.

"Looks in order. How long have you been in the stockade?"

"About . . about seven months, sir."

"What'd you do?"

"Nothing to deserve all this, sir," Robinson answered meekly. "I had a misunderstanding with the bo's'n on my last ship. He called me a name and, dumb me, I hit'im. It was a stupid thing to do, sir, but I don't like being called a sonofabitch."

"That's all?"

"That was enough for the captain to have me locked up. I don't think he liked me, sir, 'tho I don't know why. I do my job and I'm pretty good at it."

"You're sure? You only hit the bo's'n once?"

"Yes, sir. I hit'im only once. Didn't even knock him down and he went and reported me to the captain."

"What was the argument about?"

"Nothing big, sir. He asked me to pull another eight hours after I already was up for thirty hours," Robinson lied. "The invasion, you know. We were in on the invasion here and the fighting was fierce. Shells all around us. I was beat. So was everyone else. Most of the crew had already sacked out. I was going to bed when he stopped me at my foc'sle and told me I had to work another eight. I told him no. Union rules don't permit us to work all that long."

"Union rules?" Jim asked flabbergasted. "They don't apply in combat."

"I realize that now, sir," Robinson said calmly. "I just told him that to get him off my back and he called me that dirty name. I punched him without thinking. Like I said, not very smart of me."

Jim was puzzled. Fistfights occasionally broke out on merchant ships and, as long as no one was seriously hurt, the offenders were only reprimanded. Or told to fight it out with boxing gloves. Still, hitting a boatswain is a serious breach of shipboard discipline.

This fellow seems contrite enough. Maybe he's learned a lesson after seven months in an Army stockade. We need another A. B. for a full crew complement, he seems qualified and his offense probably don't justify keeping him behind bars.

"Okay," he finally said. "We'll sign you on. But I warn you. I'm in fairly good shape and I hit back."

"Oh, thank you, sir!" Robinson said, jumping up and grabbing Jim's hand. "I ain't never gonna hit anyone again!"

Jim shook himself loose of the pumping hand.

"By the way," he said, "what was the name of your last ship?"

"Sorry, sir, you know we're not supposed to name our ships in this war," the A. B. said smiling. "It might give comfort to our enemies."

Remembering how bad he felt when he gave the submarine commander the name of the *Terrapin*, Jim did not press the issue.

30 June 1943

0200 HOURS
Nassau Bay, New Guinea

There was none of the usual horseplay among the 307 soldiers silently lining the rails of the *S. S. Andrew Bennett*, watching the yellow flashes of the cruiser's guns and the long red arcs of the shells heading for the beach through heavy rain. They were quiet, subdued, some praying, others awed by the silhouetted panorama surrounding the ship. They had readied themselves for the pre-dawn landing, their rifles cleaned, bayonets sharpened, packs with shaving gear and rations checked for the last time. The scene was repeated on other troop transports in the armada of Navy and merchant ships sitting off the northeast coast of New Guinea.

General MacArthur was on the offensive, seeking another foothold on that strategic island from which American forces could join up with the Australians to retake the coastal town of Lae, 60 miles away. The embattled Australians, with limited resources and fighting against greater numbers, were barely hanging on to their ramparts on the island, next to Greenland the largest in the world. Lae's airfield, built by the Japanese after taking the town more than a year ago, was sorely needed for American fighters in the impending battle to retake the huge air-and-sea base at Rabaul in New Britain, in the middle of the 900-mile Solomon Islands chain. The fighters were needed to support Allied bombers hitting Rabaul and to give cover for planned troop landings there.

MacArthur was already one leg up on his "I shall return" promise made in March 1942 shortly after his flight from beleaguered Correigidor in the Philippines. The first American offensive of the Pacific War began on 7 August 1942, with the landings at Guadalcanal and Tulagi, islands now secure after months of bitter fighting with an enemy that preferred death to eternal dishonor.

"This stinking rain will hamper the invasion," Captain Davis told his chief mate as the two watched the unfolding drama from the flying bridge.

The downpour had gotten heavier in the past hour.

"It's been a blessing 'til now," Speer said. "The low-scudding clouds and rain have shielded us from Jap eyes ashore."

"The men seem prepared, though," the captain said. "I've been listening to the lectures from their officers about their enemy. Some of them have already seen combat and the stories they tell about the Japanese are hair-raising. Tying themselves in trees and sniping at our boys after they've advanced into the jungle away from the beach. Holing up in pillboxes and caves where the only way to get them out is to burn them alive with flame-throwers."

"How can our troops really be prepared to meet a fanatic enemy that has no value for life?"

"They'll make it," Frank said. "Americans have a way of facing up to any challenge."

A voice blaring over a bullhorn interrupted the conversation. "Land the landing force!"

Operation Cartwheel was finally underway.

Nervous and scared, the soldiers climbed over the rails and clamored down the rope nets to landing craft below, some of them stepping on the fingers of the men below them and cursing as their own fingers were squashed by the heavy combat boots of men above. Their packs were heavier than many had thought a few minutes ago. A rifle clanged against a helmet.

"Hang on to your rifles!" the voice called over the bullhorn. "You're gonna need them!"

Grips were tightened on the rifles. One helmet fell to the water.

"And your helmets, damnit!"

The nervous men jumped from the nets to the boats, some falling on top of others.

"I don't envy them," Speer whispered. "Some won't come back."

The amphibious LCPs (Landing Craft, Personnel), with the soldiers crouching behind the gunwales, formed a line and sped to the shore, followed by LCMs (Landing Craft, Mechanized) and LCTs (Landing Craft, Tank), also loaded with men and carrying tanks, jeeps, trucks and bulldozers.

"God speed," Captain Davis said, tears falling down his cheeks and feeling as though he was losing part of his family.

The solders had been aboard for ten days and he had watched them playing high-stakes poker in the holds, singing such favorites as *Chattanooga Choo-Choo* and *Anything Goes*, reading the Bible, writing letters back home and griping about the food ladled into their tins by perspiring cooks on the foredeck.

Captain Davis thought about Lynne, Frank, Jr. and Wendy, safe at home.

These men are risking their lives to protect them.

"God speed," he said again.

0300 HOURS
On the Beach
The rain, wind and high surf swamped some of the first landing craft. Their rifles and ammunition wet, the soldiers swam or waded ashore. Grounded LCMs tried to work free from soggy sand. The grinding sounds carried far in the darkness.

"Tanks! They're coming at us!" a nervous and mistaken Japanese soldier shouted to his commander.

The tanks were not yet on the beach. They were in the next wave of landing craft struggling to make it through the twelve-foot surf. The Japanese ran into the jungle while the Americans built up their beachhead.

0600 HOURS
Aboard the S. S. Andrew Bennett
"That's the last of them," Chief Mate Speer said as an LVT

(Landing Vehicle, Tracked) was lowered to the blue bay water. "Now let's get out of here and go home!"

"We have to wait for orders," Captain Davis said, "and I don't think they'll say 'go home.' We've become a fixture in the Southwest Pacific. I haven't figured out why the Army brass likes this ship so much."

"Maybe it's the Navy," his brother, Billy, chimed in.

"They should want us the hell out of here," Frank said. "Seems like we always need repairs when we come into a port. Last time it was a set screw that backed out and was digging a trench in the casting of the steering system."

"The time before that our compass was twenty degrees off," the mate complained.

"There's a pox on this ship for sure," Frank sighed. "Maybe they've heard about Bib's ghost and don't want us to take it back to the states. I'm beginning to believe that."

"What? That there's a ghost aboard?" Billy asked.

"No. That the brass thinks there is."

1 July 1943

1000 HOURS
On the Beach
Amid mortar fire and exploding grenades, the American troops moved inland and linked up with cocky Australians who had come down from the surrounding mountains after stoutly defending, for more than a year, their positions surrounding Wau, twenty-five miles from the coast. Together, the Allies began a push toward Lae.

1100 HOURS
Aboard the S. S. Andrew Bennett
The orders were crisp:

Standby to take on prisoners!

"If that don't beat all!" Chief Mate Speer said. "We've been a hospital ship, a troopship and now a prison ship! What more can we be, Frank?"

"They can put us back to carrying only cargo," Captain Davis answered.

"I'd like that," the mate said. "We'd get home every now and then."

1400 HOURS
On the Beach
The single file line moved slowly as the Japanese prisoners, many naked, boarded the barge that would take them to the *Bennett*. Australian soldiers, wearing short-sleeve shirts, shorts and traditional felt hat, prodded them with bayonets. There were 62 Japs and five Diggers guarding them. Nervous American soldiers stood off, watching, wearing the new leopard-spot jungle camouflage uniform, their M-1 rifles ready, just in case.

"We didn't take many prisoners," the Aussie sergeant told the bargemaster. "Their buddies preferred to die."

A jeep drove up. Two kimono-clad women, at gunpoint, got out and joined the end of the line.

"Comfort women," the Aussie explained. "Prostitutes. They're found in every Japanese camp. To improve morale. Sure wish we had some women with us. It's been lonely here."

He smiled at the women. They didn't smile back.

1430 HOURS
Aboard the S. S. Andrew Bennett
The eyes of the prisoners were vacant as they climbed over the ship's rails and headed for the number two hold under the watchful eyes of their Australian guards and the ship's crew.

"They don't look so invincible," Chief Mate Speer observed. "They look half-starved."

Rib cages showing, frightened and forlorn, many suffered the ravages of dysentery, scarlet fever, malaria and dengue. Some wore ill-fitting bandages, covered with dried blood, over festering wounds. A few limped with tree limbs as crutches.

"Is this the enemy we're fighting?" the mate asked.

"They don't look so good now, but they're bloody fighters, Yank," the sergeant said. "Sneaky bastards. They stack up the bodies of their dead like we do sandbags to protect our positions. Some of them lie down with their dead and wounded and wait for our boys to pass. Then they shoot or knife them in the back. We've taken to bayoneting every body, dead or not. We should of stuck these and saved ourselves this trouble, but they waved the white flag and now we're ordered to take them home to Australia. They're not fit to breathe our air!"

He fingered his bayonet.

Behind him, the comfort women were helped over the rails.

"Where do we put these sluts?" the guard asked, pointing a finger at the women. "We don't want them in the hold with the men."

"Why not?" the mate asked.

"Because they'll ply their trade there."

"Even now?"

"Sure, Yank, even now," the Aussie said. "They're supposed to give comfort and these bastards need it now. Wouldn't you?"

"Put 'em in the sickbay," the mate said. "They can't do it there."

"Maybe," the guard smiled, pushing the women aft.

1700 HOURS
On the Bennett's Bridge
The Army major boarded the *Bennett* with last-minute instructions.

"You'll leave in an hour and you'll go it alone," he told Captain Davis. "We can't spare escorts."

"Cargo not valuable enough?" Frank said, speaking of the prisoners and not expecting an answer.

"Be careful, Captain. You'll have good weather all the way to Brisbane. No storms forecast, but the Jap navy is in force around these waters. There already have been a couple of sea battles and their submarines are crawling all over. Keep an eye out for their planes, too."

"Thanks," Frank said. "We'll put on extra lookouts."

"If I were you I'd do more than that."

"What?"

"Pray."

2 July 1943

0530 HOURS
In the Bennett's Galley
The shadowy figure appeared out of nowhere and stood only a few feet from the second cook and baker, swinging an arm in a motion indicating Bib should turn around and walk back out of the galley.

"Ah ain't goin' back," the cook said. "This is ma galley. Yo' get out of here!"

The figure pointed to the aft bulkhead and again signalled a turnaround.

"Yo' means the ship should go back?"

The figure shook its head up and down.

"Somethin's gonna happen?"

The figure shook its head again, then disappeared.

"Ah'll go tell the captain," Bib said, scared.

1800 HOURS
In the Coral Sea

The blue water of the Coral Sea stretched in front of the *Bennett* as the Liberty steamed ponderously at nine knots, zig-zagging and rolling lazily, curving around the eastern tip of New Guinea and charted for Brisbane, Australia. The setting sun was a brilliant orange, low on the horizon off to the west, bleeding pale hues on rows and rows of tiny whitecapped waves. A painted ocean. Ordinary Seaman Durante stood lookout on the bow, basking in the loving relationship a man has with the sea in much the same way he embraces the tender loving of a woman ashore.

"Lord, it's beautiful!" Tony said aloud. "Who'd know there's a war on?"

Only the Japanese prisoners squatting on the foredeck and the captain's warnings to keep a sharp lookout for enemy submarines and planes were reminders that the ship was in a war zone. Although he had been sailing on it for months, he was still in awe at the spell cast by the Pacific Ocean. He remembered from school that the ocean covered one-third of the Earth's surface. Even when he had studied it on the twelve-inch world globe in the bedroom of his home, he could not fully visualize its size. He could see the North and South American continents, so big, and Africa and Europe and Asia, even bigger, and other oceans. Here and now, looking at this sea within the ocean from the bow of his ship, he was overwhelmed by its sheer immensity. Water in every direction as far as he could see.

How big can the Pacific be and how many days would it take to completely cross it in a ship that travels at only nine knots?

The question itself was so big his young mind couldn't fathom an answer. Tony loved to stand alone on the bow to fill his lungs with the clean, salty air and to marvel at the blue water. He felt the strain, though, of searching for signs of an enemy lurking below the surface, a forced fear that took away some of the pleasure. Despite it, he still enjoyed the sea's allure. He lit a cigarette, not worrying about showing a flame for the sun was still high in the sky and there was no danger of an enemy seeing the sparky flash. He took a deep drag and momentarily closed his eyes.

So peaceful, he thought. *The whole world should know this peace.*

He jumped up with a start, the cigarette burning his fingers, and was briefly disoriented. He must have dozed. Remembering his duty, he scanned the water around the ship and thought he saw a flashing movement far out to starboard. He picked up his binoculars to magnify the movement. The white ribbon appeared, disappeared, and showed up again, heading toward the ship.

"Torpedo!" he screamed into the telephone to the bridge, scared and uncertain what next to say.

He had never seen a torpedo's wake, but he knew he had to report its position. *Tell the bridge where the damn thing is!* he scolded himself.

"Torpedo! Torpedo off the . . Torpedo two points off the starboard bow! About seven thousand yards!"

On the bridge, Chief Mate Speer sounded the call to battle stations and ordered "Hard left!" He hoped the turn would be fast enough to dodge the lethal missile. His eyes searched the water to starboard. He could see nothing.

"Where away?" he shouted into the telephone.

Durante's eyes tried to fasten on the mysterious white foam as it disappeared for a few seconds, then bobbed up again.

"Where away?" the mate demanded again, tormented that he could not see the incoming danger.

"Heading straight for us! Five thousand yards now, bearing five points off the bow!" the seaman called back, frightened. "It's gone! I don't see it any more!"

His eyes strained to see the torpedo.

"There! It's back! Three thousand yards!"

Speer's eyes caught a momentary flash of white to starboard. It disappeared before he could focus his binoculars.

"Keep that rudder hard left!" he ordered the helmsman.

"Far as I can turn it," Able-Bodied Seaman Jones

responded calmly. "If I hold it much longer, we'll come about in a complete circle."

"Five hundred yards!" Durante yelled, his voice higher pitched. "It's gonna hit the stern!"

The officers and seamen on the bridge braced themselves. So did the Navy gunners and their ammunition loaders in the guntubs. The nervous black gang in the engine room, standing at their stations below the water line, held tightly to pipes and stanchions, praying the torpedo would miss or be a dud. Eight seconds passed. Ten. Twenty. There was no thud, no explosion.

"I don't see it any more," Durante said more calmly.

"Be alert," Captain Davis ordered. He had raced to the flying bridge at the clamoring bell of general quarters. He could not see any streaking white flashes in the water headed their way or traveling away from them, nor could he see any sign of a periscope.

"You may have turned her quick enough," he said to Speer. "That was some maneuver. I thought you said she responds slowly."

"Sometimes," the chief mate said. "Maybe she knew she was in danger and worked fast to get out of the way."

"Submarines don't fire just one torpedo," the captain said, perplexed, his eyes still searching the water's surface. "They get off two, quickly, then fire more if they miss with the first salvo. Maybe this guy's conservative. Keep a good lookout for more torpedoes. On all sides. Our turn was fast enough he may be on our port right now."

He asked the engine room for more steam to enable the ship to reach its maximum speed of eleven knots. He knew their only chance to lengthen the odds against a submerged submarine getting an accurate sighting to unleash another torpedo would be to push the boilers to their fullest and increase the frequency of erotic zigzagging. A sub could outrace them on the surface, but beneath the waves it could only do about eight knots. There was no sub on the surface; it had to be submerged.

That gives us a momentary advantage, he told himself as he scanned the water far out, close in.

"Maybe . . " he started when he heard the chief mate laughing.

"I don't believe it!" Speer howled. "We've got a playful porpoise!"

He pointed.

"Look! Down there!"

The sea mammal glided about six feet from the ship, jumping in and out of the water, now and then darting to touch its nose against the steel hull.

"A goddamn porpoise!" the mate roared.

The gunners in their tubs and seamen on bridge lookout joined his laughter. So did some of the Japanese prisoners.

"Stand down from G. Q.," the mate ordered. "Jones, continue our chartered course and let's give that bow lookout our Purple Porpoise Award."

"No," Captain Davis said reproachfully. "He'll get enough grief from the crew. Let's not make it worse with some sorrowful joke from the bridge."

He felt empathy for the man on the bow, left the bridge and walked there.

"Sharp eyes, Durante," he said kindly. "You'll take a lot of ribbing from the crew, but thank God you can see something in this fading light. Many lookouts can't. You did the right thing."

"No, it was stupid!" Durante protested. "Calling a porpoise a torpedo. Stupid! I've seen porpoises before. I should have known better."

He was ashamed about his momentary nap, but didn't dare tell the captain.

"Not stupid," Captain Davis said, his tone reassuring. "Porpoises often make tracks that look like a torpedo's wake. I understand this kind of false alarm happens often out here. You were unlucky enough to be the first to call it on this trip. Believe me, there will be others."

He put a hand on Durante's left shoulder.

"Best you call out any time you see any streak or object in the water, whether you're sure or not. It could be a torpedo, a real one. Better safe than sorry, son. If that had been a real one, we could all be dead now. What happened tonight will keep the other lookouts on their toes from now on."

The captain wanted to say more, to make the seaman talk, for that was what Durante needed.

Tony wasn't so sure. He bent his head and cried.

One of the prisoners saw the tears and laughed, pointing to the seaman and jabbering in the strange tongue no one aboard could understand. An Australian guard warned him to stop laughing. The man laughed harder.

"Yellow slime!" the Aussie shouted, plunging his bayonet into the man's stomach. Its point stuck out of the back. He lifted the struggling and screaming Jap like a sack of potatoes and wiped the bayonet across the rail. The man fell off, plunging downward, a blood-curdling scream cut off when he hit the water.

"Did you see that?" an astonished Jones called to the chief mate.

"I did, but I wish I hadn't," the mate said.

"That's cruel," Jones said. "I thought the Japs are the only ones who treat prisoners of war like that. They and the Germans."

"The Australians have been fighting a lot longer than we have and I suppose they've seen a lot of bizarre things happen to their comrades. Men do some strange things in war they wouldn't do at home."

As tough as he was, Jones hoped he would never do anything like that. It was plain murder.

3 July 1943

0600 HOURS
Aboard the S. S. Andrew Bennett

"My God, that's a Jap Zero bearing one seven zero!" Seaman Third Class "Rabbit" Ellard shouted as he studied the horizon with his binoculars. "He's coming in fast!"

He called the bridge, his voice filled with suppressed terror. General quarters sounded. The Armed Guard scrambled to their gun tubs. Merchant seamen assigned as ammunition loaders followed. Others raced to their fire stations. The Jap prisoners, panicked, ran to the number two hold, some ignoring the rope ladder and jumped in, screaming as they fell.

"This is the real thing, Guns," Captain Davis told Lieutenant Taylor. "Your men ready?"

"We'll know in a few seconds, Captain," the Navy gunnery officer said.

"He's coming straight at us!" Rabbit said. "Fire at will!"

The forward three-inch gun blasted. Black bursts filled the sky eight thousand yards away.

"He's coming through!" Rabbit screamed, swiveling his gun a hair to the right.

The Zero's machine guns spit deadly fire. The forward 20-millimeters hammered back. The plane kept coming.

The bridge twenties opened fire. Bullets from the Jap's machine gun raked the forward deck. Seven prisoners fell, hit by the fire.

"He's killing his own men!" Lieutenant Taylor cried as one bullet hit him in a leg.

The Zero burst into one huge fireball and it fell into the sea a few points off the starboard bow.

"We got him!" Rabbit shouted. "We got him!"

"Another Zeke at three four zero!" roared another gunner. "He's almost on top of us!

The aft five-inch pounded, shaking the ship. The Zero swooped up and the men on the bridge could see the five-hundred-pound bomb released from its undercarriage. Too late. The bomb struck the water off the stern, hurling tons of water across the men in the aft five-inch gun tub. One merchant seaman, an ammunition loader, was washed over the side,

"Man overboard!" the lead gunner shouted.

Number eight 20-millimeter, Hunt's gun, fired into the plane's canopy. A. B. Wilson, his ammunition loader, saw the pilot's face snap back, blood rushing from his forehead.

"You got him!" Wilson shouted.

The plane dove to fifty feet off the water, flames gushing from its engine and trailing smoke. After skimming the water for a mile, it plunged into the sea.

"Nice shooting, Charlie!"

Hunt nodded, took a cigar from his shirt pocket and lit it.

"That's not important," he said. "We've got to find the man who went overboard. And keep our eyes out for any more Zekes."

Purser Tanner ran to the bridge.

"Any casualties?" he asked.

"We've a man overboard," Captain Davis said, troubled. "From the aft five-incher. I've ordered the ship turned around to find him."

"Jesus! Did he have on his lifejacket?"

"I think so. Everyone's to wear a lifejacket at general quarters."

"That's a break if he doesn't panic. Any others?"

"Guns took one in the leg, but he's still standing. Better look at him."

"I'll get him to the hospital," Tanner said, turning away. "Oh, hell! The comfort women are there!"

"Put them in the hold," Chief Mate Speer said. "Some of the Japs also got hit. They'll need comfort now."

0620 HOURS
In the Water
Ordinary Seaman Donald Everingham bobbed in the calm water. It was, thankfully, warm. He was about four miles behind the *Bennett*. He waved his arms, hoping he would be seen and wishing his lifejacket was a bright color instead of gray. Yellow or orange could be seen easier, he was sure. He was not afraid. His lifejacket could keep him afloat for ten hours, maybe longer, before it became too waterlogged to hold him up any longer. He was confident he would be picked up before then. *Take deep breaths*, he told himself, remembering his mother's advice whenever he became excited or upset over a troubling situation at home or in school.

"Deep breaths help calm you," his mother had promised.

He felt something brush the prosthesis of his right leg. *Seaweed?* Another brush, this one stronger. *No, not seaweed.* There was a sharp jab at his right calf and he felt a numbness. Seconds later, there was another knife-like tear at his left thigh.

"Shark!" he screamed.

That was the last thing he remembered as darkness closed his mind.

0900 HOURS
On the Foredeck
After the memorial service on deck for Everingham, Captain Davis met with Chief Mate Speer in the saloon for a late breakfast. He was depressed and picked at his pancakes. The ordinary seaman was the first fatality on the *Bennett* and, somehow, Frank felt the ship would never be quite the same again.

"We've had bad luck ever since we left San Francisco a year and a half ago," he said. "But the crew has held together. Now, I don't know. They're not talking much and there's no excitement about downing the two planes. Bib told me and I'm sure he's told others he saw that damn ghost again just before this happened. He claims it warned that the ship should be turned around. Seems like every time he sees that thing, we run into more trouble."

"You can't believe a ghost is causing all this," Speer chastised. "You don't believe in ghosts. I don't believe in ghosts. There's no ghost on this ship. There's a war going on around us. All around us! That's what's doing it! Not a ghost! Get off it, Captain!"

"You're right. I'm letting Bib's imagination get to me and I'm tired of it. All this talk about a ghost is spreading hysteria among the crew. It's even affecting me."

He took a bite of cold pancake.

"I wonder if there's any more I could have done to save Everingham."

"Don't blame yourself, Frank," the mate said. "You couldn't have acted faster with that second plane coming in. Besides, human lives are the inevitable price of war. You have to learn to take it."

"I'll never accept a death on this ship. When will all this end?" Captain Davis asked, frustrated.

"When God, with our help, stamps out all evil in the world," Speer answered.

It wasn't what the captain wanted to hear. "Then this will go on forever," he said.

6 July 1943

1900 HOURS
Brisbane, Australia
Except for a skeleton crew, the men of the *S. S. Andrew Bennett*, including the Armed Guard in their white uniforms, walked into the Lennons Hotel, glad to have discharged their cargo of prisoners and relieved to have time for relaxation and recreation. They needed it as much as the soldiers and Marines brought to this city for R and R from the islands to the north and the Lennons was where all the action was for the military. Merchant seamen were not excluded as they were from Red Cross Canteens or U. S. O.s. Except for colored people.

"We don' want no niggas in here," a GI snarled in a Southern drawl as the second cook and baker came through the front door.

Gunner's Mate First Class Hunt put a hand on the soldier's shoulder and pushed him down.

"He's with us, Mate," Charlie warned firmly.

The soldier sat quietly. Bib Overall nodded graciously.

"Thas alright, Charlie," he said, "Ah's used to it."

"It's not all right, Bib," Hunt said. "Not here, not any place. We're all in this war together. Right, soldier?"

He poked the GI on the shoulder.

"Right, mate, anything you say."

The GI obviously didn't mean it, but apparently was afraid of the menacing looks from the rest of the *Bennett*'s crew.

Messboy Mitzell walked over to the piano in the corner. It was a baby grand. He tapped a few keys.

"Needs a tuning," he said to no one in particular.

"Yo' play?" Bib asked.

"Some."

"Well, sit down and let's hear somethin'. Ah'll get yo' a drink. Whaddaya want?"

"Oh, a Coke."

"One Coca-Cola comin' up," Overall beamed, heading for the soft drink bar.

Gilbert sat down uneasily, cracked his knuckles a couple of times, tested a few keys and then moved gracefully into Tchaikovsky's *Concerto Number One in B-Flat Minor*. Conversation in the bar slowed. Gilbert closed his eyes, nodded his head every now and then and played on. All talk stopped. No one seemed to move. Gilbert, like the composer, charged to a grandiose finale and a compelling coda that rose to the height of a brilliant bombast. Applause rocked the crowded room.

"Bravo, kid!" a soldier called. "I've never heard Tchaikovsky played as well."

"I never heard whatever you call it played at all," the cook said, handing Gilbert a glass of Coca-Cola. "But it sounded real good. You been playing long?"

"Since I was three," Gilbert answered.

"Know any more?" a Navy man shouted.

"Only concert piano," the boy replied.

"No popular music?" a GI asked. "We wanna sing."

More applause.

"No. I don't know any. But, if I had sheet music I could try," Gilbert promised.

"Find some sheet music," the solder ordered the bartender.

"I do know one song you might be able to sing," Gilbert said hopefully.

"What is it?"

The boy didn't answer, but after the first few chords

almost everyone in the bar had picked up the lyric.

" . . . *where the deer and the antelope play. Where seldom is heard a discouraging word and the skies are not cloudy all day."*

A large group surrounded the piano and, while many of the voices were off key, no one noticed. Or cared. It was a song that reminded them of home.

"More! More!" the group chanted. "Someone give the kid a drink."

"My Coke's fine," Gilbert said.

"Coke?" questioned a boisterous voice. "Spike it someone."

Someone did. With rum. Gilbert took a sip, choked and held his chest as the fiery liquid flowed into his body. "Wow!" he exclaimed. "That's strong!"

"You'll play better!" one of the soldiers encouraged.

"But I can't play any popular music, not without a song sheet. I probably won't be much good at that. My mother wants me to be a concert pianist." He began to play Edward Grieg's *Concerto in A Minor.* The bartender pushed his way through the crowd with a handful of songsheets.

"Take your pick, son," he said.

"I'd rather you pick," Gilbert said, stopping the concerto.

A soldier grabbed the sheets, leafed through a few and pulled one out. "Try this," he said, handing one to the young pianist. *As Time Goes By.*

Gilbert studied the music a few moments, keyed a few chords slowly, shook his head and keyed some more.

"Give me a minute."

His eyes looked up and down and across the sheet. Then, as if he had memorized the notes, he began to play.

"Beautiful," a voice said softly and almost everyone began to sing. Most did not know all the words and hummed.

Three, four, five more songs and they would not let him stop.

"More, more!" they shouted, getting into a jolly fraternal mood. Soldiers, sailors and merchant seamen had their arms around each other's shoulders. It was as if they were in a bar in San Francisco, Dallas, Chicago or Brooklyn. There was, for these moments, no alienation between the military men and the civilian seamen.

"Give the kid another drink!" a voice said and, before

he could object, Gilbert had another rum and Coke thrust at him. He took a long swallow. It went down more smoothly. Some of the men began putting nickels, dimes and quarters into a bowl a soldier had placed on the piano.

2100 HOURS
Still in the Bar
The crowd around the piano began to dwindle.
　"Got to stop," Gilbert pleaded. He had played some of the songs three times.
　"Just one more," a soldier prodded.
　"No. No more," Gilbert protested, standing up. "I feel dizzy."
　Rum and Coke had taken its toll of his balance, his fingers, his mind.
　"That's enough," Bib said, picking up the bowl of money and stuffing the coins in Gilbert's pocket. "The kid's beat. He's got to get some rest."
　He took one of boy's arms and steadied him.
　"Come on, we's goin' back to the ship."
　"I feel woozy," Gilbert complained.
　"It'll pass."
　"I had fun tonight. Never thought playing this kind of music would be so much fun."
　"Good," Bib answered. "But play it only fo' fun. That classical stuff yo' started with is great. Stay with it. Yo'll be a famous pianist some day."
　Gilbert hiccuped and smiled.

7 July 1943

1315 HOURS
Aboard the S. S. Andrew Bennett
Bib waited until Captain Davis had finished desert, fresh apple pie with ice cream, before entering the saloon.
　"Great pie, Bib!" the captain said. "You've outdone yourself this time."
　"Thank yo', suh. Ah couldn' resist the fresh apples in the market asho' an' we's loaded the frige wit' ice cream. There'll be enough fo' the crew fo' two weeks."
　"Excellent!" Frank commended.
　"Excuse me, Captain, suh, but now youse finished

lunch we's need yo' help with a problem."

"Problem? What problem?"

Bib shuffled his feet, then walked closer to the captain's table where his brother, Billy, also sat.

"Suh, we wants to put a piano aboard."

"A piano?" Billy asked quickly. "I've never heard of a piano on a merchant ship."

"There's always a first time, suh. If'n youse had heard Messboy Mitzell play the piano las' night, yo'd want to hear 'im all the time. So the crew, all the crew an' Armed Guard, every last man, chipped in to buy a piano fo' 'im. We's found a small upright one in a church. They's getting a new one. It's goin' to be a surprise."

"Where would we put it?" Captain Davis asked mildly.

"We kinda figgered, suh, the bes' place is right here in yo' saloon. We's already measured an' it can fit right nex' the snack frige. Like ah said, it's a small piano."

Captain Davis was amused.

"How will you keep it from rolling in a heavy sea?"

"Oh, it doesn't have wheels, suh, an' the donkeyman says he can weld some steel bars aroun' the legs to hold it in place."

"Have you also figured when he can play it?"

"Oh, yes, suh," Bib answered without pausing. "Not all officers eat at the same time so's he'll work in the galley from eight to twelve mornin's, then practice an hour durin' lunch, addin' a nice touch fo' that meal. He gets two hours off to nap or do whateva he wants. He goes back to the galley 'til five. Then he plays again fo' the officers durin' the evenin' meal. That way, youse all get to hear 'im."

"You've got this all figured out, haven't you, Bib?," Frank asked. "Suppose I said we can't have a piano on this ship?"

"Oh, we discussed that, suh, an' figgered youse wouldn' refuse. We figgered youse the kind of man who'd like good music durin' dinna."

The other officers chuckled.

"Okay, Bib," Frank smiled. "You've outfoxed me. I guess there's nothing else to figure out. You've got all the answers."

"Not quite, suh. Rememba, the whole crew's involved. The piano cost thirty bucks an' another five fo' tunin'. So, we's still got two problems."

"They are?"

"The crew'd like to hear the boy play, once in awhile."

"Hmmm," Frank mumbled.

The non-licensed crew wasn't allowed in the saloon except to clean it and except at the end of a voyage when they checked through immigration and customs and picked up their pay. The captain looked at the other officers.

"I don't see any real problem if they come in after the evening meal," he offered. "If they're orderly."

The others nodded agreement.

"All right, Bib, that's settled. What's the other problem?"

"Well, suh, the piano's in a cardboard box near the fo'ward paint locka. We's put it there so's yo'all wouldn' see it whiles we waited to talk to yo'. Anyways, it'll be ruined if'n it rains. An' they's callin' fo' rain tonight."

Frank stood and began rolling up his sleeves. "That's easy to solve," he said. "The officers will help move it in right now. On one condition."

"What's that, suh?"

"Mitzell plays a few numbers for us. Tonight."

1720 HOURS
In the Saloon
The sounds of Bach's *Concerto in B Minor* filled the saloon as some of the officers ate dinner. Happy with himself, and beaming, Bib waved a fork like a conductor's baton.

We's bringin' some life back to this morbid ship, he told himself. *Maybe this music'll chase away Major Bennett's ghost.*

8 July 1943

0700 HOURS
Aboard the S. S. Andrew Bennett
"That was some concert last night, John," Captain Davis remarked to Chief Mate Speer over breakfast. The two had become closer in the last several months and had begun calling each other by their given names.

"It was good, but I'm still not used to the idea of a piano on a Liberty ship," the mate answered. "A passenger ship, yes. A merchant ship, I don't know."

"Well, like you said a while back, we're also a passenger ship, carrying troops and prisoners."

"Yeah, but they're not the paying kind." the mate said sourly.

He went to a cupboard, took out the bottle of Dewar's Scotch and brought it back to the table. He filled his coffee mug to the top. No water. No ice.

"Mind if I have some medicine?" he asked.

"Looks like you've got some already. Kind of early in the day, isn't it?"

"Anytime's okay," John said. He took a swallow. "It eases the pain."

"What gives, John? You're more sour today than when I came aboard seventeen months ago. You're not happy about anything. You never go ashore when we pull into a port. Why? Brisbane is a great place and there's plenty of available women. It would do you good to go ashore today and meet one."

"Don't want one."

"I don't understand, John," Frank said. "You were always the ladies man. During our days at the academy you couldn't get enough of them."

"I've had enough now," the chief mate said quickly.

Frank looked a long time at his second in command, asking with his eyes if the man was serious and seeing that Speer was.

"Why?" he asked.

"You sure you want to know?"

"Wouldn't have asked otherwise."

The mate fidgeted with the one-inch fiddlestick at his end of the table, moving it up and down. In rough weather, the sticks were pulled up to provide a protective edge around all mess tables, preventing dishes from sliding off onto the deck. The small sticks worked most of the time.

"Wonder why they call these things fiddlesticks," he mused. "Someone once told me it's because people fiddle around with them like I'm doing now. Think that's true?"

"Stop stalling, John," Frank said patiently.

The mate turned up his mug and half-emptied it, wiping with his sleeve some of the whiskey running out of the corner of his mouth.

"When I was fourteen I dated this goodlooking girl several times," he said slowly. "I thought we had good times, going to the movies, bowling and all, 'til I asked her for a fourth date. Then she told me."

"Told you what?"

"'Girls,' she said, 'want it just as much as boys. You haven't even tried to feel me. You're no fun,' she said. I was heartbroken when she walked away."

Frank was silent.

"I decided right then and there I'd screw every girl I took out, the first night and, you know, it worked. None of them turned me down. Not one."

"Most guys don't have that kind of luck," Frank said. "So why the bitterness today? You always got what you wanted."

"Problem is, Frank, that isn't what I want. I never respected any of them. If they let me do it the first night, they'd let anyone do it. Who wants a steady girlfriend who'll do that?"

"A good point," Frank answered.

"Then I met Mary Jane."

"Mary Jane?"

"Yeah. In Shreveport, while my last ship was being loaded. She was sitting on a bench in a park and her boy was playing in a sandbox. I made a comment about the kid and, before you know it, we were talking. We were still there three hours later. By then, her boy was sleeping on my lap."

"Must've been some conversation."

"She was some woman."

"Guess you felt bad when she had to go home to her husband," Frank volunteered. It was more of a statement, but Frank posed it as a question.

"Her husband died on the *Arizona*."

The *Arizona* was one of the battleships sunk in the Japanese attack on Pearl Harbor.

"Sorry to hear about that. Must've been tough on her."

"It was."

"So, go on. What happened?"

John took another drink.

"I fell in love. For the first time, Frank, I really fell in love," John admitted. "Mary Jane has everything a man wants. Attractive. Not beautiful, beautiful, if you know what I mean. Attractive. Loaded with personality! Serious but with a great sense of humor. We laughed a lot. Sincere. Educated. Smart, but she don't lord it over you, not like most women with college degrees. She talked sense, yet she was timid. I liked her immediately."

"Go on."

"Well, I signed off the ship and spent eighteen days with her."

"You lived with her?"

"Hell, no, Frank! She's not that kind. I stayed in a hotel, but we were together every day. Oh, what great times we had! Together. And with her son, Tyler. What a good kid. Two years old. Mary Jane plays the piano and, you know, she's already giving him lessons!"

"Sounds like a good mother," Frank said. "It must have been difficult for you."

"In what way?"

"Well, with you staying in a hotel and her kid in the way all the time, it must have been hard to make out."

"Christ, Frank, we had such a good time we had sex only once! Eighteen days after we met. I never saw her after that."

His voice broke.

"What happened?"

"Dumb me," John answered, embarrassed. "I asked her to marry me that night. Right after we made love. She said 'no.' Flat out 'no.' Then she asked me to leave her bed."

"Why?"

The chief mate took a long breath.

"Told me she lost one husband to the sea and wouldn't do it again. If she ever remarried, it would have to be with a man who hates the ocean."

"I can understand that feeling," Frank sympathized. "Hell, John, you met her only a couple of weeks after her husband was killed. She wasn't over the shock. That will take a long time. I mean, man, have some understanding!"

"If she loved me, she wouldn't have told me to get out of her bed that night and never come back. She'd have said let's write each other and see what happens. Instead, she said it'd be better if we didn't see each other any more. Asked me to get dressed and leave right then. I pleaded with her, but she insisted. So I left. I called her for two days, but she wouldn't let me see her. I went to Frisco and signed on this bucket."

He pounded his fist on the green linoleum-covered table.

"I shoulda laid her the first time we met! Then I coulda left and forgotten her, like all the others. Now I can't get her off my mind."

Frank thought a moment.

"Have you written her?"

"No."

"You should. I'll bet she's had second thoughts."

"Doesn't matter," John said dejectedly.

"It's not bitterness you're feeling, John. It's ego. Your ego's hurt. You won't enjoy being the big man around town again. You've got her under your skin and you won't be able to get her out until you marry her or are sure she doesn't love you. One gets you twenty she does and wishes she knew how to get in touch with you."

"Maybe you understand women better than I do," John shrugged.

He went to the cupboard again and pulled out a writing tablet and a pen.

"I'll write her."

11 July 1943

0100 HOURS
In the Mediterranean

"I've never seen anything like it," Commander Barnschmidt called to his executive officer. "So many ships! There must be thousands!"

He was right. There were more than 3,300 ships of all shapes and sizes in the enormous flotilla converging on the southeastern and southern coasts of the island of Sicily off the toe of Italy. Dull-covered camouflaged troop transports. Sleek warships. Landing craft. Merchant vessels. They had departed at different times from Oran, Algiers, Bizerte, Sousse, Sfax and Tripoli in North Africa, Alexandria, Port Said, Haifa and Beirut in the Middle East, England, Scotland, Iceland and the United States and, like a welltooled machine, joined up at the same moment in the carefully planned *Operation Husky.*

The Allies had wangled for months over the exercise. General George C. Marshall, the U. S. Army Chief of Staff, argued that a bold stroke against Germany, across the English Channel and through France, would be the quickest way to end the war. English Prime Minister Winston Churchill disagreed, arguing that the Allies weren't ready for such a venture, that it would be better to weaken Germany by nibbling away at the edges of its empire. Besides, he said, an assault on Sicily could knock the Italians out of the war. Marshall wanted to tell the prime minister that, if he persisted in that view, the Americans would divert most of their forces to the Pacific in the fight against the Japanese. Roosevelt restrained him. To add to the turmoil, there was sharp disagreement about command. The British felt that the Americans, who had suffered some embarrassing defeats early on in North Africa, were not experienced enough to lead a major battle. The proud Americans thought they were better strategists and tacticians than the redcoats they had defeated in the American Revolution. In a compromise, Lieutenant General Dwight D. Eisenhower was named supreme commander and all of his principal subordinates were British. At the front, General Sir Bernard Montgomery's tested Eighth Army would land on Sicily's southeast coast and the American Seventh Army, led by General George S. Patton, Jr., would land a few miles further up the coast, at the beaches near Licotti, Gela and Scoglitti, protecting Montgomery's left flank. It was a secondary and distasteful role for the flamboyant Patton.

"We can't do anything against a convoy this size!" Barnschmidt admitted, ordering his U-boat to be turned around and headed toward the Strait of Messina. He was running for his home port in La Spezia, ashamed. He had never before run from a battle.

2230 HOURS
Aboard the S. S. Elihu Nicholson
German and Italian bombers had pummelled the convoy off Gela all day, damaging and sinking a dozen ships. More than 100 planes came over in the darkness, dropping parachute flares that illuminated the ships. Gunners answered with streams of 20-millimeter cannon tracers and shells, hitting and knocking down plane after plane. More parachutes floated down, dark objects dangling from them.

"They're dropping mines!" someone yelled.

The gunfire became more fierce.

"There's so much scrap iron up there we can't tell if we hit him!" a gunner on the *Nicholson* shouted as one plane erupted in a ball of flame and crashed into the nearby water. "But it sure feels good to see him downed!"

The ship's gunners continued to pound away at the wreckage and the men struggling to free themselves from it.

"Stop firing!" called Boatswain Jim Davis, surveying the scene with binoculars. "That's a C-Forty-Seven and those are American paratroopers!"

"Oh, gawd!"

It was one of the first disasters in a series that plagued the invasion. Twenty-three of the planes were shot down. Dozens of others were heavily damaged. More than 200 paratroopers of the 82nd Airborne Division were killed.

"It wasn't us!" a gunner said limply. "It was shot down by another ship!"

2300 HOURS
On the Gela Beach
The Germans counterattacked with tanks, moving toward the Seventh Army's beachhead. General Patton had counted on the paratroopers and antitank guns to thwart any such move. He had lost twenty per cent of his airborne reinforcements. Now he desperately needed the guns.

"Get them off the *Maddux*!" he commanded.

"Sir," his orderly said, concerned. "That LST has been sunk!"

More problems for the orderly general.

"There's more ships out there with antitank guns!"

"There are some on a Liberty ship, sir!"

"Get them off! Now!"

The orderly raced to the beach to order the unloading of the guns from the *S. S. Elihu Nicholson*

12 July 1943

0015 HOURS
Aboard the S. S. Elihu Nicholson
The first barge bounced against the *Nicholson's* steel hull and two soldiers tried to hold the craft close with their hands. A. B. Howard Robinson was on starboard watch.

"Toss us a line!" one of the soldiers shouted. "We've come to get your guns!"

"Wait 'til morning," Robinson called back. "We're off duty now."

"Off duty?"

"Yeah. Everyone's in the sack except me and a few Navy gunners."

The soldier, overwhelmed, radioed for instructions. A nearby destroyer moved alongside the *Nicholson.*

"Get your captain!" a voice boomed over the bullhorn.

"You get him," Robinson called back. "He's in the sack."

"Get him the hell up! Patton needs those guns now."

"He'll have to wait. This is a union ship. We don't unload at night unless the captain authorizes overtime."

"Overtime?" the flabbergasted voice said. "You've got to be kidding! There ain't no union rules here and there ain't no overtime. Look, mister, we're backing off a few yards, then we're opening fire with our guns unless you begin unloading. You have two minutes!"

Frightened, Robinson said he'd call the captain. Right away.

0016 HOURS
On the Gela Beach
Sixty German tanks had moved to within two thousand yards of the beach. The American situation was desperate.

"Where are those guns?" General Patton demanded.

"They're being unloaded from the Liberty now," his orderly said enthusiastically.

"Good! Move them up here fast when they come ashore!"

0017 HOURS
Aboard the S. S. Elihu Nicholson
"What happened?" Jim asked as the first guns were lowered over the side. "These Army guys seem madder than hell!"

"They couldn't take a joke," Robinson said.

"What joke?"

"I was kidding them. Told them that union rules didn't allow us to work under these bright lights at night."

"What?" Jim was dumbfounded.

"Oh, when they didn't laugh I apologized, but I guess they're pissed because I held them up for a few seconds. It's okay now, Boats."

"Jesus Christ, Robinson, that was stupid! It's no joke to them or the men ashore. I warned you about this kind of thing when I hired you on. Don't let me ever hear you talk about union rules again!"

0700 HOURS
On the Gela Beach
With the guns, Patton's forces quickly knocked out most of the tanks and the Germans beat a hasty retreat. Italian resistance folded. The Americans moved inland to the north and northwest. General Patton saw his chance to shed his secondary role in the campaign. He flew to Tunis where he challenged General Sir Harold R. L. G. Alexander, commander-in-chief of the British army and Montgomery's boss.

"My boys can take Palermo!" he shouted, pointing on the map to Sicily's largest city and port, in the north. He was determined to take that prize before Montgomery could.

Alexander agreed to let Patton try.

17 July 1943

1400 HOURS
Aboard the S. S. Elihu Nicholson
The Liberty ship, unloaded, was ordered back to Oran.

"We're to pick up some more guns, jeeps and other vehicles and swing around Sicily to Palermo," the captain said. "Word is that Patton is making a move to that port, 'tho the British want it too. It'll be a race to see who gets there first."

"I'm glad we're heading back to Oran," Boatswain Davis said.

"Got a lady friend there?" the captain asked, smiling.
"My wife's back home, sir."
"Oops! Why in a hurry, then, to get back there?"
"I want to put Robinson back in the stockade."
"For the practical joke he played on those soldiers?"
"Wasn't a joke, sir."

Jim explained he had talked to the soldiers on the barge and they told him what really had happened. That the *Nicholson* had nearly been blown up by an angry crew on the destroyer.

"He told them union rules prohibited us from unloading at night."

"That's damn close to mutiny!" the captain exploded.

"That's what I think, sir. He endangered the safety of this ship. I talked to him again and he told me his last ship was the *Andrew Bennett*. That's my youngest son's ship. Frank wouldn't have had him locked up for a little misunderstanding with the bo's'n, as Robinson told me. It had to be something bigger."

"Any ideas?"

"I tried to get it out of him, but he clams up. No sense in taking any more chances, sir. If he does what he did to those soldiers again, we might all be dead meat. We've got to dump him."

"You're the boss, Jim."

22 July 1943

1700 HOURS
Palermo
After a lightning advance that began three days ago and was met with little resistance, Patton's soldiers on foot and in tanks and jeeps moved effortlessly into Palermo. Italian soldiers, without guns and waving white flags, surrendered by the thousands.

Civilians cheered.

German soldiers fled toward the east where the mountainous terrain, with steep cliffs and nearly impassable unpaved roads, could more easily be defended.

23 July 1943

0800 HOURS
The Port of Oran
A. B. Robinson, suspecting the mood of the boatswain, jumped ship and fled into the Arab quarter. He thought he could hide out the rest of the war there.

In civilian clothes, he stole a bunch of bananas from a cart in the market. He was nabbed by three Arabs, mistaken for a German despite his dark hair. They had seen Nazi soldiers lift fruit and food from the market during the occupation.

The Arabs didn't ask questions.

While Robinson jabbered he was a United States seaman lost from his ship, they cut off his hands.

0830 HOURS
Aboard the S. S. Elihu Nicholson
"I hope we've seen the last of him," Boatswain Davis said after learning Robinson had jumped ship. "I imagine the army or someone will find him and lock him up forever. He's a disgrace to the Merchant Marine."

"Well, it's good riddance," the second mate said. "We've got enough to think about now. They've changed our orders. The Germans have sunk dozens of ships in the Palermo harbor, making it impossible for us to get in there. Patton will have to get his guns some other way. We've been ordered to sit it out here until we're needed someplace else. God only knows how long that'll be. The captain says to tell the men to divvie up duties and take some time ashore."

"They'll like that, sir," Jim said. "They'll want to get ashore and find some women."

"Tell them to be careful about lifting the veils of women," Slim cautioned. "Arab men don't like that!"

26 July 1943

0700 HOURS
Aboard the S. S. Elihu Nicholson
"Italy is falling apart!" the radio operator shouted as he raced across the ship's main deck. "Mussolini was kicked out yesterday!"

The news was met with cheers.

"Maybe we'll go home now!" a jubilant seaman yelled.

"No chance," Jim said. "The Germans control Italy. They won't run because that fat slob has been knocked over. Trust me, they'll put up a good fight. This war ain't over by a long shot. We're still fighting in Sicily."

14 August 1943

0900 HOURS
In the Strait of Messina
U-361 bobbed on the ocean surface, its commander watching the orderly Axis retreat across the two-mile wide straight to the Italian mainland. The troops brazenly loaded their barges, ferries and motorboats in broad daylight, protected by devastating fire from hundreds of guns

that blasted away at air and surface targets.

"This is what we've been relegated to," a despondent Commander Barnschmidt told his exec. "A policemen watching boys run away! It's disgusting! And humiliating!"

It was a massive evacuation. Hundreds of tanks and guns and thousands of vehicles joined the more than 110,000 German and Italian soldiers who safely made it across to be ready to fight if and when the Allies made new landings on the mainland.

3 September 1943

0500 HOURS
The Toe of Italy
Montgomery's Eighth Army encountered no opposition as they crossed the Strait of Messina and landed at the toe of Italy's boot. It was a movement to divert Axis attention from later planned invasions at other points on the mainland. The Germans didn't bite. They had already withdrawn to the north. Italian soldiers, weary of war, offered to unload the British landing craft. At this rate, the Allies figured, World War II would be over quickly.

8 September 1943

1830 HOURS
Gulf of Salerno
The *S. S. Elihu Nicholson*, its holds stuffed with thousands of tons of ammunition from mortars to artillery shells to M-1 bullets, was among the hundreds of ships rolling toward the invasion beach when the radio announced the surrender of Italy.

"It's all over!" the radio operator shouted with sheer joy.

The Armed Guard and merchant crew happily raced to their foc'sles and carried cases of beer back to their gun tubs. Some of the officers pulled bottles of bourbon and scotch from the medicine chest. The captain and Boatswain Davis tried to curb the celebration.

"It's premature!" Jim shouted. "The Germans are still there!"

He pointed to the beach.

"Doesn't matter, Boats," a gunner shouted back. "Without the Eyeties, the Germans can't stand up to us!"

10 September 1943

1200 HOURS
Salerno Beach
The American invaders were stalled. German resistance was stubborn, the beachhead was less than two miles, casualties were heavy and some thought was given to withdrawing the Americans to the British sector which was having an easier time. The idea was discarded when someone pointed out that empty landing craft could make it to the beach but, loaded with men and equipment, they'd be too heavy to move away from the sand.

Lieutenant General Mark Clark, the American commander of all Allied ground forces at Salerno, could only hope his 5th Army would ward off repeated German counterattacks and that the British would come up soon to bolster them.

13 September 1943

1500 HOURS
Aboard the S. S. Elihu Nicholson
The unloading of the ammunition had begun early in the morning and the number one hold was now empty. Army longshoremen and merchant seamen moved to number two, grappling with the dangerous cargo and gingerly hoisting it with the wooden booms over the ship's rails to waiting barges below.

Except for the screeching noises from the winches and occasional shouts from the boatswain, it was peacefully quiet. There was no air alert. The gun crew was standing down, most of them in the crew mess taking a break after a night and morning of incessant bombing of the harbor by German planes. Others watched from the bow the white puffs of artillery smoke on the beach.

A searing explosion rocked the stillness.

"What's happened?" yelled a soldier.

Showers of shrapnel rained on the decks and into the sea around the *Nicholson*. Men ran for cover.

"Something's blown up aft!" another shouted.

More explosions tore the afternoon air.

"It's not us!" Jim called, trying to calm the panic. "Something hit that British cruiser over there! To port!"

The men looked. Fires raged on the cruiser's decks and smaller explosions rocked the water all around. General quarters was sounded and the *Nicholson's* gunners ran to their tubs.

"There aren't any planes," one of them said. "One of her ammunition lockers must have exploded."

Another violent explosion ripped from the starboard side. All eyes looked there. An English battleship was engulfed in thick smoke. There was a whistling sound overhead and, a second later, an American cruiser dead ahead met the same fate. A nearby landing craft burst into flames and sank.

"What the hell's happening?" a gunner asked.

"Those ships are blowing up by themselves!" another answered.

"Try to be calm," Lieutenant Taylor called fore and aft on a bullhorn. "The Army thinks it's a new German weapon. A radio-controlled glide bomb they release from high-flying planes, miles away, that comes in quietly to its target. They tried a few in Sicily. It looks like these pilots have better aim."

The men looked skyward but could see nothing.

"Let's get this ship unloaded fast!" one of the seamen shouted. "They hit us we'll never know it!"

"That's the best way to die," another said softly.

14 September 1943

0815 HOURS
Palermo Beach

General Clark realigned the American positions during the night. The Germans mounted a morning counterattack at the points where they thought the line was the weakest and were stunned. Fire from antitank guns and 105-millimeter howitzers stopped dozens of tanks in their tracks, destroying most of them. Rifle fire from Yank infantrymen mowed down some of the proudest of the Hermann Goring Division which had been airlifted to the action.

The Germans withdrew.

The Americans and British joined up for the bitter struggle to cut through mountains and hills to Naples, thirty miles away.

27 September 1943

1000 HOURS
La Spezia, Italy
Commander Barnschmidt was adamant in his telephone conversation with Admiral Donitz.

"I want to go back to the Atlantic!" he shouted. "I'm being wasted here! "The Allies own the entire Mediterranean and we're holed up in this damn port. We don't dare go out!"

"You've lost your courage, Barnschmidt!" the admiral shot back.

"I have not! I just don't believe in committing suicide!"

"Maybe I should send Luth down there," the admiral taunted. "He takes on anything!"

That hurt Barnschmidt. Wolfgang Luth had finally surpassed Barnschmidt in ships and tonnage sunk. Thirty-four ships, 186,100 tons. So had three other U-boat captains. Victor Schutze had 30 ships, 151,300 tons. Erich Topp had 29 ships, 165,300 tons. Barnschmidt, stuck at 27 ships, 148,300 tons for more than a year, was tormented by the inaction.

"Luth wouldn't take his boat out here!" he countered. "He doesn't believe in suicide either!"

"It's that bad?" the admiral asked condescendingly.

"You know its bad, sir," Barnschmidt said more calmly, sensing a weakness in the admiral's voice. "We go out on the surface, the Allies' new radar picks us up almost as soon as we leave port. Then they pile in on us. Their sonar picks us up submerged. So do their planes. It's just as bad in port. They're bombing every day now. It seems like they never stop. I don't know where they're getting so much fire power. Or ships. And planes."

"It's the Americans," Donitz said. "Their factories aren't under the bombardment our plants suffer. They never close and more of their convoys are getting through. What's your assessment of the situation, Commander?"

"We're losing it in Italy, sir," Barnschmidt said frankly. "Oh, our ground troops will put up a good fight and maybe we can stop them in the mountains. Our boys are good at that kind of fighting. They're blowing up bridges and holding them off. For awhile. But, frankly, Admiral, it's going to be tough. We have no way of getting supplies to them from the sea. I don't know how much we can get in across the Alps."

"Not much."

"We've got to stop them, Admiral. We must go after their convoys."

"Yes. I suppose you would do more good in an Atlantic wolfpack than sitting it out down there."

It's about time you admitted that.

"I suppose I could recall your old boat, the U-Eighty-four-B."

You're damn right you can! You're an admiral.

"It's new commander hasn't sunk one ship since he took over."

Karl Schultze never did have much savvy.

"Okay, Barnschmidt. You fly up to Brest. That's safer than Wilhelmshaven these days. I'll have your boat there in four, five days."

"Thank you, sir," Barnschmidt shouted into the phone. "You won't regret it, sir. I'll sink one ship a day!"

"We need more than that to win this war!"

19 November 1943

0900 HOURS
Off Tarawa Atoll

"You've taken us here before," Captain Davis told Third Mate Franklin in the *S. S. Andrew Bennett*'s wheelhouse. "We've just passed that point where the Equator crosses the international date line."

"I know, sir, but it's a lot different this time," the mate said.

The Liberty had joined some 200 other American ships as Vice Admiral Raymond A. Spruance readied the attack on the horseshoe-shaped Tarawa Atoll, just northwest of that junction. For nearly six months, after leaving Brisbane, the *Bennett* had continued to ply the Southwest Pacific, carrying equipment, supplies and troops to support the landings at Munda and Viru on New Georgia, and to resupply the garrison at Port Moresby.

"I have a jittery feeling, Captain," the young mate said.

"What about, Mister?"

"I know it's ridiculous, sir, but Seaman Durante claims he saw Bib's ghost -- Major Bennett's ghost -- on the foredeck during the four-to-eight watch."

"He what?"

"He said the ghost stood on top the number three hatch and held up a hand like a stop sign. He thinks it was a warning for us to go back."

"Did the second mate see the ghost?" an incredulous Captain Davis asked.

"No, sir. By the time Durante called Mister Turner's attention to it, the ghost had disappeared."

"Sounds like Durante's becoming unhinged, just like the cook," the captain said, dismissing the report. "There's no ghost on this ship."

But Captain Davis was worried. Others of the crew had begun displaying signs of war neuroses.

20 November 1943

0430 HOURS
Betio, Tarawa Atoll
The battleships bombarded the half mile square coral-fringed island of Betio on the southwestern side of Tarawa Atoll. Dive bombers and fighters from the carriers *Essex*, *Bunker Hill* and *Independence* gave the island and its single airstrip an intense low-level bombing. Troops scrambled from a dozen transports into Higgins boats and amtracs for landings on beaches inside the island's lagoon. Beaches thought to be the least defended sectors of what was one of the most heavily fortified islands of its size in the Pacific.

The Japanese began firing when the boats were about 3,000 yards from shore.

"How can they be alive after all that bombing?" a Marine cried as bullets ripped through and exploded his amtrac's fuel tank.

He had earlier joked, during the three hours of bombardment from ships and planes, that all he'd have to do when he got on the beach was to use his shovel to bury the dead. He toppled to the water and, with two other survivors, waded neck deep to Red Beach 1, machine gun bullets raking around them. A shallow-draft LCVP (Landing Craft, Vehicle and Personnel), more popularly known as a Higgins boat, following the amtrac ran aground on the lagoon's reef, its shallow draw not enough to carry it over the sharp coral. Other Higgins joined the melee and Japanese guns blasted the Marines transferring to amtracs or wading ashore in the deep water.

Those men of the 2nd Marine Division who finally reached the beach found themselves pinned by withering fire from a battery of Japanese machine guns and fixed gun emplacements. The heavy bombardment had little effect on the steel rod reinforced blockhouses and pillboxes covered with more than ten feet of crushed coral.

0500 HOURS
Aboard the S. S. Andrew Bennett
A single Japanese Zero came out of the rising sun, almost at water level, and headed for the *Bennett* at anchor on the ocean side of Betio. It was the only plane to take off from the prized airstrip before its 4,000-foot runway was destroyed by the pounding shellfire from the battleships, cruisers and destroyers and by the low-level bombing from planes of the Fifth Air Force.

"Bogey at two zero five!"

The forward three-inch gun thundered. The two forward 20-millimeters hammered. The Zero's machine guns flared as it crossed over the monkey bridge, just missing the smokestack, bullets pounding into the number six guntub which had not opened fire. The screams of two men penetrated through the battle noises.

"Get him!" someone yelled.

Gunner's Mate First Class Hunt fired one short burst from his number eight 20-millimeter. The plane's left wing tore away and it tumbled into the sea.

"Nice shooting!" yelled Lieutenant Taylor.

"We should have gotten him when he was four thousand yards out!" Charlie called back. "How're the men who were hit?"

The gunnery officer jumped into the number six tub.

"My God!" he screamed. "They're dead!"

0630 HOURS
On Red Beach 1
The invasion was botched from the outset. Aerial photographs had indicated the heaviest guns were on the ocean side of Betio, largest of the atoll's 47 islands. Coral reefs

and man-installed concrete pyramids, mines and barbed wire would block landing craft from reaching shore there. The lagoon side of the 296-acre island, with reportedly fewer gun emplacements, was chosen for three landing sites. Old maps, charted by the U. S. Navy in 1841, indicated five feet or more of water lay atop the lagoon's coral reef. The fully loaded Higgins boats drew three and one-half feet.

The maps were wrong.

Most of the boats got stuck. Marines, many of them seasick from the choppy water, were slaughtered by machine gun fire in the terrifying confusion as they tried to find a way ashore on other boats that had made it over the sharp reef. Or by wading through a fast current, their rifles held over their heads. They still had to make it over a four-foot seawall of coconut logs over which the defenders fired more than 100 machine guns. Those lucky enough to reach the beach found themselves with practically no equipment to wage war. No radios to call for naval or air support. No mortars, no artillery to defend their slim positions. Some rifles and machine guns were waterlogged. Many men were without leaders, their officers having been killed or wounded. Most of their landing craft lay wrecked on the reef. Dead bodies lay sprawled, some atop each other, in shallow water or on the beach.

The water in the lagoon was tinged pink from their blood.

0645 HOURS
Aboard the S. S. Andrew Bennett
Navy Seaman First Class Cookman was dead. So was his ammunition loader, Ordinary Seaman Henderson, the graduate of the U. S. M. S. training school at Sheepshead Bay. Ordinary Seaman Benson took both deaths hard. The ship's philosopher had loaded 20-millimeter magazine's on Cookie's gun until the arrival of Henderson on the *Bennett* last October. Henderson had been trained to load and fire the antiaircraft gun. Benson was transferred to pass three-inch shells in the forward gun tub.

"It should have been me, not Henderson" he cried to the gunnery officer. "I should have been with Cookie. He was my closest buddy."

Lieutenant Taylor pointed to the shore.

"A lot of good buddies are being lost over there," he

said. "Those of us who survive must keep on going to make sure they didn't die in vain."

"That's patriotic mumbo-jumbo. Cookie wouldn't have died if it weren't for that damn ghost!"

Word had spread on the ship that Durante had seen the ghost. The fantasy was now more than just Bib's imagination. It worried the lieutenant. He reported his concerns to the captain.

Captain Davis tried to laugh it off.

"Ghosts just don't exist!" he said but he, too, was worried.

21 November 1943

1200 HOURS
On Red Beach 2
The tide in the lagoon changed and Higgins boats easily made their way over the reef to carry more troops ashore. A few 37-millimeter antitank guns and Sherman tanks also made it. Major William Yardley had been partly wrong when he said, a year ago, that the huge tanks could not be used in the Pacific fighting. True, they weren't much good for jungle warfare, but they could move easily on the flat surfaces of a coral island once they got past the reefs.

In fierce hand-to-hand fighting, the Marines punched their way to the airstrip and beyond to the ocean shore on the southern side of the island. Betio was only a half-mile wide at that point. The going was tough and the call went out to rush more men into the battle.

1900 HOURS
Aboard the S. S. Andrew Bennett
Gloom pervaded the *Bennett* as her cargo of Marsten landing mats was loaded onto barges and rushed ashore to help rebuild the airstrip. Two more men were dead. The only talk was about them and about Major Bennett's ghost stalking the ship. Captain Davis was sick about the casualties and he had heard enough about the ghost. His religious upbringing taught him that such apparitions do not exist, except in fantasy books written by authors who themselves are a bit unfringed.

"We've got to put a stop to this!" he told his brother as they had coffee on the monkey bridge.

"I agree, so why haven't you talked to Durante about what he saw two mornings ago?" Billy asked. "You've been avoiding it. Are you afraid, Frank, he'll convince you the ghost is for real? Durante's been holed up in his foc'sle most of the time since he saw whatever he saw, but he might be able to shed some light on this mystery."

"I will, damnit, I will!" Frank said angrily.

He summoned the ordinary seaman to the bridge.

"Tell me what you saw," he directed the seaman.

"I'm not sure, Captain."

"What do you mean you're not sure? You've started a serious rumor that a ghost warned the ship not to proceed in the invasion task force. Now you're not sure?"

"I did see something, sir, but it was all hazy like."

"Come on, son," Frank said more gently. "I need to know."

"It was sort of shadowy on the number three hatch covers, sir. The figure, I mean."

"What was it wearing?"

"It looked sort of like the Civil War uniforms I've seen pictured in history books," Durante said. "But I'm not sure about that. It looked torn in several places. Sort of tattered so it was hard to tell."

"Could a member of the crew have been wearing the uniform?"

Durante thought a moment.

"I don't think so, sir. I could see the number two paint locker right through him."

Frank looked askance at his brother.

"A shadowy character with a body and a torn uniform you can see through," he said. "Sounds like a dream to me. Maybe a nightmare."

He turned back to Durante.

"You sure you didn't fall asleep? Just for a second?"

"I've thought about that, sir. It's possible, but I don't think I did. It's not right to go to sleep at the wheel."

"Okay, then. Did he do or say anything?"

"He lifted his right hand, sir, like a traffic cop stopping traffic, you know."

"What time was all this, Durante?"

"Just a few minutes after I took the wheel, sir."

"You had just gotten up for your watch then?"

"Yes, sir."

"Did you have any coffee?"

"No, sir."

"Nothing to wake you?"

"I don't drink coffee, Captain. I drink cocoa, but the cook doesn't make any at that hour."

"Where was Mister Turner?"

"He was getting a cup of coffee from the hot plate."

"Did you tell him about the gho -- about the figure?"

"I called to him, but by the time he turned around it was gone."

"How long would you say you saw this thing?"

"About two seconds, sir. Then he just melted away. Like he wasn't there at all. I was scared, Captain. Do you think it was a real ghost? The major's?"

Frank took awhile to respond. He thought about a passage in a book he had read, *How to Win Friends and Influence People*, Dale Carnegie's archetype of self-help and self-promotion. *Show respect for the other person's opinion,* Mr. Carnegie urged. *Never say, 'You're wrong.' Don't criticize, condemn or complain . . .* He had done just that when he half-accused the seaman of falling asleep at the helm.

"I personally don't believe in ghosts," he finally said, "but some people do."

When Durante left the room, Billy spoke quietly to his brother.

"I don't think he saw anything," he said. "Except in his mind. Look, Frank, he had just gotten out of his bunk, probably with all his clothes on. All of us sleep that way. He went right to the wheelhouse, probably still half asleep. He thinks it had on a Civil War uniform, tattered and torn, and he could see the paint locker through it. He saw this apparition for all of two seconds, hardly enough time to blink an eye. Or to see what he described. You want my personal opinion? I think, like some of the others in the crew, Durante is suffering from some kind of somatic disorder."

The captain agreed but still had reservations.

"Neither of us believe in ghosts or that Major Bennett is haunting this ship, Billy," he said slowly. "On the other hand, I no longer can treat this as a fantasy of the cook. A second seaman has seen something. Even if it's in his mind. It seems to me we have to do something to take their minds off this ghost, to make them feel good about themselves."

"Any ideas?" Billy asked.

"One for now. Tomorrow I'm going to get them to

paint three Jap flags on the smokestack!"

22 November 1943

1315 HOURS
On Red Beach 3
Much of their equipment and tanks now ashore, the Marines moved quickly against the Japanese headquarters building to the northeast of the airstrip. The two-story, concrete structure was bombproof, hardly scathed by the shells from the offshore ships and bombs from the dive bombers. Leathernecks stormed the roof of the building. Gasoline, grenades and dynamite charges were dropped into air vents. Dozens of Japs ran from its doors and were killed by blistering rifle fire. Scores of others, including Rear Admiral Keiji Shibasaki, the island's commander, were trapped inside and burned to death.

A Navy Hellcat landed on the airstrip and the island was declared secure.

Captain Davis and his brother took a lifeboat to the shore.

"My God!" Billy exclaimed as they stepped onto the beach. "Look at the bodies!"

As far as their eyes could see, and that was across the entire island, thousands of bodies lay inert, some in the shallow water, some lying atop each other. American and Japanese. Marine medics examined each one.

"This one's alive!" they heard a corpsman call.

Two other medics raced to his side and began administering plasma. The wounded Leatherneck groaned.

"Who are you guys?" a Marine major challenged the two seamen dressed in khakis with no rank insignia. "Where are your weapons?"

"We're off that Liberty ship out there," Frank said hastily. "I'm the captain."

"Jesus Christ! You shouldn't be here."

"We brought in the landing mats for the airstrip," Frank explained. "We wanted to see what was happening here."

"Well, you're seeing it," the major said less authoritatively. "It isn't pretty."

"It's not," Billy said, his mouth and throat dry. "We've sat off on other invasions, wondering what it was like for you guys, but I never imagined it was this bad. How many were killed?"

The major shrugged.

"I don't know about the Nips. There's only a few of theM alive. I do know we lost more than a thousand of our boys and more than two thousand are wounded. Some of those won't make it either."

"It's slaughter!" Frank said. "Pure slaughter!"

"Yeah. They chopped us up pretty good just to take this fucking small chunk of coral no one ever heard of!"

1530 HOURS
Aboard the S. S. Andrew Bennett
Messboy Mitzell, artistically inclined everyone agreed, cut two stencils and, swinging precariously from a boatswain's chair, began painting rising sun flags on the gray smokestack, symbols of the kills of three Japanese planes. First a white rectangle. Then, the streaming rays in all directions from a red ball. It took him a long time to finish the first one and he planned to paint three on each side of the stack.

"Don't make those flags too big!" taunted A. B. Jones. "An American sub might mistake us for a Jap ship!"

"Wowie!" yelled Ordinary Seaman Durante. "Does that ever look great! Don't it, guys?"

"They seem happy," Billy told his brother.

"Seems like it," Frank said, pleased to see his crew in such good spirits.

"You should paint Bib's ghost next!" one of the men shouted.

"Damn!" the captain said. "They can't leave that ghost out of it!"

29 November 1943

1230 HOURS
Milne Bay, New Guinea
The crew of the S. S. *Andrew Bennett* rushed to the foredeck when Purser Tanner returned from ashore with a sack of mail.

Dear Tony,
Something's wrong. I can tell by your letters, the two you sent me in the past year. Can't you write more than that?

*You don't seem as tender or loving as you used to be.
Have you stopped loving me? Or is this war changing
you? I know it's changing me. I cry a lot.
Do you miss me? Your letters never say so. You just talk
about how much you're needed by the soldiers and
Marines. The newspapers tell us all about the invasions,
and the killings. Are you in any of them? I hope not.
Nothing can happen to you. We'll get married when you
get home, won't we? I hope so. I love you very much.
All my love,
Marilyn*

*Dear Gilbert,
Your letter from Australia arrived today. I am still upset
about your running away, but am happy that the crew on
your ship gave you a piano. It gives you a chance to keep
practicing. I dream of your being a concert pianist,
playing in Carnegie Hall some day. I hope that will
happen.
I hope even more that you will return safely to me. This
war is dreadful.
I pray for you every night.
Love,
Mother*

*Dearest Frank:
Wendy is one year old today. We're having a small party
with the neighbor kids this afternoon so I'm dashing this
off quickly. She took her first steps last week and was it
ever funny! Her legs were so bowed she looked like she
just got off a horse. But she did take four steps before she
fell down. She didn't cry though. Just picked herself up
and tried again. Made only two steps that time and fell
flat on her rump. You should have seen it! She's doing a
lot better today. She took eight steps across the kitchen
floor, grabbed a table leg and looked up at me as if to say,
"Okay, I've done that. Now where do you want me to go?"
Then she fell down. Hard. We both rolled with laughter.
You would love her, Frank. She's a lot like you. Full of
spirit.
Junior is having a difficult time. He keeps asking about
you and I've tried to tell him that you're fighting a war. At
first, he marched around like a soldier. Now he sulks and
goes to his room. He doesn't say much, but when he does
he talks about death. "People get killed in wars," he says.*

Then he asks if you will be killed. I tell him no, but he doesn't believe me. He cries.
I cry a lot, too, thinking about you, darling. It's been so long and I pray every night that God will return you safely to me. I've started going to church every Sunday and it helps a bit. I miss you so very much.
Your ever-loving Lynne

The chief mate took a letter to his cabin before opening it.

Dear John,
Oh, how marvelous it was to hear from you! I acted like a fool. When you proposed to me, I became frightened. I feared that if we did marry I would lose you, just as I lost my first husband. To this war. So I turned away from you. Then I ran away. I came back to Little Rock and am living with my parents. But I miss you. I'm sorry about what I did. Will you write to me again? I'd like that. Very much.
Mary Jane

Speer read and reread the letter, looking for hidden meaning in her words. He was convinced the "I miss you" really meant "I love you." He sat at the small desk in his cabin.
I love you, too, he wrote.

LOG BOOK THREE
31 May - 12 November 1944

"A coward turns away, but a brave man's choice is danger."

- Euripides

31 May 1944

1300 HOURS
In the North Atlantic
The S. S. *Elihu Nicholson* had been ordered to return to the States for reconditioning. One of her boilers had acted up on the last run from New York to Portsmouth, England, and, although it would still fire, there was concern that it might blow at any time. Repairs could not be made in any English port. All shipyards were tied up with a mounting naval presence in preparation for what everyone expected would be a momentary channel crossing.

"You can make it to New York on one boiler and you'll go alone," the Navy commander had said when he handed the orders to the captain. "German U-boat activity is practically non-existent. There's plenty of Allied traffic, sea and air, and you should have no problems."

The seamen were disappointed. They were aware of the mounting military might, despite the German buzz and glide bombs that devastated London and the English countryside, and had hoped their ship would be among those helping the invasion to finally crush the Nazis.

1330 HOURS
Aboard the U-84-B
The submarine had darted from the naval base at Brest late yesterday and was churning water on the surface, heading for a rendezvous with a small wolfpack three hundred nautical miles west of Ireland. Commander Barnschmidt had finally conceded to Admiral Donitz's orders that he stop traveling alone.

"A wolfpack can do more damage," the admiral had said. '"We must reassert ourselves at sea and put a stop to those damn convoys arriving from America! Your orders are to meet that wolfpack as soon as possible, stopping for nothing, and to display the courage you showed earlier in this war. I know you can do it, Barnschmidt.

Sink ships! Lot's of ships! If you have to, team up with another U-Boat in the wolfpack and both of you fire as many torpedoes as you can. I don't want you to report a damaged ship. Every ship must go to the bottom! There's not a moment to lose."

Barnschmidt thought the admiral was being overdramatic but, then, it was true the German war machine was hurting. Of course, he'd sink ships. That was his job, but he wasn't about to let another captain share the credit for a kill. He'd join the wolfpack, but he'd act alone when it came time to fire his torpedoes.

"American Liberty ship on the starboard horizon, just aft!" a lookout called.

Barnschmidt searched the horizon with his eyes.

"I don't see it," he told his exec. "Give me your binoculars."

Grabbing them quickly, he looked to starboard. The tiny speck aft his stern could hardly be seen.

"How do you know it's a Liberty?" he shouted to the lookout atop the conning tower.

"I can see it's outline clearly from here, sir. It is a Liberty and she's steaming on a course parallel to us."

Barnschmidt ordered half speed and, as he waited for his boat to slow down, he studied the speck. It's silhouette grew larger.

"It is a Liberty!" he joyously told his exec. "She's moving slow. Looks like about four, five knots. I wonder why."

He ordered all stop to the engines.

"We'll wait for her to get closer and then, boom!"

He rubbed his hands together.

"We'll blast her out of the water with our deck gun!"

The exec was stunned. He thought that risky.

"The admiral's orders were that we're not to stop for anything until we join the convoy," he said. "It'll take hours for that ship to catch up and for us to get into position. It'll be nearly dark then and I don't think using the deck gun is a good idea. Sir!"

"That's why you're not the commander!" Barnschmidt remonstrated. "The admiral asked me to show courage on this patrol. Damn him! I got three ships last patrol! What else does the bastard expect from me?"

He ignored the fact that he had used all fifteen torpedoes aboard, nine of them for the three ships sunk and completely missing two other ships. He didn't accept

31 MAY 1944 / 269

that he had missed those, blaming the failure on "duds."

"Besides, Lieutenant, it should be fun punching a few shells into that lumbering ship. Obviously, there's something wrong with her. She's hardly moving in the water. I guess that's why she's alone. They couldn't risk her in a convoy."

"You're the skipper, sir," the exec said admiringly but grudgingly.

1500 HOURS
Aboard the S. S. Elihu Nicholson

"I'm glad we're going home," Boatswain Davis told Second Mate Stevens as the two walked the main deck. The ship was empty. There was no water in the ballast and she rolled heavily in the mild sea.

"We'll be in drydock a few days and that'll give me a chance to see my wife. It's been a long time. Besides, a couple of buzz bombs hit just outside Portsmouth before our sailing yesterday. You know, it's strange. Even without a Navy, and a terribly weakened air force, Germany has found a way to destroy cities. And ships with their glide bombs. It's haunting! They're losing the war, but their scientists keep coming up with new weapons. They must be brilliant. They're so far ahead of our guys."

"One good thing, though," Slim said. "We don't have to worry about subs on this trip."

"I wouldn't bank on that, Mister Mate," Jim said, shaking his head. "Those Nazis are crafty. And nasty. I wouldn't bank on that at all."

1630 HOURS
Aboard the U-84-B

The Liberty ship was parallel to the submarine, ten thousand yards apart. There were no other ships or aircraft in sight.

"This will be easier than I thought," Commander Barnschmidt rejoiced. "She's riding high. That means she's empty, no ballast, but her broad hull gives us a bigger target for our gun."

"Sir, I think we should submerge and use our torpedoes," the exec objected.

"Where's your spirit of adventure, Lieutenant? Some of the other U-boat commanders have good records knocking off ships with their deck guns. Saves the torpedoes. Remember, we have only fifteen and I don't want to waste any on an empty ship. We've plenty of shells!"

"But ---"

"Man the deck gun," Barnschmidt ordered, ignoring his exec's protest.

1640 HOURS
Aboard the S. S. Elihu Nicholson
The ordinary seaman was on his regular bow watch. He spoke into his telephone to the lookout in the crow's nest.

"Got a funny feeling in my gut," the seaman said. "I keep looking to port and I keep seeing something. Then I don't. Even with binoculars. But then it bobs back up again. Take a look, will you."

The topside lookout scanned the horizon carefully.

"There is something out there," he called back. "I can barely see it."

He raised his binoculars again.

"I don't believe it!" the crow's nest lookout called to the bridge. "A sub is tracking us! She's on the surface!"

"Must be American or British," the captain said, sweeping the sea with his binoculars and spotting the sub. "Take it easy everyone. The Germans wouldn't be crazy enough to have a single sub in these waters."

"Should we identify ourselves?" Second Mate Stevens asked.

"Good idea! Run up the flag!" the captain ordered.

1635 HOURS
Aboard the U-84-B
"Look! She's raising the American flag!" the lookout called.

"Fantastic!" Barnschmidt said. "Her captain must think we're a friend. Fool! Okay, friend, we'll get a little closer to you."

He ordered the sub to within eight thousand yards of the Liberty.

"We'll make mincemeat of you!" he shouted.

1640 HOURS
Aboard the S. S. Elihu Nicholson
"I don't like it," the crow's nest lookout said aloud. "The

shape of that sub. Doesn't look American. Or British."

He closed his eyes momentarily, rubbed fingers over his eyelids and opened them quickly to peer through his binoculars at the black speck creeping closer.

"Holy mother of Jesus! It's German!"

He shouted the warning into his telephone.

1650 HOURS
Aboard the U-U-84-B

"She's in our range, Capitan!" the lookout shouted.

"Open fire, broadside!" Barnschmidt ordered, brandishing an arm into the air. "Put three shells into her!"

The deck gun belched three times.

"It's like the Coney Island shooting gallery!" he laughed gleefully.

1651 HOURS
Aboard the S. S. Elihu Nicholson

"Holy mother of Jesus!" shouted the crow's nest lookout again. "She's firing at us!" He scrambled down the mast. The captain belatedly sounded general quarters.

"Hard right!" he ordered the helmsman. "Bring her to bear on that pirate so our guns can get her!"

"Hard right, sir!"

The ship lazily veered starboard. The first shell crossed over the bow and dropped to the water two hundred feet away.

"You missed!" the bow lookout laughed. "You gotta aim better!"

A second shell hit the bow, ten feet above the waterline. The explosion knocked the lookout to the deck.

"Sonofabitch, we're hit!" he shouted, but his voice was lost in the deafening bark of the three-inch fifty overhead. The ship's gunners were in action.

A third shell hit midships, still far above the waterline. The aft five-inch gun spat fire. The bridge 20-millimeters opened up, tracers seeking the sub in the fading light.

1652 HOURS
Aboard the U-84-B

Commander Barnschmidt could see the belches of smoke

and tracers from the Liberty's guns. The shells fell two hundred yards short.

"They can't hit the broad side of a barn!" he shouted.

He took a quick look at the damage his two shells had done to the enemy.

"Put a couple more shells into her!" he commanded. "And lower your sights! Hit her at the waterline!"

1653 HOURS
Aboard the S. S. Elihu Nicholson
"Elevate your guns!" the Navy gunnery officer commanded the Armed Guard crew. "You're two hundred yards short!"

1654 HOURS
Aboard the U-84-B
Commander Barnschmidt saw one of his shells fall short. The second hit the stern at the waterline.

"Good!" he called to his gunners. "You got her just where - - " He cut short his words. A shell from the Liberty's aft gun hit ten feet off the stern, throwing up a huge geyser of water and violently rocking the boat.

"Now we're really having fun! Throw a couple more shells at her!"

Before his gunners could fire, another shell from the *Nicholson*'s forward gun hit the sub's bow. One gunner was thrown overboard.

"Ow!" the commander jumped. "They're aiming better! We better get out of their way! Dive! Dive!"

His deck crew and exec scrambled toward the hatch.

1658 HOURS
Aboard the S. S. Elihu Nicholson
Boatswain Davis raced to the stern to assess the damage.

"It's not a big hole, but we're taking in water!" he called to the captain. "No damage to the screw. We should close the watertight doors. I think we can pump the water out."

The aft gun overhead belched flame again.

1659 HOURS
Aboard the U-84-B
The five-inch shell hit just forward the conning tower and

threw steel and men into the air. The exec screamed as he fell on the deck, then was washed into the sea as the boat tossed wildly about. Shrapnel pierced Barnschmidt's left upper arm and shoulder. Blood gushed over his uniform. He touched it with his right hand and it felt warm. Dazed, he knew his wounds were serious and he could see the wounds to his boat were mortal.

"It's too late!" he shouted. "Abandon the boat! Abandon!"

Deflated rubber liferafts were passed up through the hatch, pins were pulled to inflate them and sailors began jumping after each other into the water. More shells threw up geysers around them.

Barnschmidt was the last to get off. Two seamen helped him into one of the rafts. One ripped off his shirt and, with the sleeve, hastily tied a tourniquet around the captain's upper arm.

"You're losing a lot of blood, sir," the man said.

"It's Aryan blood," Barnschmidt smiled weakly. "I've plenty of it."

1700 HOURS
On the Nicholson's Deck
The thunderous booms bursting from the ship's guns rolled the Liberty abruptly.

"Hold your fire!" the captain ordered. "They're abandoning the sub."

"That means there will be survivors, Captain," Jim said apprehensively.

The captain thought about that.

"We'll have to take them aboard," he said slowly, ordering the ship to make way for the three rafts bobbing in the water.

Scared men huddled in the rafts and shivered. More hung to ropes on the sides, trying to beat off sharks with wooden paddles. They had seen other men in the same frightening situation, men from ships they had sunk, but they had not anticipated this for themselves. Soon to be taken prisoners of war, or perhaps machine gunned to death, it was a blow to their pride. They looked with fear at the crew of the Liberty, the Armed Guard still pointing guns at them, the merchant seamen lining the rails menacingly.

The second mate and boatswain were ordered to the ship's starboard rail to expedite the rescue of their foes.

"The captain with you?" Slim called down.

"Yes, right here," Barnschmidt replied, his English perfect, his voice weak. He had lost so much blood he could not stand.

"All your crew get out?" Jim asked.

Barnschmidt counted the men on the rafts and clinging to them.

"Not all. I think twenty-six are missing. Some went down with her. Some drowned after they got out. Others have been . . There are sharks in this water."

"That's a heavy loss," Jim said.

"It is war," Barnschmidt answered.

That phrase sounded familiar to the boatswain. So did the voice but he couldn't place it.

A German sailor in the water screamed. His hands rose into the air and, suddenly, he was sucked under the surface. His head came back up, his voice letting out a bone-chilling cry, and he disappeared again. For the last time. Blood surrounded the bubbles from his last breaths. The twenty-seventh victim.

"Shark!" Barnschmidt shouted. There was urgency in his voice.

Jim looked at the second mate.

"We'll take you aboard," the mate called down. "As prisoners of war."

"Thank you," Barnschmidt said formally. "Without your help, we'll die down here."

The mate ordered a Jacob's ladder hung over the side. Jim tossed it and the Germans quickly scrambled aboard. One sailor remained with the submarine commander in the last raft.

"Our captain's hurt bad," the sailor said. "He can't climb that ladder."

A boatswain's chair was rigged up and lowered, the top end of the line wrapped around a winch. Carefully, respectfully, the sailor helped his captain into it.

"You can bring him up now," the sailor called.

The winch was turned, slowly, and the boatswain's chair raised the grimacing sub captain. His head appeared over the gunwale and Jim saw the small mole on the left cheek. Familiar.

Two seaman lifted the man over the side and unstrapped him from the chair. He tried to stand erect, propping himself up against the gunwale. He stiffly saluted Jim.

"Commander Barnschmidt, Commander, U-Eighty-four-B."

"Reinhard Barnschmidt?" Jim asked quickly.

"In the flesh," Barnschmidt answered, trying to act cool. He felt like falling down. He shivered, belying his mask of arrogance.

"U-Eighty-four-B?"

"U-Eighty-four-B. You've heard of us?"

Jim was incredulous. His mind went back to February 5, 1942.

You were clearly silhouetted against the horizon, the sub captain had said. *An easy mark. Easy. Like knocking over ducks in the shooting gallery at Coney Island.*

It all came back in a rush.

Tell your Mr. Roosevelt that U-Eighty-four-B is out here. Reinhard Barnschmidt, lieutenant commander. U-Eighty-four-B. Remember that.

Jim remembered. He searched the man's face. His anger at Reinhard Barnschmidt had been smoldering for more than two years and he couldn't believe the man was standing there in front of him.

"You sunk unarmed ships without warning!" he shouted beligerently.

"Were you on one of them?" Barnschmidt asked, feeling weaker.

"Yes. *The S. S. Terrapin.* You killed twenty-seven unarmed men."

"But it is war, no?"

That phrase again. Barnschmidt had bragged the same way when he talked to the survivors of *Terrapin*'s sinking. *But it is war, no?* Jim had sworn then to get even. The boatswain lunged, grabbing the man's uniform chest and Barnschmidt collapsed, lapsing into unconsciousness. Jim's anger crumbled. This was just a shadow of the man he had hated for so long.

"Take this man to the hospital cabin," he said, softly, to two seamen. "I want him to live."

1730 HOURS
In the Sickbay
Jim went to the *Nicholson*'s stern to further inspect the damage and to try to get his mind off the prisoner a few feet away in the hospital cabin. Inspecting was easy. Forgetting the man was not. He relived the nightmare of the sinking of the *Terrapin*.

There was no warning. Two torpedoes hit the S. S. Terrapin within four seconds of each other, the explosions tearing through the tanker, flinging men overboard or to the decks. Flames leaped four hundred feet into the dark night air. Burning oil cascaded back down with the water to ignite the ship from bow to stern and engulfed several men struggling in vain to swim clear of the fiery furnace. Jim was on the fantail, taking his customary inspection stroll around the deck before turning in, when the torpedoes struck near the bow and midships. Tying the ribbons on his lifejacket, he ran across the steel catwalk toward the bridge, flames licking at his every step. Blackened bodies, bursting like cooked sausage, sprawled across the deck. He did not recognize any of them. Jim visualized the terrible fate that befell the black gang, the men below decks in the engine room where the second lethal torpedo hit. Crushed by collapsing steel. Scalded to death by the steam from ruptured boilers. Or drowned by the in-rushing sea.

You killed twenty-seven unarmed men, he had told the submarine captain.

But it is war, no? the captain had answered.

Angry again, Jim walked briskly to the hospital cabin. He pulled his six-inch knife out of its sheath.

"I'll kill him!" he said aloud.

In the cabin, the purser was leaning over the patient.

"He's still unconscious," the purser said, hearing someone come in and not looking up. "He's lost a lot of blood and needs a transfusion. I can't give it to him. No plasma here."

He stood up and turned around, immediately spotting the knife in Jim's hand.

"Oh, it's you, Boats. I thought it was the captain. He said he was coming back here. What's the knife for?"

Shamefaced, Jim sheathed the knife.

"That bad?" he asked.

"He won't live if we don't get some blood into him soon. We don't have any on board and we can't break radio silence to ask for help. The captain's turning the ship back to port and I hope we can get there before this guy croaks."

Jim studied the patient's ashen face.

"I thought when he surrendered it was all over, but even now the sonofabitch is conjuring up more problems for me."

"For us, Jim," the purser said. "For us."

1 June 1944

0930 HOURS
Portsmouth, England
The prisoners were taken off an hour ago and, as the *Nicholson* rode at anchor, workmen feverishly welded plates over the gaping holes in the hull. Except for the one in the stern. There, they were plugging up the hole with wood, above and below the waterline.

"That should hold long enough for what we want to do with her," the Army colonel said.

"What's that, Colonel?" Second Mate Stevens asked.

"We're going to use this ship to help form a breakwater."

"A breakwater?"

"Yes. We've got a bunch of damaged ships for it. You're now one of them."

"Where is this breakwater?"

"Can't tell you," the colonel said. "You'll find out soon enough."

1020 HOURS
Aboard the S. S. Elihu Nicholson
Second Mate Stevens and Boatswain Davis stood on the fantail, watching the workmen lace the twelve-by-four boards into the hole, inside and out.

"Intricate work," Slim said.

"They know what they're doing," Jim said. "I wish I knew what we're doing or where we're going with that makeshift covering."

"It's easy to guess, Boats. We're going to be in on the invasion of France."

"Where?"

"I don't know," the mate answered, "but there is one thing I do know. The English Channel has big tides, much of the French coast is rocky and the water there is rough. The troop landing craft could be swamped. That's why they're talking about this ship helping form a breakwater. There'll be a helluva lot of other ships for sure."

"Will they sink us?"

"I imagine we'll scuttle her ourselves. I'm only guessing, of course."

"That'll be a helluva way for her to end," Jim said. "The Germans couldn't sink her on her run to Murmansk."

"They sure tried."

"And they've tried several other times. We took a few hits this last time, but the lady held up."

"Speaking of holding up, I think you did well yesterday when you came face to face with the sub captain. What's his name? Barnschmidt?"

"That's right."

"It must have been hard for you, Jim, seeing the guy who sank your other ship. Were it me, I probably would have punched him out."

"I thought about that, sir. And about worse. But, you know, when they took him off the ship this morning in that stretcher, he looked like a broken man. Not the way he looked and talked to us after that sinking. He wasn't so arrogant. Not arrogant at all. I felt sorry for him."

"Sorry?"

"Yes. At first I was so happy that twenty-seven of his men died. That was the same number killed on the *Terrapin*, you know. But, today, I regret they had to die. It doesn't make up for the men killed on that tanker. Not at all."

"But it's war, Jim."

The boatswain looked sharply at the mate. *Did he have to say that, too?*

5 June 1944

1500 HOURS
The English Channel

In the gray predawn light, nearly 5,000 ships of all kinds -- battleships, cruisers, destroyers, assault landing craft, troop transports, merchant vessels and hospital ships -- started their journey to the beaches at Normandy. They came from ports all over the British Isles. Belfast, Ireland. Loch Ewe, Scotland. Falmouth, Plymouth, Slapton, Plymouth, Portland, Portsmouth, New Haven, England. Even all the way from New York, Boston and Portland, Maine.

Operation Overlord, the long-awaited second front, was underway.

More than 3.5 million troops had been assembled in

England over the last two years, American. British. Canadian. French. Belgian. Dutch. Norwegian. More than 170,000, the first assault wave, were now aboard ships in that armada, driving through a moderate sea with the wind blowing up to 20 miles per hour. Many were prostrate with seasickness.

General Eisenhower, the Allied Supreme Commander, had assembled in the ports and English countryside over five million tons of invasion supplies, including 8,000 airplanes, 450,000 tons of ammunition, 50,000 vehicles including tanks, trucks, jeeps, half-tracks, 1,000 locomotives, 20,000 railroad cars, miles of railroad tracks, pontoons to span European rivers, countless barrels of motor oil, prefabricated Nissen hut sections, boxes after boxes of dried eggs and other food supplies, and 124,000 hospital beds. And rows on rows of stacked up coffins.

Many of those supplies were on the ships heading for the Normandy coast,

Perhaps the most thought out plan of the operation was the movement to take a port to the rugged French coastline. *Operation Overlord*'s planners had early recognized that it would be suicide to the invaders to try to take one or more existing ports, so well were they protected by what Adolf Hitler called his "Atlantic Wall," a formidable barrier from the Arctic Ocean to the Bay of Biscay. Massive coastal guns in heavily-fortified steel and concrete emplacements. Tetrahedal antitank obstacles. More than a half million mines planted in open beaches. Field Marshall Erwin Rommel, who had designed many of the obstacles himself, repeatedly warned the Allies not to challenge this "zone of death."

The British and Canadians had learned early in the war -- at Dunkirk, Boulogne, Saint-Nazaire and Dieppe -- that the Atlantic Wall was an almost impregnable barrier and that a massive invasion at one or more port cities probably would be doomed to failure. The Second Front landings would have to be elsewhere along the French coast and plans had to be made to create artificial harbors, providing sheltered waters through which the Allies could pass thousands of vehicles and tons of supplies each day, vehicles and bulk cargo that could not easily be landed on open beaches.

The British came up with a way to take such harbors to the beaches by combining a suggestion by Winston Churchill in 1917 and a 1943 plan devised by then-

Captain John Hughes-Hallett, a creative Royal Navy officer. In proposing an invasion of Flanders during World War I, Churchill suggested building "a number of flat bottomed barges or caissons, made not of steel but of concrete, which would float when empty of water and thus could be towed across. On arrival the sea cocks would be opened and the caissons would settle on the bottom. By this means a torpedo- and weather-proof harbour would be created in the open sea." Hughes-Hallett, declaring that "if we can't capture a port we must take one with us," proposed that a large area of sheltered water could be created by sinking a line of ships, blockships, in shoal waters off the invasion beaches.

More than 200 steel and concrete caissons measuring 220 feet long, 55 feet wide, 60 feet high and weighing over 6,000 tons, were constructed along with numerous pierheads, steel and concrete floats and ten miles of steel roadway. These huge parts were part of the invasion convoy, being towed by American and British ships along with 74 merchant vessels and obsolete warships to be used as blockships to form a breakwater at the invasion beaches. Twenty-two damaged American Liberty ships, concrete poured in their bottoms, were in the flotilla. They were scheduled to arrive on 7 June, the day after D-Day.

The *S. S. Elihu Nicholson*, with a skeleton merchant crew and a full complement of Armed Guard, was among them.

6 June 1944

0430 HOURS
Aboard the S. S. Elihu Nicholson
The crew of the Liberty ship watched and listened as more than 1,000 Royal Air Force bombers flew over the Channel and dropped their lethal bombs to soften up the coastal defenses for the early morning landings. Orange flashes from the guns on battleships, cruisers and destroyers, standing four to six miles off the Normandy coast, added to the deafening roar. Fast fighter planes, crossing the Bay of the Seine in an endless wave, strafed the beaches code-named Utah, Omaha, Gold, Juno and Sword.

"They must be tearing up the Germans," Jim said. "I

sure hope the French in those coastal villages are getting out of the way."

"How can they?" Second Mate Stevens asked. "They couldn't know the invasion is starting today. The weather has been so foul no one in his right mind would send soldiers onto those beaches. I don't understand the thinking."

"Eisenhower must have known something," Jim said. "It's stopped raining and the wind has slowed."

"Thank God for little favors. I hope it lasts."

The two kept their eyes skyward. The light of the moon allowed them to see many of the bombers, crossing over and coming back.

"That looks like gliders there, about two o'clock," Jim said, pointing.

"They'd be carrying our paratroopers. They'll probably land first, behind the enemy lines. Well, I guess I don't mean quite that. The Germans are all over France. Those guys probably have drop zones a couple of miles beyond the beaches."

The mate was right. The gliders carried 22,000 men of the British 6th Airborne Division and the American 82nd and 101st Airborne Divisions. Their targets were the bridges over the Caen Canal at Benouville and the Orne River and the village of Ranville to the east and the villages of Sainte-Mere-Eglise and Saint Martin-de-Varreville and the bridges over the Merderet to the west of the fifty-nine mile long invasion beach.

"This ain't going to be no picnic!" Jim said. "Where do we fit?"

"The captain got our orders about an hour ago. We sit out here until tonight when we get towed to Utah Beach. Believe it or not, this ship is going to help build a port in a couple of hours."

"I still can't figure out how they'll do it," Jim wondered. "It takes months to build a port with all the docks they'll need. And they probably need docks in a matter of days."

0631 HOURS
Utah Beach
Three hundred men of the 2nd Battalion of the 8th Infantry Regiment walked off the ramps of their landing craft into waist-deep water and waded one hundred yards to the sandy beach. They were the first amphibious troops

to land in France on D-Day. Resistance was light. Many Germans had been killed and their guns destroyed in the naval and aerial bombardment during the night. The GIs were elated.

"This is like picking strawberries!" one soldier rejoiced. "They didn't tell us it would be this easy!"

But they were in the wrong place. Their landing craft, clouded by a dense screen of smoke laid down by the naval bombardment, had been forced off course by a strong current. They were more than 2,000 yards from their intended target where the German defenses were much stronger. That stroke of good chance buoyed the Americans who rapidly swung inland, and north and south along the beach, giving space for the more than 30,000 men and 3,500 vehicles scheduled to land in the next few hours. Army engineers and Navy demolition teams blew up the mines buried in the shallow water, and, with bulldozers, cleared a path for the incoming stream of landing craft. More troops, tanks, guns, ammunition and vehicles poured on to the two-mile long beachhead.

0900 HOURS
Aboard the S. S. Elihu Nicholson
Three barrage balloons sailed over the Liberty ship, dancing as German shore batteries fired at them.

"Those things are supposed to be protecting the assault landing craft at the beach," Second Mate Stevens told the boatswain. "Their lines must have been blown away by the gunfire."

He didn't know that the assault boat commanders had cut the balloons loose themselves after noticing that German artillerymen concentrated their fire on the helium-filled bags. That spared most of the boats and the troops.

1030 HOURS
Utah Beach
The Americans widened their beachhead, taking strong points along the roads inland and pushing to the west and southwest over causeways in a race to link up with the airborne solders struggling to capture coastal villages. There was still little resistance from the German defenders. Their guns blew up trucks to create massive

traffic jams, but American casualties were light.

"We're better off here than they are at Omaha," a platoon commander told his troops. "The radio says our boys are having a rough go there. Heavy wooden stakes are staving in the bottoms of the landing craft and the few guys getting ashore have to pick through tons of mines. There's a lot of dead down there."

"Still, I'd rather be home," one of his men said.

1100 HOURS
Berchtesgaden, Germany
Adolf Hitler huddled with his war staff. They pointed on a table map to the Allied beachheads in Normandy.

"Those Dummkopfs!" he said laughing. "They're making fools of themselves landing there!"

He hastened to tell his generals that Normandy was not the site of the "big" Allied invasion. This is a diversionary feint, he said, expecting their full force to be thrown at another spot.

"At Pas-de-Calais, I bet! "

His generals didn't believe him. They were sure this was the real thing.

"Hold all our troops where they are!" Hitler screamed. "Our forces in Normandy will trap them!"

2300 HOURS
Aboard the S. S. Elihu Nicholson
The tug began towing the Liberty ship to Utah Beach from its anchorage twelve miles offshore. The going was rough.

"This lady doesn't like all that concrete in her bottom," Jim said. "She can hardly move."

"You wouldn't like it in your stomach either!" Slim chuckled.

7 June 1944

1100 HOURS
Aboard the S. S. Elihu Nicholson
German resistance had stiffened during the night and counterattacked the 82nd Airborne across the Merderet River. Boosted by reinforcements flown in by glider, the paratroopers held firmly while the flood of troops and vehicles extanded to more than six miles deep and eight

miles long on the beachhead.

"Look at that!" Jim shouted. "Looks like monkeys on a conveyor belt!"

He pointed to the thousands of men pouring from their landing craft and wading almost shoulder to shoulder to the sandy beach.

"That conveyor will get bigger," the second mate said. "It's time to pull the plug and sink this lady, Boats."

"Yes, sir!"

Jim headed below to direct the flooding of the compartments. He wasn't happy. The *Nicholson* had become like a second home to him, second after the *S. S. Terrapin*. That ship had gone to the bottom off the coast of North Carolina. This one would go to the bottom off the coast of France, but enough of it would stay above the surface to help form the temporary breakwater.

"Let's pull the plug!" he told the below decks watch.

"Christ! Do we have to, Boats?" the watertender asked.

"You know full well we have to."

"Swell! Damn swell! I just can't bear to think of her resting on the bottom here. It's igno - - ignominious for this lady. She's suffered lots and, now, to put her at the bottom makes me sick."

"It makes all of us sick," Jim said. "But there is one comfort. We're helping those guys ashore and those guys still to get there. They're going to need a lot of equipment, tons of equipment, ammunition and tanks, if we're ever to put a stop to Hitler. We can rest easy that, in her final days, the *Nicholson* is going down in glory."

"Yeah, I suppose so. But it still don't seem right."

The two walked aft a few feet. A section of the fourteen-inch line between the low sea suction and the main circulator pump had already been removed in preparation for the scuttling. The watertender opened the sea suction valve by a reach rod and valve wheel on a platform eight feet above the engine room floor plate. The sea water rushed into the compartment in a high velocity stream.

"Let's get topside!" the watertender sighed. "It won't take long before the engine room is filled and she's sitting on the bottom."

1400 HOURS
On the Bottom

The *Nicholson* settled on the coarse bottom of Bay of the

Seine in a wavy line with more than thirty other blockships forming the temporary breakwater.

"It's working!" Second Mate Stevens said. "Look how much calmer the sea is getting inside."

Jim studied the water.

"Yep, it's calming down. I guess they'll start bringing in those caissons."

No sooner had he spoken when tugs moved in one of the huge steel and concrete caissons to begin forming the outline of the artificial harbor. It was more than six stories high.

"I can't figure how that damn thing stays afloat!" Jim said.

"Same as we did," Slim acknowledged. "When they get her into place, they'll pull the plug and she'll settle to the bottom."

"Who'd have ever thought we could build a harbor like this, from the sea?"

"Our engineers are pretty sharp, Jim. Those German scientists are pretty good coming up with new weapons, but our guys have the savvy, real ingenuity, to design something like those big blocks."

Another 6,000-ton caisson was towed in front of the *Nicholson*.

"Just how long will it take them to put all those pieces together?" the mate wondered aloud.

8 June 1944

0600 HOURS
Utah Beach
The GIs woke in their foxholes and blinked at the rising sun. The beachhead itself was congested with men and materials. Amphibious-land vehicles raced out to the merchant ships, loaded and then raced back to the beach with more men, guns, shells, gas, tires and crates. Most were directed by an MP to the roads leading inland.

The soldiers saw French women walking around their field guns and tanks, stepping over shattered corpses, picking through broken boxes for tins of food. Children stared at the waking soldiers.

"Chocolate?" one GI, reaching into his pocket, numbly asked a small girl.

She ran off.

"Merci," a boy said, grabbing the candy bar. He choked as he devoured it hastily, then stood quietly. The soldier gave him another one and, more slowly, the boy ate it. His face opened to a wide grin.

"I'll bet he hasn't had chocolate for years," the soldier said to his buddy.

"Looks like he hasn't had a steak in years either," the other said.

"Hell, neither have I. Not a good one anyway."

1000 HOURS
Berchtesgaden, Germany
"I tell you again and again, this thing up in Normandy is not the real invasion!" Adolf Hitler shouted to his war staff. "They're going to hit us here, in the Pas-de-Calais area. You will hold the Fifteenth Army there! That's an order!"

The Fuhrer had tenaciously held to that position since the first word reached him two days ago of the Allied landings at Normandy.

"Stupid!" one of the generals muttered to himself. "You're holding back 200,000 men we need in Normandy!"

9 June 1944

0800 HOURS
Aboard the S. S. Elihu Nicholson
The German bomber flew low, almost skimming the masts of the blockships. Machine gun bullets raked the *Nicholson*'s deck. The plane climbed quickly, overhead, and dropped a string of phosphorus bombs. They hit the Liberty ship in the row in front and Armed Guard in the gun tubs screamed as they dove overboard, burning phosphorus clinging to their kapok lifejackets.

"Where in hell did he come from?" the gunnery officer shouted, running to the number four tub where two of his men had been hit. He accused himself of not being more alert. The lieutenant knew he had concentrated his eyes more on the German shore batteries which had pounded away at the blockships with 88-millimeter fire since early dawn.

No guns on any of the ships had fired. The Americans controlled the air over the beach and the last thing anyone expected was a German plane.

"How bad are you hurt?" he asked the Navy gunner still standing in the 20-millimeter tub, blood flowing from his right upper arm.

"It's just a scratch on my arm, sir," the gunner shrugged. "But Waco is hurt real bad."

The lieutenant bent down to examine the 18-year-old from Waco, Texas. Bullets had penetrated his abdomen and legs. Blood poured from the wounds and the boy was unconscious.

"He needs blood!" the officer shouted to the captain.

"We don't have any!" the captain said, racing to the scene with a first aid kit. "Even if we did there's no one on board who knows how to transfuse it."

"What can we do?" the lieutenant pleaded, feeling the boy's pulse. "He'll die without blood."

"I'll signal the hospital ship. Think we can take him over in one of our boats?"

"I don't think so, Captain. His wounds are serious and it'll kill him for sure if we move him."

"All right, then," the captain said. "Maybe they can get someone over here quick."

He headed toward the bridge. The lieutenant stood up.

"It's too late, sir. He's gone."

Stunned, the captain stopped in his tracks.

"At sea, there's no way we can get a doctor," he said softly. "But here we are with doctors all around us. A hospital ship only a thousand yards away. Medics on the beach and in the landing craft and, still, we're all alone and our men die. What a goddamn way to fight a war."

The lieutenant cried. He felt guilty again. He knew he had a responsibility to tend to his men, even medical attention if they needed it, and he hadn't known what to do. It didn't matter that even if he did there were no blood products on the ship.

"Let me look at your wound, son," he said to the other sailor, wiping tears from his cheek.

"It's really nothing, sir. The bullet just creased my arm. I'll wash it off."

"No, let me put some sulfa on it," the lieutenant insisted, grabbing a package from the first aid kit.

He had to do something for one of his men.

Anything. Even a sprinkling of sulfa. And a small bandage.

10 June 1944

1100 HOURS
Along the Normandy Coast
The Americans had solidified their beachheads. From Utah, the men of the VII Corps had moved relatively easily inland until they met stubborn German resistance at Montebourg on the road to one of their principal targets, Cherbourg. The situation at Omaha had improved tremendously, despite the heavy casualties, and had penetrated deep behind the German defensive line along the River Aure. The British and Canadians, moving up from Gold, Juno and Sword, had taken the town of Bayeux two days ago, the first important French town to be liberated from the Germans.

Things were looking up for the Allies.

1400 HOURS
Aboard the S. S. Elihu Nicholson
"Look, they're running the amphibious craft onto the beach!" Boatswain Davis pointed out to Second Mate Stevens. "They'll get stuck there!"

"You should know better, Jim," Slim replied. "They'll wait till high tide, then float them off."

"You're right, I should have known better. But why are they doing it anyway?"

"I'm not sure, but I'll take a wild guess. They can't wait for this harbor to be built and they're pushing the boats up there where they'll be easier to unload. See there, that one has a bunch of anti-tank guns. It's quicker to get them off on the beach than it is to push them through knee-deep water."

"That makes sense," Jim said. "But they won't be able to get off the locomotives and railroad cars that way. Too damn big and too damn heavy."

"Those trains are some of the reasons this artificial harbor is being built. Soon as they get all these caissons into place, the Army engineers will move in with those floating pierheads and push them into place. In a few more days, this whole area will be as large as any big city port. Then the real offloading from the merchant ships will begin."

"Yeah, if it's ever finished. Those German bombers gave us a good pasting last night."

"True, but we were lucky. They didn't hit us."

12 June 1944

1100 HOURS
Along the Normandy Coast
The German lines buckled under the American pressure. The American V Corps had captured Caumont, ten miles inland, was about to join up with the British who were moving on Villers Bocage and had already linked up with the VII Corps at the crossroads town of Carentan. The two corps readied their next move toward the port city of Cherbourg.

Supreme Commander Eisenhower visited the front lines and was happy with the progress of the GIs. But he was severely disappointed with the British Eighth Army which he felt was moving too slow in its assignment to take Caen, a city the Germans looked on as a key to holding the eastern flank of the Allies' bridgehead. General Bernard Montgomery, who had commanded the Eighth in North Africa and who now commanded all Allied ground forces in France, defensively maintained the British were intentionally drawing the main thrust of the Germans in the east so that the Americans could break out in the west.

There was division in the upper ranks of the Allied command. The foot soldiers in all the armies suffered.

1555 HOURS
Margival, France
Since 0900 hours, Hitler had listened patiently to Field Marshals Erwin Rommel and Gerd von Rundstedt explain the situation in Normandy. They were meeting in a bombproof shelter constructed in 1940 at a time when the Fuhrer dreamed of invading England. The Fuhrerbunker was his headquarters in France. The two officers wanted the German leader to recognize that the situation in Normandy was virtually hopeless. Rundstedt declared a counteroffensive could not be launched because the Allies had total air supremacy. Rommel wanted to pull back to the Orne River, arguing that there he could reorganize his panzer divisions. Hitler told them withdrawal was impossible.

"There can be no question of fighting a rearguard action," he ordered, "nor of retiring to a new line of resistance. Every man shall fight and fall where he stands."

Rommel argued that the situation was desperate, that the Italian and Russian fronts would soon fall and that the new Allied forces in France would inevitably sweep their way into Germany.

"We should end the war," he said matter-of-factly.

"Surrender is out of the question," Hitler said, surprisingly controlling his rage. "You worry too much, Rommel, about everything. You should concentrate your worries on Normandy. Let me worry about the rest and the course of the war. It's about to change. We have some new wonder weapons that will bring them to their knees."

He told them that the Luftwaffe had newly-developed and swift fighters, powered by jet engines, that would soon be in the air and would knock the much slower Allied piston aircraft from the skies. That more powerful glide bombs would be used against the ships off Normandy. And that advanced V-1 flying bombs, by the thousands, would be rocketed against London.

"England will fall!" he boasted. "And the Americans with it!"

The two field marshals were not convinced.

"But, as you have asked," Hitler said soothingly, "I will go to the Western Front and talk to the troops. That should encourage them to hold their lines, then beat the enemy back!"

Rommel and Rundstedt left the bunker, dejected.

As Hitler prepared to leave for Normandy, an errant V-1, which had done a U-turn over the Channel, flew over Margival and exploded near the bunker. The Fuhrer was scared but not hurt. He cancelled his visit to the front and flew back to Germany.

16 June 1944

0700 HOURS
Aboard the S. S. Elihu Nicholson
"I thought things would get easier by this time," Boatswain Davis said while having a mug of coffee with the second mate. "But the Germans have increased their

bombing runs on us at night. What happens to our planes after dark? They afraid to come out? We only see them during daylight."

"It is puzzling," the second mate said. "We seem to have control of the skies except at night. I wonder how long that will last, though. Did you see that strange plane that wooshed over a few minutes ago and strafed the beach? It was gone before anyone could say 'Jack Robinson.'"

"I saw it. The thing didn't have any propeller and it looked like flame coming out of its tail. A rocket?" Jim offered.

"I sure as hell don't know," Slim said. "It's probably an experimental type."

"These German scientists come up with the most weird weapons," Jim agreed. "I hope we don't see any more of those planes. That one moved so fast the gunners couldn't even track it."

"I had a helluva time seeing it!" the mate exclaimed.

1600 HOURS
Along the Normandy Coast
The embattled German troops, still hoping for an infusion of reserves and tanks, fought with skill in the hedgerow country just south of the beachheads, slowing the Allied advance and sometimes pushing it back. Caen, scheduled on the *Overlord* battle plan to be taken by nightfall on D-Day, was still in German hands. The Americans were far from Cherbourg which the planners had said must fall by D-plus-8. The offensive was slowed to a crawl in a terrain of patchwork fields enclosed by thick hedges of hawthorn, brambles, vines and trees growing out of thick stone walls four feet high that favored the defenders. Cold, rainy weather turned the fields and the dirt roads into quagmires of mud, almost putting an end to vehicle traffic. The Germans flooded large areas of the low country with water held back by dams built as a part of Hitler's Atlantic Wall.

Encouraged, Rommel and Rundstedt began to think they could hold the line and asked that more divisions be sent to them. Hitler, however, persisted in his belief that the main Allied attack was still to come up the coast in the Pas-de-Calais area. He ordered that the 200,000 men be held there. But he did dispatch some troops from the

Russian front and from southern France.

Eisenhower did not lose faith in his commanders or troops. The march to end the Third Reich, he was confident, would win.

19 June 1944

0800 HOURS
Aboard the S. S. Elihu Nicholson
"We're going home today, Jim," the second mate announced. "First to England, then on a ship back to the States."

"Going home? What's this all about?"

"They've finished building this makeshift harbor. Took them less than twelve days. Merchant ships already are heading in to begin offloading the big stuff. Locomotives. Railroad cars. Big howitzers. Parts for barracks buildings. All the stuff the Army needs to move across France and into Germany. They don't need us any more. Or the Armed Guard. We're all being relieved by Army guys who've been trained to use our guns."

"You're kidding!"

"No, and I'm glad I'm not. The captain just got the orders. We'll be out of here by noon."

"It don't seem right," Jim said reluctantly. "Leaving this girl after all this time. I'd like to stay on her."

Slim put his a hand on the boatswain's shoulder.

"She'll be all right, Jim. She don't need any more steam in her boilers and she won't be going any place for a long, long time. If ever. Her job is finished and she's done her part. So have you. It's time someone else looked after her."

21 June 1944

0900 HOURS
A Prisoner of War Camp in England
Unsure of his feelings after a troubled night's sleep, Jim walked into the orderly room of the camp surrounded by high fences topped with barbed wire.

"You have a prisoner, Reinhard Barnschmidt," he said to the corporal on duty. It was not a question but a statement.

"I don't know," the soldier said. "We have so many. They're bringing in another five hundred today. Our boys must be sweeping them up over there."

"He's a commander in the German Navy, a submarine captain. I'm told he's at this camp and I want to see him."

The corporal eyed the boatswain suspiciously. Jim was in civilian clothes.

"For what? What kind of business do you have with a sub captain? Are you from intelligence or what? You talk like an American."

"I am," Jim said. "A merchant seaman. I just want to see the guy that sank my ship."

"Oh! That's different."

He ruffled through a card index file.

"Barnschmidt. Reinhard Barnschmidt. Yeah, we've got him."

He turned to Jim.

"He's in the hospital. Took some heavy shrapnel in a shoulder, but I guess he's doing okay. He's still alive."

He called to a private at a nearby desk.

"Williams. Take this guy to the hospital, will ya? He wants to see a patient."

He looked searchingly at Jim.

"No funny stuff, you hear? We don't like our prisoners mistreated. You got a gun?"

"No."

"Good."

Jim walked with the private to the hospital, wondering what he would say to the man who had sunk one of his ships. For two years, he'd wanted to kill the U-84-B captain if he ever saw him again. Then, when he did just a couple of weeks ago, that feeling of hate disappeared. Now it had returned. He wanted to kill the man again. Last night, while tossing and turning in his bed, he relived the horrors of the sinking of the *Terrapin* and could not get it out of his head that Barnschmidt was still alive while twenty-seven Americans were dead, at the bottom of the ocean.

Fish bait. And this damn Nazi killer is enjoying American food under the care of American doctors! Life isn't fair. War isn't fair.

He walked into the ward.

I will kill him. With my bare hands. No, I can't do that. It's murder! Damnit, what's wrong with me? I feel like a yo-yo.

"Only a minute, sir," the nurse cautioned. "He's not doing well. He lost a tremendous amount of blood and the shrapnel caved in one of his lungs. The doctors have taken off his left arm. Gangrene."

Jim looked down at the patient, lying still, a tube in his nose, an IV in a right arm vein. The man was pale and it appeared to Jim that he had lost a lot of weight. His face was thin, pinched, and the mole on his left cheek had shrunk.

Barnschmidt opened his eyes and stared, glassily, then in recognition.

"You're the one who brought me here," he said.

"Yes."

"Thank you. I would have died out there."

His gratitude shook the boatswain. There was no arrogance.

"I remember you," Barnschmidt continued. "You were on a tanker I sank a couple of years ago off the coast of North Carolina. I'm glad you got off."

"Twenty-seven men didn't," Jim countered.

"I'm sorry about that."

There was real remorse.

"I've had a lot of time to think about it since I got here. A lot of time. I was younger than, pig-headed, and I didn't play by the rules of war," Barnschmidt said. "Sure, we were ordered to sink ships without warning despite the London Protocol. But that's no excuse for what I did then and with other ships. I could have given you a warning and gotten you off the ship before we sank her. I would have had to do that, you know. Sink her."

Jim didn't know what to make of this confession. *Is he really telling the truth? Is he truly remorseful?*

"I've been lying here thinking how Hitler had me fooled. He has all Germans fooled that we are the master race. Masters? Hell, you Americans are the masters. Look what you've done in such a short time. You've built an Army from almost scratch and your factories are churning out war materials enough to bury all of us Germans. We're going to lose this war, you know. It won't be long now. Your people already are talking about trying us for war crimes. Do you think they'll try me?"

"I don't think so. You were acting under orders. They'll probably go after the one who gave those orders to sink any ship, armed or unarmed."

"Yes, but I could have been more humane."

"But it was war, no?" Jim said quickly.
My God, now I'm using his words. And forgiving him.
He touched Commander Reinhard Barnschmidt on the forehead.
"Get well," he said and turned away.

4 July 1944

1010 HOURS
Baltimore, Maryland
Jim stepped off the southbound train at Baltimore's Penn Station, hoisted his seabag over his left shoulder and climbed the concrete steps to the upper level. The sun was shining brightly and he was dressed in civilian clothes. At the taxi stand facing Charles Street, he jerked a finger at the first cab, quickly opened the back door, threw his bag on the floor and climbed in.

"Where to, Chum?" the driver asked indifferently.
"Bel Air."
"Bel Air? Whew! That's way out in Harford County." He turned around to look at his passenger. "That'll be five bucks."
"Okay," Jim said nonchalantly, more interested in the coming and going train passengers than the money.
"And five more for deadheading back."
"Get going!" Jim said angrily.

He didn't care about the money, but it seemed like everyone he met since he returned to the States two days ago was looking for the fast buck. *Make it while you can. Bastards!*

The driver swung the taxi into Charles Street's northbound traffic. There wasn't much. *Gas rationing must be squeezing folks at home,* Jim thought. The taxi turned right at North Avenue, going through a red traffic light, and sped east toward Belair Road and Route 1.

"There's gonna be a big time in this old town tonight," the cabbie said.
"Yeah?"
"Yeah. It's the Fourth of July and everyone'll be celebrating the way our boys are plowing up the Nazis in Europe. There's gonna be plenty of fireworks at Fort McHenry. All over the city."
"I'm sure."
"You visiting?" the driver asked.

"Yes."

Jim didn't want to get into a conversation by telling the cabbie Baltimore was his home.

"Where you from?"

"England," Jim replied.

"You ain't got no English accent."

"I just came from there."

"Um. But where are you really from?"

Jim thought for a moment.

"Russia," he finally said gruffly.

The driver turned his head quickly.

"Come on. You're joshing. You ain't a Russian."

Jim laughed.

"What if I told you I really am?"

"I'd feel sorry for you. Christ, those Nazis have killed thousands of your people. But from what I read you're turning the tables on them."

Jim didn't say anything. He looked out the taxi window at the rolling Maryland countryside.

"I'm not from Russia," he finally said. "I've been there, though. Baltimore's my home."

"You in the Army?"

"No."

"The Navy? You ain't got on a uniform."

"No."

"Work for the government, then?"

"In a way."

Perplexed, the driver tried a different tack.

"Whadda you do?"

"Merchant Marine."

The driver chuckled.

"Oh, that explains it."

"Explains what?"

"How you can afford a taxi to Bel Air. You guys make big money."

Damn you! Jim said to himself. *Some of my own countrymen have the idea merchant seamen are wealthy guys. Little do they know.*

"Shut up and keep driving," he said aloud.

The driver eyed his passenger in the rearview mirror and decided to be quiet. No sense risking a big tip. He didn't say a word for nearly half an hour, until they had sped north on Route 1 and a sign welcomed them to Harford County.

"We're getting near Bel Air," the driver said cautiously.

"What's the address?"

Jim gave it to him.

"Don't know where that is," the driver said. "Do you?"

"I'm not really sure. Been here only a couple of times but it's so countrified I don't quite remember. I think it's not far from Mountain Road, though."

"Well, I'll have to ask around. May take some time."

"Doesn't matter to me. You won't get more than ten dollars no matter how long."

"No tip?" the driver asked testily.

"With all the money in my pocket, I might give you a dime."

Chagrined, the cabbie pulled into a gas station, got out and asked directions. A moment later, he was back in his seat.

"Not far from here. A half mile north, then a short right and another right. Quarter of a mile and we're there. Easy as pie."

The taxi's tires churned on the gravel as he pulled away. Five minutes later he drove into a private lane and inched his way to the first driveway on the right.

"Three seventeen," the driver said, reading the numbers on a sign post and starting to pull into the gravel driveway. It was curved, more than six hundred feet long and dozens of trees stood proudly on both sides. Jim could hardly see the house.

"Stop here," he ordered. "I'll walk."

"Okay, mate."

Jim got out and handed the driver a ten-dollar bill. The man looked at the money, then anxiously at his passenger. Jim reached into his pocket and handed the man a quarter.

"That's more'n a dime, man," he said cooly. "Don't spend it all in one place."

He walked up the driveway.

Lynne saw him first. She was looking out the window at her favorite birdhouse atop a two-inch pipe raised five feet above the ground. Two finches were inside the large house and a striking red cardinal was on the rooftop, pecking away at the seeds she had placed there that morning. With Frank away for two years, the birds brought her comfort in the days.

"Dad! Dad!" she called, running out the front door and racing across the lawn. She flung her arms around her father-in-law's chest, causing him to drop his seabag unceremoniously on the driveway stones.

"Dad!" she cried, kissing him over and over again on the cheek. "Geez, it's good to see you."

"Good to see you, Lynne," Jim half-whispered, trying to unwrap her arms to regain his breath. "But don't squeeze too tight. You're crushing my lungs."

She dropped her arms.

"I'm sorry," she said, embarrassed. "I'm so excited. You're here . . . and, I can't wait for you to see Junior and Wendy."

"I can only stay a couple of hours, Lynne. I'm on my way to see Alex in Wilmington."

"That's great, Dad! If only Frank could be here!"

"Have you heard from Frank? Or Billy?"

"I've gotten a few letters from Frank, none from Billy. They're still on the same ship, you know, but it's been two years since they've been home. I've talked to Captain Weatherby at the shipping company a couple of times, the last time a week ago. I've been so worried. But he said not to worry. Nothing bad has happened to the *Bennett*. She's still somewhere in the Pacific. Lord, Dad, she's been out a long time."

"She'll be okay, Lynne."

"I don't know, Dad. I saw a movie -- *Action in the North Atlantic* with Humphrey Bogart -- and I didn't know things were that rough on ships. I hope it's not that bad in the Pacific."

"Hollywood always makes things more dramatic than they are."

"There's one thing I don't understand, Dad," she said. "In one of Frank's letters he said the ship was in 'MacArthur's Navy.' What does he mean by that?"

"That's a tag the war correspondents have put on the ships MacArthur has commandeered for himself. It's mostly Admiral Kinkaid's Seventh Fleet, a collection of tired old battleships, some small escort aircraft carriers plus a bunch of merchant ships. And, like some other generals, he thinks some of those cargo ships are his own personal property."

"You mean Frank has to stay over there until MacArthur wins the war?"

"I hope not, Lynne. But the war is wrapping down. It'll be over in Europe soon, I think, and things are moving well in the Pacific from what I hear. Maybe everyone'll be home by Christmas."

She wrapped her arms around him again.

"Oh, Dad, you're wonderful! You say just the right things, even if I don't believe you. Come on, let's find the kids!"

14 October 1944

1700 HOURS
Hollandia, New Guinea

The sun was low on the horizon as the *S. S. Andrew Bennett* sailed once again into this New Guinea port. The crew saw it six months ago as part of "General MacArthur's Navy." The general had masterminded successful landings on the Admiralty Islands, to the northeast, and moved quickly to take the town of Hollandia away from the Japanese. He wanted this port, with the largest anchorage on the north coast of New Guinea, as a stepping stone for his plan to invade Mindanao, the southernmost island of the Philippines. He was determined to "return."

"Has this place ever changed!" Ordinary Seaman Benson said, looking over the ship's starboard rail at the docks and buildings stretching along the beach of Humboldt Bay.

"It's like a huge city except there's no skyscrapers!" said Ordinary Seaman Durante, marveling.

Hollandia had been a small town of native villages when it was occupied by the Japanese nearly two years ago. The Nips built three airfields for fighter planes in the nearby primeval jungle and used them to support their forces in other parts of New Guinea as well as on nearby islands. They had not done much building in the town. MacArthur's troops took Hollandia with relatively little fighting in a move that surprised its defenders and, recognizing the importance of the port to future invasions in the Pacific, they hurriedly built it into a city of more than 100,000 men. The building effort was hampered by more than one difficulty. Engineers discovered that the soil at the airfields could not support the weight of heavy bombers critical to the general's strategy to advance his control over the huge island's north coast and to support the drive of Admiral Chester Nimitz to the Mariana, Caroline and Palau island groups. The airfields needed complete rebuilding and this took a lot of men with heavy equipment. Although the Americans still planned to take other islands first, MacArthur also figured on Hollandia as a major staging port for his thrust into the Philippines. That meant docks and repair facilities for the armada of ships he planned to pull together. More men. More equipment. More barracks. More hospitals. More churches.

"I wish Cookie were here to see this," Benson said, wiping a tear from his eye.

He missed Seaman First Class George Cookman who had been killed almost a year ago when the *Bennett* took part in the taking of Tarawa Atoll. "We often talked about the growth of the Merchant Marine and how the United States had geared up to build so many Liberty ships. There's more Libertys, more merchant ships here than I've ever seen. The Japs could almost wipe out our Merchant Marine with an attack like the one they pulled on the Navy at Pearl Harbor!"

"They couldn't have that many planes left." Tony argued.

"Oh, they've got 'em. Maybe not around here, after what our Air Corps and Navy dive bombers have been doing to their fields in Rabaul and islands north of us, but they've still got a lot of planes. You can bet on that. They still hold a lot of islands and we still have to take them."

"Don't you feel good about how we're helping win this war?" Tony asked.

"Yeah, I feel good," Benson said, "but, damn, I'm tired and now it looks like we're going with the biggest invasion fleet of all. To the Philippines. I'm not as keen as MacArthur about going there. I'd rather be going home."

He was not alone in that wish. After being at Tarawa Atoll eleven months ago, the *Bennett* had supported landings at Kwajalein Atoll in the Marshall Islands, Saidor and Hollandia in New Guinea and the offshore island of Wakde, Manus in the Admiralty Islands and Morotai in the Molucca Islands. Some of the crew felt their ship was the most important one in "MacArthur's Navy." There had been no letup in the action, but there had been no other deaths on the ship. Major Bennett's ghost had made only one appearance since the landings at Tarawa. That was on 22 April, D-Day at Hollandia, when a Japanese Zero strafed the foredeck two hours after the ghost showed itself to the cook in the galley, again waving its arms in a motion signalling the ship to turn around. A Navy Armed Guard was wounded, superficially, and there was relief that no more blood had been spilled on the ship's decks.

Still, Captain Davis thought the chain of the ghost's appearances was strange.

"That thing, whatever it is, only shows up just before something bad happens on this ship and someone gets wounded or killed," he complained to his brother, Billy, as the two also looked from the flying bridge at the huge buildup that had taken place in Hollandia. "That happened last time we were here. Remember? I get the feeling it knows when something bad is going to happen again."

"Get off it, Frank," Billy said. "When did you start believing in ghosts?"

"Well, there is the Holy Ghost."

"That's different and you know it!"

"I'm not so sure, Billy."

"I don't believe you! You're more level-headed than that!"

"There may be something to Bib's stories. It all seems so real to him. Or maybe he has some sort of intuition that warns him of impending trouble for us. Some people have pretty good intuition, you know. Or premonitions."

"What about Durante? He's seen the damn thing. You think he has premonitions, too?"

"I don't know what to think any more," Frank said. "I'm concerned, Billy. There's no doubt MacArthur is going to take us all the way to the Philippines this time. There's bound to be air attacks on the ships. I'm sure the Japs have really built up their air force on the islands and they'll come at us tooth and nail. I hope neither of those guys see the damn thing before we go in."

"Like I said before, Frank, maybe the two of them have some sort of neuroses. No one else in the crew has seen Major Bennett. Or his ghost. Why don't you take those guys to a hospital ashore and let a psychiatrist examine them?"

"Not a bad idea, brother," Frank said, thumping Billy on the back.

The two had long ago given up the pretense that they were not related. They called each other by their given names and were not ashamed to say "brother." It was more comfortable for them to act as the kids they once were on the docks in Baltimore's Canton neighborhood.

"Not a bad idea, brother," Frank repeated. "I'll take them ashore tomorrow. The doctor may help us get to the bottom of things."

15 October 1944

1300 HOURS
A Field Hospital
"Your boys tell me they've been over here for a year and in North Africa before that," the Army psychiatrist said to Captain Davis after examining Bib Overall and Tony Durante. "That's a long time out for a merchant ship."

"MacArthur likes us," the captain said.

"Dugout Doug? I didn't know he likes anyone. Many don't like him," the major confided. "The man is a pompous windbag."

"I thought the Army idolized him."

"His staff does but others think he talks too big. And too much to the press. He thinks he can win the war that way. You know, he's complained that he's not getting any real support out here. Hell, Washington's poured men and equipment into this war zone and the general has made tremendous advances. I don't know what more he wants. He's ready to take the Philippines and he's still bitching he needs more. That doesn't help the morale of the troops."

"I didn't come here to analyze MacArthur," Captain Davis said curtly. "What's the story with my men?"

"Interesting cases, both of them." The major picked a folder from his desk and thumbed through four pages of notes. "Interesting."

He licked his thumb and looked inquiringly at the captain.

"They've seen a lot of action?" he questioned.

"Lots. Not as much as ground troops, of course, but we've supported seven landings out here and the North African invasion."

"Hmmmn," the major murmured.

He drummed his fingers on the desk.

"They tell me some of the crew has been killed."

"Unfortunately."

"Hmmmn."

"What does that mean, doctor?" Frank asked.

"Frankly, Captain, I haven't seen anything like this out here. Your men don't exhibit the normal symptoms of war neuroses. No physical manifestations. No twitching, blinking eyes, far away look, hypertension, not even signs of depression. The cook says he does get anxious when you fellows approach a combat area, but that's to be expected. Everyone does. Including the young ordinary seaman. True, they're war-weary. So am I and I've only been out here six months."

"We're all tired, but we're all not psycho cases," Frank said.

"I just don't understand it unless I'm missing something. They seem absolutely normal, as if the things that have happened to them, to your ship, were to be expected. Is that true of most merchant seamen?"

"I can't speak for most," the captain answered, "but my crew's pretty well adjusted. They see the enemy as just one more danger to be faced at sea. Like reefs and storms. Except for this talk about the ghost, of course. While these two are the only ones to have seen it, some of the others have been influenced by what these guys say they see. I don't know if the rest of the crew believes a ghost really haunts the ship, though. He hasn't been around for months and one would think if he is on the ship we'd see more of him."

"Have you seen it, Captain?"

"Of course not!" Frank answered defensively.

"Have you ever had a vision?"

"You mean like some people say they have seen Jesus or the Virgin Mary?"

"Yes."

"No."

"Where do we go when we die, Captain?"

"The church has taught me that if we follow God's word we go to Heaven. If not, we go to hell. But I think, metabolically speaking, we just cease to exist."

"Good answer, Captain, good answer. All right, then, but when a loved one dies, what do we have? I mean, the people who are left behind."

"Memories, I guess. There's nothing more than that.""

"Indians believe we have more. They believe the spirits of the dead come back to help guide us. Do you believe in spirits?"

"Damnit, doctor, I didn't come here to be analyzed either!" Frank said impatiently. "What did you find out about my men?"

The doctor shuffled his papers again.

"I find it strange that two men who otherwise seem normal claim to have seen this creature. The older one, the cook, may have something in his history that leads him to believe there may be such things as ghosts. He tells me an uncle believes in black magic and often tells stories about dead Africans coming back to life to haunt members of their families they didn't like. He says he never believed those stories, but enjoyed them, found them amusing. Perhaps, though, his uncle's ghosts have revisited him over here. He could have had hallucinations, seeing a form when no one is there."

"Hallucinating? That's bad!"

"Not necessarily so, Captain. Most of my colleagues would agree with you, but I don't go along with that school of thought. Seeing such a form may happen to perfectly normal people in normal circumstances, but also may be elicited under stress. He certainly has been under stress the last couple of years."

"No doubt about that. We all have."

"It doesn't mean he's crazy, seeing this thing, having hallucinations. I think it's perfectly normal for normal people to think they hear the voice of a dead one or see a form when no one else can. It's part of being human. I remember, as a child, hearing the voice of my grandfather long after he died. I loved him, loved him a lot, and thought about him often. It makes sense that at times my brain would retrieve a recollection of his voice."

"That seems logical," Frank said.

"Logic plays a role in psychiatry. Those revisits by the cook's uncle could be a serious problem, if they happen every day, but he says he hasn't seen the ghost for six months or more. He admits he gets tense when he knows your ship is going into harm's way and worries about you and the rest of the crew. It's nice to know he thinks that much of you. Many soldiers don't think that much of their officers."

Frank nodded gratefully.

"Look," the doctor continued, "the cook says he may have let his uncle's stories about ghosts affect his imagination when he saw something in his galley. It may just have been a reflection of light. He's a pretty rational man. He says he gave more credence to his own story when others on the ship said they believed a ghost could be aboard. Even if they couldn't see it. That's a form of mass hysteria. It doesn't seem to me to be a serious problem, though, Captain. I think it gives your men something to talk about other than the routine of sailing a ship."

He drummed his fingers again.

"The young boy is different. No such ghosts in his history. He had a normal childhood, an upbringing in a Catholic school. He insists God doesn't send people back to earth. Says people wouldn't come back anyway. They're too happy up in heaven."

"But he claims to have seen the ghost!" Frank said.

"Maybe. He's not so sure now. He saw it only once when he got up to go on watch at four o'clock in the morning. He admits he may have been a bit groggy and also influenced by the cook's description of the ghost. That led him to think he saw something. Imaginations do run wild when you're tired, you know. Listen, he's more concerned about something else than he is about the ghost."

"What's that?"

"That his girl friend will find out he's been laying around with prostitutes in most of the ports you've visited. That's a normal guilt reaction. Since I couldn't find anything psychologically wrong with him, I suggested he confess to the priest at the Catholic Church here. That should cleanse his sins and wipe away the ghost."

Captain Davis was relieved. There was no ghost on the *Bennett*. Just some wild imaginations.

1700 HOURS
Aboard the S. S. Andrew Bennett

Captain Davis walked into the saloon where Chief Mate Speer was eating dinner alone and reading a letter.

"Another letter from Mary Jane, John?"

The mate shook his head up and down and kept on reading.

"I guess all your personal problems are resolved now," Frank said, sitting down.

"Let's just say they're cut down to size, Frank."

"Good! You know, John, I've seen a vast improvement in your attitude since you began writing to her. Love has a way of mellowing a man."

"Oh, hell! I'm not getting soft, skipper. Can't get too soft with the crew after all this time out. We've still got a lot of problems on this ship."

"There's one problem we don't have any longer."

"What's that?"

"There isn't a ghost on board."

"For crying out loud, Frank, I know that! What's convinced you all of a sudden?"

"The Army psychiatrist. He says it's just the imaginations of Bib and Durante."

"Some imaginations! Now all we have to do is convince them."

"And the rest of the crew!"

16 October 1944

0700 HOURS
Aboard the S. S. Andrew Bennett

Army barges bumped off the hull of the Liberty ship, forward and aft, starboard and port, holding position just long enough for hooks dangling from four booms to be laced to bundles of thin sheets of steel, punched with holes that made them look like Swiss cheese. Soldiers of the port battalion hoisted the cargo topside, then down into the holds.

"You know what those Marsten landing mats mean?" Ordinary Seaman Benson asked Durante.

"What?"

"We'll be one of the first merchant ships in the invasion fleet."

"Why?"

"Well, our Army boys will be taking some airfields and it's a sure bet the Japs will destroy them as they pull back, if our own bombers already haven't torn the fields to pieces. There'll be a lot of bomb craters on the runways. It's also the rainy season, the monsoon season, and there'll be a lot of mud in those holes."

"It does look like we're in for some rain. Do you think it'll be heavy?"

"No doubt about it!"

"Geez! The damn place will be a muddy quagmire!

"That's for sure," Benson said. "So, the Army engineers will do everything to fill them in and then lace these mats together to form a solid landing strip for our planes. They're only temporary, though. They'll be used only until the engineers repair the concrete runways."

"I'll be damned!," Tony said. "MacArthur has thought of everything. Just think, he's carrying cement with an invasion force. Who would have thought that?"

"Well, I'm not sure MacArthur was the one," Benson said. "He's got a staff of planners whose job it is to think of everything the Army's going to need, not only when they hit the beach but for days and weeks after."

"Since we're carrying the landing mats, do you think we'll also carry the cement?"

"No, that's going on other ships. But we are going to fill a couple of holds with bridge parts. Second Mate Turner told me that. It'll take a couple of days to load us out here. It'd go faster if we could get into one of the docks, but they're needed to load tanks and other vehicles."

"Well, I can understand those bridge parts," Tony said. "After all, bridges are about the first thing our Air Corps goes after. And you can bet the Japs will blow up any that are left, if there are any."

18 October 1944

1100 HOURS
Aboard the S. S. Andrew Bennett

Captain Davis met with all his officers on the bridge. The *Bennett* had left Hollandia at dawn in a convoy of more than 200 merchant ships, guarded by three cruisers, nine destroyers and fourteen destroyer escorts. The main invasion force with more than 200,000 troops of the Army's Sixth Corps had sailed four days earlier.

"I have our orders," he announced, unfolding again the yellow sheet of paper. "They require strict attention from each of you and from the entire crew."

The officers echoed their support.

"The target this time is Leyte," he said.

"Leyte? Where in hell is that?" Billy asked. "I thought we were going to the Philippines. Why to another island?"

Frank looked with dismay at his brother.

"If you had studied more in geography class, Billy, you'd know the Philippines are an archipelago of more than seven thousand islands stretching more than one thousand miles from north to south. The largest are

Luzon in the north and Mindanao in the south."

"Hell, Frank, my geography teacher had trouble pegging where Chicago is," Billy quipped.

The others laughed.

"Well, anyway, fellows," Frank continued, "Leyte is a small island in the south central Philippines archipelago, to the east, and lying between the islands of Samar and Cebu. We're to proceed up the eastern coast of Mindanao and then into Leyte Gulf. We'll steam at ten knots in a straight line all the way. No zig-zagging. Got that, Billy?"

"Heard that, skipper! Ten knots!"

"Our troops will land on Leyte day after tomorrow, the twentieth. This convoy will reach the island the morning of the twenty-fourth. By then, our boys should have moved inland and taken the airfields near Tacloban, the capital. They're going to need our cargo of landing mats and bridge parts. That's why, as you can see, we're in the convoy's front row. We'll move into the docks, if they're still standing, the moment we get there and the Army will start unloading right away."

He looked at the deadpan faces of his officers.

"The weather's not going to be too good the next couple of days," he went on. "This is monsoon season here. No monsoon is expected, at least right now, but there'll be a lot of rain."

"What about the Armed Guard?" Navy Lieutenant Taylor put in. "Do you want us at battle stations now or when we get there?"

"Now," Frank said quickly. "There are reports that a Jap fleet is gathering around Luzon and may be headed south to Mindanao. They probably think we're going to hit that island. After all, it's the closest to New Guinea and were I them I'd figure on that too. Everyone's to be at their gun stations."

"I'll go tell my men," Taylor said, turning and leaving the bridge.

"This is going to be our biggest trip ever," Frank told the others. "I expect the Japs will throw everything at our troops and at us. They're getting desperate the way MacArthur and Admiral Halsey have been moving up the Pacific. I think they're beginning to smell that their days are numbered. We've got to be on our toes and be sure our cargo gets off."

"Don't worry, captain," Chief Mate Speer said. "You know our motto: 'We Deliver!'"

"That's the motto of the Armed Guard on these ships," Billy objected.

"Same thing!" the mate shot back.

1700 HOURS
Luzon, Philippines
Japanese Imperial Headquarters had hesitantly agreed with Tokyo war planners that when MacArthur returned to retake the Philippines he would strike the southernmost island of Mindanao. They concentrated on building up defenses there and on Formosa, another possible MacArthur target. But when the report came in to headquarters that an invasion fleet was moving into Leyte Gulf, Field Marshall Hisaichi Terauchi recognized the danger.

"They will not strike Mindanao," he argued firmly. "They will hit Leyte and then move north and south to take the Philippines. We must stop them there!

19 October 1944

1900 HOURS
Luzon, Philippines
"As you know, the war situation is grave," Vice Admiral Takijiro Onishi told his First Air Fleet staff at the evening meeting. "The Americans have secured New Guinea and are getting ready to invade the Philippines. Our army and air force have suffered severe losses during the last few months. Nearly six hundred planes of the Second Air Fleet were lost a week ago in American fighter sweeps over Formosa. Our Air Navy and Air Army are weak."

With troubled faces, his staff hung on to every word.

"I have studied ways to turn the situation around, to put us on the offensive again," he continued gravely. "One thing has struck me: The damage caused the enemy when one of our brave pilots, wounded or in a damaged plane, crashdives his aircraft onto an American ship. The results are devastating. We know that one plane flown by a pilot intent on suicide can cause more damage than an entire squadron intent on living again."

He paused with a grim look at his officers.

"There is only one way of assuring that our meager strength will be effective to a maximum degree. That is to organize suicide attack units composed of Zero fighters armed with five hundred and fifty-pound bombs, with each plane to crash-dive into an enemy carrier."

His officers were shocked. They thought the admiral crazy to suggest losing valuable planes, and pilots, in an official suicide operation, but they saw he was serious.

"We shall name this special air corps the Kamikaze," the admiral said.

The word meant "Divine Wind," named after the legendary typhoon that saved Japan from a Mongol invasion in the Thirteenth Century.

20 October 1944

1100 HOURS
Leyte, Philippines
Waiting for MacArthur at Mindanao, the Japanese were not prepared for the huge force of GIs that hit the beach on the east coast of this island a couple of hours ago. Resistance was so light that the troops moved inland quickly and the encouraged MacArthur, on the cruiser *Nashville*, put on a fresh, starched uniform and, with staff and newsmen, boarded a landing craft for a choppy ride to the beach. With them was Philippine President Serio Osmeria who had fled his homeland when the Japanese invaded.

MacArthur carried a revolver in a pocket, just in case he faced capture alive.

21 October 1944

0700 HOURS
Aboard the S. S. Andrew Bennett
"Ah's got to get off this ship!" an agitated Bib Overall pleaded with the captain. "Ah's gonna get killed if ah stays!"

"Get ahold of yourself, Bib," Captain Davis told the second cook and baker. "Nothing's going to happen to you. The Navy's giving us a lot of protection in this convoy."

"We's don' stand no chance, Captain!" Bib cried, grasping for the captain's arm. "Major Bennett says so!"

Not that damn ghost again! Frank thought.

The psychiatrist had convinced him the ghost was a

figment of Bib's imagination. He put a hand on the Negro's shoulder.

"Look Bib," he said consolingly. "You remember what that Army major said. The ghost is not real. It's in the recesses of your mind, put there by your uncle's stories of black magic when you were a kid. Those stories are resurfacing now, making you believe there really are ghosts when you're under a lot of stress. I assure you, there's no such thing as Major Bennett's ghost."

"But ah see'd 'im again, Captain," the cook persisted. "He come to ma galley an' youse should'a see'd 'im. He was wavin' his arms frantic like. He kept pointin' at me, warnin' me to get off this ship!"

"Did he talk to you, tell you that?"

"He didn' have to talk, suh. He pointed straight at me an' swung his arms wild like. Ah knows what he was tellin' me. Get out of here! He's warnin' us, Captain. We's all in fo' big trouble!"

For a moment, Frank didn't know what to say.

"Ah walked right up to 'im, tellin' im to go back where he came from. Ah wasn' gonna listen to 'im. That Army docta said he wasn' real so ah reached out to touch 'im. Ma hand went right through 'im. He was cold but he stood right there, wavin' his arms to turn back."

"Is he still there, Bib? Do you want me to go down and tell him to go away?"

The cook lowered his head, a bit shamefaced.

"Youse won't believe me, Captain. He's gone. He left soon's ah left the galley to come up here. But ah did see 'im, honest ah did, suh. In his tattered uniform. He's real. suh. No mistake 'bout that! Ah knows ah'm gonna die."

Good Lord! Frank said to himself. *Bib is so scared. Now he's predicting his own death. How can this be his imagination?*

0800 HOURS
A Suburb of Tokyo
With American troops already inland ten miles on Leyte and controlling the airfields near Tacloban, Admiral Soemu Toyoda convinced the Imperial Navy Headquarters that his combined fleet could destroy the invasion before it moved any further. He was mistakenly assured that the U. S. carrier-plane force had been severely weakened in

its attack on Formosa on 12 October. He devised a plan to direct the Navy from his underground headquarters here, dividing the Combined Fleet into three parts and sending them in different directions to Leyte Gulf where Admiral William F. "Bull" Halsey's Third Fleet would be "wiped out."

He proposed that the powerful Center Force, commanded by Vice Admiral Takeo Kurita, steam from Singapore through the San Bernardino Strait between Luzon and Samar and hit the American invasion force in Leyte on 25 October. That group consisted of the two largest battleships in the world, the *Musashi* and *Yamato*. The Southern Force with seven warships, commanded by Vice Admiral Shoji Nishimura, would come up to Leyte Gulf from the south on the same day in a pincer movement. Supporting this force were seven cruisers and destroyers under the command of Vice Admiral Kiyohide Shima.

The key to this divided fleet maneuver was to be the Northern Force with four aircraft carriers, two battleships and eleven light cruisers and destroyers, commanded by Vice Admiral Jisaburo Ozawa. Ozawa's force would sail from Tokyo and try to lure the American Third Fleet away from the gulf so the other parts of the fleet could strike the American positions on Leyte unopposed.

"It will be our last chance at survival," he implored, "and I tell you with this plan we will succeed."

Imperial Navy Headquarters bought it.

23 October 1944

0115 HOURS
Aboard the U. S. S. Darter
Blips on the submarine's radar screens revealed Kurita's Center Force steaming north in the dangerous waters off the western Philippines.

"Radio Halsey!" the sub commander ordered. "We've found the Jap fleet!"

He signalled another sub, the *U. S. S. Dace*, to join in a torpedo attack.

"Fire one!"
Pause.
"Fire two!"
Pause.
"Fire three!"

Pause.

"Fire four!"

In rapid succession, the four torpedoes struck a cruiser. The mighty ship sank in eighteen minutes.

"Got him!" the estatic commander shouted.

Another huge explosion rocked the submarine.

"Holy Christ! The *Dace* got another! The damn fleet isn't positioned to defend against a sub attack!"

He focused on another cruiser in his scope.

"Let's go after that one!"

Four more torpedoes crippled the second cruiser. The sea battle of Leyte Gulf had begun.

1500 HOURS
Luzon, Philippines

The first squadrons of Kamikaze pilots were fully formed. Hundreds had volunteered for the suicide missions, but Admiral Onishi had dictated that only young, inexperienced pilots could be enrolled. The older ones would be morre valuable for training the impetuous ones willing to die for their Emporer.

"In training," he said, "all will wear a hachimaki."

The headband worn by samurai warriors was a symbol of coolness and courage.

24 October 1944

0530 HOURS
Aboard the S. S. Andrew Bennett

The Liberty ship led the merchant convoy into Leyte Gulf and steamed through San Pedro Bay toward the docks at Tacloban inside a smoke screen laid down by Navy warships. Japanese light bombers, flying high overhead, dropped their bombs aimlessly, some of them hitting the water only 200 yards off the starboard bow.

"Jesus Christ! It's starting already!" Captain Davis shouted. "They won't even let us get to the dock!"

"Four Zekes bearing one six zero!" the gunnery officer called. The Zeroes could barely be seen through the smoke. "Four meatballs, four thousand yards!"

He was referring to the red circle emblems on the planes' wings.

The forward and bridge 20-millimeters opened fire.

So did the guns on the other forward ships in the convoy. The staccato roar was deafening, the sky punctured with black flak.

"I can't see them!" one gunner yelled, his own guntub veiled in smoke as he emptied the sixty rounds in his magazine.

"We got one!" another called back as one of the attackers rolled over twenty feet above the masts and somersaulted into the bay. The others disappeared in the smoke screen and then out of gun range over the island of Samar.

"Can't give credit for him," Lieutenant Taylor told the gunners. "Too many ships firing. He may have been downed by the entire Navy for all I know."

"We should get an assist!" one gunner grumbled.

0600 HOURS
Aboard Halsey's Flagship
Alerted by the radio message from the *Darter*, American carrier-based search planes spotted Admiral Kurita's Center Force in the Sibuyan Sea, between Mindoro and Luzon, and Admiral Nishimura's Southern Force in the Sulu Sea west of Mindanao. A Fifth Air Force patrol plane picked out Admiral Shima's Southern Force steaming toward the Mindanao Sea.

"Let's cut them off at the pass!" Halsey said elatedly, giving orders for a carrier-air strike in broad daylight against Kurita's ships.

Hellcat fighters from the carrier *Princeton* were the first to clear the flight deck.

0605 HOURS
Luzon, Philippines
Admiral Fukudome had the same idea as Halsey. He ordered more than 200 of his planes, based on Luzon and Formosa, to punch the American Third Fleet in the rain-swept waters east of Luzon.

He still didn't expect much air opposition.

0630 HOURS
Aboard the S. S. Andrew Bennett
"Get a move on!" the sergeant barked to the Army stevedores ambling up the gangway of the Liberty ship.

"This one's got a priority cargo and we've got to get it off fast!"

The soldiers moved more quickly to the Number Two and Three holds, tearing off the hatch covers and tossing them helter-skelter on the deck.

"Goddamnit!" the sergeant bellowed. "Stack those covers so they won't get in your way! Now!"

The GIs jumped and, in cadence time, stacked the hatch covers, lowered the hooks from the booms and began spewing the landing mats on the dock below. Trucks lined up to carry the cargo to the airfield. The ship's crew, still at battle stations, looked on in awe at the precision "down, up, swing, down, up, swing" movements.

"That's more like it, sergeant," Chief Mate Speer said. "It's bad enough having the Japs shoot us up without having your guys batter our hatch covers to death."

0938 HOURS
In Waters East of Luzon
American radar picked up the approaching planes sent by Admiral Fukudome and were ready. Navy Hellcat fighters bore into the huge squadrons, guns blazing, and shot down more than 70 before the Japs turned tail and ran. All but one.

The Judy bomber swooped down on the *Princeton*, evading the thick antiaircraft fire and dropped a 550-pounder on the carrier's flight deck. The bomb tore through the steel layering and detonated amid torpedo planes on the hangar deck. Exploding torpedoes, one after the other, sent smoke and fire reeling across the ship. Wounded climbed over the bodies of the dead only to find they were trapped below decks. Fire hoses were played out on the flight deck and on a destroyer that pulled alongside to help.

"All but essential personnel abandon ship!" the captain ordered, wanting to save lives and hopefully his ship.

0945 HOURS
Aboard the S. S. Andrew Bennett
A wave of Jap bombers flew over the harbor, dropping their lethal weapons. An oil dump ashore exploded into flames. An LST laden with tanks sank three hundred yards from the beach. A tug split in two and sank. A near-

by Liberty leaped upward when a bomb hit the foredeck. Geysers erupted as more bombs plunged into the water, missing their targets.

The planes were gone almost as soon as they arrived.

"Now, listen up!" Lieutenant Taylor called over the loudspeaker. "They're gone and here are the warnings you'll need if they come back: 'Flash White-Control Yellow' means there are no planes in the area. We can relax a bit but I want the Armed Guard on all guns at all times. Merchant seamen ammunition loaders can leave the guntubs to perform other work, but they're to be back at their posts when we need them. Understood?"

The Navy gunnery officer didn't wait for or expect an answer.

"'Flash White-Control Green' means that only friendly planes are in the area. That means no shooting. None! We don't want to hit any of our own guys! That could be a problem when we go to the 'Flash Red-Control Green' condition. That tells you both friendly and enemy planes are in the area. You've really got to be on your toes then. Don't fire unless an enemy plane comes straight at you."

That won't be easy, he thought, but he wasn't about to say that aloud.

"You can fire at will when you're told the condition is 'Flash Red-Control Yellow.' That means only enemy planes in the area. Remember that. 'Flash Red-Control Yellow.' Repeat it now."

He could hear his men shouting the words.

"Flash Red-Control Yellow!"

"There's one more condition you may hear often. 'Flash Blue-Control Yellow.' That means there's an unidentified plane in the area. Pay attention to it and listen for the next condition. It'll either tell you there are friendlies or enemies coming in."

He paused, knowing that what he had next to say might create more fear than he wanted to see.

"Now for the bad news," he continued somberly. "You won't see many friendlies, at least for the next couple of days. The Army has to straighten out the airfields before they can bring the Air Corps in so the only air support this invasion's got are planes from our Navy carriers. The carrier planes are pretty well tied up with their own problems. There's a big naval battle shaping up just outside us. They're needed there."

He let that sink in.

"It'll be up to us, and the other ships, to take care of the Jap planes until the Army can get its planes in here. Every round will count. I know you can do it, men. Good shooting!"

1000 HOURS
Above the U. S. S. Princeton
The five Hellcats hung above the clouds of smoke curling from their burning carrier.

"No chance of landing there," the flight leader spoke calmly into his mike.

He looked at his instrument panel. Two hours of fuel left.

"We'll try to make it to land," he told the others. "The Army's taken the airfield at Tacloban."

"I sure hope they've cleaned up the potholes!" his wingman called back.

1005 HOURS
Aboard the S. S. Andrew Bennett
"Hurry up!" the sergeant encouraged his men. "We've got to move faster! A carrier's been sunk and we've got to get these mats down on that airfield so's its planes can land! They got no other place!"

The stevedores worked feverishly. Trucks raced to the airstrip carrying one bundle at a time. Army engineers laid the steel strips quickly, lacing them together tongue and groove fashion.

"Friendlies are in trouble and, without a long strip of mats, those carrier planes can't land safely. They'll be comin' down in less'n two hours!"

1030 HOURS
In the Sibuyan Sea
The first wave of Hellcat fighters, Helldiver bombers and Avenger torpedo bombers from the carriers *Intrepid* and *Cabot* flung themselves against a wall of flak put up by Admiral Kurita's Central Force. The wall seemed impenetrable, but some of the fighters got through, straffing the decks of the warships and opening a path for the skimming torpedo bombers. One torpedo hit the cruiser *Myoko* but only slowed her down. Another struck the mammoth battleship *Musashi*, but bounced off her 16-

inch thick steel hull. She ploughed forward, shrugging as if a small dolphin had nosed her armor.

1145 HOURS
Over the Tacloban Airfield
The flight leader swooped over the airfield, watching the engineers laying down the Marsten mats and measuring the length of the strip.

"It's longer than the flight deck, but there ain't no hook to slow us down!" he told the others in the formation.

"Can we make it?" his wingman called back.

"Got to. We've only a few minutes of fuel left."

"Roger that."

1216 HOURS
Aboard the S. S. Andrew Bennett
All eyes on deck were on the Hellcat formation, small specks circling at ten thousand feet. The seamen could not see the airfield.

"They'll make it," Captain Davis said hopefully to his brother, Billy.

The first plane banked, headed down, then disappeared from view. There was a minute of nothing.

"He must'a made it, Frank," Billy whispered.

"Must have. Look, the second one's going in."

Again, the hills blocked the plane from sight. Breathtaking stillness. Then an explosion ripped the air and black smoke rose into the sky.

"My God!" Frank said. "He bought the farm!"

There was no hesitation. Another plane peeled off. And another.

"They must be running out of fuel," Frank said. "They ain't waiting. I hope that downed plane ain't in their way!"

1330 HOURS
In the Sibuyan Sea
The second and third waves of American carrier-based planes hit the Jap fleet, taking aim at the *Musashi*. Torpedoes hit her bow, where her armor was the thinest, and huge geysers of water spurted upward, slowing her. Other torpedoes hit Kurita's flagship, the *Yamato*. He

ordered the formation's speed reduced to 22 knots so the two battleships could keep up.

The captain of the *Musashi* finally ordered the firing of his secret weapons. He had wanted to save his 18-inch guns, the largest in the world, to hurl 3,220-pound shells at ground targets in Leyte tomorrow, but the gunfire, bombs and torpedoes from the American planes were doing devastating damage. Nine of the super guns were elevated and, aiming at the incoming planes, hurled special shells called "sanshikidon." Each sprayed 6,000 steel pellets into the sky.

Their marksmanship was poor. The American planes kept coming in.

1400 HOURS
Aboard the S. S. Andrew Bennett
The crew jumped up and down with joy.

"All of the Navy planes, all fifty, got down!" Captain Davis reported over the loudspeaker. "Two crashed at the end of the mats, but both pilots got out! Alive!"

"We did it!" Ordinary Seaman Durante slapped the second cook on the back. "We did it! Thank God for the *Bennett* and its cargo! All those pilots got down safely."

"Maybe they did, but ah don't know if we'll get out alive," Bib groaned.

1530 HOURS
Aboard Halsey's Flagship
The admiral admiringly received the reports from his fliers. The *Musashi* had been sunk along with nine cruisers and destroyers. The *Yamoto* and two other battleships were severely damaged. Admiral Kurita's fleet had reversed its course and was headed away from the San Bernardino Strait.

"They're running!" Halsey said happily as he was handed another report from planes that had spotted the carriers of Admiral Ozawa's Northern Force about 300 miles north of the strait. "That's the threat now," he said pointedly, unaware that Ozawa, who had sent only a part of his force forward, was trying to lure Halsey from Leyte Gulf.

He pondered his next move, figuring that Admiral Kurita's retreating fleet posed no threat and sensing he could make a final kill by taking his entire armada to thwart Ozawa's ships. So sure of himself, he didn't leave a destroyer behind to give warning if any other Jap ships approached the zone. He assumed carrier planes from MacArthur's and Kinkaid's Seventh Fleet would keep their eyes on the approaches to the Leyte landings.

He hadn't figured on the craftiness of Admiral Kurita who had no intention of running.

"At nightfall," the Jap officer said, "we'll swing our ships around and head through the San Bernardino to Leyte Gulf!"

1700 HOURS
Aboard the S. S. Andrew Bennett
The condition was "Flash White-Control Yellow." No planes in the area. The Armed Guard relaxed in their guntubs, smoking, shooting the breeze. The merchant seamen ammunition loaders had gone to the crew mess for coffee or to their foc'sles for a catnap. There was sporadic artillery and mortar fire on the beach, light sounds that the land invasion was moving ahead.

Without warning, four Judy bombers plunged down on the harbor, out of the sun, and streaked over the ships, dropping tons of bombs at anything in their paths.

"Where did they come from?" a forward gunner shouted, grabbing his helmet and reaching for a magazine of 20-millimeter shells. "There ain't no Flash Red-Control Yellow condition! Where's my loader?"

A bomb hit the deck between the Number Two Hold and the Number Three antiaircraft gun, ripping the guntub off its steel supports and tossing the weapon and gunner overboard onto the dock. He was killed instantly.

"Flash Red-Control Yellow!" the gunnery officer bellowed belatedly.

General quarters sounded throughout the ship.

A second bomb glanced off the bow and exploded when it hit the dock, lifting the ship up and shredding the wooden planks. Cries from wounded port battalion soldiers penetrated the late afternoon air.

Captain Davis raced to the bridge, calling to the boatswain for a damage assessment.

"It's bad, Captain!" the boatswain called back. "The ship's not hurt too much, but there's a lot of dead and wounded up here! I count seven, eight soldiers. One Navy gunner has been killed and Bib's hurt bad. Real bad!"

"Bib? What was he doing out on deck?" the captain asked, not waiting for an answer but running to the ladder to take him down to the foredeck.

"He was serving coffee to the Armed Guard," the boatswain told an unhearing captain as he ran alongside him.

Frank knelt over the cook, taking a quick look at the man's wound. It was ugly. A huge piece of shrapnel, maybe a piece of steel from the guntub, was lodged in Bib's abdomen. Blood spurted over his clothes, onto the deck, and perspiration covered his forehead.

"Ah didn't duck fast enough, Captain," Bib grunted.

"No, you didn't, Bib," the captain said gently.

From the looks of the wound, there were only a few minutes.

"Ah tole yo', suh, Major Bennett warned me 'bout comin' here."

The words came slowly.

"But ah had to. We's had a 'portant cargo an' it's already saved a lot of lives. Hasn't it, suh?"

"It has, Bib. But why were you up here giving coffee to the gunners? You didn't have to do that."

"Yes, ah did."

More slowly, short breaths.

"Major Bennett tole me to bring the coffee."

"He told you?"

"Yes, suh. He come to ma galley an' pointed to the coffee urn. Then he pointed a hand to the foredeck. Ah came right away. Did I do the right thing, suh?"

His eyes pleaded for understanding.

"Yes, you did, Bib. Yes, you did."

The cook pushed himself up on one elbow.

"He's callin' to me now, tellin' me to come."

"Who?"

"Major Bennett, suh. See 'im. He's right there."

Bib pointed to the port railing. Captain Davis didn't see anything.

"Ah's comin', Major," Bib said and slumped back on the deck. He stopped breathing.

25 October 1944

0330 HOURS
In the Surigao Strait
Admiral Nishimura confidently moved his small Southern

Force into the choppy waters of the strait, the southern approach to Leyte Gulf, relishing the idea of taking on the Seventh Fleet. On either shore, Filipino coastwatchers kept Admiral Kinkaid informed of the Jap fleet's whereabouts and helped him set a trap.

The Jap vessels moved north in single file.

"Hit them now!" ordered Vice Admiral Jesse B. Oldendorf, commander of Kinkaid's fighting ships.

American and Australian destroyers, zigzagging and throwing up smoke screens, raced down both sides of the line, each firing a salvo of torpedoes before turning around and speeding out of range of the Japanese guns. Nishimura's flagship, the battleship *Yamashiro*, took several hits. Another battleship blew up and two destroyers were sunk. Nishimura stayed his course until a murderous barrage of shells hit his ships from a line of U. S. battleships, cruisers and destroyers. The *Yamashiro* blew up, capsized and sank. All but one of his ships was sunk or damaged.

No American ships were lost.

0335 HOURS
Aboard the S. S. Andrew Bennett
White flashes sprinkled the horizon outside San Pedro Bay, illuminated by a brilliant moon and a cloudless sky.

"Heat lightning," Chief Mate Speer ventured. "I hope."

Captain Davis searched the horizon with his binoculars.

"That may be shellfire, John," Frank said.

"It is, Captain!" the radioman ran up, gasping. "A helluva naval battle is going down and the Army says we may have to leave the ship!"

"What?"

"That's right, sir," Sparks said, obviously scared. "The Army's rounding up rifles now. They tell us to get ready to leave the ship in case. They'll issue rifles to the crew."

"My God! Is it that bad, Sparks?"

"I think so, Captain. The Japs are only seventy miles away!"

Frank winced. "I'll tell the crew."

0645 HOURS
Off the East Coast of Samar
Admiral Kurita's Center Force emerged from the un-

guarded strait and steamed along the coast of Samar in a dash toward Leyte Gulf. On the horizon, in the southeast, he sighted what he thought was "a gigantic American task force with six or seven aircraft carriers protected by many cruisers and destroyers." He misread the silhouettes.

He had come across a group of thirteen ships, six of them 498-foot-long escort carriers with short flight decks, hardly larger than Liberty ships, commanded by Vice Admiral Clifton A. F. Sprague. "Taffy 3" was one of three escort carrier groups assigned to provide air cover for the Leyte landings and its bite was about that of a puppy dog. It had only three destroyers and four destroyer escorts with a total of 29 five-inch guns that, even fired all at once, could not put a dent in the armor plate of the enemy battleships. The six "Baby Flattops" carried only 28 planes each and the pilots had been trained to support ground operations, not air-to-ship combat.

Alerted to the danger by the pilot of an antisubmarine patrol plane, Sprague swung into action. He turned his small carriers into the wind, launched every plane at the ready and had all ships throw up smoke screens. Then he told the radioman:

"Radio Halsey for help! Tell him we're outnumbered and that battleships are bearing down on us. We need Task Force Thirty-Four's battleships. We're going to need all we can get!"

Just as the big guns of the Japanese battleships opened up, dropping salvos all around the small American ships, a rain squall plunged the area into near darkness. Sprague changed course, taking advantage of the rain cover, and sped south toward the other two Taffy escort groups. But he sent every available plane into the fray until they ran out of torpedoes and bombs. Then they strafed the larger ships and Kurita still thought he was facing a gigantic force. Sprague's destroyers and destroyer escorts moved into range for their five-inch guns, peashooters in the battle against 14- and 18-inchers.

The *U. S. S. Johnston* came out of a smoke screen and found herself dangerously close to a battleship. The destroyer took three 14-inch shells in her hull and ducked back into a billow of smoke. She came out the other side to see a line of Japanese warships pounding away at an already damaged baby carrier. Undaunted, its commander blazed away with his lighter guns, but he couldn't save the *U. S. S. Gambier Bay*. The carrier sank with its only five-inch gun still firing. The *Johnston*, too, was beginning to sink. A second destroyer was severely damaged.

0940 HOURS
Aboard the S. S. Andrew Bennett
"We better start packing, Captain," the radioman said. "The Army says the Navy is taking a beating just outside and we may get the order to abandon ship in a few minutes!"

"It'd make more sense to stay on board," Captain Davis said. "We've got three-inch and five-inch guns."

"So's most every other ship in the harbor," Sparks rejoined. "But if the Jap ships come in they've got fourteen-inch guns and bigger. They could stand off way out of our range and tear this place to shreds!"

1000 HOURS
Aboard Halsey's Flagship
The yeoman handed Admiral Halsey another urgent message asking for help for the embattled Taffy 3 group. Halsey had already received several urgent messages from Kinkaid and Sprague calling for the fast battleships of his Task Force 34 to head for Leyte Gulf "at once." But he was already engaged in a carrier-based air battle with Admiral Ozawa's decoy Northern Force and he figured that by noon the pasting being given the enemy by his planes would leave crippled ships in the water as easy targets for his own ships' guns. Leyte Gulf was 300 miles away and he figured Kinkaid's full Seventh Fleet would come to Sprague's rescue. He didn't know Kinkaid wasn't close.

"What is this?" he asked the messenger.

"An urgent one from Admiral Nimitz himself," the yeoman answered.

Halsey unfolded the paper.

"WHERE IS RPT WHERE IS TASK FORCE 34 RR. THE WORLD WONDERS."

Halsey growled when he stood up. He was insulted, infuriated. *How dare Nimitz send a message like that?*

Still, like the trained sailor he was, Halsey turned around his fast battleships, including his own, and headed for the Gulf.

1005 HOURS
Luzon, Philippines
Flight mechanics had spent the night polishing the airframes of twelve Zeroes. Now, they began loading 550-pound bombs. Admiral Onishi had ordered the first flight of Kamikaze pilots to Leyte Gulf to crash dive into the American ships that apparently were pummeling Admiral Kurita's battleships and cruisers.

In the ready room, the twelve pilots nonchalantly busied themselves with last-minute details of their lives. Another look at the navigation charts. A final goodbye letter to their parents. A laughing farewell to a friend. A cup of saki. A certainty they would be remembered with others of their country's martyred dead at the Yasukuni Shrine. All were willing, anxious to die.

"You are already gods without earthly desires," Onishi told them as they ran to their pre-arranged coffins.

1030 HOURS
Just Outside Leyte Gulf
"Look, admiral, they're getting away!"

Stunned by the words of one of his officers, Admiral Sprague peered through the smoke at the retreating Japanese ships.

"It can't be!" he said. "They've got us beat!"

Jap Admiral Kurita, on his flagship, didn't know that. He still believed he was facing a superior force and he had intercepted a message that Task Force 34's battleships were only two hours away. Not wanting to be caught between the two American naval forces, Kurita decided to get out of the way. Fast.

"They are running!" Sprague shouted with glee.

A pint-size U. S. Navy battle group had stopped one of Japan's largest fleets.

The battle for Leyte Gulf was over.

1300 HOURS
Aboard the S. S. Andrew Bennett
"Stand easy, men!" Captain Davis called over the ship's loudspeaker. "The Navy's clobbered the Jap fleet in Leyte Gulf! And listen to this! They did it with a couple of destroyers and some Liberty ships converted into baby aircraft carriers. There wasn't one American battleship or big aircraft carrier around!"

The crew cheered.

"Hot damn!" Ordinary Seaman Durante shouted. "We don't have to join the Army ashore. I don't know how to fire a rifle anyway!"

1130 HOURS
Above Taffy 3
The Kamikazes looked down at the tiny aircraft carriers.

"They don't look like much," the flight leader said. "I thought we'd have bigger targets."

Not one to question the orders of his superiors, he peeled out of formation and dove straight onto the deck of the escort carrier, *St. Lo.* Ten other bomb-bearing planes crash-dived into that ship, sinking it, and damaged four other baby carriers. One Kamikaze missed and crashed into the sea.

The Japanese had come up with a new and terrifying weapon too late to win the battle for Leyte Gulf, but sending a chill through the U. S. Navy.

26 October 1944

1200 HOURS
Aboard the S. S. Andrew Bennett
"We're finished here," Chief Mate Speer told Captain Davis on the flying bridge. "All our cargo's off and the Army has ordered us to anchorage in the middle of the harbor. We're to wait for a Navy convoy."

"Any idea when, John?" the captain asked.

"They didn't say. We're the first ship unloaded. I guess they'll wait for a lot more, then bundle us up for home."

"Home? I doubt that, Mister. I bet they'll send us back to Hollandia for another load. This battle for the Philippines is going to go on for awhile."

"I can't wait to get out of here, Frank," the mate said. "We're here less than two days and we've seen more action this time than in any other landing. There's a big hole in our foredeck and fifty-four tons of landing mats have been torn to pieces. Six soldiers have been killed, two others wounded, and we've lost an Armed Guard. And Bib."

"Losing Bib is real tough," Frank said, trying to steel himself against tears. "He was a good seaman, a good cook. Most of all, he was a friend to everyone on board."

"Damn! Why are all the good men killed in a war?"

"It seems that way, doesn't it? You know, John, he had a premonition that he would die."

"I wonder how many more will die before this thing's over?" the mate asked.

"A lot," Frank said solemnly.

5 November 1944

0900 HOURS
In Leyte

Without sufficient air cover, the invasion was crawling at a snail's pace. MacArthur hadn't wanted to invade Leyte without a massive land-based air force within range of the island. He bowed to Navy boasts that the fleet's carrier planes would provide all the support needed for the ground forces. But the Seventh Fleet's carriers had to be withdrawn after the damage inflicted on them during the battle of Leyte Gulf. Halsey's Third Fleet carrier planes were tied up bombing Japanese convoys heading to the island. Only a handful of American planes were based at the captured Tacloban and Dulag airstrips and they took a daily pounding from a persevering Admiral Fukudome who shifted planes from Formosa and northern Luzon to bases within range of Leyte. To make the going tougher, the Japanese ground commander brought in 45,000 reinforcements on the western and northern sides of the island.

The weather didn't help the Americans in ground combat or in developing the airstrips. Nearly 40 inches of rain from the long-predicted typhoons and monsoons turned the island into a muddy quagmire. The GIs were slowed.

11 November 1944

0700 HOURS
At Anchorage

"I swear, Frank, the U. S. Army is holding us as prisoners of war!" Billy told his brother. "We've been locked up out here for two weeks, nothing in our holds, and they won't let us out of here. All the ships are being attacked every hour or so by Japanese planes. Where in hell is our Air Corps? God, if we stay here any longer I think the crew'll go stir-crazy. I already have!"

"Get hold of yourself, Billy," Frank said. "The Army's having a tough time ashore and the Navy, well, the Navy is doing all it can to protect us with its carrier planes."

"Some protection! Bombs hit something every time the Japs come over. And they come over every few minutes, night and day."

"They're doing the best they can."

"Best? Jesus Christ, Frank, a half dozen Libertys have been smashed up and, from what I hear, they're really creating havoc on the airstrips we took. One of these days, their bombers are going to get us again like they did the first day we got here. Only the next time it'll be a lot worse!"

12 November 1944

0900 HOURS
Luzon, Philippines

Admiral Onishi handpicked another nine young pilots for the day's suicide missions.

"Three of you will go in glory in the first wave over Leyte harbor," he said tersely. "The others will follow every several hours in flights of three. That constant harassment will worry the Americans who won't be expecting you. Your targets are the merchant ships. There are many and you have been assigned a particular ship. Find it and hit it!

"But please keep in mind the first order of the Kamikazes:

"Do not be too much in a hurry to die. If you cannot find your target, turn back; next time you may find a more favorable opportunity. Choose a death which brings about a maximum result."

The first three suicide pilots downed a final cup of saki and swung into their cockpits. Two older pilots in escort planes taxied out with them to help fend off any American planes they might encounter and to report back with the results of the mission.

Onishi looked on as the planes lifted into the air.

"I don't think history will justify what I have done," he said mournfully.

1115 HOURS
Aboard the S. S. Andrew Bennett
The condition was "Flash White-Control Yellow." General MacArthur had announced earlier in the morning that Leyte was secure and the crew took advantage of the reprieve. Some sacked out in their bunks. Some went to the messhall for an early lunch. A few lounged on the foredeck, soaking up the hot rays of the sun. Others went skinny-dipping off the fantail where the bay waters were calm, unmoving. The gunnery officer led a Sunday church service on the monkey bridge.

". . . He leads me to still waters . . ."

Rat-a-tat-a-tat-a-tat-a-tat! The roar of a plane's engine and the clatter of a machine gun blasted the serenity.

"Watch out! It's a Jap!" the gunnery officer yelled and his congregation dove under ready boxes for cover.

The plane plunged into the Number Three hold, its bomb penetrating the bridgehouse bulkhead into Billy's unoccupied cabin. There was a pulverizing, crashing explosion. A dense sheet of flames rose, followed by clouds of black smoke and showers of a million pieces of aluminum and steel on the decks and into the sea around the *Bennett*. Part of the pilot's body flew over the bridgehouse and landed inside the Number Four hold, its hatch covers off for cleaning.

"What --- ? What was --- ?" a merchant seaman tried to ask, lying on the bridge deck, one leg gone, blood pouring from his abdomen. Other seamen and Armed Guard lay around him, wounded, dazed and terrified.

"A Kamikaze," Captain Davis said soothingly, wrapping a tourniquet around the man's thigh. "That pilot dove his plane right into us and killed himself."

"A dead Jap's a good one," the man grunted. "How about our guys, Captain? Did he hurt many?"

Frank surveyed the scene around him. Twenty or more men lay wounded, or dead, on the bridge, some trying to pick themselves up. Another dozen lay scattered on the foredeck, most of them dead.

"I don't know, son," Frank grimaced. "There are barges pulling up alongside and we'll be getting some medical help. A doctor will be up here any minute."

1430 HOURS
Luzon, Philippines
Admiral Onishi waved to three more pilots as they

zoomed into the sky. He was heartened by the report from the first wave's escort planes. One of the three Kamikazes had severely damaged a Liberty. The other two hit the water only fifty feet from their targets.

He had told these three eager young men not to waver.

"I know you will choose your targets carefully and save our Emperor from defeat. It's up to you. Go with the wind!"

1715 HOURS
Aboard the S. S. Andrew Bennett
The Zero flew unerringly through a wall of antiaircraft fire, hit its right wing on the Number Three boom and tore into the lower wheelhouse, its bomb dropping to the engine room and exploding in a thunderous roar. Bodies were thrown into the air like matchsticks and men lie on the decks, up and below, screaming and writhing with pain. Plywood bulkheads burst into flames, sending billows of smoke through the passageways.

Captain Davis was thrown to the wheelhouse deck, his head and arms peppered with shrapnel, his chest and legs crushed under several tons of steel beams.

"The captain's been hit!" an able-bodied seaman cried. "Holy hell! He's pinned under some beams!"

The seaman tried to lift one of them.

"I can't do it!" he huffed. "Someone help me!"

Chief Mate Speer ran in, followed by the captain's brother and Purser Tanner.

"Billy," the mate said, "we've got to get them off. He's being crushed."

"Don't . . . Don't bother with me," Frank coughed. "What about . . . the rest of the crew? Are many hurt?"

His breathing was labored.

"It's tough, Captain," Tanner said. "Ten or twelve are dead. I don't have a full count yet. Seaman Durante's among them."

"Oh, no!" Frank moaned, the word of Tony's death causing more pain than he felt in his chest.

"I got to him seconds before he died," the purser said. "Last thing he said was not to tell Marilyn what he had done. What'd he mean by that?"

Frank shook his head slowly.

"It . . . It doesn't matter now. He told her . . . he'd be a virgin when they got married. He wasn't."

"Oh!"

Frank coughed again. A frothy mixture of saliva and blood rolled from his mouth and trickled down his chin.

"What about . . . the others?" he sputtered.

"Third Mate --- "

"Cut out all this crap, damnit!" Billy screamed at the purser. "Can we do anything for him?"

"This isn't . . . crap, brother!" Frank said quickly. "I want . . . a full accounting of the ship."

Purser Tanner took the captain's pulse.

"It's racing! We've got to do something quick!"

"The others?" Frank demanded hoarsely, concerned about his crew.

"Third Mate Franklin bought it, too," Tanner said nervously. "Seamen Wilson and Benson and three Armed Guard that I know of. I haven't looked at the other dead. There's at least a dozen wounded. Thank God we've still got two Army corpsmen aboard. They're looking after the others. We'll get one for you."

"It's too late for me -- "

The thunder of bass piano notes rose over the noise of the crackling fires.

Dum . . . dum . . . de dum . . .

"What the hell is that?" Billy shouted.

Dum . . . de dum de dum de dum . . .

It was a slow, deliberate movement.

"Sounds like some sort of dirge," the chief mate said.

Mr. Tanner recognized it as Handel's *Death March from Saul.*

"Who would be playing something like that?" he asked.

"Must be . . . Seaman . . . Mitzell . . ." Frank said slowly, in time with the music.

"God!" Tanner burst. "I saw him lying on the deck with a corpsman treating a terrible wound in his chest. I can't believe he made it to the saloon he was hurt so bad."

"No one else plays," Frank said.

More blood flowed from his mouth. He listened a moment and then looked around at the destruction of his wheelhouse.

"How bad . . . How bad is she hurt, John?" he asked, troubled for his ship.

"We're taking water in the engine room," the chief mate answered. "The bomb blew a hole in the hull big enough to drive a truck through. It's a flood down there. I don't think we can keep her afloat more than an hour or two. We'll have you off before then."

"No, you can't lift these beams."

"We'll rig up a block and tackle."

"Where?" Frank asked, his eyes pointing to the empty space overhead. "The beams . . . from up there . . . are atop me."

His face was contorted in pain.

A corpsman ran in, knelt and examined the captain.

"Nothing I can do for him," the corpsman announced to the others, wiping the blood from Frank's chin. "He's not for long."

"You've got to save him," Billy said, tugging at the medic's sleeve. "He's my brother."

The soldier gave the chief engineer a piercing look.

"A lot of brothers are dying over here," he said crisply.

"Damn you!" Billy shouted, shaking the man. "You've got to save him!"

"I can't even if we get those beams off him. He's lost two much blood and I'm sure one lung's collapsed if not both. His ribs are crushed. We could try to get these beams off him so he can rest easier."

The corpsman put his strong arms under one of the beams. Billy and the chief mate did likewise.

"Now, on three, lift together! One. . . two. . . three!"

The beam didn't budge.

"We can't lift it!" the corpsman said.

"Try! Damnit, let's try lifting this other one!"

That didn't budge either.

"It's no use . . . Billy," Frank shuddered.

His breathing was more labored. "Your arms . . . are pushing this one . . . more down on me. It hurts a lot."

"I'll give you a shot of morphine," the corpsman promised, pulling a needle and syringe from his medical bag. "That'll ease the pain."

He stuck the needle into Frank's arm and pressed the plunger. Frank felt like drifting off to sleep but fought the temptation. With his free right arm he sought his brother's hand.

"Billy . . . do you remember . . . the game we played . . . when we were kids?"

"What game, Frank?"

"Whenever it rained and we were . . . were on the docks . . . in Canton? You would . . . let me play captain of the ship. And we . . . we pretended we were . . . in a storm at sea. I'd hold tight to a lamp post . . . hollering the waves . . . were washing over the ship. Remember?

Remember how I told everyone . . . to abandon ship?"

"Don't, Frank!" Billy appealed.

"Then I'd . . . I'd fell off the dock . . . and pretend I drowned?"

"Stop it, Frank!"

"Well, brother . . . it's now . . . almost like it was then. We've got . . . to abandon the *Bennett*."

There was a disjointed crashing of piano keys. The music stopped abruptly.

"Good Lord! . . . Mitzell's gone too!" Frank cried, tears welling in his eyes, his voice weaker.

He turned to his chief mate.

"John, listen to me. Prepare to . . . abandon ship. Get everyone off, the wounded . . . the dead . . . everyone."

"I can't leave you like this, Frank," Speer protested. "We've got to get you off too."

"That's an order, Mister!"

Frank gasped for air.

"We may be . . . in a harbor, but you've got . . . lives to save . . . and I'm not one of them. You've . . . I'm turning command . . . of the ship . . . over to you. Take over now!"

John knew his old academy roommate meant it.

"Yes, sir!"

He bent down and kissed Frank on the forehead.

"Good sailing, skipper!"

He turned and left, fighting back tears.

"That goes . . . for you too, Billy!" Frank said tersely.

"I ain't leaving, kid brother!"

"To hell you're not!" Frank snapped.

The excitement pained him.

"You've got . . . to get back home . . . to tell Lynne what happened. Tell her . . . I wasn't afraid."

"I won't!"

"You will, Billy!" Frank summoned all his strength to shout the words. "Look . . . there's a letter . . . on my desk. I want you . . . to take it to her. I wrote it last night."

"You wrote her last night?"

"Yes. I had a premonition . . . a premonition that something . . . terrible was going to happen. After we talked yesterday . . . you know . . . when you said you were afraid . . . a bomber would get us again . . . I thought I saw -- "

He stopped and closed his eyes, not wanting to tell his

brother of the vision he saw in his cabin.

"You thought you saw what?"

"I meant . . . I didn't expect . . . two Kamikazes to hit us today. But I had a sinking feeling . . . I wouldn't see her . . . or Junior again. I won't . . . I won't ever see Wendy. You know . . . how feelings like that go. You've got to go back there . . . and look after them . . . big brother. Promise me you will."

"But, I --- "

"Promise me, Billy."

"Okay, okay," the chief engineer said reluctantly.

He wrapped his hands endearingly around Frank's head, holding him tight and kissing him softly.

"I'll be fine," Frank whispered. "I'm ready . . . for whatever happens."

"Whatever," Billy mumbled.

"Look, Billy . . . when you get the letter . . . do me another favor. Open the . . . right hand bottom drawer under my bunk . . . and bring the picture . . . of her to me. I want . . . I want Lynne to be the last thing I see."

"Goddamnit, Frank, I --- "

"Go, Billy, and get it!" Frank commanded.

Billy did.

No words were spoken when he came back with the photo. Billy looked for a long time at his brother, saluted smartly and left the wheelhouse. He went to help the others get off the ship.

Frank stared pensively at the naughty but nice photo of his wife dressed as he had never seen her in real life. In flimsy see-through panties and an open lace bra that barely concealed her breasts.

"I don't know . . . if I could have stood it, Pugnose . . . seeing you really dressed like this."

He kissed her face in the photo.

"Take care of yourself, Lynne . . . and the kids."

He sighed heavily and looked over the beams to the far bulkhead. A shadowy figure in a tattered Civil War uniform gently waved to Frank to join him there.

"I'm coming . . . Major Bennett! I'm coming!"

*